THE BEASTS WE BURY

D.L.TAYLOR
THE
BEASTS
WE BURY
FIRST INK

First published 2025 in the US by Henry Holt and Company

First published in hardback 2025 in the UK by First Ink, an imprint of Pan Macmillan

This paperback edition published 2025 in the UK by First Ink, an imprint of Pan Macmillan
The Smithson, 6 Briset Street, London EC1M 5NR
EU representative: Macmillan Publishers Ireland Ltd, 1st Floor,
The Liffey Trust Centre, 117–126 Sheriff Street Upper, Dublin 1 D01 YC43
Associated companies throughout the world

ISBN 978-1-0350-4184-8

1 3 5 7 9 8 6 4 2

A CIP catalogue record for this book is available from the British Library.

Printed and bound in the UK using 100% Renewable Electricity by CPI Group (UK) Ltd
Book design by Meg Sayre and Aurora Parlagreco

FOR THE FAMILY OF MY BLOOD,

THE FAMILY I CHOSE,

AND THE FAMILY FORGED IN VELVET AND STEEL

1

Prospective Seconde Mancella Amaryllis Cliff

|15 DAYS UNTIL THE ASSURANCE|

My father waits until halfway through breakfast to announce that I'll be killing something again today. Presumably he did this so my mouth would be too full to scream at him, but I try to anyway and end up choking on my croissant. My sister thumps me on the back and my mother dabs her mouth with a silk napkin as though she finds the whole thing distasteful, but my father just keeps talking, blathering on about what a beautiful creature he's found and how strong this quarry will make our family.

Just beneath my skin, the animals I've killed before writhe in anger, squirming and thrashing until I feel like an overfilled sack that will rip at the seams any second. I imagine a tear starting at my forehead and splitting my body in half until everything inside of me is spilling onto the tablecloth, staining the porcelain plates and desecrating the elderberry tea. I picture my empty skin collapsing into a puddle at the base of my chair. And I wonder if my father would even stop talking. I wonder if my mother would start.

"The Assurance is in two weeks," I protest, once I manage to force the bread down my suddenly dry throat. "You'll name me as your Seconde in *two weeks*. Why now?"

My father scrunches his heavy brows, making a pronounced V in the center of his forehead. And even though he launches into another speech—one I barely listen to—his deliberately exaggerated confusion is more than enough to convey how ridiculous my question is to him.

The impending Assurance *is* why we're doing this now.

And I should have known that.

My barely chewed croissant sinks to the bottom of my stomach as another protest rises from my lips.

"But I thought . . ." That's all I get out before the sentiment dies on my tongue and bitter embarrassment burns the back of my throat.

I'd thought that Father finally naming me his heir meant I was done with all the killing. That he'd decided I was strong enough at last and I could put it all behind me. Move forward. Conduct myself in my new role the way *I* saw fit.

Clearly, I was just kidding myself.

"Excuse me," I say, scraping my chair away from the table and throwing my napkin on the plate.

I make it all the way to the grand foyer before Mara catches up. I cross my arms at her approach, but she only quirks a smile at me with the half of her mouth that's visible. The other half, along with her left eye, is covered by a brightly colored scarf.

"Did they send you after me to make sure I don't run away?" I ask.

"Of course not," she says. "They sent me for emotional support."

I snort, and the joke eases the pressure in my chest a little. I drop my arms and let her fall into step with me as I pass through the grand double doors and out into the courtyard.

I want a breath of fresh air, but the towering stone walls that circle the grounds make the air outside taste just as stale as the stifling indoors. I frown at them, hating their polished gleam, their ridiculous height, their copious fortifications and well-manned guard posts. Hating how small they make my world feel.

"So," Mara asks, her voice synthetically cheerful. "*Are* you going to run?"

I glance at her and then away.

"That depends," I say. "How suitable are your shoes for an extended chase?"

She lifts her skirts and checks.

"They're slippers," she tells me, in the patronizing manner of an older sister merely entertaining a younger sister's ridiculousness. "And they look pretty flimsy. But I can always kick them off."

"And are you prepared to tackle me if it comes down to it?" I ask, wheeling on her. "Would you take the scarf off your face to bind me and force me back? Would you use violence if violence was necessary?" My tone is harsher than our banter warrants, as chilly as the autumn frost that coats the rock mosaic beneath our feet.

Mara grabs my elbow, pulling me to a stop. "Are you being serious right now?"

"Are you?" I counter. "If I ran, would you really pursue?"

She studies me, considering the question, her one visible eye raking my expression and picking it apart, like someone squeezing fruit at the marketplace, trying to decide if it's spoiled.

"No," she says finally.

But I don't miss that she had to think about it.

I shake free of her grip and quicken my pace, rubbing my arms against the cold, and she lengthens her own steps again to keep up.

"So are you going to?" she presses.

I tilt my head back and look at the sky, noting the thick, smothering blanket of clouds. The sun is merely a dull smudge behind them, gasping for life.

And yet the clouds aren't dense enough—could never be dense enough—to obscure the slimy green glow of the magic on the northeastern horizon. Even on such a murky day, it manages to creep over the walls like a caustic patch of green corrosion eating away at the steely gray heavens. Its light is bright enough to cut through the gloom, and sharp enough to carve into my mind, never letting me forget how much has changed since I let it devour me.

"No," I say. "After all, that was the deal, wasn't it? Kill one creature a year? Endure one sacrifice in exchange for peace the rest of the time? I'd hoped this year I could stop, but clearly that was just wishful thinking. Why would Father ever stop honing his favorite tool?" I spit the last word, sourness sharpening the sentiment.

"It's better than before," Mara murmurs. "When he'd lock you in a room with a fox or a badger and not let you out until it was dead."

The fox and badger within me stir, raising their little heads.

Heads that I bashed into walls with childish, imprecise hands, sobbing and screaming and afraid.

"Yes," I say. "Better."

I change direction and she follows, dogging my steps.

"So where *are* you going?" she asks.

I point to a corner of the grounds and her shoulders relax. "Oh. Right." She plays with the necklaces tangled around her throat, clinking them together as we walk. "You want me to get some twine?" she asks finally.

"Please," I say.

She heads back inside and I angle my steps toward the expansive rectangle of grass that borders the courtyard. It's pristine. Every blade the same height, the green appropriately verdant, and the perfect amount of moisture to make it grow thick and lush.

There's absolutely no sign of any little white flowers that might break up the uniformity, but that's only because they are wrenched from the dirt and burned daily.

Where I'd pointed, there's a stone incinerator belching black smoke into the sky, and, beside it, today's stack of limp white blooms, scheduled for destruction at sunset. They're called starsprouts, for their pointed petals. Although if you ask my father, they're called weeds.

I kneel and comb through them, plucking up the nicest ones and twisting their stems together, a little more viciously than warranted. When Mara comes back, I take the twine she hands me and wrap it around the bundle twice before tying a bow.

At least, I try to make a bow. But my scar-covered hands are shaking too badly, and the knot keeps slipping loose.

"Want me to?" Mara asks, reaching out.

"No," I say, jerking away from her. "I have to do it myself."

She frowns but doesn't try to reach for it again.

I will my hands to still, squeezing them into painful fists, and a few moments later I finally press a miniature bouquet into the palm of Mara's hand.

"Give it to the Captain, will you?" I ask. "And then tell Father that I tried to flee but you dragged me back by the hair and I'll be there shortly."

"You don't have to go in right away," she says. "You could take a few hours . . ."

But I shake my head. "I'd rather get it over with." Because until I do, I'll only be torturing myself about it. Imagining it, dreading it, wanting to run. Remembering all the times in the past that I *did* run. All the times I was hunted and hauled back like I was an animal myself. I wouldn't call complying easier, but at least it's faster.

Mara nods, fingering the petals of the flowers before standing and taking her leave. I watch her go, leaning against the incinerator and feeling its heat beneath my cheek, a few degrees shy of blistering.

Before me lies the stack of flowers I didn't choose, drooping and dejected.

Doomed.

❧✻☙

My father is waiting by my door with a maid when I get there. I curtsy low to the ground and he peers down his nose at me like he's trying to figure out if the gesture is sarcastic.

It is.

I wave the maid into my room, but when my father tries to follow, I hold up a hand.

"I have to change, remember?" I say.

"There are things I need to tell you," he counters. "To prepare you."

"So talk through the door," I say, shutting it in his face.

Just shutting. Not slamming. The line between surly teenage attitude and high treason is a thin one, but I dance it well.

I pick up my skirts and rustle them loudly to make it clear I'm about to get undressed, and thankfully he leaves the door closed. I can practically feel him frowning, though.

"So what kind of animal is it this time?" I ask, holding out my arms to the sides as the maid steps forward. She sets to removing my overwrought, crystalline corset, first tugging on ribbons to loosen it, then wrenching the contraption open on its little metal hinges.

I have my grandfather to thank for this torturous fashion statement. He was Prime when the magic reappeared, and he came out of the Broken Citadel with the power to grow trees made of unbreakable glass. Which means that ever since then our family has had to have glass adorning every wall, dripping from every ceiling, and compressing every female's bodice.

Once the monstrosity has been pried free, the maid begins plucking out pins with busy fingers until the fabric that envelops me at last begins to fall away. My lungs expand gratefully and my shoulders lift as the weight of my garments is blessedly stripped off.

"It's a jaguar," my father says.

The maid slips and accidentally jabs me. A pin digs deep into my side, just beneath my rib cage. She squeaks and looks up at me with scared eyes, but I shake my head to tell her it's fine. Like I'm going to make a big deal out of a pinprick when I'm about to be ripped apart by a giant, untamed jungle cat.

"Lovely," I say out loud. "I was really *hoping* for something with claws."

The maid breathes a sigh of relief and keeps working, more cautiously now.

"It's not the claws you have to worry about," my father tells me matter-of-factly. "It's the fangs. Make sure to wear your helmet because her bite could crush your skull."

Nervousness skates down my spine, but I refuse to let any of it enter my voice.

"Good tip," I say. "Anything else?"

"Don't turn your back on her. They usually attack from behind. And keep in mind that she can jump. She's also faster than any of the larger predators you've already fought so try to cripple her quickly."

Bile rises in my throat, but I swallow it down.

"Your people appreciate your sacrifice," he continues. "By increasing your own power, you increase the power of the whole realm. You protect us all."

"Through slaughter," I say bitterly.

"Hunters and butchers provide for their families the same way," he points out.

I glare at the door, and he sighs as though he can feel it. This argument is so familiar to both of us that we could switch parts and still know every line.

"I'll let you finish preparing," he says. "Be careful out there."

Careful. Right.

I don't dignify his platitudes with a response.

When the maid finishes gathering up the fabric, she bows and leaves the room with a swish of chiffon and a sympathetic look.

As soon as the door clicks shut, I fall backward onto my bed and cover my face with my hands. They're shaking again. In fact, my whole body is shaking. The animals within me are rioting, absorbing the tumult of emotions I'm feeling and reflecting it back. I remember when it was only a handful of bugs and mice, but there are scores of creatures now, and it feels like they're stampeding, pounding the inside of my body as they try to run, slither, and fly as far away from this situation as they can. If I close my eyes, it feels like I am fleeing with them. Wind on my face, dirt under my feet, the arena far behind me.

But when I open my eyes, I am still lying on my bed, staring at the ceiling. And though my creatures are still running, they are running nowhere. They are as trapped as I am.

I shove my feelings down until the animals settle enough for me to sit up without feeling sick. I can't fall apart yet. I'll have to fall apart afterward. Right now I need to be . . . strong. All Father's ever wanted of me.

I get up from the bed and fling open the doors of my closet with one forceful shove. On the left side, there's a row of floaty dresses in bold, vibrant hues, complete with a rack of aggressively shimmering corsets to strap on top of them. Precise and flawless, just like the lawn out front.

On the right is my battle suit, looking like a limp and headless corpse hung from the railing.

I reach for it, suppressing a shudder. The suit is from Prime Gerdis, former ruler of the Jungle Realm. His magic was to grow armor on his skin and then shed it like a snake. When it's off my body, it retains the shape of his, forming the outline of a man now long dead. But when I put it on, it tightens to my flesh like a second layer of skin. I try not to think about the fact that that's exactly what it is.

It's black, but its shine is green and iridescent, like a beetle shell, and when I wear it I look like a creature myself. The only parts that aren't covered are my head and my clenched fists.

I don't attempt to cover the latter. My magic likes a fair fight, so I have to kill with my own bare hands, which is why they're so littered with scars. Armor on the rest of me doesn't seem to mess anything up, fortunately, but I can't use weapons or traps, I can't tie an animal down, and no one can weaken the creature for me in advance. All of this we learned through a horrific sequence of trial and error.

My childhood was truly charmed.

I'm allowed to cover my head, though, and if what my father said is true, it seems like an incredibly good idea. We have healing magic in stock, of course, but I don't think it could fix a punctured skull.

I pick the helm up and fit it over my head, making sure it's resting securely and fastened firmly. Then I take a couple unsteady, gasping breaths, because the animals are squirming again. Right up my throat.

I can do this. A couple hours from now, it will all be over, and then I'll have a whole year of peace. I am strong. I feel nothing. I am *fine*.

But the girl in the mirror looks nothing like fine. She looks pale and resigned.

She looks weak.

I turn away from her and stride out into the hall, shoving the door shut and locking her behind it, along with my feelings, my fears, and my hesitations.

I'll deal with them later.

Right now I have to do what must be done.

With a straight back and a raised chin, I make my way to what used to be the ballroom.

When I was younger and still listened to my mother's stories, I heard all about the opulent parties my grandfather used to throw there. She spoke at length of the gorgeous dresses, the luscious food, the intoxicating music, and the way it felt to dance and dance and dance.

The room's purpose is a little different now.

When I get to the entrance, two soldiers stand ready. They unlock the double doors and hold them open for me, both their mouths widened in what I'm sure they think are encouraging smiles. Any comfort I might have gained from their expressions, however, is negated by the snap of the bolt locking me in once I've stepped through.

Gone are the drapes and tapestries that adorned the walls when I was a child. The plush carpet, too, has been stripped away. Too many bloodstains. The wall of windows is boarded up, except the very highest ones, which let in either dim sunlight or eerie moonlight depending on the time of day. Where there was once a grand chandelier, dripping with sapphires and gold filigree, there is now a bare hook in the ceiling. The only decoration, if you can call it that, is a giant cage installed at the far side of the room, on what used to be the dance floor. It extends to the ceiling and protrudes deep into the room, so cavernous that it chills me to wonder what kind of beast Father imagines it will one day need to fit. The bars, however, are extremely close together in case the animal is smaller.

The lithe form of a large feline paces behind them. I can hear her growling low in the back of her throat. Her head is close to the ground and her paws pad softly. Her tail whips from side to side. She's ready to pounce. She's scared.

A lump rises in my throat.

"I'm sorry," I whisper.

The door of the cage swings open just as she passes in front of it, triggered by a lever in another room. Luminous yellow eyes swerve toward me.

I meet her gaze, but she doesn't hold mine, instead swiveling her head from wall to wall, looking for an exit.

She won't find one. This room was a ballroom once, but now it's a place of execution.

She's cornered.

When she realizes it, she bares her teeth. They're long and yellow, glistening with saliva, sharp and well used. I remember what my father said about their strength, and I swallow.

For a breath, before everything starts, I allow myself a small moment to feel helpless. To feel sadness. Because this wild beast is absolutely gorgeous, and there's nothing I can do to save her. If I win, her body will be stuffed and mounted on my father's wall, and her spirit will become my slave. If I lose, the soldiers watching from the next room will kill her anyway.

There is no scenario in which she wins.

Then she charges me, and I inhale sharply. She's so fast. I barely have enough time to brace myself before she leaps at me, claws extended and jaws gaping. When she slams into me, she clamps down with her teeth and digs in with her claws, but neither will penetrate my suit. This makes her grip slipperier than she anticipated, and I'm able to use her own momentum to shove her past me, panting.

My advantage is short-lived. In the span of a heartbeat, she lands on silken paws, spins, and lunges again, this time managing to throw me down onto my stomach. My nose smacks against the marble and I both hear and feel a sickening crunch as my blood spatters onto the floor.

I rear my head back, more in alarm than in a coordinated attack, but she's still on me. She wraps me in her paws and buries her fangs into my helm from behind. I writhe beneath her, trying to get away, but her jaws are too powerful. The metal starts to dent, starts to press into my skull.

At the feel of it, my mind blackens with panic, and I fumble with the chin strap. It feels like it takes hours to undo, but in reality it's probably only half a second. As soon as it pops open, I duck out of it and squirm from her grip, letting her crash to the floor with my helmet. Her teeth finally penetrate, and she snaps through the reinforced metal like it's nothing, then spits it out and stalks back toward me.

My heart is racing. My creatures are shifting. I need to calm *down.*

It was a mistake to let sadness in too early.

I shove all my soft sentimentality to the very depths of my heart and wall it off until I am focused and steadfast. Present. Deadly.

I fall back into a fighting stance, a movement that feels as natural as breathing. With carefully placed feet and vigilant eyes, we circle each other, both assessing, both deciding our next move.

I want the fight to be over quickly, not because I fear pain but because I don't want to inflict any more on her than I have to. So I feint to the left and charge her haunches as she jerks to defend her neck.

The move is successful, and I catch her off-balance, pinning her lower half to the floor. But then her torso thrashes above me, and I have to bury my head in her stomach to avoid her swiping paws. Her claws rake my back, but they only ricochet off. That should make me feel confident, but my head feels so exposed now in the open air. It's only a matter of time before she figures out it's not as impenetrable as the rest of my body.

I have to find a way to end this soon.

Her head lashes around, jaws open and teeth snapping. I ball a fist and plunge it at the space between her eyes, hoping to at least stun her, but she's quick. She throws herself forward and catches my fist in her mouth.

Then she slams those long fangs straight through my flesh.

Pain explodes and I scream. It echoes through the cavernous room. I think I feel something crack. Encouraged that she's finally doing damage, the jaguar bites down harder and I feel the deep, seeping sickness of serious injury wash over me. Is she going to rip the whole thing off? I've never lost a hand before. Some distant part of my mind wonders if they'll be able to reattach it, like they did when the bear tore off two fingers.

Most of my mind is not occupied with rational thought, however. The pain is all-consuming, and it ignites something primal in me, something I hate but can't help. It's like my body is made of deadwood until pain acts as its ignition, and then I'm inflamed.

It's the magic, twisting in my gut. I don't like the fight, but *it* does, and it blazes to life, raging through my veins and roaring in my ears. It's a powerful thing, but not like a sword or an arrow is powerful. Like a disease. Like a rot in my flesh, the same rot that lights up the sky. And it changes me, transforming my insides into something monstrous. Something hungry. I grasp for the pain, trying to hold on to it and let it ground me, but I can barely feel it. All I can feel is the bloodlust that isn't mine, and the nausea that is.

Propelled by the ravenous magic, I bear down on her, my free hand at her neck, my fingers digging deep into her throat. Her fur is matted with my blood now, and that makes it slippery, but I hold firm. My knees ram into her midsection, ruthlessly forcing the air from her lungs while I maintain my vise grip on her throat. As I press down with my full weight, she goes feral, bucking and snarling and ripping through the skin of my other hand. I feel the pain like one might register the background noise of a busy street, but it has no hold on me anymore. All that matters is her increasingly strangled breaths.

And the long pauses between them.

One paw swipes me in the head, knocking me to the side, but I catch myself on my shoulder, enough to somewhat soften the blow when my unguarded skull slams into the marble floor. Still, I manage not to let go, to keep clinging to her neck, squeezing with all the desperate, ravenous fury that burns in my veins until the breaths dry up completely. Until her body slumps next to mine.

And then this is the hardest part.

As the bloodlust starts to fade, I force myself to hang on even longer, pushing the now-helpless creature past the point of mere unconsciousness and into something deeper and darker.

And the darkness cuts me just as deeply. As the jaguar's spirit desperately clings to life, my magic wrenches that life away and thrusts it into me instead. It rips my soul open and it plants new teeth and new claws there, impervious to how they shred my insides.

That's when I know it's done, and I drop her and flinch away, bracing my body for what's coming, knowing no walls I put up will be strong enough to shield me from it.

When I claim a new animal, I usually get a flash of who they are, who they were, just before they settle and blend into the rest of me. This happens now, and for a moment I am the jaguar, living her life and seeing the world through her eyes. I know the smells of the jungle, the way it feels to stalk its shadows.

And I know the soft, fuzzy warmth of her cubs snuggling at her side, only a couple months old. It was because of them she was so scared, because of them she fought so hard. Two boys, the older one feisty and the younger shy unless pushed. I have an image of one tackling the other and the two play-wrestling in an adorable ball of rolling fur.

Tears fill my eyes, because they feel like my cubs, and I have no idea what's happened to them. They were too young to survive on their own.

As I'm filled with her life, her memories, and her spirit, the bloodlust dissipates completely, like it was never there. The magic fights with me, but when the excitement is all over, it abandons me to deal with the aftermath on my own. The injuries that I ignored so easily before are now overwhelming. My hand is shredded. My head is throbbing. But the guilt and self-disgust in the pit of my stomach is what causes me to crumple in on myself, sobbing in harsh, wet gasps.

Somewhere in the distance, I hear the door open and medical staff come rushing in to pump me with other people's magic and stitch me up again. I'm a windup doll who has come unwound and their whole job is to wind me back up.

Before they reach me, I lay my head next to the jaguar's and let my tears flow into her fur. My throat is thick and constricted. She's so limp now. So lifeless. It hurts to even look at her, but I force myself to do it.

There's a hand on my shoulder. The Captain of our guard kneels next to me, her salt-and-pepper hair falling into her face. Despite her stocky, armored frame and habitually militaristic posture, her expression is soft.

"You all right?" she asks gruffly.

I shake my head and hold out the hand that isn't ripped apart. She riffles through a pouch at her waist, then presses a small bundle into my palm: the starsprouts I gave Mara earlier.

I clutch them and press the pointed petals to my lips. Then I prop myself on my elbows and lay the bundle gently on the jaguar's chest. Blood soaks the soft white blooms, and another sob escapes my throat. I feel dizzy, and my ears are ringing with the howls of my creatures, storming past the walls to share my grief.

The jaguar within me mourns, too, lamenting her own destruction through the secondhand grief of her killer. It's not right.

It's not *right.*

"We have to knock you out," the Captain says. "So we can sew you up." She gestures at my broken hand, but I don't look at it. I just nod. Right now, oblivion doesn't seem so bad.

The medical staff and soldiers all cover their faces with scarves, before one of them opens a large teal bottle shaped like a crescent moon. Pearl-colored mist streams out of it, and I inhale, coaxing the cloud toward me. As it fills my nostrils, my brain fogs and my limbs go slack. Blessed blackness seeps into my vision and I fall into the Captain's ready arms.

As consciousness slips away and the image of the jaguar's fallen form blurs and disintegrates before me, one question fills my mind.

Am I strong enough yet?

2

Silver

|15 DAYS UNTIL THE ASSURANCE|

Breaking into the palace is a terrible idea, but that doesn't mean I'm not going to do it. Impossibility is negotiable. Inadvisability depends entirely on execution. And irrationality? It's where I live.

But besides all that, I'm desperate.

I leap from one mossy boulder to the next, combat boots thunking against the rock as I land.

"You know there's a giant wall around the castle, right?" Vie snipes as she crouches and eyes the distance I just jumped, preparing to follow.

"I do, yes," I tell her. "It's not overly subtle."

She makes the leap, landing behind me like a cat, but I'm already hoisting myself up the next one, using a patch of shrubbery as leverage, my forearms chafing against the rock.

"Okay, but do you know about the forest of wickedly sharp, magically unbreakable glass trees around that?" she calls after me.

"Yup," I grunt. "Totally aware."

As soon as I clear the top of the rock, she huffs and scrambles up after me, her cheeks reddening with the exertion.

"Are you also aware, Silver, that to get to either one of them, you're going to have to scale an *entire freaking cliff*?"

I smirk. "You mean that one?" I point to the towering ridge in front of us, the one we're heading toward. It's steep, slick, and probably near five hundred feet. "It doesn't seem so bad."

"Tell that to the guy over there."

She waves at a flock of carrion crows picking at something splayed on the other side of a tree stump. Something with a very human-looking hand.

"That's different," I say. "He was probably pushed."

"Pushed by the man whose castle you're about to break into? Great, I feel so much better."

She glares at me with eyes like storm clouds, always thundering against something. Close-cropped black hair slices across her forehead. Her tattooed arms are flexed, and her square jaw is set, her mouth a downturned slash in the middle of it. As small as she is, she can be intimidating when she wants to be.

I flick a pebble at her.

"You're not gonna change his mind, Vie," a voice interjects.

Both our heads whip toward a cleft in the cliffside as a boy our age ducks out of it, practically bent in half because of how tall he is. He swats a clump of springy curls out of his face as he straightens and frowns at me with the air of a father who isn't angry but is extremely disappointed.

"Hey, Rooftop!" I say cheerfully.

Vie scrunches her face up at him. "What are you doing here?"

Rooftop dusts himself off before coming over. "Me?" he asks. "Just following through on a hunch. See, when Silver told us he was going to try to break into the castle, I thought to myself, 'Now what would be the most ridiculous, ill-conceived, and frankly unhinged way to pursue that already outrageous goal?' It was a toss-up between this and seducing the Prospective Seconde, but I know Silver thinks she's obnoxious."

"It's all the pouting," I confirm. "What's she got to be so upset about? One of her dresses is worth more than our entire neighborhood, but she always looks so freaking miserable."

"Right," Rooftop says dryly. "So here I am. And . . . here you are, too." He looks entirely unamused at his own accurate assessment.

"Well, I for one am happy to see you," Vie says, clapping her hands together. "You grab one arm and I'll grab the other. Between the two of us, we can drag him back, easy."

Rooftop lifts one angular shoulder in a half-hearted shrug. "Nah," he says. "He'd just jump out a window while we were sleeping."

"We'll take turns watching him, then," Vie says through gritted teeth.

But Rooftop only shakes his head, springy curls bouncing over green eyes as docile as the moss dusting the boulders around us.

"Then why'd you even come?" Vie growls, impatient.

Rooftop takes a cloth-wrapped package out of his bulky, patchwork coat. "I brought breakfast, actually," he announces with a lopsided grin.

"Breakfast?" I ask. "It's almost noon."

"Yeah, well, you took longer than I thought."

"Vie tied me to a chair."

"That checks out."

Vie pouts as Rooftop finds a sunny patch and lays out his coat like a picnic blanket before unwrapping his flimsy bundle on top of it. Inside are three flaky pastries, each one the size of two fists.

"Whoa!" Vie says, her surliness evaporating immediately at

the prospect of food. "Where'd you get those?"

"Stole them," Rooftop says.

"*You?* No, you didn't." I squint at him, detailing every scrap of his appearance. Ratty shirt, dirty pants, and . . . no shoes. I stomp over. "You sold your boots? You can't survive in the Outskirts without boots, Rooftop."

"Please, tell me how dangerous it is to go without shoes, Mr. About-to-Scale-a-Cliff-with-No-Harness."

I narrow my eyes. "Fair point, but . . . you sold them for a handful of desserts? Why?"

Rooftop's expression darkens with a menace that is uncommon on his face. "I sold them for a final meal with my blockheaded friend before he falls pointlessly to his entirely predictable death and leaves me forever," he says. "Now shut up, sit down, and tell me how much you value our friendship."

I sit.

But I'm still looking at his feet.

"Vie?" I call. "Do you think—"

"Already checking," she says, skipping over to the body behind the stump. There are some scuffling noises and then she reemerges with a pair of shoes. "They're froofy loafers, but they're better than nothing," she says, tossing them at Rooftop.

He wrinkles his nose as he catches them but slips them on his feet without protest. They fit okay.

That taken care of, I relax and reach for a pastry, the other two following my lead.

And it's incredible. Flaky, buttery, melt-in-your-mouth deliciousness, with dollops of sticky-sweet jam. They're not warm anymore, but that doesn't matter. They're the best thing any of us has had in weeks.

"When I finish this job, we're going to eat these every morning," I say. "In our own kitchen, in our own house. And we won't have to sell *any* of our possessions to be able to afford them."

"Yeah, yeah," Rooftop grouses. But I see a wistful smile curling the corner of his mouth.

We eat mostly in silence, with Rooftop giving me mournful glances and Vie glaring at the cliff over my shoulder. When we've consumed every tiny crumb and licked away all hints of jam on the packaging and our fingers, Rooftop stands up.

"Wait until I'm out of sight, will you?" he says.

"You're not staying?" Vie asks, leaping up after him.

"I almost fainted last month when he jumped out of that tree. There's no way I can watch this. Goodbye, Silver. I hope you turn out to be slightly less of a harebrained nitwit than I believe you to be."

"I have valued our friendship greatly these many years," I say solemnly.

He punches me in the chest, mumbles, "Me too," and heads back toward the Outskirts, his back slumped.

I look at Vie and she squares her shoulders at me, hands on her hips and feet firmly planted.

"Fair enough," I say. "Someone's gotta bury me if it all goes wrong."

"No way," she says. "If you actually end up dying because you decided to scale a freaking cliff with no ropes and nothing to catch you, I'm gonna leave your body to rot."

"Okay, then," I tell her.

"I'm serious," she insists. "You're gonna get picked apart by scavenger birds like that guy over there. They're gonna peck out your eyeballs. And your innards."

"I'll try not to fall, then."

"You freaking *better* try not to fall." Her voice catches and I put a hand on her shoulder.

"My very hardest, I promise."

She makes a face and lapses into silence as I let my arm fall back to my side.

"What do you think is the best path?" I ask, because I know that's what she was trying to figure out when she was glaring at the mountain like she could intimidate it into becoming stairs.

She points. "That crack will take you halfway up. Then there's a ledge where it ends that you can follow to the left and get up a little higher. It gets kinda rough after that and you'll have a couple long reaches, but you can make them if you stay steady. Then it's a pretty clear shot to the top from there."

I follow her line of sight and even though it's obvious that it's not a clear shot at *any* point, I don't correct her. She knows as well as I do.

"All right, then," I say. "When the crows come to eat me, try to grab one so you guys can eat, too."

"It's not funny!" she says, even though she's the one who started it.

I take off my shoes and rub my feet in the dirt to give them better traction, then tie the shoes around my waist. Vie pulls on the knot to test it and it holds. But she doesn't let go of the rope. Instead she steps closer and bites her lip.

"I know you're doing this because of me," she says quietly.

"Hey," I say. "I'm not doing this because of you. Or because of Rooftop. I'm doing it *for* you guys, but that's different."

"It isn't," she insists. "And if you die, I'll blame myself forever."

"Oh, yeah?" I press my fingers lightly against her stomach and she hisses and flinches back, wrapping both arms around her midsection as she shoots me an acidic glare. "And what if you die fighting people three times your size for a handful of loose change?" I demand. "You think I wouldn't blame myself for that? You think either of us would ever get over it if Rooftop was caught and killed for moonlighting at a bakery without the proper papers? Academy runaways like us don't *have* a path that's free of danger. But if I pull this off . . . then we will. So Rooftop was right, you're not going to talk me out of it, Vie. Don't try, okay? Because I don't want to fight."

She winces and looks at the ground. "I don't either," she says, voice small.

I hold out a hand. "Tell you what, go ahead and write down all the names you were gonna call me on little slips of paper and when we see each other again you can ball them up and chuck them at my face one by one. Deal?"

She takes my hand, gives it a firm shake, and then forces herself to drop it, uncurling her fingers with noticeable effort.

"Fine," she chokes out. "But no dodging." It seems like she wants to say something else, but instead she purses her lips together and takes a step back.

"No dodging," I promise.

She nods.

And then there's nothing left to do but step up to the rock and start climbing.

The gray stone is cool beneath my palms, and the first bit, when I follow the split in the rock that Vie pointed out, isn't too difficult. I climb every day to get around, so it's mindless at first. Just one move after another, a series of incremental steps. By the time I reach the end of the crack, though, my muscles are burning.

I take a moment to breathe before I edge onto the rock shelf. It's narrower than it looked from the ground, but still definitely wide enough for my toes and the pads of my feet. I ease my foot sideways, feeling confident, but then I accidentally look down and the mountain seems to lurch.

I dig my fingers into the rock and close my eyes. The height doesn't matter as long as I don't fall. This part isn't even hard. If I hadn't looked, I would've been on the other end of the ledge by now.

But I did look, and it was so much farther than I thought, so much farther than it seemed from below. Vie is a tiny doll peering up at me. I can't even read her expression. And I don't remember those rocks being quite so pointy when I was on the ground.

Pushing all of that out of my mind, I focus on the taste of breakfast pastry in my mouth. Tart strawberry. Browned butter. Flaky crust. The traces of mint and rosemary that I'm only able to identify because Rooftop pointed them out to me. Eventually my heartbeat slows.

Careful now to keep my eyes on the ledge and nothing below it, I creep sideways, then up. The handholds here are deep and easy. I gain some distance and some of my confidence back. But then I hit that smooth patch Vie pointed out. My hand gropes around for any kind of purchase, but there's none. The closest divot in the rock face is way too far. I look at the hole, assess at the distance I need to reach, and my limbs lock up.

I don't look down this time, but I know the height isn't survivable. Not a chance.

My leg starts to shake.

"Oh, come on," I say. "Not now."

This happens to me sometimes with heights. I'm *not* afraid of them. But my leg is, I guess, because every now and then when I get too high it starts to lose it.

Loose gravel falls out of the pocket I wedged my foot into and I try not to listen to the sound of it skittering down, down, down, down.

"You shouldn't have been so quick to dismiss that 'seduce the Prospective Seconde' idea," I grumble to myself. "Flirting wouldn't end in shattered bones."

Then again, she did rip apart a menagerie of animals with her bare hands, so maybe this was the safer route after all.

I inhale through my nose and exhale through pursed lips. If I can't get my traitorous leg under control, it will buckle when I put weight on it.

"What kind of fear response is this anyway?" I ask it. "Do you think this is helpful? In what scenario would you shivering like a wet kitten be of any use to me at all? Huh?"

My leg does not answer. It just keeps banging against the rock. My knee's probably going to have a bruise, which is just great.

It is also, quite definitely, the least of my problems.

Vie shouts something and her voice echoes off the rock, but I can't make out what she's saying. Despite the chill of the stone, my fingertips are getting sweaty. I have to move.

I don't think the pastry will work again, so this time when I clear my head I think of safety. Four walls around me, a roof over my head, and solid ground beneath my feet. I think about walking around barefoot with no fear of glass in the dirt. I think about Rooftop cooking and Vie not feeling like she has to keep guard all night and a door that can shut out everything in the world that we don't want to let in. A place where we make the rules and where nothing can hurt us. Real jobs we don't have to hide. A real future.

Bit by bit, my leg relaxes. I take four more deep, steadying breaths. As I exhale the last one, I steel myself. I am calm. I am impenetrable.

I reach.

Only to come up short. The next handhold is too far, and I can only graze it.

I lean out as much as I can and try again.

This time, I can grasp the lip of it just barely, but it's not enough. I won't get a good grip unless I let go with my other hand.

And if I think about that too much, I know my leg will start up again and I'll never get it to stop. So I don't think.

I let go.

I know that the moment I'm holding on to nothing can't be more than a second or two, but it feels like forever. My stomach scrapes on the rock as I thrust myself sideways, grabbing at the handhold with a desperation I haven't felt since I was first on the streets, before I learned to steal and thought starving might be the only way. But when I dig my fingers in, the rock is solid. It holds. I can pull myself up and swing my leg into another foothold.

And from there I don't stop. I can't take any more time to contemplate what an insane thing I just did. I scuttle up the rest of the cliff until I'm finally pulling myself over the edge and clenching fistfuls of grass like I'm still dangling and they're my only anchor.

It's only when Vie's whoop echoes behind me that I cough out a laugh and unclench my fists.

"It's not over yet," I say under my breath.

Rows and rows of glass pines stand before me, an army as formidable as any battalion of soldiers. Each individual tree is decked with thousands of sinister points, like a bouquet of crystal knives glittering in the muted sunlight. But together, crowded so close that they form a near-solid mass of edges and spikes, and towering so high that I almost can't see above them, they form a forest that looks impenetrable.

I hold up a finger. "If you guys could give me just a minute, that would be great."

The forest of death doesn't move, so I flop on my back and close my eyes, once again trying to slow my heart and my breathing. My mom used to tell me I was reckless. If she hadn't died in the war, she probably would have had a heart attack watching me do that.

Then again, she wouldn't have let me.

Then again, I wouldn't have had to in the first place.

I sit up, this time looking at the castle beyond the pines, a barely visible collection of dark towers and edged spires laying its claim to the cliff's highest points.

The monster in there took everything from me.

And I'm ready to take a little back.

I push myself to my feet and approach the glass forest. Prime Elod, the current Prime's father, grew these, but he had to be standing on the ground to do it. Which means as close together as these trees look, there must be some paths between them.

I walk up to them and try to fit myself between one tree and another. I can do it, but barely. One slip, one fall, and I'm impaled.

"Good thing my leg doesn't have a thing about glass," I mutter.

I go agonizingly slowly, placing careful footsteps on soft, overgrown grass, and keeping my spine ramrod straight. At one point a hawk's shriek makes me flinch and my arm gets a few new gashes, but I've had worse. I keep going, leaving my blood glinting on the crystal branches.

When I get to the wall, I press up against it with an eager grin. This last obstacle seems like nothing after the two before it. I scale the sleek surface in what feels like two strides, ready to swing my leg over it and finally enter the castle.

And that's when someone grabs my wrist.

Panic surges through me and I jerk back, wrenching my hand free. But that motion tips me off-balance and I fall into a shock of empty air.

With frantic clawing motions, I grapple for purchase on the wall as I plunge downward, only a mere breath away from the sea of sharpened glass when I manage to dig my fingers and toes deep enough into mortar-filled cracks to stop my descent. But even then I don't relax.

I expect the sound of an alarm. Or an arrow through my head. I brace myself to be scraped off the wall like a bug and unceremoniously dropped into the waiting jaws of the forest below at any moment.

But nothing happens. Finally, cautiously, I tilt my head back and look up.

The soldier is leaning over the edge, regarding me with amusement, and I can't figure out why he's not attacking me until I take in the features of his face.

Sharp cheekbones, light stubble, keen eyes the blue of ice.

It's . . . Guerre.

As in the guy who offered me this job. The guy who said he *needed* someone who could get into the castle for him.

"So you're perfectly capable of breaking in on your own, then, huh?" I grumble.

He pulls me up with a chuckle. "Of course I am. But I already know what *I* can do. I needed to know what you could do. It was a test, and you passed."

"I'm thrilled," I say dryly, rubbing a knot in my shoulder.

He gives me a smirk that's halfway between friendly and mocking. "You know, there's a servant's tunnel on the other side of the grounds. One you don't have to clamber up a cliff to use."

"Oh, sure," I say. "I knew. I just thought this way would be more fun."

He laughs and claps me on the back. Then he strolls toward a guard tower nearby, clearly expecting me to follow.

But I hesitate.

I don't completely trust Guerre. There have been rumors circulating about him for months, passed through back alleys and whispered in Outskirt shacks. Rumors that he had under-the-table jobs for kids without papers, but that those jobs were always . . . sketchy. Dangerous. *Odd*. The general consensus was to stay away.

And if Rooftop hadn't lost his bakery gig, I probably would have. But then the Prime announced the Assurance, an event that not only formally establishes the heir and second-in-command, but also usually comes with several other internal appointments and promotions. Suddenly, all the Prime's soldiers got real interested in proving themselves, and smoking out Academy runaways like us is an easy way to do it. Kids were disappearing right and left, then showing up dead in the town square, their employers right beside them. So Rooftop's boss got spooked and threw him out. Of course, Rooftop didn't argue, and he still insists that his boss was a good guy. But personally, I don't have a lot of respect for cowards.

Since then, all we've had to live off of is what I could steal and what Vie could win in the ring. And it's not enough. Vie started fighting more often, throwing herself into new fights long before she'd recovered from the last ones. When she came home spitting blood last week, I decided it was time to seek Guerre out.

And to my surprise, he'd been watching me, too.

He offered me something big. Academy graduate papers, ones that would get us whatever jobs we wanted. And a house that isn't in the Outskirts. Somewhere safe and comfortable where we could build a real future. It's everything we could want, everything we need—everything the Prime took from us in the first place.

But he wouldn't tell me what he wanted in exchange, only that the first step was to break into the castle.

And now that I've done it, I feel more anxious than elated. There's something about this guy that I can't put my finger on. Like some core part of him, something important, is missing. He gives me shivers whenever he talks.

But I've come this far.

And like I said, I don't have a lot of respect for cowards.

So let's see what kind of mess I've gotten myself into this time.

I make my feet move and follow him into the guardhouse, swallowing hard. If he notices my reluctance, he doesn't show it. He just takes a bundle off a shelf and passes it to me, his expression unconcerned.

"What's this?" I ask as the fabric unfolds in my hands.

"A servant's uniform," he says. "It will come in handy for the next part."

"The next part being what exactly?" I say pointedly. "You said you'd tell me."

"I will." He levels his cool blue eyes on me. "I need something with the Prime's seal on it. I need *you* to steal it."

I almost drop the uniform completely.

"The Prime's seal?" I gasp. "But that's—"

"Impossible, I know. So is breaking into the palace. But here we are."

I blink at the folded waistcoat and crisp white shirt bunched in my hands. They're nicer than anything I own. "Are you sure you don't already have twelve seals in your back pocket or something?" I grouse.

This time, he doesn't laugh. "I assure you, every task I give you from here on out will be vital. This is the first of three. You'll get details on the other two when it's appropriate, but you can expect them to be of a similar difficulty."

Well, that's great.

I don't care what this guy does to the Prime. Whatever it is, I'm sure the brute deserves it. Guerre can burn down the whole castle with everyone in it, and as long as I get paid I'll be perfectly happy.

But as reckless as I may be, I'm not trying to get killed for someone else's scheme, and if this first task is only the beginning of the danger, then I'm not sure it's worth it. I sincerely consider climbing back down the cliff when Guerre pries open the shutters of the guard tower with a clatter and sweeps his arm over the realm below us. "Do you see the house with the green roof?" he asks me.

I lean out, the wind on my face. And the whole of the Cliff Realm is spread before me. Bulging bluffs surrounded by scraggly forest. Homes, storefronts, and meeting places crammed along a steep, narrow road zigzagging to the top. Most of the roofs are thatched, but one near the middle has painted green shingles.

"I see it."

He places a heavy hand on my shoulder. "That's the one I'll give you if you successfully complete all three tasks. That"—he unfurls a scroll that somehow appeared in his other hand—"and these." I see my name in neat calligraphy, and then he slides his thumb so I can see Vie's and Rooftop's names on scrolls behind it. The language of the documents is exact, and the lettering is perfect. If they're forgeries, they're very good ones. Except . . .

"They're not sealed," I protest.

He makes an exasperated noise. "And why do you think that is?"

Oh. Duh. "Because . . . you need me to steal the seal."

"There it is," he says, rolling the scrolls back up. "For a second you made me doubt you were clever enough for this after all."

I watch the scrolls disappear into his pockets, resisting the urge to snatch them out of his hands. Seeing tangible proof of the future I'm fighting for has done a lot to shore up my resolve. So it's without any lingering trace of reluctance that I say, "All right, I'll do it."

"Good," Guerre says. "Then report to the kitchens. As it happens, the head of the serving staff is taking on temporary new hires to help prepare for the enthroning of the Seconde. You're one of them. Good luck."

He smiles in a way that makes me feel small, and I look down, my gaze drawn back to the house he promised. As I greedily soak in its ivy-covered walls, wrought iron lanterns, and burgundy shutters, I know I made the right decision, and the last of my unease is snatched away by the wind whipping my face. I'm doing this, no matter what the risks might be.

But when I turn back to say so, Guerre is gone.

3

Prospective Seconde Mancella Amaryllis Cliff

|14 DAYS UNTIL THE ASSURANCE|

I am eight years old, and my father has brought me to a ghost town.

We trudge forward, my hand in his. Desert sand bites at my cheeks as a hot wind rattles the loose, broken shutters of empty houses. It makes my skin crawl, like the sand isn't sand at all, but ants that burrow into my clothing and my eyes and my mouth. Worse, there's no life here. Not even a lizard or a spindly shrub. The whole city feels like an open wound.

And still we keep walking.

In front of us lies the Broken Citadel. Squinting into the sun, I can almost imagine the grand castle it must once have been. That gritty, charred masonry was probably a blend of warm, inviting earth tones when it was constructed. Those spiraling columns must have been stories high. But now it is only a jagged set of walls jutting out of the ground. The rest of the castle is gone, as if it were made of nothing but more sand, and someone walked up and kicked it over, spilling its innards into the wind.

And if the castle had stayed that way, it wouldn't be scary. There's nothing to fear in empty ruins.

But these ruins aren't empty. Something grew there, like a fungus in its festering corpse. Within the open, gaping shell of the Citadel is an amorphous green ball of light so intense it should hurt to look at it. But it doesn't. It has a strange, sickly draw, such that it isn't the looking that's difficult. It's the looking away.

"I'm supposed to go in there?" Mara asks, clutching Father's other hand so firmly that her knuckles turn bone white. Her posture is rigidly regal, but a note of uncertainty weaves itself into her voice, and I tear my eyes away from the Citadel to look at her sharply.

"Yes," Father replies, squeezing her hand hard enough to force her fingers to release. "All you have to do is walk in. The magic will accept you, and you'll walk out again with a piece of it to keep."

This is enough for Mara, and she nods solemnly, her expression set.

But it isn't enough for me.

"What about Uncle Edwarn?" I ask, tugging Father's arm so he'll look at me. "He didn't get magic. He never came back out at all."

Father's face goes slack and I shrink into myself, regretting my blunt words. It's been almost a year since Father and Uncle Edwarn entered the Broken Citadel and only Father came back out, but it's still a sore subject. Everyone in the castle knows not to mention it. Even Edwarn's wife and son—my aunt and cousin—have avoided his name. At least they did before they suddenly disappeared a few weeks ago, something no one has been willing to explain to me.

But I know my cousin Alect, and he wouldn't have left willingly. At least, not without saying goodbye.

He was one of my best friends.

"He . . . wasn't worthy," Father says, and it takes me a second to realize he's talking about his brother.

I bite my lip. "But . . . why not?" I press. "Uncle Edwarn was good! And brave, and kind, and—"

"We don't know," my father snaps. "We never know. The magic decides."

A shutter clatters in the wind, and it draws my attention back to the yawning desolation around us. The silence feels so loud, so heavy in its emptiness.

"Did it decide this whole city wasn't worthy, then?" I ask quietly. "Because we've yet to see a single person."

For a second, he looks at me like he wishes I would disappear, too. Like if the sand below our feet turned into quicksand, if it started to suck me in, he would drop my hand and keep walking. But then he turns away from me and his expression clears.

"In a way I suppose it did," he says distantly.

My mother comes up and clasps my shoulders, rubbing small circles with her thumbs.

"Magic was common once," she tells me. "Did you know that? But then one realm tried to harness the magic to use against another. They only wanted to use a little, but then the magic started feeding on them and they didn't know how to stop it. It just kept going, draining every drop of power they had. First everyone in the castle, and then the city, and then the realm. In the end, it took the magic of everyone in the world, and the blast it created was so large it destroyed six whole realms completely. Those who were left thought the magic was gone forever. But then, just a few years ago, it appeared again. As a glow on the horizon."

"And ever since then, the magic has been wrong," the Captain snaps. She's been tromping stonily at the back of our party, and this is the first I've heard her speak on the entire journey.

My father scowls at her. "It isn't wrong*, it just requires strength to handle. To tame. As I said, not everyone is worthy. The magic knows to reject those who are not up to the task."*

"Then perhaps we should not be tossing it children," the Captain hisses, but softly enough that only my mother and I can hear, and my mother pretends not to.

I peer at the Captain over my shoulder, but she doesn't say anything else. She merely keeps marching, her every muscle tensed like she's expecting a threat.

"I don't have a good feeling about this," I say, loudly enough to be heard by everyone. "I don't think Mara should go in."

"That's not up for debate," Father tells me.

Mara ducks behind his back and pokes me in the shoulder. "Don't worry so much," she says, with big-sisterly confidence. "I'm strong. I'll be fine." Her eyes shine with newly acquired purpose, and I have to admit that it suits her. If she gets magic she could become eligible to rule today, and that's a powerful and important thing. In a mere handful of years, Father could name her his Seconde.

On the other hand, in a mere handful of hours, she could be dead.

The heat suddenly feels stifling, searing. I have the irrational thought that it may soon burn me alive. I want to get away from it. I want to go home.

But before I can express the wish, our party comes to an abrupt halt.

The Citadel looms above us, its strange green flames licking at the edges of its empty doorway like a starving man might lick his lips.

Mara takes a step forward, and it feels too fast, too soon. I grab for her arm, but my mother pulls me back, her pretty nails scraping my wrist, and my father's grip tightens uncomfortably.

"Don't—" I say.

But before I can even finish the plea, Mara takes off, running through the great archway and instantly swallowed by its light.

My breath catches in my throat. Dread creeps down my scalp. I pull away from my parents and stare into the curling flames so hard that my eyes start stinging.

"Why can't I see her anymore?" I demand.

"That's normal," my father says. His gaze is also riveted on the twisting magic light, but his expression isn't one of worry. It's . . . hunger.

"Well, how long will she be in there?" I push.

"It varies," he tells me, unconcerned.

The Captain's armor creaks as she shifts. My mother returns her hands to my shoulders, but they feel heavier this time and I fall silent. There's nothing I can do now anyway. Whatever happens next has already been set in motion.

So we wait.

Each minute feels like a lifetime as the sun sinks lower on the horizon. Soon the sky is a brilliant orange, clashing with the green of the blazing, radiant magic contorting before us. It feels like too much color. The vividness is inescapable, suffocating.

And Mara still hasn't come back out.

My mother sniffs behind me and it's only then I realize she's crying. Silent, desolate tears making wet tracks in the sand on her face. Why doesn't she make any noise? I want to pinch her, just to make her scream.

Then my father detaches her from me and plants a firm hand on my lower back, shoving me forward.

"Your turn, Mancella," he says.

I whip around, angry, as the Captain stalks toward us.

"Mara could still come out," I protest. "She will come out."

"Your turn," he repeats. Something about him has hardened, and it makes my skin go clammy.

Mother sees it, too, and tries to encourage me. "You'll get magic!" she says, but she can't make her mouth smile, and tears still darken her cheeks.

And she can't really tell me what will happen, anyway. She's never gone in herself. As the fifth child out of seven, she was never expected to rule her native Coast Realm. It was safer and more useful to secure an alliance with my father by marrying her off, rather than keeping too many contenders for the throne in one castle.

"My Prime," the Captain says, stepping between us. "You cannot throw both children in today. Think it through! If what you say is true and the magic looks for strength, then perhaps it is rejecting them today when it would not do so later on. You could lose them both, senselessly! Just . . . give Mancella time!"

"I do not have time!" my father shouts, wheeling on her. "You know why."

I look between them, startled. "Why?" I ask. Because if there's a reason that Mara and I are going in at eight and ten years of age when Father and Uncle Edwarn didn't visit the Broken Citadel until well into adulthood, no one has told that reason to me.

But my father keeps talking as though he didn't hear me. "More importantly," he says. "This is not your decision to make. And you would do well to remember your place."

"I cannot watch you sacrifice these children for nothing," the Captain shoots back. "I—"

Her hand twitches toward her sword, and in a cold moment of clarity I realize she might actually attack.

My father could die. Or my Captain could. And I can't lose either one.

I take off, running toward the castle, questions forgotten.

"Mancella," the Captain cries. "No!"

Heedless of her cries, I speed up, until I'm hurtling forward as recklessly as Mara did, straight through the doorway and into the beckoning light.

Just before entering the Citadel, I look back. I see my father's puffed-out chest. My mother's head buried in her hands. The Captain running after me.

But when I cross the threshold, everything goes black.

Black black. Not black like someone has snuffed the lamp but moonlight still streams through the windows. Black like light has never existed. Black like the world was only chalk on a chalkboard and it's just been wiped away.

It feels like a force, the blackness. Like it's solid and alive. Breathing.

I'm afraid to move. Afraid of what my hands might hit if I do. Afraid that if I open my mouth, the darkness will rush into it.

The force around me rumbles. Suddenly, I know that a closed mouth will do nothing to stop this darkness if it wants me.

Which it does.

It rushes in all at once, filling every pore of my skin, coating every strand of my hair, flowing through every vein. I don't know where I end and it begins. I don't even know what it is, and yet it knows me. Every part of my body and corner of my mind feels splayed open for the magic's viewing, like I'm a bug pinned to a wall and then sliced apart and studied bit by bit by bit by bit by bit. I scream and writhe, but there's nothing to attack but my own body. I don't even feel solid ground beneath my feet anymore. There is only blackness. There is only invasion. There is only the magic and me.

Then, in a moment, there is stillness.

And in that small moment, that absence of anything, I feel something within me break.

I couldn't have told you what it was beforehand, as I'd never noticed it before. But as soon as I feel it altered, I know it to be the most core part of me. It's as though my very soul has bent. My self, my being, is twisted now, ever so slightly.

And that small, brief, infinitesimal moment of twisting terrifies me more than the rushing, consuming force that preceded it ever could.

A doorway appears behind me, with moonlight streaming through it, but the girl who walks out of that door is not the same as the girl who ran in.

My parents fall upon me, kissing me and embracing me, but even my love for them is bent a little. I still feel it, but it isn't the same. I can't stop thinking about the fact that they sent me in there, and my father, at least, knew what was waiting. I feel as though he's killed me.

"Did Mara make it?" I ask, in a voice that doesn't quite sound like my own.

Their faces fall, and my stomach along with them. I wrench myself free of their grasp and run back to the doorway, hoping for a glimpse of black hair or pale skin. Which part is she trapped in? Is the magic still consuming her, or is her soul being broken more than once? Twisted and retwisted like hair around a finger?

The green of the magic is paler now, ghostly and translucent in the night.

I can't see Mara anywhere.

"Mancella," the Captain says. Her voice is gentle, but her grip on my arm is firm. "It's been hours. She's not coming out."

"It's time to leave," my father says.

But I won't go, I can't. I'm about to say this, to fight him, when Mother cries out. She's pointing behind me.

And then Mara is there. A cry of joy fills my throat, only to die on my tongue when Mara steps out of the magic's glare.

In the eerie green glow, her face looks like it's melted. One eye is completely missing, and the skin around her mouth is red and raw. Her lips seem as though they've been peeled away, revealing all her teeth on one side. She leans heavily against the doorway, like she needs it to stand.

Then she looks up.

And the scars on her face are nothing compared to the stark horror in her hooded gaze.

I wake screaming, my sister's terror even more upsetting than my own. My blankets are wrapped around my limbs, and in a moment of hazy panic I think the tightly wound comforters are the fiery tendrils of the magic reclaiming me, pulling me back in. I fight it, arms flailing, frantic when I can't easily break free.

But then a cool hand touches my forehead. I stop thrashing long enough to realize that the room is chilly instead of scorching hot. The light is white and soft instead of green and searing. And that's Mara next to me. Safe.

"They told me they gave you Uncle Veras's sleeping magic," she says.

I swallow and nod against her hand. The pearl-colored gas is imported from the Coast Realm, from my mother's brother. It knocks you out, speeds your healing, and enables you to endure all manner of surgeries without feeling a thing. But it gives you horrible nightmares as you slumber. And they're always true.

Mara smooths the hair from my face and tucks it behind my ear. "Did you see the Broken Citadel?"

"Yes," I whisper hoarsely.

She makes a humming noise in the back of her throat. Then she leans forward and the moonlight catches her features. In the unguardedness of nighttime her face is uncovered. The scars from that day are still there, webbed across what's left of her skin in puckered white lines.

I feel a pang of nostalgia. Mara and I haven't been close since the Citadel, not like we used to be. It isn't as if we're enemies, but we don't talk the way we did before. These days our jokes have barbs and our hearts have walls. I think we both dealt with what happened in our own ways and didn't realize until it was too late that the way we each chose was "alone."

But she always seems to appear in the aftermath of my darkest moments. She always knows, and she always sits with me until everything feels less terrible.

And that isn't nothing.

I lean into her, and she strokes my hair until I fall back asleep.

*

Hours later, I wake again, to the swish of fabric and the clack of hangers. I crack an eye open to see Mara riffling through my closet, discarding one dress after another. With a sleepy groan, I pull the covers back over my head, hoping she'll take the hint, but the clatter only gets louder. I whip the covers off again and catch her slamming one of the hangers against the back of the closet.

"Oh, hello!" she says, acting surprised. "I hope I didn't wake you."

Glaring, I prop myself up, inadvertently putting weight on my injured hand, then hiss at the resulting jolt of pain. Yesterday's events come rushing back to me as I take in the fresh bandages that wind around my palm.

I can't stand the sight of them, so I rip them off. Underneath, my flesh is red and angry. Black thread weaves through it in so many places it looks more like chunks of meat strung together than it does a hand. But I flex the fingers, and although it feels like sticking my arm in a meat grinder, everything bends like it's supposed to.

"What do you think?" I ask Mara, waving my mess of a hand at her. "Pretty gruesome, huh?"

She turns toward me, holding a dress of midnight blue. Her face is still uncovered, the teeth on one side of her mouth exposed. "Not bad," she says, "but still not on my level. Keep trying."

I chuckle. "Maybe next time."

She puts the blue dress back and grabs one in forest green. "If you *really* wanted scars as cool as mine, you'd stop dodging so much."

"Duly noted," I return. "Next time something comes at me with fangs as long as my forearms I'll just stand there."

"Very good." She studies the gown in her hand, then holds it up to me. "How do you feel about this one?"

It's a floor-length wrap dress with silver embellishments and a plunging neckline. And I mean *plunging*.

"I hate it," I tell her frankly. "It's too low-cut."

"That's why I picked it. Father said to dress aggressively."

"My breasts are the least aggressive part of me."

"Then you're not using them right," she says, tossing the dress at me.

For herself, Mara chose a severe black dress with stark lines and a high collar that frames her face. I note that it shows no cleavage at all, which really doesn't seem fair. And, as usual, in lieu of a corset she wears several oversized necklaces strung with glittering glass gems.

I raise an eyebrow at her. "What if I told you I don't care what Father thinks I should wear today?"

To my surprise, Mara laughs and gives me a pitying look. "You know I'm always here for a tantrum, but I would advise you to pick another day to throw it."

Something in her tone makes me sit up straighter, throwing my blankets off. "Why?"

"Because the Prime of the Grasslands is here," she tells me, like she's divulging a secret.

"Oh," I say, slouching again. "Sangua *is* pretty creepy." She can manipulate blood, and instead of looking a person in the eye, she will usually focus her attention on your jugular or the veins of your wrists. No wonder Mara chose such a high-necked dress.

"Wow, you really haven't been paying attention, have you?" Mara says, flipping her hair over her back smugly. She loves knowing things other people don't.

I roll my eyes. "Whatever you're preening about, why don't you just spit it out?"

"All right, fine," she says, affronted. "Sangua's *dead*."

Whatever I was expecting, it wasn't that. "What?!" I gasp. "Are you sure? When did that happen?"

Mara plops down next to me on the bed, pleased that I'm finally showing some interest in her gossip, and lowers her voice to a conspiratorial whisper. "Seems like it happened about a month ago but they kept it under wraps for a while, so Father only found out last week," she tells me. "I overheard." Translation: She was spying.

I lean back on my elbows, processing. "I can't believe I didn't know this. How did she die?"

"That's the weird thing," Mara says, leaning forward. "From all accounts it sounds like she did it herself. When they found her body, it was completely bloodless. Not a drop left inside of her, but it looked like blood had burst out of her mouth and her eyes and even exploded from under her fingernails. It was *everywhere*. And no one could have done that to her but *her*."

I feel my own blood drain from my face. "That's horrible."

"Isn't it?" She doesn't say it with the same sincerity that I do.

"Wait, but then . . . who's coming tonight? Sangua didn't have any children. And she didn't name a Seconde. Who was her heir?"

"That's where it gets even weirder!" Mara exclaims, throwing her hands up. "She had no blood relatives at all, but a week before she died she tossed a bunch of her servants into the Broken Citadel to see what they came out with, and then she picked her favorite to inherit. Some kid barely older than us. Her name's Azele."

"But that doesn't even make sense!" I burst out, cutting her off. "What about the treaty?"

When the magic came back, for a while everything was chaos. Primes would cart their citizens up to the Citadel in droves and come back with destructive, overpowered armies. War was rampant, and it was more breathtakingly vicious than ever before. Casualties were high, borders were constantly shifting, and many families started running out of successors. My grandfather was one of the only Primes who survived the whole turbulent period.

Finally, after a few years of chaos, the standing Primes of the six living realms made a treaty to limit Citadel access to royal bloodlines only. But because this agreement was reached by a group of Primes who had already attained magic, they also decided that no one could run a realm without it. It was to be an aristocratic rite of passage. Which means if a Prime dies before naming a Seconde—the formal title for an heir and second-in-command—then rule of the realm would pass to their closest magic-wielding blood relation, and no one else.

It's the reason Father's naming me his Seconde instead of Mara. Because despite what the Broken Citadel put her through, it never gave her anything back.

Her magic never manifested.

Mara plucks leftover pins out of my hair, making my tangled

tresses unfurl around my shoulders. "Apparently she altered their blood before having them enter to make them all her cousins, and then undid it if she didn't like what they came out with. Azele is the only one she didn't change back, which means she's the only one left eligible."

I shiver, imagining what it must feel like to have the very blood in your veins altered, most likely against your will. "And they counted that?" I ask.

"They kind of had to," she says, combing through my hair with her fingers in search of any pins she missed. "They've got no other heir. And if the rumors are to be believed, the girl didn't even know she was set to inherit. She was mucking out the stables when they told her she'd just become the ruler of the entire realm. And then her Ascension was the very next day."

"Wow," I say. "That must have been quite the adjustment."

"No kidding," she says. "Although maybe she knew the whole time and just kept it to herself. I would." Once the last pin is free, Mara braids along my scalp with nimble fingers, smoothing strands into submission effortlessly. Then she stabs the pins back in to keep everything in place.

"Ow," I mutter. "So what's her power?"

"Oh!" Mara says, brightening as the last pin slides into place. "She can turn any inanimate object into ash. And she's got this bodyguard with magic, too. One of the other servants Sangua tossed in. His name is Rift and they say he can turn into shadows." She wiggles her fingers dramatically.

"So they're really keeping the creepy theme going, huh?"

"Well, sure, it's tradition. So anyway"—Mara pushes off the bed and heads back for the closet—"because Sangua wasn't really one to make treaties, everyone's scrambling to convince her successor to be more amenable. Including us. So . . . now that you understand the circumstances, will you *please* wear the flattering dress?" She holds it up, shaking the skirts at me so that the fabric shimmers. "As I have just clearly outlined for you, it is of great importance to inter-realm relations."

"I see how the *meeting* is of importance to inter-realm relations," I tell her. "I'm still not entirely clear why my breasts are. But I'll wear the red one. All right? Red like the blood of our enemies."

She sniffs but seems satisfied. "I'll see you in there, then," she says, returning the sparkly monstrosity to my closet.

Before she leaves, she grabs a scarf from the vanity and winds it around her face. It's black, like her gown, and makes her look even more austere.

"See you at dinner!" she calls as she shuts the door. "You have twenty minutes!"

Dinner? How long have I been sleeping?

I look out the window to see the sun already low on the horizon. The clouds are the same color as my dress, a red that is both bright and deep. Like gashes in the open sky.

The same color Sangua's blood must have been when it exploded out of her body and coated her room.

I shudder and draw the curtains shut before I change.

❦✻❦

The dining room is as dressed up as we are, with oversized goblets, wine-colored tablecloths, and all four candelabras lit and shining brightly. As usual, glass plays prominently into the decor, framing the plates, encircling the napkins, and dangling from the chandeliers above. My mother's dress is crafted entirely out of glass beads stitched together, and it makes her look like a curtain, or perhaps a lamp.

My father is seated at the head of the table, with Mother at his left and Mara beside her. The empty seat on his right is for me.

Across from him sits the new Prime of the Grasslands. Just like Mara said, she's young, but she looks convincingly regal. Her posture is rigid, her hands are folded, and her eyes are intelligent. She's wearing a cinder-colored silk dress that contrasts stunningly with her dark skin. Her cheekbones are highlighted with ash.

Beside her is her bodyguard, presumably the one who can turn into shadows. Rift, was it? His gaze snaps to mine as though he can sense my attention, and his eyes are startlingly lifeless. They're gray, but one of them has a jagged orange line slashed through it, like a vein of quartz in granite. It feels as though someone carved a statue out of stone and painted it to resemble a living human, but entirely forgot to paint over those cold, stony eyes.

I sit.

Father smiles at me warmly, which puts me even more on edge. It almost never means something good when he smiles like that. I shift in my chair, wishing I'd told everyone I was still recovering and taken dinner alone in my room.

He claps his hands and servants appear behind each chair, carrying dome-covered plates. I regard the one placed in front of me, hoping for salad, or corn soup, or roasted sweet potatoes stuffed with a black bean relish. My father knows I won't eat meat, that with all the killing I'm forced to do I refuse to endorse any more for something as trivial as my meals, but sometimes when we have guests, he "forgets."

The dome is lifted.

And my stomach roils.

Sitting on my shiny glass plate is a steak. Rare. No sides, no garnishes, just a giant slab of steaming, bloody meat. My hands fist in the tablecloth as I fight back the urge to vomit, but it's not until Prime Azele takes a bite and draws her eyebrows together like the flavor is something she can't quite place that I realize the situation is even worse than I thought.

I study the meat meticulously, hoping I'm wrong. But the color is slightly off. The texture is different, too, tougher and grainier than a steak would typically be.

It's no cow on my plate.

"How do you like it?" my father asks, barely containing his glee.

Prime Azele looks unsure. She cuts another slice but doesn't raise it to her lips. "It's a unique flavor. What kind of meat is it?"

I flinch and make an involuntary noise in the back of my throat.

"It's jaguar," my father declares, as though revealing a delightful surprise.

I knew before he said it, but even so, the words are like a slap to my face. I am shaking with anger. Within me, my animals rear up on hind legs, clawing at the underside of my skin. And among them is a new voice, a new roar, a new set of furiously swiping paws.

The pressure is unbearable.

My father leans forward conspiratorially. "Mancella killed the beast herself," he gloats.

Everyone's eyes flick to me. Azele's look startled, but her bodyguard's are cold and flat, like he could kill me and it would barely even register.

Under their gazes, my body feels even tighter. They *must* be able to see my struggle. It feels like my skin is bulging with the riot it's holding at bay. Can't they hear the snarls? Can't they sense the jaguar herself breathing down their necks as she watches them feast?

But Father just keeps beaming.

I can't stand it. His boasting, his pride. The delight he takes in that which causes me the most pain. The gusto with which he slices into the flesh, juices spilling onto his plate and flecking the front of his shirt.

"It's very interesting," my mother says, mulling over a dainty bite. "Sort of like wild boar in taste, but with the texture of goat."

Mara nods in agreement, even though she hasn't touched hers. She's trying to catch my eye, warning me to keep my temper in check in front of our guests. And with good reason, because Prime Azele is still looking right at me, as though whatever I do next will form her opinion of me, my family, and my realm forever.

Which is a pretty big deal. It's been drilled into me from birth that the success of a realm depends heavily on its relations with the other five, and my father is diligent, sometimes even ruthless, in maintaining them. His marriage to my mother guarantees good standing with the Coast Realm, the Jungle Realm is secured by a longstanding alliance based heavily on militaristic promises, the Forest Realm hasn't been an issue since we decimated half their population in the last war, and the Swamp Realm keeps mostly to itself.

Which makes the Grasslands the only realm we're not sure of.

The only realm with whom war could be on the horizon if tonight ends in disaster.

And that is the only reason I stay still and silent. Because if I move even a little, I know I will break.

My father swallows a hearty bite and frowns down at me.

"Eat, Mancella," he says, steel behind his jovial tone.

I give my head the tiniest shake.

He slams the end of his knife on the table. "*Eat!*" he roars.

I feel something rise in my throat again, but it's not bile. It's a roar much worse than my father's. The roar of a creature slaughtered too soon.

Rage blinds me, and before I can think better of it, I let the jaguar surge free. As always when I summon, it feels like my skin is the surface of a lake and she bursts through it, creating ripples that run across my whole body, though there's nothing actually visible.

She lands on the table, scattering silverware and sending the giant glass goblets careening toward the floor. Instead of merely tickling my mind, her roar fills the room, echoing as harshly as it did in the arena. Her luminous, yellow eyes are narrowed and accusing. Her lengthy fangs are bared.

I meant to shame them, I think, but their reaction is the opposite. My father bellows in approval and my sister gapes, hands at her throat. My mother looks frightened instead of chagrined.

"What is this?" Azele asks, her lips twisting like she's suppressing a snarl. "Are you trying to intimidate me?"

My father smiles as though this was all in his plan. "I am trying to show you the strength of our realm. It need not intimidate you if you intend for our realms to cooperate. But if you intend to make us your enemy, well . . . then perhaps it should."

Rift lunges out of his chair, but Prime Azele lays a hand on his arm and he stills.

"I believe we are done here for today," she says. "I will consult with my advisor about your proposal, and you will receive my response to it within the week." She sounds as formal as any other noble, like she was born into it.

Maybe Mara's right. Maybe she really did know. Or maybe this advisor of hers kept her a secret for the last month because they've been training her, drilling the proper etiquette into her until she could maintain it in the face of a predator baring its fangs at her from across the dining room table.

"Of course," my father says. "May I walk you out?"

Prime Azele inclines her head in a stiff nod, and Father rises to join her. The two Primes make stilted but cordial small talk as they exit the room, but I notice her bodyguard's gait is tense. Controlled, but . . . displeased.

My stomach takes a nosedive.

What did I just *do*?

"Interesting performance," someone says.

I'm startled to find that the words came from behind me, from someone leaning in surprisingly close. Close enough that I can feel the vibration of his voice on my skin. It's a servant, one with a jagged haircut and an easy grin that is completely at odds with the present situation.

"E-excuse me?" I stutter.

He juts his chin at the plate in front of me, and I turn as directed, too stunned to do anything else. The meat is gone, replaced by a small bowl with a colorful salad.

In front of that, a note, folded over three times. I snatch the parchment from the table and look to see what my mother and sister might have witnessed. They are both still focused on my jaguar, my sister reaching fingers out to touch its snout, and my mother inching her chair away as she grasps the neckline of her dress with white knuckles.

I turn back to the boy, questions now fully formed and ready to be deployed, but he's already headed back into the kitchens.

So I open the note.

It doesn't contain any explanations. It doesn't tell me who the boy is or what he wants with me or why he thinks it's appropriate to smirk at me like that when I'm in the middle of destroying any hope we have of establishing a positive relationship with the Grassland Realm.

There are only five words:

Kitchen. Midnight. See you there.

4

Silver

|14 DAYS UNTIL THE ASSURANCE|

The decision to target the Prospective Seconde was not a premeditated one.

I have to get the seal from someone, of course, but it didn't have to be her. It could have been her reclusive older sister. It could have been her wilting wisp of a mother. If I was feeling ambitious, it could even have been the Prime himself. I studied all of them as I circled the table, serving them costly, imported drinks in sculpted glass bottles. I broke them down to bits, analyzing every expression and every word. I saw the ferocity in Mancella's eyes as she struggled to suppress her reaction to the meat. I caught how Lady Wespa's hands shook under the table as the conflict rose, but the smile on her face didn't crack. I noticed Mara pulling back whenever someone almost touched her, like she disdained human contact. And I studied the cold calculation in the Prime's expression as he prodded the conversation to the point of explosion and then reveled in the fallout.

They did not return the attention. As I poured, I stood close enough to kill any one of them, and yet none of them spared me a glance.

But it wasn't until I locked eyes with the jaguar that I made my decision. I was halfway through filling Prime Azele's goblet when the last four I'd filled went careening to the ground, their expensive contents spattered across the marble floor, and then suddenly I was staring into the acid yellow eyes of a predator, and the breath in my lungs evaporated.

But not because I was afraid.

Because the beast's expression held exactly the same desperate ferocity as Mancella's.

And I found that *fascinating*.

The next thing I knew, I was throwing together a salad in the kitchen, scribbling out a note on a page torn from the back of a cookbook, and approaching the future ruler of the realm as casually as I might approach a girl in the local tavern.

Now, hours later, sneaking back into the kitchens after the rest of the staff have gone to bed, I wonder at my own audacity. I'm probably going to get myself killed one day. *This* day, even. As the lock clicks open and the door swings wide, I stretch my arms over my head, wondering how much I'll miss them if they end up down the jungle cat's gullet.

"This is amazing," Rooftop whispers beside me. He rushes forward, brushing his fingers over kitchen appliances like they're works of art.

"It's an oven," I tell him. "Can you use it or not?"

I say this to goad him, and it works. He gives me an outraged splutter, like I might have forgotten for a minute that his parents were bakers before they were shipped off to war with mine and Vie's, that he was raised in flour and salt and that he can do more with a pinch of either than most people can do with a full pantry.

"What do you want me to make?" he asks, rolling up sleeves

that match mine. Once dinner was over, I stole a second uniform from the laundry and snuck away to the Outskirts. Vie was off fighting, probably working out her anxiety in the ring. But Rooftop was there and, after enduring several minutes of vigorous hugging, I smuggled him in through that servants' tunnel Guerre neglected to mention to me earlier. It would have been infuriatingly easy to break into if I'd known about it, but I guess that doesn't matter now.

"Can you make the pastries we ate yesterday morning?" I ask.

He scoffs. "I can make you something way better than that."

"Then have at it, my friend," I say, clapping him on the back. "Whatever your heart desires."

His face lights up, and he riffles through cupboards, muttering to himself with glee. He grabs chocolate, sugar, and jars of spices. I grab an apple and scarf it down as I watch him work. An hour and a half later, there are five trays of thin, circular biscuits in the oven, a giant bowl of cocoa whipped cream on the counter, and a tray of chocolate shavings and candied nuts on the island in the center of the room.

"Thanks, man," I say, tossing my apple core in the trash bin. "Now unfortunately, you have to leave."

"Huh? *Leave*?" He looks at me, stricken. "But it's not done yet."

"I'll finish it," I tell him. "It's just that I told her to meet me roughly now-ish, and if she actually deigns to come, you can't be here when she does."

"She?" Rooftop raises an eyebrow. "She who?"

"She Mancella," I say with a smirk.

Rooftop's mouth falls open. "You're *not*."

"What?" I ask innocently. "It was your idea."

Rooftop tears off his apron, throwing it on the countertop

forcefully enough to awaken a cloud of white powder. "I was joking!" he hisses. "You're seriously going to try to seduce the girl who rips animals apart with her bare hands? Using *my* torte?"

"Not seduce," I tell him. "Just . . . persuade. I mean, probably. We'll see how it goes. I don't have that much of a plan yet."

Rooftop pinches the bridge of his nose and takes several deep breaths. "Do you ever think about taking a night off from giving me heart attacks? I could really use one."

"Sometimes," I admit, "but what would you do with all your time if you didn't spend it worrying about me? I would hate to deprive you of your favorite hobby."

Rooftop mumbles something about the things he'd like to deprive *me* of, and I cordially pretend not to hear as I push him toward the door.

When we get there, Rooftop casts one last heartbroken glance back at the ovens. "I can't believe you had me make all that and you're not even going to let me eat it."

I toss him a second apple and he catches it with a glare.

"You're lucky I'm still overwhelmed with relief that you're alive or I'd kill you myself," he grumbles.

"Noted," I say, shoving him out. "Now beat it!"

As I shut the door, he gives hurried instructions on the last few steps of the recipe, detailing measurements and techniques that I have absolutely no intention of following.

Just as I click the lock shut again, there's a soft knock on the kitchen door that leads to the dining room.

I grab Rooftop's abandoned apron from the counter, throw it on, and then dash some flour on my cheek to make it look convincing. "Come in!" I say.

The door creaks open.

And there she is.

Mancella Cliff.

It's kind of an unreal moment, to be honest. I've spent my entire life jostling to get a glimpse of this girl across crowded squares. I watched her grow up, from a gangly kid to a scowling, terrifying figure wrapped in glass and silk. And even though the boyish admiration I had as a child has soured into contempt and disgust, she's always been larger than life to me.

Meanwhile, until today, she didn't even know I existed.

Yet here she is, responding to *my* invitation, blinking at *me* through wide, lash-framed eyes.

I'm struck by the fact that she doesn't have any makeup on. At dinner, she was as ornamented as the candelabras, but now she's wearing only a simple shift dress, with her hair in an oversized braid. She looks startlingly human.

Her ears, nose, and chin are all just as pointed and assertive as they looked from a distance, but when she isn't glowering there's a softness to her heart-shaped face. Her eyes are enormous, even without the benefit of kohl around their edges, and her mouth seems disproportionately small, giving her whole face an endearingly off-balance feeling I never noticed before. She's also got knobby knees and elbows, frizzy hair, and a slight smattering of freckles across her nose.

I was expecting a glittering monster, but she's . . . just a girl.

Which means I can break her.

"Have a seat," I say. And as if on cue, the timer Rooftop set begins to clang.

I twist the dial and stuff my hands into two oven mitts. She doesn't take a seat, but instead hovers by the door and watches, frowning, as I take tray after tray out of the oven and set them on the kitchen island.

"What's all this?" she asks.

"A cinnamon chocolate torte," I recite.

"For whom?"

"For you."

After a pause, she narrows her eyes at me. "Why?"

I take off the oven mitts and toss them at the counter. "You didn't eat much at dinner," I say, my tone carefully friendly. "So I figured you were hungry." I stick my hands in the apron's pockets and flash her a dimpled grin that has never failed to get me attention when attention is what I want, and then wait for her eyes to melt gratefully at my thoughtfulness.

"*That's* why you called me here in the middle of the night?" she asks, folding her arms over her chest. "As it happens, I am not a child and am therefore perfectly capable of feeding myself. I ate hours ago."

I blink and my smile thins.

Maybe this won't be so easy after all.

Seeing my expression, she sighs and slides a hand down her face, then looks back up at me with a grimace.

"Look, I'm sorry," she says. "This is a very, uh . . . *kind* gesture, and I appreciate it. I do. But in the last forty-eight hours or so I've had a horrific fight, a disturbing dream, and a truly disastrous dinner, so I'm pretty exhausted, and to be frank with you I think my problems are slightly bigger than your deconstructed confectionary can fix."

My mind races, trying to figure out how to keep her here long enough for me to find another angle, because if she leaves now I doubt I'll get a second shot.

"Well, we have to put it together," I say awkwardly. "In, like, a tower."

Brilliant, that should do it.

She scowls at me. "My problems are also bigger than a confectionary *tower* can fix, but thank you again for the thought."

She turns to go, her braid swinging behind her, and I'm almost dazzled by how little she cares about my efforts. To any girl in the Outskirts, a torte of this decadence would have been impossible to turn down, but I guess a spoiled brat like Mancella can gorge herself on sweets whenever she pleases and therefore has no incentive to eat this particular one at this particular hour.

A flash of familiar and long-harbored hatred sears through me.

"What do you want me to do?" I burst out. "Eat the whole thing myself?"

It's a ridiculous question because that actually sounds amazing, but she whirls back toward me, her eyes dark and sparking.

"Well, I didn't ask you to make it and I don't want it, so that's a fairly logical next step, yes," she snaps. "I hope you enjoy it."

"But I didn't make it for me," I protest. "I made it for you."

"You did that without *asking* me, though," she spits through bared teeth, advancing on me. "And, to be honest, what I would like most today is for everyone to *stop* presuming what I would like or what I should do or what's best for my life and just *leave me alone*."

I open my mouth to snap back when something creaks in the next room and I still instinctually, straining to listen.

Maybe the noise was nothing.

Or maybe it was someone coming to see why there are raised voices in the kitchen. And it suddenly occurs to me how bad it would look if someone did see me yelling at an already infuriated future Seconde.

My heart hammering, I swallow my protests and manage to wrench my lips into a placating smile instead, doing my best to act like this tantrum Mancella's throwing doesn't bother me at all.

"Okay," I say, putting both hands up in surrender. "Let's start over. I apologize for not asking you in advance whether a torte might be something you'd enjoy tonight. That's my bad. All I ask, although I acknowledge that I haven't earned it, is for you to try one little spoonful before you go. A dollop, if you will. If you do that, then it will be completely up to you whether you want to finish making the torte with me, whether you want to leave and continue on with your original plan of sulking alone in your room, or whether you'd like to dump the entire bowl on my head, snap the biscuits into tiny pieces, and then light the whole kitchen on fire. I promise I'll be fine with whatever choice you make."

I stick a spoon in the bowl and thrust it toward her, hoping I can count on Rooftop's skills to bring this home for me, since I clearly can't count on my own.

She scrunches up her mouth, making it look even smaller. Her eyes are two dark chasms boring into me. And it's strange, but I can almost see the jaguar lurking just behind them, ready to leap through her skin and attack. If she opened her mouth, I wouldn't be surprised to see fangs.

"I'd let you leave first," she says finally.

I shake my head, confused. "What?"

"If I decided to burn down the kitchen," she explains. "I'd at least give you a head start."

In spite of myself, I bark out a laugh, surprised by this

concession. "Really? How long of a head start?"

"That depends on how bad this goop is."

She grabs the spoon and pops it in her mouth, swishing it around a little before swallowing.

There's a tense beat of silence as my hand drops back to my side.

Then she marches past me and sits down in front of the biscuits, arms crossed.

"Fine," she says. "It's delicious. Show me how to make it a tower or whatever."

Spiteful triumph washes over me and I allow myself a small, smug smirk before I turn around to follow her with an expression considerably more benign. I sit down on the other side of the island, scoop up a biscuit from one of the baking sheets, and plop said biscuit on a plate. Then I slide the plate toward her.

"Put some of the whipped stuff on there," I say blandly. "If you want to, of course. Absolutely no pressure. My head is still an option as well."

She eyes me, and I wonder if perhaps I've been *too* bland and she's picking up on the sarcasm dripping from my every word. But then she takes a healthy scoop and dumps it on the cookie, spreading it around with the back of the spoon. I put another cookie on top of that and she does it again.

We get into a rhythm, building layer by layer until the dessert is a tower of crisp wafer cookies and gooey cream. By the time we arrange the nuts and dark chocolate curls on top, the scent of cocoa, butter, and cinnamon is making my mouth water.

I hand Mancella a fork.

"Good job," I say. "Now dig in."

"Only if you join me," she insists.

Now she's being nice? After practically biting my head off earlier? So obnoxious.

But also, yes, obviously, I am going to eat this. It looks fantastic and if she didn't give me any I would set this kitchen on fire myself. And whether I'd give her a head start is *debatable*.

Placid smile still in place, I grab a second fork.

The torte crunches as we dig into it, and it melts in my mouth, the perfect blend of cool smoothness and crispy warmth. Sweet, but with a bite as well.

For a few minutes, there's nothing but the sound of biscuits cracking and metal tines clinking against the glass plate. She seems calm now. Pleased, even. She certainly seems to be enjoying the dessert. Her sharp features actually soften as she tries each component, easing into an expression that's more like the beauty of a flower than the beauty of a knife.

It's not until her tongue flicks over her thumb to remove a dab of icing that I realize I'm staring. I start, embarrassed, and focus back on the plate in front of me, because gawking is absolutely *not* how I want to play this.

I have to admit, though, it's weirdly intimate watching her enjoy something. It's been ages since I've seen her looking even remotely happy, and even longer since I heard her laugh. I mean, she isn't laughing. She isn't even smiling. The difference in her expression is barely perceptible, just an unclenching of her jaw and a lowering of her chin and a general relaxation of her features. But it makes me feel like a door has been cracked, and some part of me wants to see what's on the other side.

"Do you wanna talk about it?" I try.

She looks at me with eyes so dark I can't tell exactly where her pupils are. "About what?"

"About whatever's bothering you."

"Nothing's bothering me."

"You screamed a few things to the contrary when you first got in here," I point out.

She stiffens, and her expression gets tight, her angular features once more pronounced. Her chin could slice me in half. "I'm not sure it would be appropriate to discuss any of those things with you," she says primly.

"Yeah, but you already did, so there's no real point in holding back now, right?" I ask.

"You're awfully pushy for a servant." She doesn't say it in a mean way. More like she's trying to figure me out.

"And for someone who lives in a castle, you seem awfully unhappy," I shoot back. "So maybe there's a little more to both of us than meets the eye."

Her dark eyes study me, and I feel like I see the slightest flicker in them, like the spark of a match. "Maybe so," she muses.

"Besides," I say. "It's healthy to let things out sometimes."

"Like I did at dinner?" she says wryly. "You're right; that went great."

"What happened at dinner probably happened *because* you keep everything bottled up. When all you do is press everything down, it will eventually explode into a jaguar-sized outburst. But if you process things in more, I dunno, rodent-sized chunks, then it won't get so out of control."

She looks thoughtful. And then the next thing I know, there's a squirrel on the counter in front of me, its tiny nostrils flaring like it's trying to puzzle me out.

"I, uh . . . I didn't mean literally," I say, trying to pretend that being so close to her magic doesn't thrill me.

Both Mancella and the squirrel stare at me, their eyes equally dark and unreadable.

Which is *super* creepy by the way.

"Does he want, like, a nut or something?" I ask, plucking a candied walnut off the top of the cake and holding it out. The squirrel does not move toward me.

"He's dead," Mancella says. "He doesn't need to eat."

"Right."

She picks up the squirrel and puts him on her shoulder. He settles in, wrapping his bushy tail around her neck, but his eyes are still trained on me.

"All right," she says. "Let's have a . . . rodent-sized conversation. I'll let you know afterward if I feel it changed my life and solved all my emotional problems."

No pressure.

I cough and skim my fork over the top of the torte, gathering the rest of the rejected nuts into one enormous, creamy forkful.

But instead of feeling intimidated, like I should, I'm excited for the challenge.

"So you didn't have a good dinner," I start. "Obviously, that's because of what your dad pulled, but it's still bothering you so there must be more. Is it the guest? You're worried about what she might think?" When she was trying to control herself, I noticed a lot of glances in the new Prime's direction, so it's a safe bet.

Mancella looks down, playing with some shavings that have fallen onto the countertop. "Well, yes," she acknowledges. "Very much so, actually."

I lick chocolate off my wrist, partially as revenge for the thumb thing earlier, and partially to unbalance her so she keeps answering my questions. I'm absurdly gratified when her gaze flicks up and then quickly down again. "Why's that?" I ask.

She shakes her head. "That's not a rodent-sized question."

I cannot resist glaring at the top of her head, but I manage to snap my features back to placidity by the time her eyes meet mine again.

"All right," I say. "You're worried about what the guest might think, for reasons that are entirely your own and none of my business. So what are you going to do about it?"

She blinks at me like she doesn't understand the question. "*Do* about it?"

I raise an eyebrow at her. "I'm sorry, was pouting alone in your room the *entire* plan?"

Mancella doesn't move, but the squirrel flings itself onto the table, gnashing its teeth at me and whipping its tail back and forth with this weird, guttural growl that doesn't seem like it should come out of a creature so small.

With admirable restraint, I just barely manage not to launch myself out of my chair and flip the table.

"Could you, uh . . . make it stop?" I ask through clenched teeth.

"Don't make me sound weak," she snaps at me. "If I could do something, I would. But it's not like I can just call on a foreign Prime myself. My father is *always* there."

"So write her a letter," I say, because even in the middle of a rodent onslaught, I am nothing if not focused on the mission. "Apologize. Put your family's seal on it so she knows it's from you." Was that too obvious?

"My father thinks apologies are a sign of weakness," Mancella protests. "He'd never allow it."

"You wouldn't have to tell him," I point out.

She looks at me like I just suggested her head was detachable. "He reviews all our letters before they're sent," she informs me dryly. "There's no way to get around him."

"Oh yeah?" I ask sarcastically. "Does he deliver them himself?"

"Of course not. We send them with a servant."

"Well, if only you knew someone on the serving staff who could sneak an extra letter in the bag."

Mancella's eyes narrow. "You do realize that would be treason, right?"

"What I realize," I shoot back, "is that nothing in your life is going to change unless *you* change it."

"Oh, so I should just disregard the rules completely, then?" she scoffs. "Throw them out if they don't suit me? Rules are made for a reason."

"I agree. And sometimes the reason is to keep the person who made the rules in power and to push everyone else down."

Her eyes widen and her mouth falls open. The statement hovers between us like a buzzing bee, poised to sting.

Some nagging voice in the back of my head is trying to explain to me that this is the point at which I should backtrack. Tell her I didn't mean it and redirect the conversation to more idle pleasantries. That's what someone with sense would do.

But then she slams both palms on the table and lurches to her feet, raising her voice over the chattering of her squirrel, which is rising to a fever pitch between us. "How *dare* you?" she exclaims.

And I'm already launching to my feet as well, too caught up in the argument to listen to that voice of sense. "If you let someone else set the rules for you, then you'll be stuck in the game they want to play," I seethe. "And you'll be a pawn, not a player. In this world, nothing is handed to you, and if you don't take control of your own life, someone else will. In fact, it seems like someone already has."

It's not until the squirrel's ranting suddenly cuts off that I realize I've gone way too far.

The silence feels thick and dangerous, and the way Mancella is looking at me makes me think I might be seconds away from getting flung off the cliffs I scraped my way up yesterday. My heart pounds in my ears and I open my mouth to take it back, but nothing comes out, like the silence is a physical force blocking my throat.

I've really, *really* messed up.

"Right," Mancella says finally. "What's your name again?"

I bite the inside of my cheek. "It's, uh . . . Marc. Marc Hillcrest." That was the name written on the scrap of paper I found in the uniform's front pocket anyway. I don't know where it came from, whether it was entirely fabricated or whether there's a real Marc out there who was somehow *deterred* from showing up at the castle when he was supposed to.

I wonder briefly whether Guerre can get me a second new identity if I manage to destroy this one, because it seems like a distinct and imminent possibility.

Mancella grips the edge of the island with fingers like claws. The squirrel runs up her arm and then blinks out of being when she dismisses it without so much as a wave of her hand.

I can't help but think it would be just as effortless for her to erase me.

"Well, Marc," she says, voice measured, "as a thank-you for the torte, which was admittedly lovely, and as an apology for unloading all my anger on you when I first walked in here, I am going to pretend you *didn't* just suggest betraying the throne and then rail at me about my perceived deficiencies. And I will refrain from sharing that information with your supervisor as well. This time. But I will also be ending this conversation here, as it's clear to me we have very different ideas of what is and isn't appropriate, and I would suggest you think very carefully before saying anything of the kind to me ever again. Good night to you."

She turns on her heel and strides out of the room, the door slamming shut behind her. My mind goes momentarily fuzzy as I replay everything I just said and barely resist slapping myself in the face. She said she wouldn't report me, but she *could*. She could have me killed. She could kill me herself. For some ludicrous reason, I was talking to her like she's a regular human, but she isn't.

She's a demon in a family of demons and I'm a bug beneath her feet.

For a minute I just stare at the door, trying to figure out what to do. Run? Hide? Follow? Drop this identity completely, construct a new one, and try again tomorrow? The new one would have to wear a mask at all times so she doesn't recognize me, but I'm sure I can come up with a reason for that. Traveling performer, perhaps?

Sliding a hand down my face, I head back to the outside door and call, "Rooftop? You still there? Hanging out to make sure I don't get executed and such?"

"Yeah, I'm here," responds a bush to my left. The leaves rustle and then Rooftop emerges through the branches. "How'd it go?" he asks.

I pluck a leaf out of his springy curls. "Not great and then okay and then abysmal," I tell him. What I don't tell him is how it felt to be alone with a girl I loathe, and how little I was able to keep my cool while doing it. Or how much that bothers me.

He scans me for injuries. Finding none, he must decide it can't have been that bad, because his stance relaxes and an easy and hopeful grin flits across his face. "That's nice. Is there any torte left?"

I jab a thumb behind me and he eagerly heads back into the kitchen, rubbing his hands together in anticipation.

"Make sure you clean everything up before you leave!" I call after him before dashing away to the sound of his affronted protests.

He'll be fine. He's better at cleaning than I am anyway, and I've got no time to help right now.

I need to figure out how to salvage this.

And *quick*.

5

Prospective Seconde Mancella Amaryllis Cliff

|13 DAYS UNTIL THE ASSURANCE|

I'm so busy mentally eviscerating that floppy-haired servant that I don't realize where I'm stomping off to until I've already arrived, and then I stop in place, surprised.

It's been a long time since I sought refuge in the east library.

My fingers, already reaching for the doorknob, now flex in irritation. That boy must have *really* gotten under my skin if this is where I ended up. And while that's perfectly understandable when one takes into account how condescending, presumptuous, and infuriatingly smug he was, it still annoys me. I don't get this upset often.

In the absence of my own pacing and huffing, the halls around me are silent. It makes my exaggerated anger feel silly. I should just go to bed.

But I slept all day and I'm not tired anymore.

Besides, I'm already here.

I turn the knob and step into the room, the shadow of every bookshelf, armchair, and table stretching toward me. I know they're just fleeing the moonlight streaming through the giant Palladian window on the far wall, but it feels like they're reaching out to greet me, to welcome me back into an old, familiar space.

When I was younger, my parents used to fight a lot. They don't now, not since the Broken Citadel gave my father the power to freeze the words in my mother's throat. But when I was a kid, their arguing always scared me, and I didn't want to be alone when it was happening. At first I'd search out Mara, but she somehow seemed to know when a fight was coming, and she'd make herself scarce for the whole day.

So I went to my cousin Alect instead.

He was older than me by about eight years and he practically lived in this library, so he was easy to find. Day or night, rain or shine, he'd be here. He wanted to know everything about everything, so he devoured the books shelf by shelf, like their words were a banquet and he was insatiable.

He never turned me away when I showed up. Never asked why I was there. In fact, he kept a pile of blankets stashed in the window seat specifically for me. He'd set me up in an armchair by the fire all cozy and snug, ignoring my continued insistence that I wasn't a bit tired and certainly wouldn't fall asleep. Then he'd go back to studying, but he'd read and think out loud.

I recognize now that he was just trying to get my mind off whatever was worrying me, but it worked. To me, there was nothing more comforting than snuggling into those blankets and listening to him tell me about other realms, other people, other ideas.

I'd wake up surprised, unsure when exactly I'd fallen asleep, panicked that I might have missed the end of a story.

But he'd still be there, still studying. Without even glancing up, he'd ring for a servant to bring me breakfast and he'd start reading aloud again.

Without him here, the space feels empty and uncared for. The stately shelves are dusty and untouched. And without his voice or the rustle of turning pages, everything feels so quiet.

When I reach the window, I lift the cushioned bench beneath it. The hinges squeak, but the blankets are still there, right where Alect left them nearly a decade ago. I pull them out and wrap them around me, inhaling the faint scent of yellowed pages and ginger tea, Alect's drink of choice.

Then I settle down in the frame of the window, fix my eyes on the dark expanse of grass below it, and wait.

When Alect grew older, his father would take him along on official trips, introducing him to the other Primes and their lands. And when he got back, I'd come running in, and he'd be waiting for me with a story and a trinket, both specifically curated to make me happy. Heat rocks from Prime Tibits in the Jungle Realm, who could warm them anywhere on the scale from "pleasantly sun-soaked" to "melt your bones" (with mine being closer to the former). Rope sculptures from Prime Artro in the Swamp Realm, who could shoot ropes out of his fingers and then move them however he liked (although Father wouldn't let me keep those, in case Artro ever bade them to strangle me).

But by far my favorite present was the starsprout. He told me he found it somewhere in the mountains, and when he first presented it to me it looked like nothing more than a pot of grass. I pretended to be pleased, but secretly I was disappointed. He could tell, but instead of being angry, he only laughed. That night, he didn't set me up with blankets and pillows. He plopped me down by the window and told me to watch the plant, no matter how late it got.

With the stubborn diligence of a child trying to impress someone older, I did. As he read to me, I stared at that plant like it might disappear if I dared even blink.

And then, a few hours past midnight, my vigil paid off. Two snow-white flowers unfurled in the pot in front of me, their petals pointed like little stars. I cried out, interrupting Alect's recitation of the line of ascension in the Swamp Realm.

He grinned and snapped his book shut. Then he blew out the candles, joined me by the window, and told me to hold the flowers up to the night sky. I did, barely breathing, and when the petals caught the moonlight they began to glow, glimmering softly in the darkness. It felt like I held real starlight in the palms of my hands.

My eyes mist at the memory, and I panic, rubbing the moisture away and then blinking at the lawn, afraid that I've missed what I'm waiting for. But the lawn is still dark, and I slump back into my blankets.

After the Broken Citadel, my father told me I'd never see Alect again, although it was quite a bit longer before he told me why.

At first, I refused to believe that the cousin I knew would abandon me, or that anything could have happened to someone so constantly prepared. I spent months checking for letters from him and scouring the library for any messages he might have left behind. But nothing ever turned up.

The day that I finally accepted he was gone, I planted the star-sprout in the middle of our lawn.

And it felt like digging a grave.

It felt like burying a body.

It felt like the funeral we'd been forbidden to hold.

Of course, my father was enraged when he saw it. To him it was a blemish right on his front lawn. He yanked the flower from the ground in one fist and tossed it into the incinerator. I watched the smoke rise with silent tears, and it felt like losing Alect all over again.

But the starsprout must have dropped some seeds because the next night, two little stars blinked open in the night.

I kept them a secret, and it took my father a few days to notice on his own. By then, wind had dispersed the seedlings to every corner of our lawn, until handfuls were popping up all over. Tiny rebels. Despite my father specifically assigning someone to pull them up by the root every morning before dawn, somehow the plant still spread, and a few would always spring up again the next night.

So every now and then, on days when everything feels like too much, I wait for them, half afraid that this time he'll finally have gotten them all.

I lean forward, pressing my face against the window so hard that my nose is uncomfortably flattened. I wait for what feels like hours. I wait until the fear that they are really gone this time feels not only real, but overwhelming.

Then, finally, there's a pinprick of light in the middle of the field. One tiny starsprout, yawning and stretching its angular petals toward the moon. Though the night is cloudy, the starsprout somehow finds just enough moonlight to catch and reflect back, creating its own little corner of brightness in the gloom.

For a moment a warm smile flits across my lips.

But the next moment it flickers away.

Because I know that each and every happy little star will be ripped from the earth by sunrise. And what's the point of hope if it never makes it through the night? Better not to have it at all, knowing that it will be plucked up and burned.

That's what the boy in the kitchen didn't get. Why strive to fix things when failure is inevitable? It's not that I don't want to try, but surviving alone takes so much effort. How can I find it in me to fight even harder when my head's barely above water as it is?

I grip my legs so hard that my nails dig into my knees.

Nothing in your life is going to change unless you change it, the boy had said.

But what does he know of the life I've lived? What does he know about anything?

My skin squirms with anger, my creatures restless and fuming, but below me the flowers continue to glow softly, sweetly oblivious to their scheduled destruction.

Suddenly, it's all too much.

I push myself away from the window and wrap the blanket around my shoulders like a cloak, rushing out of the room.

Five minutes later, I'm on my knees in the dirt, hacking away with a spade I stole from the gardener's shed. I'm making a mess, and I know it, but when I plunge my fingers into the ground and cup a single glimmering bloom between my palms, it feels worth it.

I'll save this one.

It's a start.

And later, once I've planted the shrub in a saucepan from the kitchen, once I've watered it and washed the evidence off my hands . . .

I sit down to draft a letter.

Just to think about what I might say if I *did* decide to fight.

⁂

Most of the servants sleep in communal barracks on the back of the grounds, but the temporary hires we took on for the Assurance preparations were only given bedrolls and a section of floor in the cellars. It isn't too hard to figure out where they put Marc.

When I find him, he's curled on his side, back shoved up against a shelf full of jams, smothered by a heavy woolen blanket.

In sleep, he looks much younger. Instead of a tight smirk or a bland, careful smile, his face is relaxed and unfortified, and instead of falling in his face, his choppy hair is sticking out at all angles around his head. It's kinda cute, actually, and for a second I almost lose my nerve as I think about how incredibly inappropriate it is for me to be seeing him like this. But then I remember that *he* was inappropriate first, and that he's an infuriating, treasonous miscreant who is not cute at all and I feel better.

I don't know how best to wake him, though. Touching him in any way seems far too intimate, and I didn't think to bring a stick to poke him with. Eventually I summon a pair of beetles on his face hoping the feeling of them creeping across his skin will be enough to rouse him. But then one of them heads for his nose and I panic and dismiss them immediately.

Before I can come up with a new plan, his rust-colored eyes shoot open and latch onto mine, so suddenly that my breath catches in my throat.

For a second, neither of us moves. I watch emotions flit through his gaze as he puzzles over where he is and what exactly I'm doing there with him. Then, slowly, without breaking eye contact, he sits up. The muscles of his shoulders contract, and the blanket falls enough to reveal that he's shirtless.

Shirtless at *minimum*.

I ignore the blush creeping up my neck and raise a finger to my lips, gesturing at the other sleeping bodies around us. In return, he narrows his eyes, a clear question in his expression.

I hold up a folded-over note between two fingers, until his eyes finally leave mine to focus on it. Then I chuck it at his face and flee, too embarrassed to stick around while he reads it.

It doesn't say much. Just:

Roof of the Lonely Tower. Sunrise. See you there.

❧✻☙

He's late, but I expected that. It's hard to find the entrance to this tower. I picked it because I wanted to make him sweat a little bit, but now I'm regretting it because the waiting is making me anxious.

The Lonely Tower is set apart from the rest of the castle, which is how it got its name, but it's also one of the tallest buildings on the grounds. As I walk along the parapet, brushing the rough stone edges with my fingertips, it feels like I can see the entire world.

In one direction, the whole of the Cliff Realm is speckled against the rocky bluffs, looking like it might slide into the forests below at any moment. Beyond that lie miles and miles of multicolored trees, ones we stole from the Forest Realm a decade ago.

I don't remember much of the war, but I do remember standing here with Alect, watching my grandfather's glass trees burst up among the scarlet oaks, only to have Prime Gore's black explosions rip them apart. At six, I was too young and too far away to understand the scale of the death I was witnessing, but old enough and close enough for it to make me feel uneasy.

"Why are they fighting?" I'd asked Alect.

At fourteen, he had just hit a growth spurt. He was leaning over the high part of the battlement, gangly arms folded over the edge, and I was sticking my head through the lower notches reserved for archers, hands primly propped beneath my chin. He looked down at me as though unsure how to answer.

"Grandfather didn't feel comfortable living near a Prime with such powerful magic," he explained. "He was afraid Prime Gore would try to invade and that we wouldn't be able to defend ourselves. So he's beating the Forest Realm back from our borders."

"That doesn't make sense," I said, shaking my head. "He didn't want war, so he started a war?" Adults were so strange.

"He thought it was better to attack when he was prepared than to *be* attacked when he wasn't," Alect said. "But I think it would have been better to avoid war altogether. Don't you?"

I nodded solemnly, glad that at least Alect seemed to understand.

But then we just continued to stand there and watch, two children unable to do anything to stop the bloodshed.

We won that war, almost obliterating the Forest Realm in the process, but victory came at a cost.

Two years in, my grandfather got caught in one of the explosions. He died shortly after, and my father took the throne, but his new power wasn't well suited to war. He could dominate and control a single person, maybe even two or three. But not an army.

So he used his power in a different way, conscripting nearly every able citizen we had, overwhelming the opposition with sheer numbers and finally bringing the war to an end. He didn't seem to care that the citizens he sent to their deaths were the very same ones the war was supposed to protect. Then Alect disappeared, Mara and I made our own trip to the Citadel, and life has been different ever since.

When I look at the forest now, all I can feel is grief.

I turn away, but the view on the other side gives me no comfort, either. Breathtaking mountains with snowcapped peaks, the former home of the Mountain Realm. And smeared in the sky above them is the slime-green magic that once killed every single soul who lived there, along with the populations of five more realms beyond it: Desert, Valley, Island, Moors, and Canyon.

Graveyards. In every direction. Death and desolation, no matter which way you turn.

I want better.

I'm older now, older even than Alect was then, and I'm supposed to be named the second most powerful person in this realm in a couple of weeks. Yet I feel completely powerless. Here in the middle of the vast world, I can't help but feel incredibly small.

Nothing in your life is going to change unless you change it. The boy's words come to me again, like a gnat in my ear.

As I consider them, a flock of birds crests the cliff to the west of me, soaring and circling over my head. I wish I could join them. I wish the things that hold me down could simply fall away. I wish I could feel less . . . limited. So I focus on a different thing the boy said.

It's healthy to let things out sometimes.

Despite my resistance in the moment, there was something about the way he said those words that made me want to listen to him. The way his voice was warm, but deep, like embers, with a teasing quality to it that reminds me of the way a dying fire tends to spark, sending dancing lights into the air to distract from how low it burns.

Letting the words rumble in my chest, I release my own flock of birds. A carrier pigeon, three ravens, an owl, and a hawk all sitting on the ledge blinking at me as I blink at them.

"Fly," I tell them.

But they don't follow my commands. They only reflect what I'm feeling. If I feel like I can't fly, like I'm grounded and trapped, then that's how they will act.

"*FLY!*" I scream.

And as though a giant gust of wind has caught them, they all burst away from me in a flurry of wings, spinning up and up and up until it feels like they might fly directly into the sun.

"You're not going to attack me with those, are you?"

I whip around, knowing who said the words. The smoldering embers in his voice gave him away.

My heart is racing like I've been caught doing something I shouldn't, and I have to remind myself that I'm the one who is supposed to have the upper hand here.

"Perhaps I should," I say, leaning back against the parapet. "You *are* late."

I mean it as a joke, but his eyes get serious and he nods gravely. "I apologize," he says. "For that and also for . . . earlier. I was out of line. It won't happen again."

Imitating one of the bland smiles he gave me last night, I tilt my head. "Can you be more specific?"

His eyes probe my expression, like he's searching for the answer in the set of my mouth or the edges of my eyes. It makes me feel uncomfortable, like his gaze is chipping away at my very skin, and I don't even know what might be underneath it.

"I . . . shouldn't have talked to you like that?" he says finally. And I'm immediately gratified by how unsure he sounds.

I shake my head and turn away from him, my hands braced on either side of me as my gaze returns to the birds. They're still soaring, and the sight gives me strength. "That's not what I want you to apologize for," I tell him.

He comes closer. "Then . . . what?" he asks, and though I don't look, I can feel the warmth of his body beside me, making me wonder just how close he's standing. For a moment, the hair on my arm stands up, like there's an electric charge in the air. But then in the next moment, a sudden gale steals the sensation away.

"For not telling me your real name, as a start," I say.

He stills, and so does the air. Even my birds are motionless, their wings outstretched but not flapping.

"What makes you think I didn't?" he asks, a slight edge to his voice.

Which means I'm right. I feel a rush of satisfaction that makes my skin prickle.

"Because," I tell him. "We keep extensive records of our citizens in the library, and I looked you up, Marc Hillcrest. You're supposed to have blond hair." I look meaningfully at his ashy brown mop.

"Hair can change colors," he counters.

"And green eyes," I continue, lowering my gaze to irises the color of rust. I mean only to glance at them pointedly, but once our gazes lock, his doesn't release me. And I realize that his eyes are more vivid than mere rust. They're more like angry sunsets and rebellious autumn leaves. Like the same smoldering flames that color his voice. Beautiful, brilliant things. But also things that herald destruction.

He searches my face in a way that makes me feel exposed, even though I'm the one exposing him. My stomach flutters under his scrutiny, but I refuse to look away first.

"Records can be wrong," he says. And the embers are stronger in his voice now, burning dangerously low.

It gives me goose bumps.

"But they aren't in this case," I whisper. "Are they?"

My hawk's screech pierces the air, and the boy flinches. In spite of myself I'm pleased that I've unnerved him. When he breaks eye contact first, I feel another rush of satisfaction, even as a part of me feels disappointed. He turns his back to the wall separating us from a sheer drop and leans against it, his elbows just over the edge.

The same smile from yesterday slips over his features, like a mask against the world. Something about the way it deepens his dimple, arches his brow, and doesn't quite reach his eyes gives me the impression that he's much older than he looks at first. Or at least that he's been through too much for his age.

"All right," he says, tone challenging. "You got me. So what are you going to do about it?"

The same question he asked last night, but a completely different context. Another breeze lifts my hair, making the strands tickle my face as though his challenge has charged the very air around us.

"That depends," I say.

"On?"

"On your reason for lying. And whether it's a good one."

His eyes flare slightly in surprise and he sweeps his eyes over my face again, always studying.

"What kind of reason would you consider a good one?" he asks.

"Why don't you tell me the true one and I'll let you know if it qualifies?" I shoot back.

He pushes off the wall and walks away from me, and at first I think he's just going to abandon the conversation entirely and my flare of anger causes my birds to dive-bomb. But just before they get in clawing distance, he passes the staircase leading back inside and settles on the opposite side of the parapet, arms crossed under his chin.

"Have you ever been to the Academy?" he asks.

This confuses me enough that my birds pull up short and flap around awkwardly, unsure of which way to fly.

"No," I admit.

He raises one shoulder in a shrug, like that was exactly the answer he was expecting, and I feel a spike of annoyance. He must think so little of me. I want to rip that obscuring smile off his face and see the expression he'd make if he were actually honest. What would it be?

Why do I even care?

I shake my head. It doesn't matter. He's not going to get a rise out of me today. I'm growing more familiar with his barbed way of speaking, and I refuse to snap back. I want answers, and I mean to get them. Neither his grin nor his condescending shrugs will distract me from that goal.

Because if I'm really going to do what I think I might, then I need to know who I'm doing it with.

I touch the edge of the envelope in my pocket.

Then I cross the tower and reclaim my spot next to him, looking down at the Academy's thatched roof. Noticing for the first time that it's rotten in the middle, mold creeping toward the edges.

Based on his question, I'm guessing this boy attended there once, living and learning beneath that rot-speckled roof.

"So tell me about it," I say.

6

Silver

|13 DAYS UNTIL THE ASSURANCE|

It's hard to think over the sound of my own inner voice screaming in panic. From waking up to her dangerous, dark eyes to dancing my way through a rooftop inquisition, almost every second of this day has felt charged, like the air right before a rainstorm.

As Mancella settles on the parapet next to me, I give her a glance that I hope comes across as "thoughtful" instead of "barely reining in outright hysteria."

I actually crossed the tower so she *wouldn't* be standing right next to me. For starters, because it would be a lot more difficult for her to toss me to my death from twenty feet away if this conversation goes awry. But, more importantly, because her proximity seems to scramble all the rational parts of my brain.

She angles her pointed chin toward me, and all I can think about is the jaguar that lurks beneath her skin and the birds that claw the air above me, ready to attack. Her dark eyes are unreadable, but the message in them is clear. Whatever I say next had better be good.

Clearing my throat, I turn back to the Academy. It's weird how small it looks from here. I could cover it with one hand. And even if I didn't, it doesn't look like much. A squat building. A neatly trimmed yard.

And a large black fence littered with jagged shards of magic glass, sharp enough to shred the hands of any children who might want out.

Since she's already caught me in one lie, it seems safest to stick close to the truth.

So I tell her, "It's a waking nightmare."

Because nothing's truer than that.

She tilts her head, expression indecipherable. It's actually infuriating how hard it is to read this girl. And yet I can't stop trying, scrutinizing every flicker in her eyes or twitch of her lips, hoping for a crack.

"That's where they send kids whose parents choose to enlist as soldiers, isn't it?" she asks.

I bark out a laugh, my hands flexing. "I'm not sure 'choose' is the right word," I tell her bitterly, "but yes. Half orphanage, half prison, and one hundred percent future army recruitment."

That seems to surprise her, but I'm not sure why it should. It's not like the Academy is particularly subtle in its mission.

"And you went there." She doesn't say it like a question, but I answer anyway.

"Not for long." The smile on my face twists and turns caustic. "Just a couple years, clinging to the hope that my parents would show up again and take me back home. But the second I got the news that they were dead and there was no use waiting around for them, I ran. I've been living in the streets since."

"How old were you when you left?" The question is so gentle it causes me to jolt.

"Ten," I bite out, not sure why she's pretending to care.

"That must have been hard," she says softly.

I prickle, angry that she's acting like her family had nothing to do with any of it. Like it was just this random thing that happened to me, when—

"It was your father who conscripted them. Your father who made the Academy what it is. *Your* father who made it impossible for runaways to have any kind of life."

As soon as the words are out, I want to slap myself. What is it about this girl that makes me lose my cool so quickly? She's locked up tight and I feel like I'm just out here ripping scabs off and inviting her to crawl into my skin. I need to remember how dangerous it is to anger the Prime's daughter. I need to get myself under better control.

But when I sneak a look at Mancella, she doesn't seem angry. Her head is angled to the side and she's frowning, but not at me. "What do you mean?" she asks. "About the runaways?"

I try to make my tone more clinical. Distant. "If you don't graduate, you'll always be a criminal. No one will touch you. No one will help. You can't get a house, you can't get a job, you can't get any kind of foothold in society at all."

She shakes her head, still not getting it. "Why? Because people won't hire you?"

It's the honest confusion in her question that makes me lose it. Because it's *infuriating* that this girl should get to live in a literal tower with no idea what the rest of us are going through down in the dirt. I forget about control or caution or the advisability of hiding my wounds from her and I wheel on her with a snarl.

"No," I say, my fingers digging into the stone of the parapet. "As in, if you try and you're caught, then you and whoever employed you are publicly executed and displayed along the road as a warning to anyone else who's thinking about it. I'm talking *kids*. Kids who are just trying to scrape together a living, just trying to learn how to build a bookshelf or make a loaf of bread—" I break off and a burst of fear explodes in my chest like fireworks as I wonder if mentioning bread was too close to betraying Rooftop. If she'll storm into town questioning bakers and she'll find him. If she'll—

A loud chorus of screams derails my train of thought, and I jolt back from the wall, my head whipping around wildly to find the source of the noise. Mancella, on the other hand, seems completely unconcerned. She has both hands over her mouth, and her dark eyes are wide and haunted.

She looks . . . devastated.

The sight is so jarring that I can't look away, can't make sense of that broken expression on her normally ferocious face. I was looking for a crack in her composure, but I wasn't expecting her to completely shatter before me.

And I wasn't expecting this vulnerable sorrow.

Suddenly the air is full of creatures, as a mismatched assortment of birds—the ones she summoned—drifts down in forlorn circles around her, landing in awkward lumps at her feet. They must have made the noises I heard. They weren't screams, but avian cries of despair. Cries that reflected Mancella's genuine reaction to my words.

She drops her arms to her sides, but they're trembling slightly.

"So that's why you lied?" she confirms, voice shaky. "Because it was the only way for you to find work? The only way for you to survive?"

I mean. Not the only way, technically. I've survived this long mostly on thievery. But somehow I think she'll be less sympathetic if I explain that to her.

So I shake off my surprise and press my advantage, relieved to finally have found an angle that seems to be working.

"That's right," I say, making my voice rough for effect.

"Where's the real Marc, then?" she asks.

Mentally, I cringe. For all I know, the guy is dead in a ditch somewhere.

"He's . . . a friend who changed his mind about working here," I say, the first actual lie of the conversation. "And was kind enough to let me show up in his place."

She considers this, one finger pressed to the corner of her lips.

"What's your real name?" she asks.

"Silver," I say, and then immediately wonder whether I should have. "At least that's what I go by."

She nods, studying my face. Then her expression sets, like she's just come to a decision, and I stiffen, wondering what exactly it might be.

"Well, Silver," she says, and the birds around her stir. "You haven't made a very good first impression. You presumed my feelings, you pushed me to tell you more about my life than I was comfortable with, and you even suggested I engage in subterfuge. Now I come to find out you've already engaged in some yourself. I've got grounds to throw you back on the streets. Probably have you killed if I were so inclined."

As if I didn't already know all that. I tense at the sound of talons scraping on stone as her birds pick themselves up, clicking their beaks and emitting a babel of clipped caws.

"And are you?" I ask through clenched teeth.

"No," she says. "Even if I were so inclined to begin with, I could never go through with it after hearing your story. I think you're abrasive and shameless, don't get me wrong. But at the end of the day . . . we both want the same thing."

My brows scrunch together because that seems incredibly unlikely.

"Which is what, exactly?"

"Better," she says. Then she pulls a piece of paper out of her pocket.

One with a bright ocher seal on top.

Time seems to slow as my vision tunnels on the scrap of paper in her hand and the crest of her family pressed into the shiny wax on top of it.

It *can't* be that easy.

"I don't know if this is the right thing to do or not," she says, oblivious to my shock. "I don't really know if I can trust you when you've lied to me already. In fact, I probably shouldn't. But if there's one thing I do know, it's that I can't go on as I have been. I have to try something. Fight . . . somehow. Even if it fails spectacularly. At least . . . at least I will have tried. Will you sneak this into the bag of letters for me after all?"

She thrusts the parchment toward me, and it's a full ten seconds or so before I snap out of my stupor enough to take it.

As soon as I touch it, the birds all disappear, called back into her body.

"I'll keep your secret if you keep mine," she says, letting the paper go. Then she turns and marches down the stairs without a single look back.

I stand there for several more moments holding the letter, turning it over and over in my hands.

Thinking about how if I'm caught with it, the message might as well be a warrant for my own execution.

Thinking about how even I don't yet understand the full weight of what I'm doing.

Then, finally, I slide it into my pocket.

❦

After that, I have to book it back to my assigned tasks for the day, working double time to get them all done by the afternoon inspection. I don't feel like I breathe once until the supervisor gives me a curt nod that says my efforts are adequate. Once that's done, I'm off for the evening, since I took the dinner shift the night before.

So I basically flee the castle. Across the grounds, through the servants' tunnels, and out into the market district. It's not until I'm among the familiar, crammed-together buildings of the city, breathing in the smells of moss and dust and spicy, street vendor kebabs that my heart stops hammering in my ears. The muddy cobblestones beneath my feet feel like the first steady ground I've walked on all day.

That is, until I catch sight of a dark shadow moving between buildings.

My heart rate ratchets up again immediately and I freeze, thumbing the dagger concealed at my hip.

But then a balled-up wad of paper hits me in the side of the face. I catch it before it drops and unfurl it, only to find an impressive list of insulting names scrawled inside.

My shoulders relax. "Hey, Vie," I say.

She emerges from the alleyway and gives me a toothy grin.

"You're alive," she says, looking pleased and appraising.

"Rooftop didn't tell you?" I ask, pocketing the insults and

continuing to walk as she falls in beside me.

"He did, but it's nice to know he wasn't just so delusional with grief that he imagined you."

Rooftop drops down from an awning as we pass it. "If seeing him was only a delusion, I would've gotten to eat the whole torte myself. And I wouldn't have had to clean up alone."

I snap my fingers and point at him. "Speaking of, I've got more chores for you to do tomorrow."

"Oh, delightful."

"Don't pout. I'm gonna get fired if they're not done."

"So *you* do them."

"I would, but unfortunately I'm super busy."

He shoves my shoulder with an open palm, grinning. "Super busy wooing the Prospective Seconde, right?"

"Wait, *what*?" Vie swipes her bangs out of her face, spinning on her heel until she's walking backward in front of us, her eyes shifting from Rooftop's to mine.

The back of my neck prickles uncomfortably. "I told you," I protest. "I was just *persuading* her."

"With your body?" Rooftop asks, waggling his eyebrows. A sudden flash of Mancella crouching over my bed flits across my mind, and once again I find myself uncharacteristically at a loss for words. A pattern that is decidedly obnoxious.

"Shut up, man," I grumble, fighting a blush.

Vie unsheathes a dagger and starts to spin it in one hand, a fun and not-at-all-intimidating thing she does when she's irritated.

Gritting my teeth, I turn toward her to deliver more convincing denials, but then something over her shoulder catches my eye.

The clang of metal on metal echoes down the street as a blacksmith beats a glowing hunk of steel in front of his shop. His face is darkened with soot and streaked with sweat, but what gives me pause is that there's something familiar about the way he holds himself. I'm usually good with faces, so it bothers me that I can't place this one when I have such a strong sense that I've seen this man before. He makes me feel uneasy, and I'm not sure why. Which of course makes the unease worse.

Then his keen blue eyes flick to mine and immediately the rest of his features take on an unmistakable context.

I *do* know him.

Without warning, I halt, and the others stumble to a stop around me, giving me curious looks.

"I'll be right back," I tell them. "Wait here."

Guerre puts his tools down as I approach and wipes his brow with the back of a filthy leather glove.

"New job?" I ask. My unease lingers on the question, and I wonder if he can hear it.

"Just for the week," he says gruffly. "It gives me access to some of the tools I need." He holds up the sword he was working on, still blazing with orange heat, and my stomach lurches. But then he drops it in a barrel of cold water, making steam waft over the rim, and takes his gloves off. "So do you have it?"

It suddenly strikes me that Guerre has a full beard today, and he definitely didn't when I saw him yesterday morning. Is it fake? It doesn't look fake. Between that and the soot on his face, he looks like a completely different person. No wonder it took me a minute to place him. In spite of myself, I'm a little impressed by the intricacy of this disguise.

I pull the envelope out of my shirt and hold it up. Guerre's eyes gleam as he takes it, but not with warmth. It's more like sunlight bouncing off a lake that's frozen over completely. Somehow, even as he stands in front of the heat of the forge, his eyes still look so cold.

"I knew you'd come through," he murmurs. "Good work."

He withdraws a wide knife from the sheath at his side and in one swift jerk cuts the seal free from the paper, which collapses to the table like a butterfly with broken wings. Then he pulls a hunk of what looks like soft clay from a drawer and presses the seal into it. After carefully prying it out, he then fills the hole with some kind of liquid and sets it on a shelf to solidify.

"What are you going to do with that?" I ask.

He grunts like this should be obvious, but answers anyway. "I'm going to reverse engineer my own ring."

He's right. That should be obvious. And yet my mouth drops open in surprise. Somehow, until this moment, I didn't think about how much power Guerre could wield with a copy of the signet ring. He can make me and my friends papers, sure, but he can also make . . . anything. Anything at all.

I snap my mouth shut again as the enormity of what I'm doing hits me like a hammer to the skull. With creeping dread, I realize that I don't know anything about Guerre or his plans. Not really. Why am I helping him again?

"I had the family of that house evicted," he says, as though he can read my thoughts. Maybe they're written on my face.

"What?" I say, shaking out of it.

He pulls an official-looking document off a shelf and shows it to me. It's a deed. The stately stone house with the green roof springs to mind and I suppress the urge to reach out and run my fingers over the numbers and letters that make up its address. The words that say it's going to be mine.

"How?" I ask instead. Then I shake my head. "Wait . . . you mean people were living there?" I'd assumed it was empty. Though, come to think of it, he'd never said it was.

"You worry about your part, and I'll worry about mine," Guerre says dismissively. "I just wanted to give you some assurances that I'm ready to make good on our deal when the time comes. You've seen the graduation papers, and now here's the deed. Once this ring is finished, your future will be secured. And you're only two tasks away from claiming it."

I nod slowly, but there's still a lump in my throat. I do my best to swallow it down. After all, this is what I wanted. Everything is going smoothly. There's no reason at all to be upset or to feel so slimy. Anyone with a house like that can probably get another one just as easily. Whereas for me, it would be life-changing.

And anything Guerre plans to do to the Prime is completely deserved. After all the suffering he's caused to me and the people I care about, I won't shed a single tear if he has some suffering coming back for him. It would be nothing less than justice.

"I'll contact you when I need you," Guerre continues. "In the meantime, consider this a token of my gratitude."

He tosses me a few coins—which I catch between my palms—then goes back to work, taking the cooled sword and sticking it back in the forge to heat up again. With a flick of his wrist, he tosses Mancella's letter in the garbage, where it rests on discarded ashes and what looks like rotten beef.

It's a clear dismissal, but I feel rooted to the spot, staring at the paper as juices from the meat soak into it, seconds away from turning it into a putrid mess. Mancella's earnest expression when she gave it to me flickers in the back of my mind.

I look up to see if Guerre is watching me, but he's peering into the flames, cold eyes lost in thought. Acting more on instinct than on any conscious decision, I pluck the letter out of the bin and hurry away, tucking it into my waistcoat even though the stink of rancid meat makes my stomach turn.

"That's the guy?" Vie asks as I approach. Her dagger is sheathed again, so Rooftop must have calmed her down.

I nod and she wrinkles her nose. "I pictured him differently. But whatever. Was he happy?"

"I don't know if that guy's ever happy," I tell her. "But he said I did well. And he showed me the deed to the house."

"What house? We're getting a house?" Her tone is cautious, but her eyes are wide and excited, like she hasn't figured out yet whether I'm joking, and her face and voice have two different theories about it.

For the first time today I give a smile that's actually genuine and sling an arm around her shoulders.

"Let me show you," I say.

It takes us about an hour to find it, since I'm going off my memory of a bird's-eye view, but finally it stands in front of us in all its glory. Bigger than I thought. Classier. And even more gorgeous. So gorgeous that none of us says a word as we take it in.

It looks like something from a story. Lush, thorny roses climb up the smoke-gray stones, twining themselves around curved double doors in a dark burgundy. There's a row of cheery windows, each with a wrought iron balcony just big enough to lean out of. And the roof is gabled and ornate, just as green as I remember.

Rooftop stuffs his hands deep into his pockets and looks like he might cry.

But Vie bares her teeth at me in the glinting light of the hanging lanterns. "It's the wrong place. He must have pointed somewhere else."

I understand what she means. This house can't be real. Or at least, it can't be real and ours at the same time.

"Nope," I assure her. "This is it. Go ahead; pick a room."

Both Rooftop and Vie immediately point to the biggest window in the middle, and I burst out laughing as they break into a good-natured bickering match over who deserves it more. If I know Rooftop, he doesn't even want the biggest room, he just wants to make Vie think he does so he can get a rise out of her and then look like a hero when he steps aside.

I hook an elbow around both of their necks and drag them back down the street. "Plenty of time to work it out later," I tell them good-naturedly. "Let's go home. It'll be dark soon."

They both look at the sky and then nod. In the Outskirts, it's best to be indoors before sundown.

Rooftop ducks out of my grip. "You mean you're going to slum it with us tonight?" he asks. "Don't you have fancy new digs at the castle?"

Most people wouldn't call a bedroll shoved against a shelf of jarred fruit paste "fancy digs," but to us, any room with four solid walls and no leaks in the roof is paradise. And yes, technically, I am supposed to sleep there every night. But I'm sure I can sneak back in before anyone really notices.

"I do, but it was desolate without you," I say teasingly. "I just tossed and turned all night from missing you so much. Please let me come home so I can finally sleep knowing you're near."

Rooftop scoffs. "Not if you're going to be weird about it."

"Of course you can come home tonight," Vie says. Although, even as she says it, I catch her looking back toward one of the taverns in this part of town.

I wonder if she was planning to fight there tonight.

"Here," I say, shoving the coins Guerre gave me into her hand. "I've got room and board at the castle from now until the Assurance, so you guys should keep this."

Vie's eyes widen. What I've just given her is more than she makes in a week, even with her new, increased pace.

"I don't need your charity," she says automatically.

I roll my eyes and flick her nose. "Fine, then give it all to Rooftop. He can eat like a king this week while you starve in a corner, content in your pride."

"Sounds good to me," Rooftop chimes in.

Vie sneers, but her fingers curl around the coins and she doesn't say anything else about it.

Pretty soon the houses get less flashy and more haphazard. Storefronts become slapdash lean-tos or blankets on the ground with dirty wares set out in piles, easily swept up and carried away if some noble recognizes a bauble or a necklace that went missing last week. As we wind down to the bottom of the cliff, the cobblestone road beneath our feet starts to break up into gravel, and then dirt. And when we reach the end of the road, that dirt gets crunchier beneath our boots.

Up on top of the cliffs, the glass trees are still pretty. Even the deadly pines have a certain sinister beauty to them.

But down here in the Outskirts, we make our homes in the dark side of the magic. The aftermath.

Before Prime Elod's time, this land used to belong to the Forest Realm. But once the magic was rediscovered and everyone wanted to fight about it, it became a battleground. A war zone. Quite possibly the one my parents died in.

I've heard the crystalline hollies and hawthorns Elod sprouted were awe-inspiring, even covered with the bodies of the soldiers he skewered as he grew them. Some of the trees are still standing, but most of them were shattered in combat by Prime Gore's horrifying magical explosions. They could burst anything to bits, whether it be pines, arcane glass, or human bodies.

What's left now is a wasteland, even a decade later. The corpses are cleaned up, but no one bothered with the rest of the fallout. Jagged shards stick up from the ground, with only the remnants of bark-like patterning around their bases. The dirt is so full of broken glass that boots are a necessity, and tripping can be catastrophic. Worst of all, because the glass is magical, its sharp edges never smooth or break down. They just infest the earth, sowing pain for all future generations.

You don't live out here if you have anywhere else to go.

We clomp on. Because the ground is so hazardous, the rickety shacks that speckle the forest are built on stilts or crammed into trees. Many of them are abandoned military bunkers from the war, visible only if you know where to look for the doors hidden in stacks of logs or the staircase openings buried in leaves.

Ours is a hastily constructed guard tower in the branches of a weathered oak. It's hanging together by a thread, but it's better than sleeping in glass. Barely. The wooden sides are graying and flecked with ancient, peeling paint of an indistinguishable color, and the windows are just openings in the wood. We cut off the ladder because it's easier to defend that way. Besides, we can all climb.

We scale the trunk and swing onto the small porch jutting outward. Then we take our boots off, hitting them against the railing to dislodge as many shards as we can before setting them down on the mat.

And then I'm home, and it's easy to fall into our regular routine. We board up the windows for the evening in a mostly vain attempt to keep out the night's chill. We make a dinner of some berries Rooftop foraged and a loaf of stale bread Vie swiped from an abandoned table at the tavern last night.

It's not until I fall face-first into one of the three hammocks we strung up in the tiny back room and hear a faint crinkling in my waistcoat that I remember I still have Mancella's letter.

It's dark now. We only have one flickering candle that I made out of some beeswax I found in the woods. By its weak, wavering flame, I pull the letter out and unfold it, brushing off the ash and fetid meat that stain its pages. In the dancing shadows, Rooftop raises an eyebrow at me, silently asking what it is. But I ignore him, flipping toward the wall as I take in the words that the Prospective Seconde entrusted to my care.

It really is the apology she said it was, and it reads as though it's sincere. She speaks of regretting her actions and desiring a truce. She extols the virtues of peace. If I had read these words on the tower when she'd given them to me, when her broken expression was still fresh in my mind, I might have been tempted to believe them. There was something in the way she looked that made me *want* to, that tugged at parts of me I'd thought long dead.

But here, in the bowels of a battle that drew in hundreds of lives only to destroy them, all so we could possess land that the Prime isn't even using, the words read false. At best, naive.

I listen to the sound of wind throwing glass against the trees, occasionally punctuated by the cry of someone who didn't make it to shelter before the evening breeze turned into a gale.

It was the Prime's family who did all this, and they don't even care. Whatever happens to them, whatever Guerre might have planned with his new ring, the Cliffs have it coming. Even their

Prospective Seconde. She may have surprised me a little today, but I can't forget about her beasts, or how she came to possess them. If push came to shove, I'm sure she'd rip me apart just as cruelly.

Leaning out of the hammock, I grab a knapsack and shove Mancella's letter inside it, buried under a collection of other rejected items—mostly worthless knickknacks that I stole and couldn't manage to resell.

Then I toss that knapsack into the corner and don't think about it again.

The candle finally sputters out, and the room is plunged into darkness.

7

Prospective Seconde Mancella Amaryllis Cliff

|10 DAYS UNTIL THE ASSURANCE|

When I decided to commit arguable treason, I anticipated some kind of dramatic result in fairly short order. Immediately, if I'm honest. As soon as I left the Lonely Tower, I expected someone to jump out and tell me that it was all a test and I'd failed, and the Assurance was therefore canceled. When that didn't happen, I was sure I'd be caught and then disowned and/or beheaded. And then, after a couple days passed and no punishment manifested, my imagination swung the other way. I pictured Azele showing up with tears in her eyes ready to form an alliance because my letter had moved her so deeply. I envisioned myself receiving her with grace and gratitude, and the two of us heralding a new era of peace between our realms.

But that didn't happen either.

Nothing has happened.

I find and badger Silver nearly every day, and although he assures me he's checking with appropriate diligence, there has been no response. So eventually I have to entertain another theory.

Which is that my words just don't matter.

I worry over this as I make my way to the infirmary, bracing to have my stitches removed. By now, the skin around them has stopped feeling so raw, turning pink and white instead of an angry red.

When I arrive, Mara is already there, stretched out on a cot. I frown at her.

"Are you hurt?" I ask.

"Nah," she says, folding her arms behind her head. "I faked an injury so I could hang out with you during your big hand unstitching. You know the healers won't let anyone in unless they're a legitimate patient."

I narrow my eyes, wondering if I'm the one she's really lying to.

"What did you fake?" I ask.

Instead of answering, she props herself up on her elbows and studies my face. "You looked upset when you walked in here. Something bothering you?"

I wince, casting around for a response.

Fortunately, at that moment a healer bustles in, saving us both from any further inquiry. With a last glance at Mara, I plop down on a cot and stick out my hand.

As I do my best to hold still, the nurse methodically extracts the black threads, leaving only a jagged white gash lined with puckered spots across the center of my hand. Already the pain is barely there, more of an itch than a stab. I watch her work with a kind of melancholic detachment.

"I wish the magic didn't heal me so quickly," I murmur. "It should hurt more. What I did."

"Don't worry," Mara says, picking something from under her nails. "You're hurting yourself plenty over it."

The nurse dabs some alcohol on the wound and then flicks the gauze into the bowl with the sutures and declares me finished.

She tells Mara she'll need to stay a bit, though, and Mara makes a sour face. I ask if she wants me to stay, too, but she waves me off.

I hover for a moment anyway, toying with the idea of lingering long enough to see what the healers think they're treating. But if my sister really does have a wound and she doesn't want to talk about it, then it's probably best I let it be. Mara always has her reasons for keeping secrets. Besides, I don't have anything scheduled until this afternoon, and I've been waiting for a window of time like this.

Because even if my letter *didn't* do anything, that doesn't mean I have to give up.

It just means I need to push somewhere else. Eventually, something has to give.

And I know where I want to push next.

❧✻☙

The Academy stands below the castle, but above most of the rest of the town. I've passed by it many times, but today I feel a strange, uncertain dread as I remember the look in Silver's eyes when he talked about this place.

The giant black gates are embedded with so many jagged chunks of glass that they look like they're iced over. Constantly surrounded by glass garnishment as I am, I never questioned it before. But the shards are not smoothed down and ornamental. They're sharp as blades. It doesn't seem appropriate on a school for children.

I summon a snake, because I've been experimenting with keeping an animal or two out when my emotions start to overwhelm me. It relieves the pressure somewhat. She wraps herself around my arms, flicking her tongue at the gates, and the feeling of her cool, smooth skin sliding against mine makes me feel a little stronger.

I've never been inside the Academy before. I half expect them to turn me away at the gate, but it seems less likely with a snake around my neck.

I pull the rope to ring the bell, and a slat slams open next to it, just big enough for a pair of squinting eyes to peer through.

"Can I help you?"

"I . . . I'm the Prospective Seconde," I say. Maybe unnecessarily.

"Yes, I'm aware," he says carefully. "Did your father send you?"

At this, I square my shoulders and my snake raises her head as though shaken awake. "I don't believe I need my father's permission to make an appearance at one of the facilities my family funds and maintains. Do you?"

There's a weighty pause, and then the slat slides shut and the gate swings open. I have to step back hastily to avoid being impaled on its glittering shards. Behind it stands a muscular man with close-cropped, graying hair. He looks down at me like I'm the last thing he wants to deal with today, but when he speaks his tone is formal.

"What can I do for you?" he asks.

I sniff and cross my arms, surveying the stocky building behind him, and the dirt grounds that surround it.

"I'd like to look around," I say. "Right now."

He leans back and his jaw flexes, like he's doing his best to think of a reason to turn me down. But he must not be able to, because finally he gives a series of short whistles. A kid, probably only a little younger than I am, jogs up, then assumes a military posture with his arms folded behind his back, waiting for instructions.

"This is the Prospective Seconde," the man says. "Show her

around. Answer her questions."

The boy's eyes flash with something like panic, even as he says, "Yes, sir."

The two of them lock eyes for a brief moment, and though I can't see the man's face, whatever his gaze communicates causes the boy to look down quickly.

My snake flicks her tongue and I shift uncomfortably from one foot to the other.

"Shall we go, then?" I ask finally, when it doesn't seem like either of them will say anything else.

The boy turns on his heel and marches toward the building, so I follow.

I feel the man's gaze on my back until we're out of sight.

Inside, the furniture is decidedly utilitarian. Stone and metal. The tables are bolted down, and they each have six stone circles attached to them by metal arms to serve as seats. They don't look comfortable. Or movable. Glass lines the walls as well, in a way that makes the room feel like it could close in on itself and crush everyone inside at any moment.

A line of children walking single file weaves through the tables past us, and when we enter, their eyes all snap to me. I expect them to start whispering, but their arms stay locked in place behind their backs and their mouths stay shut, which is somehow even more unnerving. The silence is heavy, broken only by an odd scraping noise that I can't place at first. It's not until I look down that I realize many of the children have rocks tied to their ankles, which they are dragging across the floor. Some have only a few, but others seem to have a small mountain clattering behind them.

"What are those stones for?" I ask my guide.

He assumes the military posture again and responds with an immediacy that feels practiced. "We need to remember the power of the cliffs and how fortunate we are to be a part of them," he says. "When we commit an infraction, a piece of the cliffs is tied to our feet so that every step reminds us of our shame and strengthens us against future mistakes."

My snake slithers across my collarbone, unable to settle as I look back at the children. Some of them have so many rocks tied to their feet that they're straining to move. I see a boy who looks about eight walking as though he's wading through molasses, his face pinched in distress as he tries to keep pace with the others.

No one tries to help him.

"What sorts of infractions?" I ask.

"Disrespect, talking out of turn, taking more food than your portion, failing to follow any given command, failing to keep up in training, speaking ill of the Prime—"

"That's enough," I say, feeling queasy. "Who administers this punishment?"

"Instructors," he says. "And older students who have earned the privilege of participating in communal discipline."

I don't like the sound of that.

"What if the child denies the infraction?" I ask.

"Then they are given a second rock for lying."

"And if they aren't lying?"

My guide seems uncomfortable with the question. He casts me a brief, guarded glance, and I suddenly remember the way the man outside seemed to give him a warning, and I hastily tell him to forget I asked.

As the trail of children comes to an end, I fall into step behind them, my guide shadowing.

They wind outside and I pause in the doorway to watch them, not wanting to make my presence known to their waiting instructor. She's a grim-faced woman who lines them up on a track painted into the dust. When she whistles they break into a run, and she jogs beside them, setting a minimum pace.

But no one removed the rocks before the children started running, and this quickly divides the race into tiers. The ones with no rocks surge ahead, not even sparing a glance back for their companions. The ones with only a few rocks are slower but still able to stay ahead of the instructor, although their expressions are strained as the rocks bounce behind them, biting into the backs of their legs. However, the ones who are the most burdened, including the boy I was watching earlier, strain to keep up.

Instead of helping, the instructor berates them, calling them vile names and cruelly mocking their inability to keep pace, all while threatening to add more rocks if they can't catch up by the end of the race.

At one point, the young boy falls and struggles to rise, now openly weeping. His ankles are rubbed raw by the rope, and his legs are bruised and bleeding. The instructor screams at him, accusing him of faking his infirmity to get sympathy, and assuring him he won't get it, not from her.

The boy vomits into the dirt.

Nearly choking with rage, I take a step through the door, meaning to get the rocks off the boy's legs if I have to rip them free myself.

"If you help him," my guide says in a low voice. "He'll be punished worse after you leave."

I stop in place, feeling sick to my stomach, and look back at him. His eyes are straight ahead, as though he isn't talking to me, but there's tension in his posture.

I turn back to the runners in the front, the ones who run silently and never glance back. Their gazes are as fixed as his, but I see the same kind of tension in their postures, now that I'm looking for it.

"Punished how?" I ask.

He turns and continues down the hallway, but it's only when the young boy pulls himself up and starts limping forward again that I'm able to follow, my snake's tail rattling against my stomach.

My guide takes several turns, leading me past rooms crammed with unornamented bunk beds and classrooms where learning is a fast-paced, call-and-response experience that sounds more like thinly veiled propaganda than actual curriculum.

When we get near to the back of the building, I start to hear screaming.

It's raw and hoarse, like the person has been doing it for hours, but also muffled somehow. I can't make out any words, only stark, guttural noises that I didn't know a human could make. My guide keeps his head down and drops behind me, probably so it doesn't look like he led me here, and that's fine with me. I surge ahead.

When I turn the corner, there is a row of doors, each with a small window. The screaming is coming from behind the first door, where a girl is held in a chair. Her arms and legs are strapped down and there's a gag in her mouth and a blindfold across her eyes. Around her ankles is a halo of rocks, so numerous that they look like a small battlement. Her hair is greasy and matted. Her cheeks are tracked with tears. She's thrashing against the bonds like she's a wild animal, and the snake in my shoulder bares its fangs, flexing against my neck like it's poised to strike.

"How long has she been in there?" I ask my guide.

"They put her in yesterday." He's behind me, but he's speaking in a low voice, glancing frequently down the hallway behind us.

"For?"

"She attacked an instructor. That's why they're using the chair. The longer you're restrained, the more it hurts your body. And the more your mind rebels against its inability to move. And it just keeps going. It makes you—"

He's cut off by another scream that's near snarl, and he merely gestures at the door as if the cry finished his sentence better than he could anyway.

It's then I hear weeping coming from farther down the hallway, and I move past him, my snake slithering restlessly across my body.

As I look in each door, most of the rooms are filled. They're tiny, each barely bigger than a closet. Most of the children inside aren't restrained, but they look despondent, their eyes sunken and their clothes hanging loosely off their bodies, making me wonder how often they're fed. One child is humming a broken tune. One is crying. One appears to be staring at nothing. Each has a small mountain range of rocks around them, weighing down their every movement.

I feel nauseous.

"How long have these other kids been here?" I ask.

"Couple weeks. Some a couple months."

"*Months*? When do they let them out?"

"When they have . . . learned their lesson," my guide says hesitantly.

"Meaning what?"

He looks at me with dark eyes.

"Please," I say. "The truth. You won't get in trouble, I promise."

He looks back down the hallway again and then leans toward

me, his voice an urgent whisper. "Meaning when we act like good soldiers again. And after you've been alone for long enough . . . you'll say anything. Whatever they want to hear. Then once you're out, you'll do anything not to be back. Even punish other kids. Even commit yourself to the army, where you know you'll either kill or be killed. You'll obey any order you're given. Just as long as you don't have to go back to that chair or that room."

His haunted expression makes it clear he's speaking from first-hand experience.

There are footsteps behind us, and my guide's back goes ram-rod straight again, as his eyes go distant.

It's the man from the gate, and fortunately he doesn't seem to have heard our conversation.

"You've been in here quite a while," he says, addressing me, "and I'm afraid your guide needs to report for training now. Is there anything else I can do for you before you go?"

I don't miss the attempt at shooing me out the door, but I refuse to be cowed by it.

"As a matter of fact, there is," I say. "Could you send a message to my father? I'd like him to meet me here as soon as he's able."

❦✻❦

After some discussion they reluctantly set me up to wait in what is essentially a storage room, where all the books and curricula the school used before the war were packed into boxes and presumably abandoned.

Through the small window, I can see the students running through yet another round of drills, the third of the day. And it's not even lunchtime. I picture Silver there, going through the exercises in time with everyone else, and I understand a little better the bitterness in his voice when he spoke of this place. I wonder if he was one of the kids with rocks around his ankles or one of those who silently looked away.

I might as well make use of the time waiting, so I roll up my sleeves. There are shelves. And there are books. I think of the refuge my own library was at home and decide I can make at least one nice room in this monstrous place. Not that I can fix the deeper issues here with a single reading room, but it's something.

By the time my father deigns to arrive, I have three of the standing bookshelves sorted, first by subject matter and then by title.

I expect my father to be angry, but he just regards me with the kind of bemusement one might use to look upon a dog circling his bed three times and then lying down exactly where he started. And I understand how silly this must look to him, in the midst of a facility devoted to training for war.

"When's the last time you came to this school?" I ask him.

"I visit regularly."

"Oh, you do?" I say sharply. "So you're aware that it's essentially a prison? That children are *tortured* until they agree to die for you?"

He shakes his head at me with infuriating indulgence. "Children grow strong here," he says, voice deceptively patient. "Strong and obedient, the two most important traits in a soldier. And soldiers are desperately needed to protect this realm, no matter how much you would prefer to believe otherwise."

"Only," I shoot back, "if you keep entering wars with high casualties." My snake gives her tail a warning shake, the rattle underscoring my words.

My father exhales a small puff of air through his nose, and sits in the lone, dusty armchair, regarding me.

I rip the tape off another box and keep sorting.

"This place needs reform," I tell him. "It needs better facilities, a more diverse curriculum, a system of discipline that is actually *humane,* and it needs to provide real options after graduation. As in more than one."

He strokes his chin, considering. "All right. If it's that important to you, I'll give you a budget and you can propose some changes. After all, you will be Seconde soon. I'm pleased to see you taking the role seriously. If there are things you want to implement, then of course we should discuss them."

I sift through the contents of the box in front of me, waiting. Certain it can't be that easy. My snake's tail vibrates again, punctuating the pause.

"But there's something I'd like to talk to you about first," he continues. "And, actually, this is a fortuitous location for the conversation I'd like to have."

I knew it.

I run my fingers on the spine of a bright yellow textbook before sliding it in with the other sciences.

"What conversation is that?" I ask.

He gets up and pulls the book I just shelved. It's a text on biology with a drawing of an ape on the cover.

"Do you remember going over material similar to this with your tutors?"

I lean against the shelves and cross my arms over my chest. "It wasn't my favorite subject, but I remember the basics, why?"

"What is the class and order of our species?" he asks.

His voice has taken on the same lecturing tone that my tutors often had, so I answer automatically. "Humans belong to the mammalia class. We are in the order of primates."

"And our kingdom?" he asks.

"Animalia," I say, not sure where he's going with this.

"So humans are a subtype of animal, correct?"

"Yes?"

He replaces the book and turns toward me fully. "What do you think would happen if you killed a human?"

I open my mouth to respond because I was expecting another rote question with a straightforward response, but then what he's actually said hits me, and any words I might have offered evaporate in my throat.

I feel cold. Numb. My snake must feel it, too, because she slithers up my leg and curls around my torso seeking warmth.

"How could you ask me that?" I rasp.

"It might be the same as your usual process," he continues, as if I'd never spoken, "or it might be different. After all, humans have higher cognitive abilities than animals do. They dream, they love, they reason. They have deeper relationships, longer memories, and more complex plans. Perhaps they are so different that it would not work at all . . . but perhaps it would work even better. Perhaps you could truly command them, or communicate with them, or—"

"I guess we'll never know," I say firmly, cutting him off.

"For the sake of discussion—"

"But it *isn't*!" I cry, and my serpent's rattle rumbles against my ear. "It isn't just for the sake of discussion. Is it?" I start pacing, weaving a haphazard path through abandoned tomes in beaten boxes as my snake weaves around my shoulders. "I don't understand. How could a thought like this even *occur* to you?"

He returns to the armchair, steepling his hands, calm as he traces my frantic zigzag through the room with distant eyes.

"Look out the window," he says.

"I know what's there," I retort, not breaking stride. "Children who lost their parents in a war being trained to fight in some future one."

"Exactly," he says. "And you could stop the whole cycle."

I stumble to a stop and the rattle stills. "How's that?"

"If a war broke out, many of our soldiers would die," he explains, in the tone he might use to explain one of the basic math concepts in these textbooks. "They would leave children behind, and their loss would create a need for more soldiers. And on and on it goes. But what if we never had to send them out? What if you could summon an army, and every time they were killed, you had only to summon them again? No one would dare challenge us!" He spreads his arms wide, as if revealing a delightful surprise.

"You want me to kill a whole army?" I breathe. My skin feels clammy all of a sudden, and I pull my cloak tighter around me as my snake coils closer underneath it.

He waves his hands to dismiss the thought, but it's far, far too late. "Don't worry about that right now," he says. "Let's just try one and see how it goes."

Just . . . try one?

Just try one.

Like I'm trying on a dress. Or a hat.

Just try *murdering another human being with my bare hands* one time.

And see how it goes.

I feel faint, a dreadful, potent stirring in the pit of my gut. I press my lips together, genuinely afraid that if I open my mouth too wide I might throw up.

"You're right," he says. "This isn't a hypothetical. You will be

Seconde soon, and when I present you to the people of this realm, I want you to be as strong as you can be. The ceremony is called an Assurance not only because it assures your place in the succession, but also because it assures the people that they will be taken care of when I die. Beyond that"—he hesitates briefly, but then carries on—"there have been developments in our relations with the other realms that are extremely concerning to me. Another war may be imminent."

A part of me processes that information, enough that it makes my ears ring in alarm, but most of me is focused on the more immediate issue.

"I killed just last week," I remind him fiercely. "And we had an agreement. I was supposed to have a *year* before—"

"You were a child when we made that agreement," he snaps. "Now you're nearly an adult. Nearly a Seconde. You came here today, lectured me about classrooms and curriculums, because you recognize that you should be doing more for your realm. I applaud you. But you're thinking too small. If we develop it properly, your magic could fix the root cause of a lot of suffering. You could enact real, systemic change. It's time to rise to the occasion."

I lift my eyes to his, waiting for the gut punch. And he gives it. "I'd like you to choose one of the students at this Academy to test my hypothesis on by the end of the week."

My snake clenches around my stomach and I feel goose bumps erupt on my skin. "You can't be serious," I say, but my tone comes out more pleading than incredulous. "You mean . . . one of the children?"

"Many of them are competent soldiers already," he tells me, as though that was my concern.

"But they're—"

"Children without futures, without family, eager to make a name for themselves. I think you may find more volunteers than you anticipate."

I think about my guide telling me that a person would do anything to avoid ending up in the rooms at the back of the building, and I wonder if that extends to laying down their very lives. If the alternative was continuing to live in a place like this, then maybe they would. But not for the sake of glory, like my father seems to think.

"What if no one volunteers?" I press.

"Then the hundreds of lives to be saved is worth the cost of one unwilling sacrifice. Pick one by the end of the week, or I will pick one for you."

"And if I refuse entirely?" I demand, raising my voice.

"Then I will kill one a week in the public square until you relent. I hope it doesn't come to that."

I reel back, crashing into the bookcase and sending science textbooks toppling. "You're bluffing," I say. "You wouldn't do that. Your methods may be brutal, but even you wouldn't go that far."

Would he?

He doesn't answer, but he doesn't break our gaze either. I push off the shelves and make a dash for the door, thinking desperate, impractical thoughts. I'm seconds away from bursting out into the side yard and screaming at all the children to run for the mountains and never look back, to find what escape they can from the horrible proclamation my father has just made.

But then he grabs my hand.

And in an instant his magic surges through me, locking me into place.

It starts with my skin. Suddenly it feels as hard as armor, like a shell around my body. My mouth is stuck in the precursor to a scream, half agape, and my breath is shallow. I make a low noise in the back of my throat, like the yowl of an angry cat, but I can't form words. And no matter how hard I try to wrench my jaws open wider or take a step forward or just move my pinkie the tiniest bit, I can't.

I'm frozen.

My snake rears up, hissing, her tongue flicking dangerously.

"Don't walk away from me," my father says.

I can barely hear him over the rushing in my ears.

My muscles lock up next, making me feel like my whole body is tensed. Like I'm just about to fight, but without the subsequent relief of landing a swing. My snake lunges toward my father, fangs bared, but he bats her away with his free hand, then presses one boot into her side when she hits the ground, pinning her down.

Please, I want to say. *Please let go.* He usually does by now. He usually only wants to stop me in place, not hurt me. Does he want to hurt me?

If I could cry, I would, but I can't even blink. My eyes feel like sandpaper.

Please, I beg through silent lips. *Please, please, please stop!*

But he doesn't. Not this time.

And the next thing to freeze is my lungs.

My mouth goes dry as the air within it stagnates. I try to work my throat, try to draw more air in, but I can't move anything. I can't breathe. I can't even struggle, because my every muscle is trapped in place. I can't scream, because my vocal cords are immobile. I can only stand there as my lungs burn and black spots begin to enter my vision.

At my feet, my snake writhes, twisting into herself and arcing away from the ground in frantic, jerky movements. She lashes against my father, but her fangs can't penetrate his steel-plated boots. Within me, the rest of my animals mirror her desperation, contorting in desperate, anguished terror, raging against the underside of my skin.

Because he still hasn't let go. If he doesn't soon, I'll pass out. I can already feel the grim dizziness creeping up on me. And if he keeps holding on after that, after my mind shuts down even as my body remains locked in place, the last thing to stop will be my heart.

He releases me and I collapse to the ground, gasping and choking. My mouth floods with saliva, and snot runs from my nose as my shoulders shake with my rasping, miserable sobs. Everything burns as my internal organs stutter back to life.

"I hope you see now," my father says, "that I will do what needs to be done. You have one week."

Then he crushes my snake's skull with the heel of his boot and walks out the door.

And as I lie on the floor, still gasping for breath, the corpse in front of me disappears, and my snake revives within me, twisting in the deepest pits of my stomach.

As furious as I am.

8

Silver

|10 DAYS UNTIL THE ASSURANCE|

I'm cleaning one of the grand windows that looks out onto the mountains when suddenly Guerre appears on the castle wall, silhouetted by the morning sun. I jerk back, leaving a long streak on the glass. I could swear he wasn't there a second before.

He doesn't look at me, but he does angle his head in my direction enough to let me know he's aware of me. Then he ambles along the edge of the wall, casual as anything, and descends the stairs into the courtyard.

He's dressed like a gardener today. The beard is gone, but his hair is longer and stragglier. He looks tanned, too. More weather-beaten. Older, somehow.

Without ever looking up, he disappears into the gardening shed on the edge of the lawn.

The message is clear. I toss my rag into the bucket of sudsy water and head out to meet him.

As promised, my second task is just as impossible as the first.

I'm supposed to steal a sword. But not just any sword: the Victory's Herald, a blade even someone like me has heard of.

Lore has it some Prime a long time ago made the first kill of an apparently unwinnable ancient war with it, and then ultimately emerged victorious from the not-so-unwinnable-after-all campaign. Instead of crediting some superior strategy or, I don't know, the humans who did all the actual killing, I guess the Prime decided the sword should get the accolades.

So now it has a fancy name and several ceremonial functions. It's the sword the Cliff Realm has used to formally start and end every war since. It's also the sword Prime Merod will use to anoint Mancella as his heir in a week and a half. But more to the point, it's the sword the Prime keeps in a locked box in his locked desk in his locked office in the middle of a castle stuffed to the gills with guards.

Which is not ideal.

I puzzle over it all morning, but I'm not going to be able to come up with much of a plan until I can get a solid feel for the obstacles. So after lunch I start a (very small, nothing to worry about) fire in the kitchens and sneak in an attempt at unlocking the first door while everyone is distracted.

Now, usually, I'm pretty good with locks. I'm more of a pickpocket than a burglar, admittedly, but there have been a few times I've found the need to branch out. This lock is weird, though. It doesn't make sense. My picks can't even penetrate it, like the empty space inside the lock isn't really there. I can *see* it, but when I try to stick my tools into it there's some kind of invisible barrier, like—

"Like magic," I say out loud, shaking my head. "Of course it is."

I guess it makes sense that his study would have some kind of extra protection, but it's still annoying.

Because now I have to figure out how to talk Mancella into letting me in there, and I've got no great ideas.

But before I can dwell on it too much, a guard strides around the corner and I hastily shove my picks into my waistcoat and rush past him, making a show of clutching the bucket of water I'd announced I was going to get.

Hopefully no one notices it's the same one I was using to clean the windows earlier.

❧❦☙

"Prime Azele finally wrote back," I mumble to myself as I pace down one of the many glass-strewn halls later that night. "Weirdest thing, though. She says we can only read the letter in your dad's office. I dunno, Primes are kooky. Best do what she says, though, don't you think?"

That'll *definitely* work.

I glance through a door at yet another reading room or breakfast nook or solarium or whatever (I genuinely cannot tell these rich-people rooms apart) and then turn a corner, only to find that I've already paced this hallway.

Which means that since my shift ended two hours ago, I have officially looked in every room of the castle, and Mancella wasn't in any of them.

Man, she's annoying me and I haven't even started talking to her yet. I don't know why I spent the last several days memorizing her schedule if she was just going to disappear on me as soon as the information became relevant.

A night guard steps into the hallway, so I duck through the closest doorway to hide. I'm supposed to be asleep right now, since my shift tomorrow is the earliest one. There's a balled-up pair of jackets under the blankets on my bedroll in case anyone checks, but if I run into any actual people that flimsy alibi will be destroyed immediately.

The guard's footsteps echo down the corridor, getting closer. I can't close the door or he'll hear it, but the room doesn't have any great places to hide. If he so much as glances inside as he passes, I'm done for.

Just before the guard walks by, I ease open a thankfully well-oiled window and slip outside.

I crouch in the bushes below for several beats, just to be safe, but when there are no sounds of pursuit, I straighten and pull the window shut again.

It's a nice evening. The moon is bright and full, the stars are starting to come out. Maybe Mancella went for a walk. In one of the half dozen gardens.

And maybe I should just wait until tomorrow.

But I step out into the darkness anyway because I am physically incapable of quitting anything I've started.

With no real direction, I pass the perfectly manicured lawn, the greenhouse, and the hedge maze and step into the glass garden near the back of the grounds.

It's where I would go for a walk. Unlike the haphazard shards strewn around my house and the weaponized pines around the castle wall, these trees were grown purely for the aesthetic. I think about the warlord who sent my family to die growing this gorgeous garden for his own family to enjoy and I hate every sparkling inch of it, but that doesn't keep me from wanting to stroll through it, wanting to brush my fingers on the leaves that look so delicate but feel so strong.

It's genuinely breathtaking. Something about the magic in the glass catches the moonlight and refracts it, so that the whole garden is splintered with pale white light. There are magnolias covered in crystal blooms, fruit trees bursting with glittering pears and apples. There are topiaries like giant glass sculptures crafted into the shapes of animals made of thousands of intricately placed leaves. There are even palm trees that would never be able to grow here, stretching their broad fronds up to the sky. And whenever the wind rustles the leaves, they make this soft chiming noise that makes you feel like you're in another place entirely, somewhere beauty and music make sense. Somewhere . . . magical.

But then I hear another sound as the wind dies down and the leaves settle.

A scream of rage.

I whip around and scan the grounds until I find her. Mancella—her cheeks flushed and her hair loose around her shoulders. She's . . . punching a wisteria.

My shoulders relax and I approach, bemused.

The tree tinkles raucously as she hits, kicks, and yanks on its shining boughs. She's really going at it, throwing herself into the attack like the wisteria might start fighting back any minute. And each strike is punctuated by another grunt or shriek or growl.

When I picture the dolled-up Seconde who appears at formal events, this deranged, screeching child seems like a different person entirely. Yet another side of her that the public never gets to witness.

Knowing that, I observe her in silence for a minute, taking it in. Reveling in what feels like an uncovered secret.

Then finally I step out of the shadows.

"I get mad at trees, too," I say. "They can be so rude."

She startles, shifting back onto the balls of her feet like she's preparing for a blow, but when she sees it's me she straightens again and turns her back to me, tossing inky hair over her shoulder.

"I'm not mad at the tree," she grumbles, hunching her shoulders.

"You *seem* mad at the tree, though."

"What reason would anyone have to be mad at a tree?" she snaps. "That would be ridiculous."

"Of course," I say, lifting one corner of my mouth in a smirk. "I'm sure you were in a slap contest with an inanimate object for an entirely sensible reason."

She glowers at me over her shoulder, and I lean against a knotted glass oak and raise an eyebrow at her. Seeing that I'm not leaving, she bares her teeth at me like a dog defending its territory.

"Fine," she growls. "I'm mad at the tree. Are you happy? Will you leave now?"

I snort at this admission. "May I ask what exactly the tree did to offend you?"

"No, you may not."

"You expect me to just go about my day pretending I didn't witness the future leader of the realm flailing her arms and bellowing at a bunch of see-through flowers?"

"I was not bellowing."

"You were," I say. "But don't worry, it was a very ladylike bellow."

"There's no such—" She pinches her nose and takes a deep breath like conversing with me is taking all of her patience. Some small voice in the back of my head tries to remind me that I'm supposed to be getting into her good graces, but most of me is too entertained to care. "Look," she says. "I'm dealing with a lot tonight and I'd like to be alone right now. If I tell you why I was attacking the tree, will you go away?"

"If that's what you really want," I say. Even though I most certainly will not.

She looks up at the sky, biting her lip like whatever she's about to confess is difficult for her. In spite of myself, I lean forward, interested, wanting another secret about her to add to my growing collection.

"It won't break," she says finally. "I can't . . . break it. It's got these infuriating, delicate-looking leaves but they're impossible to even scratch. No matter how hard I try, I can't change a single thing in this entire, perfect garden. And it infuriates me."

I'm surprised to find that I understand that. I think about the bolted-down furniture in the Academy, immobilized to prevent us from chucking chairs at one another's heads. Some days, in an environment so aggressively controlled, the inability to even move a table an inch to the left was unbearable. It's the reason I've spent the last few days in the castle turning vases the wrong way and pushing statues slightly off-center.

I notice her hands balled at her sides and I tap my fingers against my arm, thinking.

Her emotions are a little too raw to just be general dissatisfaction with a garden's unchangeability. Something happened today. Something that made her go off on a sparkly houseplant.

But I realize she gave me the first secret to protect the second, so she probably won't tell me that one outright. I decide to take a different tack entirely.

"You can, you know," I say.

"Can what?" she asks.

"Break them. My whole neighborhood is covered with

smashed-up trees from the battles with the Forest Realm, so there's definitely a way."

"Still?" She looks puzzled. "But those battles were years ago. Why hasn't anyone cleaned it up yet?"

"Great question," I say. But there's too much of an edge to my voice so I quickly plaster on a grin to soften the statement and hurry on. "The point is, you may not be able to break it with your hands, but magic is vulnerable to other magic. Have you tried breaking it that way?"

"What do you want me to do?" she asks. "Hit it with a monkey?"

"You have a monkey?"

"Two," she says dismissively. "Neither of which makes a great sledgehammer."

I chuckle and look around. Most of the trees are gargantuan, showy pieces. But there are also tiny bonsai lining the path, each twisted into the exact same delicate arches, like a row of flawless, crystalline soldiers.

I bend over and yank one out of the ground. Then I toss it a little ways down the path where it lands with a clank, still looking infuriatingly poised, its now-exposed roots curved in perfect waves.

"Run that over with a horse," I say. "See what happens."

She gapes at the bonsai, then at the yawning hole I pulled it from. And I don't blame her. It looks like the garden path has a missing tooth now. The whole symmetry of the arrangement is completely ruined.

What I expect is for her to tell me I can't do that, to demand that I replant the work of art immediately and apologize.

Instead, she summons a stallion. He bursts into being,

stamping the ground with his feet and snorting. I can see the whites of his bloodshot eyes. As his hooves pound against the ground, his nostrils flare with his hot breath, and his ears are all the way back against his skull.

So . . . she's more upset than I thought.

I flex my fingers apprehensively and press myself closer to the strangely smooth bark of the oak, regarding her more carefully than I did before. Now that I'm looking, I can see there are tracks of tears on her cheeks and her eyes are red. Sweat makes her hair cling to her neck. How long has she been out here fighting like that?

She doesn't give me long to ponder the question. Undaunted by the rage of the beast towering behind her, Mancella buries her fingers in his mane and swings herself onto his sweat-flecked back. Then she digs her knees into his sides and he charges forward. Unconsciously, I hold my breath as the animal bears down on the hunk of glass, closing the distance pace by pace until . . .

It shatters beneath his thundering hooves.

Mancella gasps, and the horse disappears. She falls to her hands and knees directly into the broken remains of the bonsai, crying out as they cut her. I push off the tree and jog up to her as she sits back and pulls a shard out of her palm, staring with wide eyes while her hand fills with blood.

"Are you okay?" I pant, throwing myself down to my knees next to her. If anyone in the castle finds out I caused injury to the Seconde, I'm done for. Yet another fireable, if not execution-able, offense. I curse and rip my shirt off, wrapping it around the wound and pressing down with my thumb to stop the bleeding. "We need to get you to a healer. Can you walk? Did you get glass anywhere else? Are you—"

It's around this point that Mancella bursts into hysterical laughter.

"It worked!" she cries. "It really . . ."

She shoves me off and stands, pacing back and forth along the path. Occasionally she squats down to poke at the broken branches and cackle.

Which is very concerning.

I sit back on my heels and watch her, trying to make sense of this weird breakdown.

"There was a way," she mutters to herself as she stands and moves back down the path again, my bloodied shirt trailing behind her. "My whole life, I thought it was impossible, but there was a way. So there must be a way with this, too. I can figure it out. I just need to think about it from a different angle. A different—"

She turns on her heel, hair flying behind her, and something about the look in her eye makes me shrink back.

"I've got it!" she says. "Can I kill *you*?"

There are very few times in my life that I've been at a loss for words, but when the future Prime of the realm latches her eyes onto mine and politely requests the privilege of my murder, I have to admit that my mind goes completely blank.

"I-I'm sorry?" I splutter.

"That came out wrong."

"I should hope so."

"Hear me out."

"About my own death? I'm gonna be honest, I don't think I can be persuaded. But I do appreciate you including me in the decision-making process." As I ramble, I am slowly rising into a crouch, tensed and ready to make a run for it if she tries to grab me. Although if she summons that horse again, there's no way I can outrun it. Maybe if I climbed a tree? There's a fairly large willow with branches I'm sure I can scale. But what if she decides to wait me out?

I snatch a sizable shard of glass and palm it.

"Wait, wait, wait," she says, waving both hands in the air in front of her. "Let me start over. I don't want to actually kill you. I just need you to let me pretend."

What kind of sick request was that? Are the rumors true? Is she one of those people who takes pleasure in the pain of others? I grit my teeth and grip the shard harder, even as I feel it slice my skin.

Mancella reads my expression and puts her uninjured hand over her face.

"I'm not expressing myself very well at all, am I? I'm sorry, I . . . I'm not used to asking for help." She takes a step toward me but I flinch, and she must notice because she stops in place, holds up both hands, and sinks to the ground, sitting cross-legged. "Here's the situation," she says. "To summon an animal, I first need to kill it with my bare hands. I'm sure you know this." Of course I do. Everyone knows about the future Seconde's barbaric magic. I lift my lip in a sneer. "Well," she continues. "My father has a theory . . . that if I kill a human, I might be able to summon them, too. He wants to know what that might look like."

That's it.

I shoot to my feet.

I knew this family was despicable. I don't know why for even a second I thought there might be a softer side to the next generation. Her grandfather was a warmonger, her father is a tyrant, and she's no different. They're monsters. Every one.

I back up rapidly, upsetting the branches of a beech tree and causing the leaves to clang together in a series of sharp notes that sound like an alarm.

"Wait!" Mancella cries. She launches herself at me with surprising speed and latches onto my arm. I try to shake her off, but she's unyielding. I press my lips together and raise the shard, wondering where best to plunge it. "That's what *he* wants, but I don't want to hurt anyone!" she cries. "I would never kill a human. I don't even want to kill my animals, but he forces me. And I can't let him force me into this, too. It's too far. But . . . but maybe you could help. If I could pretend to kill you and then pretend it didn't work, he'd have to drop the whole thing. Right? No one would need to die at all!"

My hand stills, just short of the underside of her rib cage. With her clinging to my arm and my fingers a breath away from her stomach, it almost feels like we're in an embrace. It would take only one small movement to finish my attack, but it would be just as easy to turn the action into a caress.

She doesn't pull away from either possibility. As my mind spins over her words, she only holds her breath, grip tight and eyes pleading, seemingly unaware of the weapon hovering between us.

Does she really not want to kill?

My first instinct is not to believe her. She has so many animals. The people tried to keep track at first, but we lost count a long time ago. She *has* to enjoy it to some degree to have accrued that many.

But she said he forced her.

Could that actually be true?

Sensing that I'm no longer running, Mancella eases off my arm and raises her hands again in surrender. And my breath catches when the contorted moonlight slashes across them.

Because I've never really looked at her hands before.

They are *littered* with scars. Serried white lines score her palms and wind around her fingers like a road map of where she's been, some old, and some fresher, one still red and sickly purple along its edges.

Suddenly a part of me wonders if she's actually telling the truth. I mean . . . would anyone really choose a life that led to scars like that? What would it mean if she truly *didn't* want to kill? If she never did?

The possibility is an uncomfortable one. It doesn't fit with what I thought I knew about her. And I'm not sure if I'm ready for what it might mean.

"So?" she prompts, and I remember that she's waiting on an answer.

About playacting my demise.

I shake my head and purse my lips as I consider it. This seems like a very, very dangerous idea. She could slip up and kill me accidentally. Her father could discover the plot and kill me on purpose. There are actually quite a lot of ways that this idea could end with me dying. And whether she's a monster at heart or not, I owe her nothing. I owe the stranger she would kill if I don't agree nothing, too. Better them than me. That's been my motto for a long time.

But then a thought occurs to me.

Mancella is clearly desperate. Her fingers are flexing like she's ready to make another grab for my arm if I move an inch. Her eyes are worriedly tracking my every change in expression. Her mouth is pinched up into an anxious knot. I turn it all over in my mind.

I was hoping to win some of her trust tonight, but leveraging her desperation may work just as well.

"I'll help you," I say. "But I want something in return."

"Anything," she breathes. "Name it."

“I want the Victory’s Herald.”

The silence that follows is heavy, and I grow conscious for the first time of how late it’s gotten. How high the moon hangs in the sky and how quiet and still and thick the darkness is around us.

“Why do you want that?” she asks in a whisper.

A great question, to be fair. I’ll need a really good lie to sell this. She’s desperate and everything, but we’re talking about a blade that could literally start a war. You can’t just hand something like that out to random servants.

I shift, considering.

Usually, it’s best to tailor a falsehood to what the listener wants to be true. It’s easier for them to swallow that way.

Which means I have to take a gamble on what it is that Mancella Cliff truly wants.

I think about the cries for peace in her letter to Azele, and about what she’s just told me of her powers. It’s hard for me to believe she’s sincere, but I’ll need to decide in this moment, because whether I’m right will determine the effectiveness of my lie. And the effectiveness of my lie will determine whether my imminent death is a performance or a reality.

I don’t know why, but I decide to take a chance. “There’s something I haven’t told you,” I say. “And I didn’t ever plan to. But if we’re going to do this, then we need to trust each other.” She narrows her eyes, waiting, and I swallow before pressing on. “What I said on the rooftop was true, but there’s more to my presence in this castle than just that. I’m . . . part of a clandestine organization that seeks peace between realms. We have members all over and aren’t loyal to any particular Prime, just to our ideals. And we have reason to believe that your father is on the verge of starting a war that would be even more destructive than the last one. We believe we can divert it, but we'll need time. If you gave me the sword, then we could delay a rash action on your father's part. Its absence won't prevent him from declaring war forever, but he values tradition enough that it might buy us a couple of days. Then, once the danger is past, we could return it. Certainly before your Assurance. If all goes well, he won't even notice. But if we don't take it and things go sideways, then the consequences could be catastrophic."

She searches my face, her eyes wide. "How do you know all this?" she asks.

I don't, of course. I don't know anything. But the bluff seems to be working, so I shake my head slowly, wanting to press my advantage and keep the lie as simple as possible. "I can't tell you any more. I've probably already said too much. I just . . . feel that I can trust you. I hope I'm not wrong?" I reach forward and touch her arm lightly, fingertips tracing her elbow.

She follows the movement with her eyes, looking troubled. "I . . . I don't know," she says. "It's a big ask."

I step forward, into her space, and lower my voice. "What you're asking for isn't a small thing either," I say. "Putting aside the danger of playing at murder, to avoid getting caught we would need more people. The person who fights you needs to be in on it, but so does the person who checks the body for a pulse, as well as the person who carries the corpse away. If you insist on disposing of it yourself and don't let anyone touch it, it will raise more than a couple eyebrows. Which means if we don't have a detailed plan and a full crew, we'll be caught, and you'll be right back where you started, or worse." Her face darkens and her shoulders slump, but then I continue. "I can take care of all that."

Her head shoots up. "You can?"

I give her a sardonic smirk. "Like I said, there's a whole

organization behind me. I'm confident we can put on a convincing show. All I need from you . . . is the sword."

She crosses her arms again. Shakes me off and walks away from me.

Doubles back.

I wait, letting her work through the problem in her own mind. Letting her realize that what I'm offering is too good to pass up, and that the theft is in line with her own goals anyway. Finally, she comes to a stop in front of me.

"All right," she says, voice shaky but decided. "You've got a deal."

I feel a flash of surprise that arguing for peace actually worked. She's even willing to undermine her father's wishes in pursuit of it. In that moment, something shifts in my chest, and I find that I suddenly believe the things she's been telling me about herself.

Mancella really *doesn't* want the life of violence that she leads.

It's a shame that I could only realize this in the middle of deceiving her. But I'm too far in to back out now.

She extends a slender hand, and I take it. We both flinch as our cuts collide, but we shake anyway, ignoring the pain.

Ignoring the blood that drips onto the shattered branches of the bonsai tree glimmering at our feet.

9

Prospective Seconde Mancella Amaryllis Cliff

|8 DAYS UNTIL THE ASSURANCE|

A couple days later, Silver takes me up the wrong side of the Beholding Mountain. Not the side with the nice, well-worn path that overlooks our realm, but the side that's crammed against another mountain so it's just stark, bare rock no matter which way you look, and every step is precarious.

Silver leaps past me, skipping from boulder to boulder like an antelope, completely at ease.

Okay, so maybe every step is just precarious for me.

I slip on some loose sediment and almost fall face-first into the gravel, but I catch myself on an outcropping at the last second, watching the pebbles skitter down the mountainside behind me.

"You all right back there?" Silver crouches on a ledge that doesn't look like it has enough room to crouch on at all, and I scowl at him. He shoots me a lopsided, one-dimpled grin, and it actually reaches his eyes this time. They crinkle at the corners, and it makes their color softer, less like rust or dying leaves and more like burnt sugar, just short of caramelization.

Something in my chest flutters.

I'm sure it's just surprise.

Silver's attitude toward me seems to have shifted since our conversation in the garden. I guess conspiring to commit treason together can do that for a relationship, but I'm still getting used to it. Between our clandestine planning meetings to the faces he makes at me during dinner when no one is looking—and somehow he always knows when no one is looking—he has fit himself into the small corners of my day that I didn't realize were empty before.

It's a little disconcerting, but it's also . . . nice. I don't miss the careful phrasings or the simpering, full-dimpled smiles he used when we first met. In a castle loaded with double meanings and significant glances, I appreciate the bluntness.

"Next time wear better shoes," he calls back, executing another perfect jump. "Those slippers are ridiculous. They'll be ruined by the end of the hike."

I look down at my feet, and he's right. The sea-green silk is already filthy and one of the soles is starting to detach. "Well, you could've told me where we were going!" I remind him in exasperation. "I would've changed!"

"Next time, guess better," he says.

On second thought, the simpering wasn't so bad.

I heft my bag higher on my shoulder—the one he didn't offer to carry even though it would clearly be less of a hindrance for him than it is for me—and chuck a shoe at his head.

After another arduous half hour, punctuated by several more helpful remarks like "you probably shouldn't have worn a dress either" and "stop falling so much," we finally reach our destination.

Which, apparently, is a crack in the cliff face.

I drop my pack and do my best not to pant visibly, since Silver continues to be infuriatingly sweat-free.

"What is this?" I ask, jutting my chin at the gap in the rock.

He strides toward it, fingering the edges of the cleft. For a second, he looks strangely doleful, but in the next second his trademark smirk slides back into place like a door slamming shut. "*This* is a back entrance to what used to be the best market around," he tells me, voice light.

I scrunch my eyebrows. "A market? All the way up here?"

He shrugs. "What it sold wasn't strictly legal. But anyway, it's gone now. Come on."

He slips into the crevice like a fish flitting through water and quickly disappears from sight.

I eye my bulky bag and the narrowness of the crack, gritting my teeth, but I don't call after him. I've been pandered to my whole life, and it's refreshing not to be.

Refreshing, I think forcefully as I cram myself into the fissure and immediately get stuck.

Heaving the pack back up, I contort my body until it fits through the narrow opening. Hard stone grates against my shoulders as I edge forward. Sunlight fades away behind me, and I'm claustrophobic almost immediately. In suffocating darkness, with rock pressing against my body from every side, it's difficult not to feel that I'm being chewed up and swallowed alive by the mountain itself. But I push through. I keep going. And soon I'm stumbling into an enormous cavern, trying hard not to think of it as the mountain's gaping belly.

A bonfire crackles in a rough pit in the middle of the floor and it's burning too high for Silver to have built it in the last couple minutes, so I tense. He turns to me, silhouetted by the flames, and two other figures approach to flank him.

"I . . . didn't realize we were meeting anyone," I say nervously, taking a step back as they advance into the light.

The one on the right doesn't seem so bad. He's tall, and his eyes are the soothing pale green of an aloe vera. Not the spiky exterior of the plant, but the dewy heart of it, the part that responds to a fresh cut with healing salve. I don't know him, but I feel immediately that I could trust him. No one with eyes that kind could want to hurt me.

This girl, though.

She's pretty, with striking features and stark gray eyes, but her smile makes her seem more like a predator than a friend. She's not standing completely straight, but slightly crouched, like she's ready to pounce at any moment. Her hair is cropped close to her temples, her nails torn down to stubs. She wears no accessories or makeup, but her arms are covered with tattoos, many of them graphically violent. I felt her sizing me up when I first entered, and she hasn't stopped looking at me since. It's unnerving.

Almost without meaning to, I let a small fennec fox slip out of my inner well, sending ripples over my skin. He sniffs the air and growls, a low, gravelly sound that echoes off the walls of the cavern.

The girl growls back like it's the most natural thing in the world.

I yank the fox back inside me and his physical form blinks away. But I can still feel him, and others, stirring with apprehension under my skin.

"Relax, Mance," Silver says easily. He started calling me by the nickname a couple days ago and I've mostly gotten used to it, but the way the girl's eyes cut toward him when he says it tells me that she's not. I wonder what their relationship is. "These are friends," Silver explains. "They're here to help with the plan."

"Oh," I say, my shoulders slumping. "Of course." Other

members of his mysterious, pacifistic organization. I should probably have expected that.

Still, he could have told me.

"Let's review the logistics," he continues. "Mance, you have the uniforms?"

"Yes," I say, shoving the bag at his chest with a little more force than is strictly necessary. "But I'm not sure why I couldn't have given them to you at the *bottom* of the mountain. Or, I don't know, a different day entirely. One that didn't involve a lengthy hike."

"Because it wouldn't have been as entertaining," he says cheerfully, lifting the pack like it's made of feathers and riffling around inside. "How many did you bring?"

"Several," I grumble. "You didn't tell me your . . . *friends'* sizes."

"You didn't ask."

I glower at him. "Fine, I'll ask more questions. For example, why did we need to scale this mountain in the first place? Haven't you ever heard of meeting up at a tavern?"

"There are people at taverns."

"Yes, smart ones who realize how easy and pleasant it is to meet there."

"Or, nosy ones who would love to overhear our plot to deceive the Prime."

"Oh." It annoys me that he has a point. "Well, what about—"

"The castle is full of loyal servants and soldiers, the town has gossipy merchants and nobles, and if anyone in *our* neighborhood thought a scrap of information was worth half a meal, they'd sell you out faster than you can blink," Silver says. "But no one comes here. They sealed the main entrance a few years ago and only a handful of people know about the back way."

For the first time, I peer past the ring of the firelight, trying to make out what lies beyond it. I see the shadowy shapes of stalls strung up between stalagmites, stacks of boxes, and tables broken in half.

"What did they used to sell here?" I ask. "Weapons? Drugs?"

"Food, mostly," Silver says wistfully. "They had the best pies."

"What?" I shake my head. "But food isn't illegal."

"It is if you don't pay taxes on it," the tall one says. His voice isn't aggressive, but there's a bitterness to it. Like someone accidentally stirred some mugwort into a cup of chamomile tea.

"Oh," I say. "Well, then why wouldn't they just—"

The girl shoots forward. "Because your father hiked up the prices so high that no one could afford them," she says, getting in my face. "All to fund his constant preparations for war. People were just trying to make a living, trying to survive, but he realized he wasn't getting enough, so he sniffed this place out, and he slaughtered everyone in it. To make an example." Her sharp eyes bore into mine, daring me to snap back.

But I don't want to. I look down instead. "I-I'm sorry," I stutter. "I didn't know. I'm realizing that there are a lot of things I don't know. But when I'm Prime, it will be different. I promise."

She spits on the ground at my feet. "I've heard a lot of promises from Primes. Enough to know how little they're worth."

Silver puts a hand on her shoulder. "Cut it out, Vie. We're here to plan, not to put her on trial."

"Can't I do both?" she sneers. But she does fall back.

I shake out my arms like I've just finished the first round of a fight and I'm trying to pump myself up for Round 2. Silver said his organization wasn't partial to any particular Prime, but these two certainly seem biased *against* my father. But if they, like Silver, grew up in the Academy, then I can't exactly blame them. Silver was hostile at first, too. And it's clear that this place brings back bad memories.

I wonder how many people they knew at the market that day. How many of their friends died on the stone beneath my feet. Suddenly, the flickering flames seem ominous, and I fear what they might reveal if they burned any brighter.

"So, the plan?" I prompt, voice small.

"Right," Silver says. "You and I will fight. I hear you have a creepy death arena?"

I scrunch up my face. "That's . . . accurate, yes."

"Great, so we'll fight there. Nice and visible. Vie and Rooftop," he continues, pointing to each of them so I know which is which, "will wear the soldier uniforms and blend in. After I die, your job is to make sure no one touches me but them. They'll get the body out, you'll get your dad to back off the whole murder plan, and once everything is said and done, I get the fancy sword. Right?" He points a finger at me for confirmation.

"Right," I grit out. I know I agreed, and I believe him that his ultimate goal is peace between the realms, but I still don't think he should be talking about something this serious so flippantly. And I don't love that he won't give me any more information about the organization he works for.

But I don't really have a lot of options here. Not if I want to avoid innocent kids being murdered at my father's hand.

"Excellent," Silver says. "Let's practice."

I shift, tugging on the edge of my dress. "Right now?"

"Unless you want to hike up here again later."

I don't, so I kick off my useless slippers, which are completely destroyed at this point. The corset I ditched a while ago, but I'm not sure what to do about my dress. I try to knot it at the sides, but this particular dress is just as impractical as my shoes are, made of a filmy fabric in the same sea green, and the skirts are too billowy to be subdued. After a prolonged and embarrassing struggle, I decide to just take the whole thing off. My chemise and leggings are covering enough.

As I pull the garment over my head, I feel the gazes of all three of them tracing the movement, but no one makes any attempt to stop me. By the time I toss it to the side, Vie is scowling, Rooftop looks like he's trying not to laugh, and Silver's expression is appraising, though I'm not sure whether he's evaluating my decision to disrobe or the way I look now that I have.

Was the fire this warm before?

I resist the urge to cover myself as his gaze travels up my body. When his eyes get to my face, I meet them.

And the burnt sugar has fully caramelized.

"Okay," I say, my voice breathier than I'd prefer, "let's practice."

Silver smirks.

Our eyes stay locked for one more beat, and then he charges me. I dance to the side, making the flames flicker as I brush by them, assessing Silver's movements the way I would study a new creature. Memorizing the ways his muscles move as I try to predict what he might do next.

He swipes again, and I duck effortlessly, having read the action in the tension of his shoulders before he struck.

We keep that up for a few more strikes. He's not bad. Decent form, and quick recoveries. But I don't have too much trouble sidestepping his attacks.

"You can't dodge forever," he taunts.

And he's completely right, so I punch him in the face.

The smack of flesh connecting echoes through the cavern and he reels back, surprised. I dart forward to land another on his gut, but this time he catches my fist. And to my surprise, he's smiling.

"Didn't know you had it in you," he says, sounding weirdly impressed.

"You know I killed a jaguar, right?" I remind him.

"Sure," he says teasingly. "But I figured someone softened it up first so you wouldn't get your pretty hands dirty."

My face falls, but not because I'm offended.

With a sudden flash I remember my father locking me in a room with a dog when I was nine. The poor creature was beaten, bloodied, and whimpering, looking at me with watery eyes that begged for mercy. It tried to stand, but its legs were broken, so it toppled to the ground with a pained bark that still haunts me. I remember looking at him with tears streaming down my face, knowing what I had to do.

"It doesn't work," I say darkly. "The magic likes a fair fight." And the fact that the dog had been tortured first did not make my hands feel any less dirty.

Silver's expression sobers as he takes in mine, and his eyes latch on to my scar-covered hands.

"I'm sorry," he says. "I'm still getting used to—"

I lash out, striking his throat with my palm, right in the spot that cuts off his breath for a couple seconds. As he staggers back, I hook a leg around his in an attempt to trip him, but he flings a handful of ash in my face that leaves me coughing and retreating. I don't even know when he scooped it up.

"That's cheating!" I protest.

"Just because the magic likes a fair fight doesn't mean I do," he says.

I sense a challenge in his words.

And I grin.

What follows is not only a battle between two people but also a clash of styles. My fighting techniques come from the Captain, and they're characterized by structure, strategy, and discipline. Silver, on the other hand, is pure chaos. I'm stronger than he is, and I have much better form, but he uses the environment around him in a way I can't help but respect. One minute he's leading me away from the fire so I can't see what direction his hits are coming from and the next he's spinning me around until the flames blind me. He kicks rocks into my path, uses sparking embers to distract me, and at one point even chucks an entire flaming log at my head. I duck just in time and it lands with a thunk behind me.

Off to the side, Vie and Rooftop are sitting cross-legged on the ground, whispering back and forth. I think they're placing bets. As the log rolls to a stop, Vie's mocking laughter reverberates around the cave, bouncing from rock to rock until I hear it from every angle.

I grit my teeth and the animals within me grow restless, growling and gnashing their teeth at the indignity of losing to such cheap tricks.

So the next time Silver charges toward me, I let him get close, close enough to feel his breath on my cheek.

Then I drop to the ground.

In the space I just abandoned, the space directly in front of Silver's face, I summon my grizzly bear. She surges into being, a fur-covered giant with swiping claws and a gaping maw. Her full, throaty roar booms through the cavern, drowning out any trace of laughter. It also drowns out whatever expletive Silver utters as he scurries backward, away from the kind of beast he's probably never seen up close.

But I'm already behind him. As he stumbles away, I sweep his legs out from under him, and slam him face-first into the ground, twisting both his arms into a neat restraint behind his back. As the bear disappears, I dig my knee into his spine, making it clear that he's not going anywhere.

Beside us, Vie's on her feet, a dagger in each hand, but Rooftop is frozen, jaw dropped. It's several breaths before anyone speaks. The only noise is the crackling of the fire and the faint whistle of the wind in the crevice outside.

"All right," Silver says finally. "You win."

"Not yet," I disagree. "We're playing to the death, remember? So how would you like me to kill you? Any preferences?"

He chuckles, and I feel it vibrate through his back. "What are my options?" he asks, turning his face to fix those caramel eyes on mine.

"Let's see . . ." I scrunch my mouth to the side, pretending to think about it. "We could do a hard blow to the temple, a snapped spine, a nice strangle—"

"I'm failing to see what exactly would be nice about a strangle."

"Well," I say, leaning forward until my hair drapes across his shoulders, caging the two of us in, and lowering my voice to a whisper. "I've heard that you can also kill a man by hitting him so hard between the legs that he goes into shock from the overwhelming, vicious pain of it. Compared to that, I'd say strangling is pretty nice."

He shifts beneath me uncomfortably. "Okay, well, I'm definitely voting *against* that one."

Then suddenly he raises one knee and turns sharply to the side, throwing me off-balance. I crash to the floor behind him and he uses the momentum to push me back farther, flipping toward me in the process. I don't go down easily, though, and soon we're rolling, both of us wrestling for the upper hand, careening across the stone floor of the cavern.

It's only when a stick digs into my side that I stop, realizing how close we've come to the edge of the bonfire. In my moment of hesitation, he straddles me, pinning my wrists on either side of my head. Both of us are breathing hard.

For one heartbeat, I blink up at him, stunned, and he stares down at me with an unreadable expression. The heat of the flames washes over me, and his dulcet eyes seem to liquefy and turn molten in their flickering light.

In the next heartbeat, I am abruptly and acutely aware that his legs are wrapped around my thighs, his face is only inches from mine, and this is, by a pretty wide margin, the closest I've *ever* been to a boy. And I'm only wearing a thin shift.

Every exposed inch of skin seems to burn.

For two more heartbeats we stay there, skin blazing, breaths panting, bodies interwoven, and eyes locked.

But on the fifth heartbeat, we both launch ourselves away, Silver rearing to his feet, and me scuttling backward in a ridiculous crab walk. The cool air of the cave rushes into the void that opens up between us.

"Get off me!" Silver yells.

Which is an absolutely *absurd* thing to say.

"First of all," I yell back, leaping to my feet and waving my arms erratically at the extensive space that now surrounds me. "I'm all the way over here now. But secondly, and more importantly, *you* are the one who straddled *me*."

"Because you suddenly stopped rolling!"

"Because we were about to be *engulfed in flames*, Silver!"

"Yeah, you were," Rooftop says with a snicker.

I must not be as far away from the bonfire as I thought, because suddenly my face is scorching. Rooftop's smirk only widens.

Vie, on the other hand, is significantly less amused. She stomps over, twirling both daggers with sharp, rapid fingers.

"You know what just occurred to me?" she says loudly. "Silver can't fight you after all. Unfortunately, we're going to have to throw out the whole plan. So sorry."

I straighten and my animals snap their heads up in alarm, my argument with Silver forgotten. "What do you mean?" I demand.

"I mean," she says, stalking toward me, "if he dies in front of everyone, then he's not going to be able to work there anymore. They'll remember him and wonder why he's looking so very not dead. And I know how much the job means to him and how much he'd hate to lose it." She gives him a pointed look that I don't completely understand, and he frowns. "So you can't do it. Or do you not care how your little plan affects anyone else so long as *you* get what you want?" Her daggers speed up as she talks until they're whirling metallic discs glinting in the firelight, and she keeps creeping closer, pinning me with a glare that feels just as dangerous as the weapons in her hands.

I bristle against her accusations, but my heart thrums with panic. I need this to work. I don't have many days left before the deadline. And if I don't pick someone before then . . .

"Thankfully," Vie continues, almost preening. "There's a very simple solution here."

"And what's that?" I ask, jaw clenched.

She smiles at me with that predatory smile, her lips stretched wide and her teeth glistening. Shadows play along her features now that she's standing so close to the flames, making them look eerie and off-balance, almost inhuman.

Her daggers come to a sudden stop.

"You can fight *me*," she says.

10

Silver

|6 DAYS UNTIL THE ASSURANCE|

I'm not really sure how I managed to get sidelined in my own plan. Yet here I am, pretending to dust an oversized vase in front of the arena while I watch the guards pat down *Vie* for hidden weapons. As they rifle through her hair, pull at the seams of her shoes, and shake out her clothing, all I can think about is how the person in the arena should be me.

Well, that and how ridiculously overprotective the guards are being. When they ask her to open her mouth so they can check for needles hidden in her gums, even Mance rolls her eyes.

No one's patting *her* down, by the way. When the guards are done with Vie, they'll probably each give Mance a high five and a "go get 'em."

Vie snaps her teeth shut just shy of the guards' fingers when they finally pull them out of her mouth, and I flinch, almost knocking over the vase I'm supposedly polishing. It wobbles perilously until I grab it with both hands and force it back to stillness, my knuckles white and my heart pounding out of my chest.

Okay, so I'm a little tense.

We haven't practiced this fight as much as I would've liked. We tried, but Vie was more interested in taunting than choreographing, and the battles quickly devolved into uncoordinated brawls that I had to break up before Vie left an actual mark that could invite questions.

Today, there won't be any rules about marks. And there won't be anyone to hold Vie back.

Which I know she's been looking forward to.

I polish the vase so hard that it gleams aggressively in the light of the wall sconces. Part of me wants to shove it over and let it smash into pieces on the glossy marble floor.

"Mancella!"

My thoughts are derailed as a thin woman bustles down the hall, her skirts voluminous and her glass corset pulled so tight it's amazing she can still breathe. Mance's mother. I rarely see her apart from meals and I think this is the first time I've heard her speak. Her voice is drab and clingy, like wet clothing, and I resist the urge to wipe it out of my ears.

Mance straightens as she approaches, regarding her with an expression that seems oddly guarded. "Yes?" she asks.

The woman stumbles to a stop in front of her daughter. A couple wisps work their way free of her carefully arranged updo and she doesn't reach up to tuck them back in. Something vulnerable enters her expression as she takes in Vie, who sneers up at her obligingly.

"Is it true?" she asks, in that same soggy voice. "You're going to fight this . . . girl?"

Wow, could she be any more disdainful? I wring out my rag into the bucket, twisting the cloth until its threads bulge.

"It's true," Mance says.

"Oh." Lady Wespa fidgets, rubbing a thumb along the edge of

her corset, leaving a smudgy streak on the glass.

"Are you . . . all right?" Mance asks. "I thought you'd be happy."

"I am, of course." She says it quickly, but distantly, like it's an automatic response. "I just wish . . ."

"What?"

She parts her lips, but then Prime Merod strides up to say something to the soldiers and she pinches them back together in a stilted line. She shakes her head, dislodging even more strands, and puts a hand on Mance's cheek. "I wish you didn't have to," she whispers. "But I think you're very brave." She says this last part louder, like a proclamation, and pairs it with a tight smile.

Then she flees back down the hallway, clearly not intending to stay and watch.

I snort as her skirts disappear around the corner. Some support she was. She must have to keep her corset so tight because it's the only thing holding her upright. What with the lack of spine and all.

Rooftop, in full soldier attire, brushes past me, and although neither of us acknowledges the other, I know we're both noting each other's location, scanning the hallway for exits and potential threats, and keeping an eye on Vie.

It's almost time.

Rooftop brushes past Vie as well, with a similar lack of eye contact, and enters the side room where the soldiers watch. I'll need to find my way in there, too, but not until Vie leaves this hallway. I'd like at least one of us to have eyes on her at all times. Despite what Mance said about the magic liking a fair fight, I wouldn't put it past her father to try something underhanded. So far he's given Vie a wide berth, but you can never be too sure.

As if hearing my thoughts, the Prime shoulders past the

searching guards and lifts Vie's chin with one hand, studying her himself. I tense, and Vie straightens to her full height, returning his gaze with a glower. Whatever he sees must satisfy him because he lets her go.

"You understand the terms of the fight?" he asks.

"Yeah," Vie shoots back, rubbing the bottom of her chin. "The magic likes it fair, so no holding back. I actually had a question about that."

Prime Merod raises an eyebrow, expression detached. "Go on."

What is she doing? I sneak a quick look at Mance, but she doesn't seem to know either.

Vie blows her bangs out of her face. "Well, if I'm not holding back, then there's a chance I actually kill her, right? If it turns out I'm the stronger one? There's no fair fight if you don't allow for that possibility."

Prime Merod tilts his head back, regarding her. "In theory, yes. You'll need to give it your all, and there is a risk associated with that."

Mance wrinkles her nose at her death being called an "associated risk," and even I can't suppress a wince.

But Vie seems pleased. "Great," she says, pushing on. "So let's say I do. Kill her. No penalties for that, right? You're not gonna punish me for doing exactly what you told me to do?"

The cloth drops from my hand with a wet plop.

I know Vie, and she wouldn't ask something like that without a reason. She knows Mance isn't actually trying to hurt her, so there's no way she's afraid. In fact, she's been *excited* for this fight. A little too excited.

And a little too guarded about her reasons why.

Of course, it's not exactly a secret that she hates Mance. I mean, we all hate the Cliffs. We've spent almost every day since the Academy cursing their names, talking about what we'd do if we were ever alone in a room with any one of them. But it was just talk. Even Vie isn't reckless enough to try to murder a member of the ruling family right in the middle of their own castle.

At least, not without a guarantee that she could get away with it scot-free.

"No," Prime Merod says finally. "No penalty. If you win, then you walk."

"Excellent," Vie says.

The Prime turns away, and for a second I see a vicious, vindictive smile on Vie's face that makes my stomach clench. But before I can figure out if I should do anything about it, they're shoving her into the arena.

Mance strides in after, an uncertainty in her step now. She's probably turning Vie's questions over in her mind just as much as I am. Her shoulder slants, like she wants to turn back and look at me, but at the last moment she remembers herself and keeps her face forward.

And then the great doors slam shut, the bolt clicking into place.

I swallow, my mind racing.

Prime Merod hurries through the same door Rooftop used, eager for the match to start, but I don't follow right away.

In the emptiness of the hallway it suddenly occurs to me that if Vie *did* have some plan of her own, there's nothing I could do to stop it. Not in front of the Prime himself. My veins buzz in alarm.

Hurriedly, I slip into the side room as well, hoping it's crowded enough inside that one spare servant won't raise any eyebrows.

Turns out, I didn't need to worry. The place is packed.

There are soldiers there, but plenty of other servants, too. Cooks, cleaners, ladies' maids, groomsmen, and gardeners, all crammed into every crevice of the room. They must be drawn to the spectacle. I guess it's not every day the Seconde agrees to a death match with an unknown girl. Still, it makes me sick.

Anxious, I cast around for a spot to stand that won't be too noticeable but also grants a good vantage point. After shifting through the bodies, I end up near the Prime, because everyone else is trying to give him room, so the only free space up front is right at his elbow.

Standing that close to the man I hate most in the world makes me almost dizzy, but I shove my hatred aside for now.

Because I don't want to miss a thing.

In the arena, Vie and Mance are circling each other. Neither's made much of a move yet, and the room around me is on edge. Everyone's waiting for the first strike, me included.

"It's not too late to stop this," a woman at the front says, voice low enough that probably only the Prime and I can hear it.

I'm surprised by the opposition, so I tear my eyes away from the fight to search out its source.

The woman is squat and armored, with salt-and-pepper hair. She stands at the Prime's right hand. According to the badges on her uniform, she's a captain, and I can't help but be impressed with her because I've never seen an old lady so buff.

"Enough, Petrice," the Prime says, not sparing her so much as a glance.

But the woman is not silenced so easily. "She's still a child," she hisses.

"So are many of your soldiers. And she agreed to this."

"I'm certain she didn't agree to it without coercion, sir," the Captain says pointedly.

"I said enough!" the Prime roars, wheeling on her. "You forget your place."

Several around us make startled noises and take a step back.

The Captain, however, does not cower under his anger. In fact, she seems to stand up straighter. But she does bite her tongue with a terse, "Sir."

I take advantage of everyone's shifting to sidle farther in, closer to Rooftop and the door. Neither the Captain nor the Prime seems to have taken notice of either one of us, which is how I'd like to keep it. And no matter how interesting it is eavesdropping on the Prime, I don't want to get distracted again.

In the arena, things are picking up. Vie is employing her typical ruthless style, ducking under Mance's guard to administer brutal and efficient jabs to her vital points. I can tell she's missing her knives, wishing she could slide them into each of the soft patches of flesh she hits, but she's making a good show of it anyway.

Mance, on the other hand, adopts the same disciplined forms she used with me, every bit of her body a honed and powerful weapon. It's a different experience watching her fight from a distance. Against my will, I'm struck by the grace and precision of her movements, the way one form flows into the next, the way her footwork is so deliberate and yet so fluid. Though she never summons an animal, she seems to embody them in her attacks nonetheless, slinking like a crafty cat, dodging like a lithe gazelle, striking like a venomous snake.

She's mesmerizing.

From what I can tell, the sentiment is shared by everyone around me, and it feels like we breathe as one, gasping at tricks and sighing at escapes together. At some points it doesn't feel like anyone in the room is breathing at all.

I can see the moment Vie comes to the same conclusion I did in my own fight. Mance is better than we are, and denying it out of pride would only give her the win quicker. The only way to have any chance at all is to do something unexpected. Basically, to play dirty. But Vie doesn't have a bonfire or a sediment-filled cave to work with like I did. I rock on my heels, nervous about what she's going to do.

Quick as a flash, Vie's hand lashes out, fisting in Mance's hair, winding it around her fingers with quick, rough jerks until she's woven a solid anchor.

Then she pulls.

Hard.

Mance's scream fills the room as she claws at Vie's hands, digging in her nails. But Vie just keeps yanking, pushing Mance's head down low and ripping at her wavy tresses, clearly reveling in this moment of power over her. Mance says something under her breath that the rest of us can't hear, but Vie only snickers and slams her knee into Mance's face.

She's enjoying it, I can tell. And the pain she's inflicting now is real.

When she brings her knee up again it slams into Mance's stomach, and then her neck. Mance makes a horrific gurgling sound and then spits blood onto the marble.

My breathing shallows and sweat breaks out on my forehead.

Vie isn't actually this senseless, is she? She doesn't really believe the Prime will let her go without penalty if she murders his heir, right? What incentive would he have to uphold that promise?

Mance coughs up more blood and my stomach clenches.

I don't like seeing her like this.

The realization startles me, but it's impossible to deny the physical, *visceral* response I'm having to her pain.

It feels like I'm taking the hits myself.

Even more alarming, there's a part of me that wishes I *could*.

"Come on, Mance," I whisper under my breath.

Finally, Mance digs her thumbs into the soft part of Vie's wrist and simultaneously gives her a hard kick to the gut. As Vie lurches backward, her grip loosens and Mance manages to detach herself. She backs up, panting, her formerly pristine bun now half unwound, her hair falling in haphazard tufts around her face.

The room is alternately cheering at her escape and jeering at Vie for the cheap moves, but in the midst of their noise I go silent.

Because I see the look on Mance's face.

Fury.

It's the same look she had when she was going at that wisteria. Like she was holding nothing back. Like she'd keep going until the thing was ground to dust or her hands were a bloody pulp, whichever came first. Something about that look makes my mouth go dry and apprehension skate down my spine.

"The magic has awakened," murmurs a voice to my right. Several around me nod, pressing in closer, and suddenly the energy of the crowd is charged. Expectant.

"What does that mean?" I ask, turning toward the speaker.

She angles her eye toward me and I suck in a breath.

It's Mara, Mance's sister, and I never should have drawn her attention. I look down at my shoes, trying to act the part of a new hire embarrassed by a social gaffe. But for whatever reason, she decides to answer me, pressing in close to my back and speaking in a low voice, her gaze still on the battle in front of us.

"The magic has a bloodlust," she tells me. "And at a certain point in the fight, that bloodlust takes over. My sister stops guarding. She stops evading. She *becomes* the fight. Watch."

My eyes flick up, and my breath catches in my throat, because she's right. Mance has changed. She was a creature before, but a gentle one. A beautiful one. One that viewed the back-and-forth as a dance.

Now she's a predator. Fast, sharp, savage. Vie doesn't stand a chance. She stumbles back amid an onslaught of attacks that seem to come from everywhere at once, and in that moment an expression passes over her face that I haven't seen on her in a long, long time.

Fear.

Vie, the girl I always thought was impenetrable, the girl who regularly fights men twice her size just for a few coins and the glee of knowing that she can beat them, is afraid.

All of a sudden none of this feels right at all.

My heartbeat speeds up and the room feels like it gets twenty degrees hotter. The bodies pressed around me feel too close, too claustrophobic, like they're breathing down my neck.

And Mance just keeps going, attacking again and again. Vie is barely even trying to defend anymore; there's no time between blows.

For a second I get the wild, irrational thought to run out there and stop this. Shut the whole thing down. I look at Rooftop and he's already looking at me, and the fact that we've both abandoned subtlety in the same moment makes my stomach lurch into my throat.

Then Mance takes Vie's head into her hands and whips it to the side, and I will never forget the thunderous crack that her bones make as they snap beneath the Prospective Seconde's fingers. It feels like the sound reverberates through my very chest.

Vie's expression freezes in shock. Then she slumps to the ground, and there's a second crack—that of her skull hitting solid marble.

But Vie doesn't flinch. She just lies there . . . lifeless.

My heart racing, I remind myself that this isn't real. We're here to pretend. It's a *good* thing that it looks so realistic. It means we all did our job. Everything's going according to plan.

Right?

Jubilant applause explodes all around me, and I take a reckless half step toward them, but Rooftop's faster. He shoots forward, pushing off the wall and charging to Vie's side, all sense of decorum lost.

"Soldier!" the Captain bellows, storming after him. "You're to wait for my signal!"

"Apologies, ma'am," Rooftop says, and I hear the quaver in his voice. "I just . . ."

But he doesn't get to finish what he's saying because Mance falls to her knees, her expression stricken, as whatever came over her evaporates like water beneath the cruel sun. Her hands are shaking, and she looks at them like she's never seen them before.

"Oh no," she whimpers. "What did I do? *What did I do?*" Her whimper turns to a scream so agonized that it sets my teeth on edge. Even Rooftop takes a step back. At the movement, she whirls on him.

"Is she dead?" she asks. "Is she really dead? Tell me!"

Rooftop needs no other prompting. He bends down and puts his fingers to Vie's neck. Her head lolls limply to the side. When he lifts his face again, it's ashen. "She's dead," he says. And although his voice is deadpan, I can hear the slightest quaver. One that no one but me would be able to hear, but that hits me as hard as the two cracks that came before it, like the sound of a hammer pounding the final nail into the coffin.

Vie's coffin.

No.

No no no no no no.

At first I think the word is echoing in my head, but then I realize Mance is screaming it and I feel like I might pass out.

Prime Merod pushes through to grab Mance by the shoulders, shaking her.

"Snap out of it!" he orders.

"Why did you push me to this?" Mance yells at him. "Take her away, please, I can't even look at her. Tell her family that I'm sorry. Tell them I'm so, so sorry."

Is it just me, or did her teary eyes flick in my direction when she said that? I reach a hand out to the wall in front of me to steady myself.

"Peace," the Captain says, pressing something into her palm. Mance stares at it. Turns it over. Swallows.

"I should have made a bigger one this time," she says faintly. "I . . ." She chokes up, tries to speak again, and finally lays the item on Vie's chest with shaking hands. It's a tiny bouquet of white flowers tied with twine.

The kind of bouquet someone might leave at a grave.

Mance puts both hands over her face and sobs into them, and I am horrified to find a sob rising in my own throat as well. I jerk my head back to see if anyone has noticed my lack of composure, but most are fixated on the scene before them.

Except for Mara, whose evaluating gaze is latched solely on me, and whose mouth is quirked up at the side.

"Never seen anyone die before," I mutter to her, hoping to explain away my reaction as mere discomfort with violence. Then

I turn back to the arena, desperately trying to force my features into something safer.

Rooftop is blank-faced as he scoops up Vie's body and cradles her to his chest, a gesture she would normally hate. But she doesn't move.

And I don't, either.

I can't.

He rushes out, head bowed and expression shadowed. The medical staff floods in to give Mance an evaluation, but she seems fine. Physically, anyway. Her father must have come to the same conclusion because he swats them all away.

"Focus," he demands. "Can you feel her?"

Mance raises her head and looks at him. Then with a last sob, she closes her eyes and takes a deep breath.

My own breath sticks in my throat, my emotions churning, my feet still frozen to the floor. If Vie is really dead, do I want Mance to be able to summon her or not? The idea of Vie as one of her pets makes me sick, but the thought of never seeing her again makes me sicker. The room reels.

"I-I can't," Mance stutters.

Merod's face falls, but then he clenches his jaw. "Try. Try to summon her anyway. Maybe you can't feel her inside, but that doesn't necessarily mean she isn't there."

"I really don't want to do this right now, Father, can't I rest first?"

"No," he says. "Try."

Mance closes her eyes and scrunches up her face. I realize I now have both hands clenched. It's only the possibility that Mara's still watching me that makes me forcibly relax them.

Finally, Mance shakes her head. "She's not there. She's not anywhere."

My heart plummets.

Her father stares at her for a moment, then stalks out of the room with a frustrated snarl, leaving a wake of tense silence behind him.

Through the crowd, Mance's eyes find mine. Her cheeks are blotchy, her hands are shaking, and tears stream down her face. I don't know what she's looking for from me, but I can't give it. I'm not ready for this.

I bolt.

Somehow, I don't know how, I keep my steps brisk but measured until I'm out of the palace. But once my boots hit grass, I break into a run.

"W-wait!"

That's Mance's voice. It's still teary.

I speed up.

Behind me, her footsteps get louder, hitting the ground at a faster, more frenzied pace.

What does she want, to apologize? I can't hear it right now. I'm seconds away from a breakdown.

But where can I go? How can I lose her?

I turn on my heel, veering back toward the glass gardens. In the sunlight, the glass is glaringly bright, almost blinding. I charge toward them, driven by the irrational feeling that if I just go back to where we struck this horrible deal, maybe I can undo it. But she's gaining on me too quickly, so I dart into the hedge maze instead. I dash left, then right, then right again, making turns at random, hoping desperately to lose her. But she knows the layout better than I do, and soon her hand grabs the back of my waistcoat, pulling me to a stop.

And I can't *stand* that she's outmaneuvered me again.

I shrug the garment off and spin, pushing her backward into the shrubbery.

She has the nerve to look stunned as leaves cascade into her hair. "What are you—"

"Was this the plan all along?" I ask. "Get a willing volunteer by telling her it won't be real and then taking her life anyway once it's too late to escape? Was your original intention to kill *me*?"

I'm advancing on her, and she's stumbling sideways, toward a gap in the bushes, all innocent doe. But I'm not buying it anymore. I've seen the real creature. I've seen her darkness. She will never fool me again.

"Listen—" she protests.

But I talk over her, half because my anger is overflowing and half out of fear of what she might say, what she will confirm. "Just because we're poor, it doesn't make us less than you," I shout. "We're not expendable people. We're not your playthings!"

"I never thought you were! I—"

My hand crashes into the bushes by her head, blocking her exit. The whole wall rustles and her eyes go wide.

"So, what, it was an accident?" I growl. "You just couldn't control the monster that you are? Got too carried away by your own sick bloodlust and you're *sorry* now? Well, let me tell you something. I don't forgive you. I will *never* forgive you. You are—"

In the middle of my sentence, she takes my head in her hands and whips it sharply to the side.

I both hear and feel my own bones cracking beneath her fingers.

My words wither in my throat.

And time grinds to a halt.

I've thought about my own death a lot, but I never thought

that when it came it would make me want to laugh. It's funny, though, isn't it? I can't believe she's gotten away with this. Can't believe that after my life of defying the odds, *this* is how it ends for me. In a perfectly manicured hedge maze. On a bright, sunny day. At the hands of a teenage girl who I never, *ever* should have trusted.

At least I'll be able to apologize to Vie sooner than I thought.

I hope Rooftop will be okay without us.

A beat goes by as I brace myself both mentally and physically for whatever comes next.

But then, shockingly . . . nothing does.

Feeling foolish, I reach a tentative hand up to my throat. And my pulse is there, thrumming away. I am unexpectedly but very obviously still alive. I'm . . . great, actually.

It doesn't even hurt.

"Are you done?" Mance asks in a dangerously low voice. "Because that was a move the healers use on me when my back gets tight. It's loud and dramatic looking, but all I actually did was realign the bones of your neck. You're fine. And Vie's fine, too. If anything, she's *better* than before."

It's true; my neck feels fantastic now. Like I've never spent a night sleeping on cobblestones in my life.

I stare at her, breathing hard. She hasn't fixed her hair yet, so it's spilling out of its bun, framing her face with uneven tendrils. This close, and under the bright light of the sun, I can see that her eyes aren't actually black, like I'd always assumed. They're blue—a shadowy, impenetrable blue I've only ever seen in the depths of a midnight sky. It's her lashes that are true black, framing those eyes in inky wisps, some of them stuck together in still-damp clumps left over from her tears. I didn't realize she'd cried that much.

But she isn't crying now. Behind the leftover tears, her midnight eyes are burning.

My lips part, but I have no idea what I'm about to say.

And I guess we'll never find out, because before I utter a word, she ducks under my arm and makes a run for it, leaving nothing but the sound of rustling leaves and retreating footsteps behind her.

11

Prospective Seconde Mancella Amaryllis Cliff

|6 DAYS UNTIL THE ASSURANCE|

M*onster.*

It's not like the word is new to me. I hear it whispered wherever I go. When I make formal appearances, the name rips through the crowd like a shark in the water, chewing up any other perception of me like chum.

My father told me that was a good thing. If I'm strong, I keep us safe. If they think me brutal, they won't attack or disobey. By becoming the monster, I prevent *true* monstrosities.

But . . . I never put that mask on with Silver. I was always me.

And he used the word anyway.

I throw myself into my room and slam the door behind me, gasping for breath.

I thought it would feel better to succeed at this ruse. I mean, everything went perfectly, didn't it? So perfectly even Silver was fooled.

But there were too many parts of it that *were* real. The hatred in Vie's eyes. The way her jabs were truly designed to hurt. The feeling of dropping her limp body at my feet and having everyone cheer, exulting in her death. I didn't have to fake the sobs or the accusations I threw at my father, because everything leading up to them hit way too close to home.

I sink to the floor, rubbing the last of the tears off my face as my chest turns cold.

What if I've leaned too far into the illusion? What if I've put on this persona and, like my armor, it's molded itself into my skin until you can't tell one from the other?

What if I can't take it off again? Will I have to play this part for the rest of my life?

And if I do . . . at some point will it stop being an act?

I've always thought it was the Citadel that made my father what he is now, that stripped away the kindness he used to show me when I was younger. But what if it was power? What if the same happens to me?

Pulling my knees against my chest, I balance my chin on my arms.

When it was all over, I ran to Silver because I needed someone to remind me that it was only pretend and I'm *not* that person. I needed to take the armor off before it suffocated me.

But it turns out the armor was all he ever saw.

What do I do now?

The clouds outside shift, transforming the shadows in my room, and a flash of metal on top of my bookcase catches my eye. I squint up at it.

It's the saucepan I planted the starsprout in, nestled between a stack of textbooks and a figurine of a jeweled elephant.

I stare at it, sniffing noisily.

Then I haul myself up, drag over a chair, and stand on my tiptoes until I can grasp the handle and pull it down, because right now I could really use the reminder that I *did* save something. One starsprout. One little flower that I yanked from the earth in the dead of night to spare it from the inferno.

And a monster wouldn't do that, would they?

But when I peek over the edge, the flower is wilting and the dirt is bone dry.

My stomach sinks and my eyes burn. I almost throw the entire pot at the wall.

Instead, with a white-knuckled grip, I drag the withered mess into my bathroom and draw some water.

I don't know how much is the right amount, so I dribble careful, incremental portions until the dirt feels roughly as moist as the soil of the lawn felt when I buried my hands in it. And maybe it's my imagination, but the little plant seems to perk up.

My shoulders relax and I clutch the saucepan in my lap, sitting cross-legged on the floor. The starsprout will be okay. *I* will be okay. Somehow.

I stroke one of the petals with my finger, and, as the animals within me brighten as well, I let out a handful of butterflies. They bat their jewel-toned wings and flutter around me. One of them lands gently on my nose, and I respond with a relieved smile as I watch its wings open and close, open and close.

"Well, you certainly look happy for a murderer."

I jerk my head up, heart in my throat, to see Mara leaning against the doorframe.

I dismiss my butterflies and shove the crude flowerpot behind my back. The clouds move again, and a shadow falls across Mara's scarf-covered face as she studies me.

"Um," I say. "What happened was—"

"Save it," she says. "We need to talk. My room. Now."

My mouth snaps shut because Mara never invites me to her

room. Or anyone. I'm not sure she's let anybody in since the Broken Citadel. So when she pushes off the doorframe and heads for the hall, I stumble after her, wondering what this might mean.

When we get to her room, Mara swings the door wide and steps back, gesturing me forward. I oblige, but my steps are tentative. Entering feels like crossing some kind of metaphorical threshold.

We both live in towers, but while my room is like a showroom, frequently swept and carefully arranged, Mara's is more . . . lived in. Probably because she long ago banned any of the maids from entering either.

The first thing I notice is the smell, tingling my nostrils. Like peppermint, sage, and burnt citrus.

The next thing I notice is how cluttered everything is. Every surface—and a fair chunk of the floor—is covered with a weird assortment of seemingly useless knickknacks. I see feathers, dried herbs, broken dolls, and yellowed papers. On one table there's a pile of bracelets and busted locks. On another there's a glass vial suspended above a candle, with some kind of dark amber liquid inside. I'm guessing that's where the smell is coming from. And there are other casks and bottles scattered throughout the room as well, with liquids and powders in a variety of shades. Some are clear and light, like water but thicker, and others are as dark and crusty as dried blood.

But all of this I expected. She's always been messy. She's always collected odd, discarded things, only giving secretive smiles in answer when asked what they could possibly be for.

What I didn't expect was the paintings on the walls. I walk to the center of the room and turn slowly, taking it all in.

On the wall to the left of the door, she's depicted the mountain range in broad, deliberate strokes. The magic twists above it, eating away at the sky. She's made its edges look like pointed teeth.

On the next wall, she's painted the desert, the riven pieces of the Broken Citadel poking out of the sand, and the magic's twisting mass within them. All the lines of the painting point inward, toward its glowing center, and the greens she's used are so vivid and striking that I almost feel the same pull toward them that I did when I saw the real thing, when I struggled to avert my eyes. I tear my gaze away from it, but the next mural is worse.

The wall on the right side of the room, the one behind her bed, is painted completely black. Not the flat black that would come from only one coat and only one shade. It's layered. It breathes. I don't know how she did it, but it feels alive, like it might reach out and snatch me.

I stagger back, into a pile of lampshades, and send the stack of bracelets on the desk toppling.

"How can you sleep under that?" I ask.

"The same way you do," she says matter-of-factly. "It's there whenever you close your eyes, isn't it? The blackness. And we have to hide it so much when we're out there in the world. We have to smile and talk around it. So in this room, at the very least, I want to be honest. To stare into it without flinching. To say what I need to say to it whenever I need to say it."

Her words make sense to me. They make sense, and yet I still can't look at that wall. Nor can I fully turn my back on it. I stand at an angle, keeping it in the corner of my eye, my whole body tensed like the wall itself might attack.

I could never live in a room like this.

"So you wanted to talk?" I say nervously.

"I wanted to congratulate you," she says.

I turn from the blackness to gape at her, though I still feel it prickling my scalp. "You want to congratulate me for my first real murder?"

"I want to congratulate you for finally playing the game," she says. "Making the moves necessary to survive in this castle. It's about time."

I clench my fists. "I can't believe how callous—"

She waves an impatient hand to dismiss my admonition. "You and I both know you didn't kill that girl."

The certainty in her voice makes my heart plummet. I make a feeble attempt to look surprised, but it must fall completely flat, because her one eye shoots me a glare and I deflate immediately.

"Was it that obvious?" I ask. "To . . . everyone?"

"Nah," she says, walking toward the blackness. "I only knew something was up when that servant started having a panic attack. So when he ran off and you fled in the same direction, I told everyone to give you space and let me talk to you first. And then I followed you."

I swallow. "How much did you see?"

She tilts her chin at me, assessing my reaction. Her dark hair blends in with the paint until it almost looks like it's swallowing her. "The two of you running, the two of you disappearing into a hedge maze, and then, later, a dead girl and a soldier meeting up with that same servant. But even if I hadn't seen any of that, your little butterflies-and-flowers act would have given you away pretty quickly. If you had actually killed someone, there's no way you would've been able to smile like that so soon. And the whole walk over here you seemed perfectly fine, so . . . you'll have to work on that."

My stomach clenches as I realize she's got a point. The act isn't over. I'll have to mope around for weeks to make this look realistic. I scrunch up my mouth and sink to the ground, dragging my hands down my face.

"There you go," she says. "That's much better."

I chuck a pillow at her but she's already moving, so it bounces harmlessly off the onyx-colored paint behind her. Part of me expected it to get sucked right in, and the fact that it didn't gives me a small measure of nonsensical relief.

Meanwhile, Mara is moving things around on her bookshelf. "Here," she says, gathering various plants and powders and measuring them out into an emptied makeup jar.

I peer through my fingers at her skeptically. "What is all that?" I ask.

She pours the now bright yellow mixture into a tiny cask and puts a stopper in it, then tosses it at me. I catch it in one hand.

"If you need to cry, that will irritate your glands," she tells me. "Only use a little at a time. If you dose more than four times a day, you might go blind for a week or so. But as long as you use it appropriately, it should really help sell the act."

"How do you know all this?" I ask, holding the bottle up to the light.

She shrugs. "You're not the only one who's needed to force a tear."

I turn the vial over, watching the sediment in the bottom float to the top. I try to think of the last time I saw Mara cry so I can pick it apart for authenticity.

But I can't even think of a single time.

Not since we were kids, anyway. Not since . . .

My eyes flick up to the Citadel and then away.

"Why would you need to—" I try.

But Mara shakes her head, cutting me off. "Don't forget, you've only just stepped up to the board. I've already been playing this game for years. And anyway, I didn't bring you here to talk about stuff like that. I just want you to . . . I don't know, relax a little. Fortify yourself before you go back out there. With the Assurance coming up so soon, things are getting intense. But you don't have to play in here." To punctuate her point, she unfastens her scarf and peels it off, folding it over her hands in a practiced rhythm before hanging it up in the closet beside hundreds of others.

When she turns back, her face is bare, but her expression is sincere. I can't help feeling that she's telling me to lay my cards down even as she keeps hiding her own. But I force myself to loosen my shoulders and shove down my nerves anyway, because I do appreciate the gesture. I slip the tonic into my pocket and cross my legs underneath me, motioning for her to sit down, too.

As she does, my eyes skim over the weathered papers, the broken locks, and the bundles of herbs, before finally landing on the charred candle. The smell of the mixture above it still needles me, and I have to know.

"What's that for?" I ask, pointing. "Father's not still making you conduct those experiments, is he?"

Her expression turns grim as memories surface between us, like dead bodies floating to the top of a lake.

For the first several years after we returned from the Broken Citadel, Father tried to force Mara's magic to manifest. He found some scholar from the Jungle Realm who told him about others whose magic was delayed, and how it usually took a traumatic event to trigger it.

So he'd stick her hand in a fire to see if she was resistant to flames. He'd stir poison into her breakfast to see if she was immune to it. One cold night I had to drag her out of the well in the garden because he'd tied a rock to her foot and thrown her in, hoping she could breathe underwater. I'll never forget the cold, slimy feeling of her skin or the rasping, heaving coughs she made as I clutched her to my chest. I thought he'd stopped all that, but maybe he hadn't. Maybe he's just gotten better at hiding it. Maybe—

"No," she says, mouth drooping but voice forceful. "He gave up on me a long time ago. I use that for tea." She gives me a watery smile. "Want some?"

I'm simultaneously relieved by her words and devastated by her phrasing. My stomach is churning, but I nod anyway. "Tea would be nice."

She picks up one of the bags of herbs, which I now realize are tea leaves, and dumps it into a beaker of fresh water, swapping this with the stale one above the candle. Then she strikes a match and holds the fire to the wick. Once the tea is steeping, she pulls some crackers and jams out of the stand by her bedside and holds them out.

"We might as well make a meal of it," she says. "I'd rather not find out if Father tries to serve orphan for dinner tonight."

I snort, accepting the tin she hands me, and we sit side by side on the floor to share our makeshift dinner.

But no matter how light our conversation is or how sweet the lemon and lavender curd we spread on our buttery crackers might be, I never stop noticing the blackness on the wall. I remember sitting in this same room with Mara when we were younger, staying up late and giggling freely. There were never any secrets then. There were no shadows seeping in.

But so much has changed, and although the chat we share

now is pleasant, it's not the same. It can't be, not when it takes place against the background of that enveloping, all-consuming blackness.

Still, I feel like the magic has taken enough from me already, and I won a victory against it today. I kept my control even when its bloodlust surged. I didn't kill, and now I won't have to. So no matter how uncomfortable that mural makes me, I don't leave. I stay until the wall matches the sky outside. And then I stay even longer, until stars begin to make the darkness softer.

12

Silver

|5 DAYS UNTIL THE ASSURANCE|

We said we'd meet a few hours before dawn to get the sword, and there's no reason to change that just because I profoundly insulted a girl who didn't deserve it and have spent the last few hours berating myself for doing so.

It's not like stressing about Mance is a new experience. But it feels new, because this time I'm not concerned about losing my job or getting eaten by a jaguar or being shoved off the cliffs, probably because I've finally accepted that she was never going to do any of those things in the first place.

What I'm worried about is that I hurt her feelings.

And I don't know what to do with that. Which is probably why I've been standing in front of her door for twenty minutes and I have yet to actually knock. I've had to duck into the curtains thrice now to avoid the night guard, and there are only four minutes left before he comes around again.

"Get it together, Silver," I mutter to myself. "It's a door, not a guillotine."

Wincing as though I don't believe my own statement, I reach forward and, after another tense beat, finally rap on the door with my knuckles.

She flings it open right away, very suddenly in my space, making it clear that she was waiting for me just on the other side of the door.

But for how long?

Did she hear my mumbling?

Does she know it took almost half an hour for me to finally knock?

Obnoxiously panicked, I back up a couple steps, trying to make the action look smooth and casual. Trying *not* to make it seem like her proximity freaked me out. Because why should it? We've stood near each other plenty of times. Like yesterday, when I shoved her into a bush and screamed in her face. We were standing *very* close then. Or when we were in the cave and she was laid out beneath me, the fire warming our skin.

Nope. That train of thought is not helping.

She blinks up at me like she can hear my disjointed inner monologue, but her own emotions are locked away. She's combed her hair back from her face and smoothed it into a high ponytail, and her midnight eyes are dark and shadowy again, no sign of vulnerable blue. She seems to be waiting for me to speak first.

So I say, "Hey." Which is not the best of opening lines, but considering all the other things I've shouted at her in recent history, it could certainly be worse. Then I clear my throat. "I'm sorry about—"

"I wore slippers again," she blurts, cutting me off. I don't know how to respond to that, so I just raise an eyebrow. She crosses her arms and continues snippily. "I just wanted to ask up front whether you anticipate us scaling a mountain at any point in this outing, since evidently I need to specifically request that information at the outset of our every excursion lest I make inappropriate wardrobe decisions."

I can't help it. I laugh. But she doesn't, so I quickly sober.

"No mountains," I say.

"Am I at any point going to be lit on fire, plunged underwater, or encountering any other topographical obstacles that I may have to dress differently for?" she asks.

"Not that I'm aware of," I say. "But you know your dad's security system better than I do."

She finally notices what I'm holding—a giant lead pipe, currently propped against my shoulder, and her bristly facade cracks a little as she eyes it curiously.

"What's that for?" she asks.

"To put the sword in," I explain. "Pipes are much less suspicious than ceremonial swords."

"I don't know about that, since there's no real reason for you to be hauling a pipe around, either."

"There is, actually, since the drainpipes on the east side of the castle are in tragic disrepair."

She narrows her eyes at me. "Since when?"

"Since I took a crowbar to them a few days ago, notified my supervisor of the damage, offered to fix it, and put in an order for a replacement pipe. Which would be this."

I lean the pipe toward her helpfully, and she purses her lips. She looks like she wants to lecture me, but ultimately she just shakes her head.

"All right, then," she says. "Let's get this over with."

"Sure thing," I say, glancing behind me. "In about two minutes. But first, back up."

She furrows her brow, but there's not much time to explain, so

I push her gently back into her room and close the door behind us, as softly as I can.

She opens her mouth to protest, but I hold a finger to her lips as the sound of a full set of armor clanks up the stairs behind us. Understanding flickers in her expression and she doesn't speak, but she does flick my hand away. I try not to feel stung.

We both hold still, barely breathing as the clanking passes by the door and continues onward. Even when it fades, we stay silent a beat longer, huddled together in the shadows of her doorway. I can smell the honeysuckle soap she used to wash her hair.

Finally, she raises an eyebrow and I swallow and nod.

Without another word, she brushes past me, like she can't wait to get out of my presence. I heave a sigh and hoist the pipe back up on my shoulder, slinking after her like a dog with his tail between his legs.

We steal down the darkened staircase, our steps soundless. She's better at stealth than I thought she would be, and once again I wonder if her animals lend her some of their attributes. There's something in the way she moves that reminds me of how her jaguar crept along the dinner table the night we met. Any other time, I might be impressed by it. Tonight it only adds to my unease.

Despite me openly watching her the whole way to the study, Mance doesn't look at me once.

When we get there, she flicks something on the side of the door before turning the knob. It was a quick, practiced movement that she half shielded with her shoulder. I only saw it because I was scrutinizing her so closely.

She enters the room, but I linger, checking to see what she changed. My fingers find a small clasp tucked into the seam of the doorframe. It's attached to a cord of metal that goes all the way around the door and, I assume, under the flooring as well.

"Magical barrier?" I ask.

She pulls at her ponytail and clears her throat, clearly annoyed that I noticed. "Yes."

"And it only works if it's unbroken?"

She flips her hair over her shoulder and raises her chin without answering.

"Don't worry about it," I say. "I was just curious. What Prime makes barrier magic?"

"I'm . . . not sure, actually," she admits. "I mean, it isn't one of the Primes; I know all their powers. But I don't keep track of all the third sons and second cousins who possess magic. It's probably one of them."

Imagine having so many magical artifacts in your life that you can't even keep track of where they all come from. I shake my head and follow her into the room.

Only to stumble to a stop.

Every inch of every wall is crammed with the mounted heads of Mance's kills, from the grizzly snarling with two extended paws to the ferret staring down with beady eyes. I let out a low whistle as I take it all in.

"You killed all of these?" I ask.

She shifts from one foot to the other and nods. For the first time tonight, a flash of vulnerability enters her expression before she quickly schools it and turns away from me.

She's uncomfortable.

And, weirdly, I'm uncomfortable, too. If I had seen this room a few days ago, it would have disgusted me. I would have taken it as further evidence of her brutal and uncaring nature that she not only ripped so many animals apart with her bare hands but also made trophies of them to display.

But I can't shake the way she looked at me when I called her a monster. And I can't stop thinking about the act she put on for her father after "killing" Vie. It wasn't triumph she feigned for him. It was grief. And back in the gardens, she'd told me he *forces* her to kill. That she'd never wanted to hurt anyone or anything.

I've struggled to believe it, but after what happened today, I'm not struggling anymore. I know I was wrong.

Which means the animals on these walls might be trophies to her father, but they represent something else entirely to her. I swallow as I take them in. The sheer *multitude*.

Then I look back at Mance, whose gaze has been fixed on her shoes since we walked in here.

Gently, without really thinking about what I'm doing, I lean the pipe against the wall and wrap my hand around hers.

She flinches and scrunches her face up, but she doesn't pull away. She doesn't move at all.

Staring at her when she's trying so hard to be invisible feels invasive, so I let my gaze drift to a monkey, mid-howl, imagining what it must have been like for her to feel its life leak out between her fingers. The same fingers currently twined in mine.

"Tell me about one of them," I say.

Her grip tightens painfully. "I don't want to. I hate this room. It's full of memories I'd much rather bury."

"It's healthy to let things out sometimes, remember?" I say, half kidding. A reference to our first conversation, the one I botched so badly.

But she's not in the mood for jokes.

"You go first, then," she snaps. "Tell me about one of the worst moments in *your* life."

I tilt my head back, considering that.

And I shouldn't, because all I really need to do is get the sword and leave. But she didn't want to hear my apology, and it bothers me. Having her act so distant and curt *bothers* me. More than I'd like to admit.

So I speak.

"I was eight when they took my parents," I say. "The war with the Forest Realm had been going for a couple years already. I don't really remember anything before it."

She stills, clearly surprised that I'm obliging, and meets my eyes for the first time since we left her room.

I give her a tight smile. "They dragged my mother out, crying," I continue. "Ripped me from her arms. And then they knocked my father unconscious, tossing him in the back of their carriage like a sack of flour. I had to watch it all, had to listen to my mother screaming as she clutched my father's head in her lap. Had to see her reach for me through the windows while the carriage clattered away and multiple hands pulled her back inside. Then they carted me up to the Academy where everyone told me it was just temporary. That I'd only be there until my parents came back, and when they did, it would be as celebrated war heroes. That we'd all be together again and live happily ever after."

"But they never came back?" she asks, voice quiet.

I scoff. "They died in less than a week."

Her hand flies to her mouth in shock. "I'm so sorry."

I look at the floor, at the rich carpet that covers it, wondering if the Prime was standing among this brutal luxury when he signed the order that condemned my parents to death. My face twists into a sneer.

"They didn't even tell me," I say. "I found out two years later when I broke into the headmaster's office and discovered a ledger of the deceased in his desk. When I confronted my teachers about it, they told me it was tragic and a risk my parents took, but I now believe it was inevitable. My parents weren't trained for war. They made candles. If you put them in a battlefield, how could they possibly know what to do?" I clench my fists, annoyed that I can't keep the anger out of my voice. "So take your pick, that's three in a row. Watching my parents dragged away, arriving at the Academy, and finding out that they'd been killed and that the rest of my life had only one track forward: serving the very person who killed them until I died in the exact same way."

I cross the room to sit in the Prime's chair, kicking my feet up on his desk and jutting my chin at her in challenge. "Your turn."

She doesn't react to my anger. In fact, it almost seems to relax her. Probably because she can understand it, if the animals around us are any indication. It suddenly occurs to me that the statements I've just made are nearly seditious. Yet she doesn't appear to mind.

"When did you leave?" she asks. "And why?"

I tilt my head at her. "If I tell you that, you'll owe me four," I warn.

"I'll pay," she says simply.

Victory buzzes across my skin. I lean the chair back, running my fingers over the arms just because I can. Because with all the Prime has taken from me, it gives me a small amount of pleasure to be sitting in his own personal chair when I know he'd seethe at the thought.

But then I look back at Mance and the anger dims a little bit. I close my eyes, remembering, and when I speak again, my voice is softer.

"It was Vie," I say. "She was a small kid, even smaller than she is now, so she was always trying to fight everyone to keep them from picking on her. Would go into detail about how she'd cut them up like one of the steaks in her family's butcher shop. But I heard her crying one night—"

I break off, knowing Vie wouldn't want me to tell the story. How she sobbed into her knees when she looked up her own parents in the headmaster's book and got the same news I did, only she lost two older brothers, too. How we were both locked into adjacent rooms for weeks as punishment and almost starved, but we made vows to each other through the walls. Vows that we'd never serve the man who did this to us. That if we ever got the chance, we'd take him down.

How that moment and that promise mean something to us, even now.

"Anyway," I continue. "We became friends. Three weeks later, we were breaking into the kitchen to steal some knives, hoping to fight our way out or die trying, when we found Rooftop already there."

"Also stealing knives?" Mance asks.

I quirk a smile. "Nah. Spices. He couldn't stand how bland the food was. Which sounds silly, but I actually think it was his way of still feeling human. A rebellion of paprika. Anyway, he had better ideas about how to break out than we did. Safer ones with higher chances of success. We ended up hiding in a supply cart and then making a run for it. We've been together ever since."

"It's nice that you have each other," she says, a peculiar tone in her voice that I can't quite place.

My eyes cut to her, but she's looking at the floor.

"Your turn," I say again, but gentler this time.

Heaving a resigned sigh, she walks around the room, looking

at each animal as though sifting through her memories and deciding which to present to me.

"You were ten when you left, right?" she asks, stopping in the corner to the left of the door.

"Yup," I say. "Just barely."

She holds her hand up to the wall, walking along it until she stops just short of the next corner. "That would bring me to about here."

I take my legs off the desk. It's almost thirty animals. "You killed all those before you were ten?" I ask.

She walks back to the beginning, to the frogs and lizards and mice. "He didn't put the bugs up, but those were first," she says. "If I slapped a fly, he'd give me a cupcake. I loved cupcakes."

In an instant, the air is teeming with insects, every one she's ever killed. I sit up straight, clamping my mouth shut and holding my breath so I don't accidentally inhale a bee or a mosquito. But they're everywhere, crawling on my skin, burying themselves in my clothes and my hair, burrowing into my ears. Before my throat starts to burn, they disappear and I suck in a relieved breath.

"It was fun," she says quietly.

She turns back to the wall and juts her chin at the smaller creatures. "These were more painful to kill, but it was still like a game. He called me his little hunter and sent me out into the forests and the mountains to see what I could find and bring back to him. I didn't enjoy squishing them between my palms but he praised me so thoroughly and it was over so quickly and the rewards were so great that I shoved my feelings down."

I lean forward on the desk, quiet.

Then her hand moves to a bundle of fur on a wooden shelf, curled in on itself like it's only sleeping peacefully. "Until he brought me the kitten," she says. I wince, and her mouth pulls down as well, but she keeps going. "I was nine. One of the barn cats had a whole litter and there were too many to keep, so Father thought it would be a good opportunity . . ." Her voice is distant. The hand at her side is shaking a little.

I wait.

"When he explained what he wanted me to do, I cried so hard I almost passed out. But he talked me through it, step by step, with a gentle voice and one hand rubbing my back in encouragement. I didn't want to disappoint him. So I . . ."

Her voice gets thick, like she might start crying. I get up from the desk and cross the room to stand next to her, but she doesn't look at me. She looks down at her hands, and I take one again, feeling all the rough scars as they rub against my palm. This time, she doesn't flinch. She just folds her hand around mine.

"What I remember most is how warm and soft the kitten was beneath my fingers," she says. "How she squirmed and how her little mouth opened wide in what I could swear was a scream. And then she went limp, and . . . it felt *wrong*. It felt terrifying. I wanted to undo it, but I couldn't. She just lay there, limp and wrong and staring at nothing. I was horrified. Sobbing. Scared. But even as I was feeling all those things, there was something else, too. This sinister flicker at the back of my mind from the magic that I hadn't felt before. And it was . . . pleased."

Shivers run up my spine, and she starts talking faster.

"It was thrilled, actually. The magic *liked* how limp and wrong the kitten looked. It . . . gloried in it." She swallows and shakes her head. "I ran to the bathroom and threw up that day's cupcake, wishing I could purge every other one he'd bribed me with, too."

She summons the cat onto her shoulder and it looks at me

with luminous eyes, a tuft of fur sticking up above its forehead. Goose bumps erupt on my skin.

Then the cat disappears, too, and she moves on, to a tiny fennec fox, with ears bigger than the rest of his body. "This was the first one I refused," she says.

"I imagine he took that well," I quip, voice tight.

She gives a humorless laugh. "Oh yes, he was very understanding. Gone were the games, gone were the rewards and the praise. He locked me in the stables with it and told me I couldn't come out, couldn't eat, until it was dead."

"What about your mom?" I ask. "Didn't anyone try to stop him?"

She goes still, her hand twitching in mine.

"I asked her to," she says, voice small. "After the cat, I begged her not to let it happen to me again. And she promised she'd step in the next time. But when my father hauled me to the stables, she didn't come. I waited for her. I was *so* certain that she would follow through on her word. But she never showed, that time or any other. She never apologized. For all I know, she never even tried."

I remember the conversation I witnessed before Mance's battle with Vie, how Lady Wespa seemed as fragile as the glass on her corset.

"And Mara?" I ask. "You guys seem friendly at least. Did she ever stand up for you?"

Mance clicks her tongue. "In her own way, I guess she did. But not in the way I wanted her to. She was always there to comfort me after or prep me before, but she told me she couldn't fix it for me. I needed to handle it on my own, or I'd never get stronger. I needed to . . . play the game."

I hear the same note in her voice that she used earlier, when I talked about my friends, and it makes sense now. No one's ever had her back like Vie and Rooftop have mine. With sudden, startling clarity, I realize that the future Seconde is lonely.

The thought is unsettling.

"So the fox?" I prompt, rubbing circles on the back of her hand with my thumb.

"Right," she says, shaking her head as though casting the feelings aside to focus on the narrative. "I was in those stables for two days straight. The first day I just refused, hoping he'd change his mind, hoping my mother would show up after all. But after a cold night sleeping in dirt that smelled like manure, my stomach clenching with hunger I'd never experienced before, I felt that it was him or me, and I relented." As she talks, the fox appears at her feet, winding around her legs and butting his head against her. "Took me the whole second day to catch him. He wouldn't come down from the rafters, so I had to shimmy out of my skirts and climb up after him. Then I flung myself across the beams, just hoping to grab him without falling, not really understanding how difficult that was for someone my size."

"But you managed it?"

"No," she says. "One out of two. I grabbed him, but not the rafter. The next thing I knew I was plunging toward the ground with this shrieking, clawing creature clutched to my chest. I landed in a pile of hay and broke my arm. But I also managed to break his neck on the way down." She gives me a wry smile that turns sad. "Then I cried alone in the dirty hay, gripping his body, until one of the guards realized it was over and let me out."

Something passes over her face and her tone changes to matter-of-fact. The fox disappears and she walks along the wall, passing badgers and raccoons and owls.

"From there the training started," she goes on. "I ran. I fought. But he has legions of soldiers. They caught me, they subdued me, and they put me in a room with an animal about once every couple months. Then, when he finished stripping the ballroom to make an arena, it became once every few weeks. He pushed the boundaries of my magic to see what it could do. If I summoned a chicken, could we eat it? If I summoned a lamb, could we shear it and use the wool? No to both, by the way. As soon as I call an animal back, everything that was a part of them disappears as well. So then he moved on to creatures that would be useful in and of themselves. He made me kill my horse so I could ride it. A carrier pigeon so I could send messages. Hunting dogs so I could find and kill more and more."

She turns toward me, rows of animal eyes staring down at me over her shoulders. I feel the hair stand up on the back of my neck, but before I can think of anything to say she rushes on, words tumbling out of her mouth like she's trying to purge them from her body.

"At twelve I decided I couldn't take it anymore. I was ready to do anything just to end it. So when they locked me in the arena with a wolf, I didn't try to take it down. Instead, I provoked it. Then, once it was enraged, I forced myself to lie still, fighting my rising bloodlust even as the wolf tore at my body.

"But they just stitched me up and sent me back. Wolf after wolf. I was bedridden. Mutilated, but determined. Finally, after weeks of that, my father agreed to negotiate. One animal a year, but he could pick any he wanted. I would train the rest of the time, but I wouldn't be expected to kill. So that's how we got the wolf at thirteen, the cougar at fourteen, the grizzly bear at fifteen, and . . ."

Her hands stop at an empty plaque on the wall. "The jaguar will go here. They're stuffing and mounting it now."

As she names each animal, she summons them beside her, until I'm standing in a room with four apex predators staring me down. But she is calm, so they are, too, sitting on their haunches mildly as she explains how she ripped them all apart.

Despite my instincts screaming at me not to, I reach a hand out and stroke the ear of the bear that so terrified me a few days ago when it roared in my face, teeth snapping mere inches from my nose. He tosses his head, untroubled.

"What about Vie, then?" I ask bitterly. "If we hadn't snuck her out, would he have put her head up there, too?"

She winces. "Vie was an experiment to him, I think. One that's done now. Apparently, some increased tension with another realm spooked him and he wants more weapons. Wants to make me as strong as possible before he makes me his heir so that the other realms will be too intimidated to attack. Now that I think about it, it's probably the same tensions that your organization is worried about. The reason you want the Victory's Herald out of the way for a little bit?"

I feel a jolt of panic, because I'd made those tensions up and I don't know what it means that they're real. Is it possible Guerre actually does want to remove the sword so that he can garner peace?

I remember the coldness in his eyes, and I doubt it.

But then . . . what *does* he want the sword for?

Fortunately, Mance doesn't seem to notice my reaction. She walks to the desk, unlocks a drawer, and takes out a long case, laying it on the wood in front of her. After disengaging the latch, she lifts the sword in its scabbard and draws it, the steel blade glinting in the light. For a wild moment I think she might swing it at me, but she just looks at it, her expression inscrutable.

"I'm choosing to trust you," she says. "To trust that your secrecy is warranted, that you will return this weapon before the Assurance as you promised, and that your goal truly is peace. From the sounds of it, we've both seen far too much of the opposite. And if your organization genuinely thinks they can prevent atrocities like the ones you've just described, then . . ." She sheathes the blade and holds it out, expression determined. "I'm honored to play a part in it."

My hand wraps around the scabbard reflexively, even as my chest goes cold.

What am I . . . doing?

I've spent the last few hours worried that I've hurt Mance's feelings, but this whole time I've been betraying her. Lying to her. Playing on her ideals and the fact that she *cares* about people.

Just so I can help myself and my friends get ahead.

She's worried about the whole realm, and meanwhile I haven't even tried to find out the consequences of my actions. I have no idea what Guerre has done with the seal, and I have no idea what the plans are for this sword, either. She wants peace, and for all I know I'm enabling the opposite.

People could die because of me.

Suddenly, the stories she's told me, the animals staring down at me, and the easy faith in her eyes are too much.

For a single, ludicrous moment, I almost shove the sword back at her.

But then I remember Vie and Rooftop and how they're depending on me. I remember the house and the future we'll be able to build together when this is all over. And I yank the blade out of her hands.

Her brows crease and she shakes out her wrists like I've hurt them.

"I . . . should go," I say gruffly. "But thank you for upholding your end of the agreement. And I am . . . sorry. For . . ." Everything. Everything I thought and everything I'm doing now and everything that might come because of it. I clear my throat. "For what I said. You're not a monster, Mance. You never have been. And I should've seen that earlier."

Her eyes flick up to mine, and she seems taken aback by my sudden solemnity. But then her expression clears, like the sun dawning in her midnight eyes, and she beams at me.

And it's the strangest thing, but when she smiles, her face doesn't look off-balance anymore. The mouth that was so small broadens, and the eyes that were so big crinkle in the corners to make room. She looks so elated, so giddily triumphant, that it knocks the wind out of me for a second.

"Thank *you*," she says back, "for upholding yours. And . . ." She looks down, shyly, and my heart lurches. "For listening."

"Anytime," I choke out.

Then I drop the sword into the pipe, more carelessly than I mean to, and it careens noisily downward before finally hitting the bottom with a hollow, echoing clang.

❧✻☙

A few hours later, as the sky turns from velvet darkness to early morning gray, I approach a seedy tavern just a little too low on the cliff to qualify as the nice part of town. I think Vie has probably fought here, in a back storeroom cut deep into the rock. The Victory's Herald is strapped to my back and hidden under a cloak, but I do my best to walk like I'm *not* carrying treason. You know, with a law-abiding spring in my step.

But it's hard when the sword weighs so heavy.

"Silver."

I spin as Rooftop drops down from an awning. I swear that kid walks on rooftops more than actual roadways. Thus the name, I guess.

"What are you doing here?" I hiss.

He shoves his hands into his pockets as he ambles toward me, face obscured by his dark, springy locks.

"I need to talk to you," he says.

It's not like him to be so somber. I look over my shoulder at the tavern door, then the sun barely peeking over the horizon.

"Okay," I say. "Sure. Just give me a minute. I have to meet—"

"Guerre," Rooftop says. "I know. That's why I'm here. I need to talk to you *before* that."

A bell chimes, its notes echoing off the cliffside and ringing through the valley.

"I can't," I tell him. "I'm about to be late."

Rooftop fidgets unhappily. "Let me come with you, then?" he asks.

"Fine," I say, as the fifth and final note fades away. "Come on."

I duck into the tavern and Rooftop slinks in behind me, gaze swinging wildly from one early-morning patron to the next like he thinks the entire room is a threat.

An elderly woman spills her tea and frowns at it. A drunk who has probably been here since last night slumps across his table, snoring nasally as the server wipes up the spilled drinks around him. Rooftop jumps when the man's arm knocks into one of the few remaining upright bottles and sends it toppling.

"If you can't relax, then you can't be here," I grouch at Rooftop through the corner of my mouth.

Rooftop's face sets. "No. I want to stay. Is he here already?" He eyes the drunk suspiciously.

I'd laugh, but Guerre's definitely worn more elaborate disguises. I squint at the man closely before replying, "No."

We take a seat.

"So what did you want to talk about, then?" I ask in a low voice. "Seems we've got a minute." I position my back to the wall so I'll be able to see if anyone comes in.

Rooftop's green eyes flit to the door as well, but then land back on me. "I . . . did some digging last night," he whispers. "About Guerre."

I raise an eyebrow. "Oh?"

Rooftop nods. "How did you first hear about him, again?"

I adjust the sword on my back so it's not jabbing into me as much. "I knew some other kids who worked for him. Other Academy runaways who said he was willing to give under-the-table jobs. Smaller ones at first, but then bigger stuff. With bigger rewards."

"Which kids, specifically?" Rooftop asks, his tone urgent.

"Glib was first," I say. "And then Lock and Flay."

Rooftop sits back in his chair. "That's what I thought," he says darkly.

"Why?" I ask, finally turning fully toward him.

"Because they've disappeared, Silver. All three of them, plus another couple kids besides. All of them were Academy runaways with no family, and all of them started taking odd jobs from someone who sounds a lot like Guerre right before they vanished."

I let that sit with me, turning it over in my mind. "Well . . .

maybe he just gave them jobs out of town or something."

"No," Rooftop whispers. "I knew Glib. He would have told me if he was leaving town for a while, even if he had to lie about where. And with so many disappearing? Everyone who worked for him? It can't be a coincidence. I think they're . . . I think they're—"

"Can I get you anything?" the server asks cheerfully. We both startle, our heads snapping up. She gives us a bemused smile, like she's used to such odd behavior.

"Uh. Frosted Earthquake," I say, giving the name of the drink Guerre told me to order.

"Ah," she says. "Your companion is in the back room. You can head on in and I'll bring that Frosted Earthquake when it's ready."

She jabs a thumb at a door behind the bar, half hidden by a raggedy curtain.

Rooftop and I exchange a look. He shakes his head, but I stand, so he swallows and stands up, too.

"Sorry," the server says, holding up one hand at Rooftop. "You'll have to wait here."

"Why?" Rooftop asks suspiciously.

She swats at him scoldingly. "Because when someone pays well, and I mean *really* well, I don't ask questions about how they want things. That's why. So sit your butt down and your friend will be back in a minute." She muscles Rooftop back into his chair with one arm and nods me toward the door again.

Rooftop opens his mouth to protest, but I cut him off. If Guerre really is dangerous, then I'd rather Rooftop wait out here.

"I'll be back in a minute," I tell him. "Just like she said." Then I head behind the bar.

The door opens into a narrow hallway cut into the stone of the cliff. It angles downward, and as I plod forward, the air gets chillier.

It reminds me of the marketplace in the Beholding Mountains, only this tunnel was deliberately carved, and there are notches with torches lining the walls. Every few feet there are dark smears on the floor or the walls from fighters who had to drag themselves out. I wonder briefly whether any of the bloodstains are Vie's.

When the hallway opens up into a stark, bare room, Guerre is already there. This time he's wearing a traveling cloak, one that an out-of-town patron might sport while grabbing a quick meal on the road. There's some fake scarring on his face, and his hair is lighter, almost blond, making him look like a completely different person. It's all very realistic, though. I wonder if it's some kind of magic or if it's just dye and clay and paint.

"Do you have it?" he asks, before I'm even fully in the room.

Guess we're not chitchatting today.

I reach behind me and draw the sword out, feeling the weight of it, noticing the dark stone plating the handle, and the cold band of metal just below the pommel.

Guerre's ice-blue eyes gleam in the torchlight.

"Well done," he says. And then he's snatching it from me, wrenching it out of my grip before I've even decided whether I'm going to give it to him. "Just one task left. I'll be in touch."

His cape whirls as he spins to move a bookcase, revealing a hidden back staircase. When I realize he's about to leave, just like that, apprehension closes my throat.

"W-wait!" I cry.

He stops in place, one foot already on the first step, and I hesitate.

Should I ask about the other kids? What happened to them?

Should I ask about his plans for *me*?

But as he tucks the glittering blade into his cloak, eying me with impatience, it's the plot that might affect Mance that moves me to speak. "What are you going to use it for?" I blurt. "The sword, I mean. What are you going to do with it? Are you going to hurt . . . people?"

His face morphs into a glower, so rapidly that my breath catches in my throat. "That's none of your concern," he snarls, and the warning in his voice is clear.

"Tell me something," I say regardless. "Anything."

For a couple seconds, his expression stays dark, and I brace myself, not sure what he'll do. But then suddenly his face clears and he smirks, like he knows why I'm asking and thinks me childish for caring.

"All right," he says languidly. "I will tell you this. It's in your best interest to lay low for the next few days. At least until after the Assurance. Things are about to get . . ." His smirk turns sinister, curling at the edges like smoke curls from a flame. "Ugly."

And even as sunshine streams down from the top of the stairs, revealing that the morning outside has gotten warm and bright, his words still chill me to the bone.

13

Prospective Seconde Mancella Amaryllis Cliff

|3 DAYS UNTIL THE ASSURANCE|

It takes my father two days to realize the sword is missing.

I'm in my mother's private dressing room, holding as still as I can while she practices my makeup look for the Assurance. My eyes are stinging—partially from the abundance of powder in the air and partially from the lingering effects of Mara's useful-but-aggravating tonic, which I've already used twice today. I sniff snottily and squeeze out one final tear, just to keep up the act, but my mother rubs it away with a perfectly manicured thumb and keeps painting, her brush never pausing for a moment.

Almost like she's *used* to applying makeup to tearstained cheeks.

My father enters without knocking, and this isn't enough to break her rhythm either, although she does stiffen. For a moment, he just watches her work, tracing the lines she sketches onto my face in silence. Clingy powder along my cheekbones, a thick, claylike paste around my eyes. A line of kohl across each eyebrow. My skin feels heavy and congested, like someone's smashed my face into a bowl of dough and they won't let me just wipe it off.

Finally, she lowers the brush and takes in her handiwork, glancing sideways at my father.

But if she's looking for approval, she doesn't get it.

"I'd like to speak to Mancella alone," Father says.

My mother grips the brush in her hand. "I . . . I'm not quite finished yet."

My eyes fly to her face as a small bit of hope blooms in my chest. Her words are not exactly defiance, but they're closer to it than I've heard in a while. Does she know what he's going to say? Is she trying to protect me from it?

"Wespa," my father says. He puts his hand briefly on her arm, just long enough to freeze her in place for half a breath. She was in the middle of turning her head toward him, but he halts her just as her eyes pass over me, and there's a flash of worry suspended in them that I probably wasn't meant to see.

I open my mouth to demand he release her, but he already has, and she's already tucked the emotion away and replaced it with a vacant expression that makes my heart sink.

She doesn't finish the turn. Instead she purses her lips together, hard, her gaze still on me but unreadable now. Then she lays down the brush with a clack, lifts her skirts, and bustles out of the room.

The lump in my throat feels sharp, like choking on a shard of glass, but I swallow it down anyway as my father takes her place in front of me.

"I wanted to apologize to you," he says.

My mind is following my mother down the hallway, so it takes a few seconds for his words to penetrate. When they do, I whip back toward him, mouth open. "You *what*?"

He looks through the window above me, at the acidic green glow on the horizon, then finally lowers his eyes to my face.

"I understand your shock," he says. "But I *can* admit when I've made a mistake. Just because I am aggressive in pursuing my goals doesn't mean I don't regret it when I err."

The paint at the corners of my eyes cracks as I squint up at him.

"All right," I say carefully. "What are you sorry for? That you threatened to kill children and forced me to become a murderer, or just that it didn't work?"

"Both," he says, without hesitation. "Both. I have room for many regrets in my life."

It's not exactly the answer I was looking for, but after a short deliberation I decide that I don't want to start a fight when he's trying to make a gesture. If . . . that's what this is.

"Fine," I say instead. "Thank you. I appreciate it."

He nods, and then there's a silence that I'm not sure how to fill. I raise a kohl-darkened eyebrow, trying to figure out why my father hasn't left yet. Wondering what exactly it is that he's working up to.

"Did you take the Victory's Herald?" he asks, voice deceptively mild.

Ah.

I should have expected this.

"It's . . . m-missing?" I choke out, hoping my stuttering comes across as genuine surprise instead of the nervousness that it is. But then I register the fact that he noticed the sword's disappearance at all and frown. "Hold on. Why were you getting it out in the first place?"

"For the Assurance," he says easily. "We are all making the final preparations." He gestures to my painted face as proof.

I study his face, and I don't see a tell. What he's saying is believable, and a week ago I might have even bought it.

But Silver's warning that war might be coming rings in my ears.

"Of course," I say carefully. "Because if you *were* going to start a war, you would tell me. Right? I'll be named your Seconde in three days. I need to start being a part of these decisions."

He regards me coolly, until it occurs to me that I still haven't responded to his initial inquiry, and he's noticed.

"No," I blurt. "I don't have your sword."

The pause stretches longer, and I can't tell if he believes me or not.

Finally, he steeples his hands in front of his face. "You're right," he says. "You *should* have more of a part in these things. I reviewed your propositions for the Academy and they were thorough and well reasoned, showing an impressive aptitude. While it would be impossible to enact everything you outlined immediately, I have taken the liberty of instituting the ones that seemed most important to you. The isolation rooms are closed, the restraint chair will no longer be used, and the rocks will be put away. Moving forward, discipline will be administered more humanely. As you wished."

I blink in shock.

First an apology and then a major concession?

Suspicion buzzes over my skin, making me sit up straighter. The last time he pretended to care about my feelings was right before he ordered me to kill a human. There must be something else coming now, too.

"Thank you," I say formally. Uncertainly. "I . . . appreciate your attention on the matter."

"Of course," he says. "And as to discussions of war . . ."

I hold my breath.

"If you want to be included, then you will be. In a few minutes,

I'm taking a trip to the border to take care of a few things. Come with me, and you can ask me any questions that you'd like on the journey, about the potential for war or anything else. I promise to answer fully."

I swallow, expecting there to be more.

And yet it doesn't come. He only sits there, waiting for my response.

I narrow my eyes.

It's impossible that there's no catch here. There must be some other plan, some other atrocity he'll propose once he has me in the carriage. And anticipating it is almost worse than just having it happen, because at least then I would know what it is.

It occurs to me that I could turn him down. Refuse to go entirely. And perhaps I should.

But the truth is, if he *is* planning a war—and he hasn't explicitly said yet that he isn't—I need to know about it. Maybe I could learn something that would be helpful to Silver and his mysterious group.

Besides, even if he is leading me into a trap, it doesn't mean I have to be caught in it. I succeeded in thwarting his last plan, after all. I can find a way out of the next one, too.

As Mara so frequently tells me, I need to play the game.

"I would love to," I say finally.

He nods, standing and holding out a hand.

I don't take it.

But I do get up and follow him out of the room.

When we step into the hallway, we almost run over Silver, who is up on a ladder dusting one of our many chandeliers. He always seems close at hand lately, finding chores to do nearby, wherever I am. In fact, I'm pretty sure he was dusting this same chandelier when I stepped into Mother's dressing room an hour ago. I linger a moment to give him a secretive smile, but my father steps past me and reaches up to touch Silver's leg.

Then Silver's body locks into place.

I barely stifle a cry of dismay. What's he doing? Is he going to attack? Does he know something about what Silver and I have done?

But no. He only drones on about a chandelier in another hallway that he'd like cleaned next.

I grimace as bile rises to the back of my throat. My father does this often with servants. He says it's to make sure he has their full attention while he's speaking, but I think he likes the casual touch of dominance. The restrained violence. I dig my fingernails into my arm, willing him to let go. Unable to stop looking at the unnatural way Silver's arm hangs in the air. Thinking about how, despite the fact that his artificially immobilized stance is casual, his insides must be screaming.

Finally, Father drops his hand. Silver's features shutter immediately.

"Understood?" my father asks.

"Yes, sir," Silver answers. "I'll get right on that." His voice doesn't betray a hint of rage, but it's unanimated. Smoke only, no glowing embers to be found.

My father brushes by and keeps walking, his mind already moving on from the interaction.

I stay. Tipping my head back, I catch Silver's attention, my animals squirming in dismay within me. "I'm sorry," I mouth behind my father's back.

He drops off the ladder and approaches me, body language still deliberately casual, but his amber eyes burning.

"How often has he done that to you?" he asks. And now his voice is all ember, no smoke. It takes me a second to find mine.

"I've lost count," I tell him.

He steps up close to me, lifting my chin with one hand, eyes raking over my face. I blush until I realize he's probably just taking in my makeup. Hopefully he attributes the reddening of my cheeks to liberally applied rouge.

"You two going somewhere?" he asks in a low voice.

"Nowhere important. Just for a ride."

Silver's gaze flicks over my shoulder to my father's back disappearing around the corner, and his mouth tightens.

"Be careful," he murmurs.

I shake my head. "What do you mean?"

"Mancella?" My father must have finally noticed that I'm not following him. No doubt he'll double back any second to find me.

"Be right there," I call.

I make to go after him, but Silver grabs my hand, pulling me to a stop. His fingers are urgent on my wrist.

"Silver?" I whisper.

He starts, like he didn't realize he'd actually reached out. Then he frowns and drops my hand, stepping back.

I hesitate, but then turn and catch up to my father, mumbling something about a third dusty chandelier I'd noticed that I wanted to make sure the servant addressed as well. My instincts are screaming at me to stay and hear the rest of Silver's warning, but now isn't the time.

The last thing I want is to give my father any reason to pay special attention to the amber-eyed boy behind me, or the troubled expression on his face as he watches us walk away.

❧✻☙

The carriage Father selects isn't one of the ostentatious ones we use when we want to be seen, but one of the plainer ones we use for travel. It's all metal, with no ornamentation but spikes circling its roof like a crown. I take this as a good sign.

"After you," he says, gesturing inside. I climb up and arrange myself on one of the cushioned benches within. Father joins me, settling on the opposite side. Then the door swings shut and the wheels begin to turn. Over their rattling, my father heaves a sigh, one that's long and weary. I give him a sidelong glance but say nothing.

We rumble through the castle gates and down the front path, then depart from the main road to take a smaller, bumpier track that avoids the crowds and circles the mountains.

"So," I prompt testily. "Are we preparing for a war?"

"We are always preparing for war, in a sense."

"No," I say, cutting him off. "You promised real answers. Be direct with me. Do you have reason to believe that war is an imminent reality?"

He raises one bushy eyebrow, almost looking impressed with my assertiveness. "It is at minimum a possibility," he allows. "Our relations with the new Prime in the Grasslands have not gone smoothly. She has sent several correspondences that were decidedly aggressive. I still hope that an outright war can be avoided, but it seems unlikely at this point that mere diplomacy will be enough."

I frown, processing this. I guess that means my letter didn't work. My heart squeezes in sorrow as I realize there's no use waiting for a response anymore. "How do you plan to avert it, then?"

"With a show of force."

His words strike me in the chest, and as soon as they do I wonder why I expected him to say anything different. "Why do you do that?" I blurt out in frustration.

His other eyebrow climbs to join the first. "Do what?"

"Why do you only use your power to crush people?"

"To protect—"

"Don't give me that!" I snap. "Because it isn't just other realms. It's Mother and S—servants. Mara and me. Do you enjoy the control that much?"

I expect him to be offended by the question, but instead he considers it. "Enjoy?" he says. "No. But I do value it."

I scowl at him. "What does that mean?"

He shifts in his seat, hands clasped in front of him. "Do you remember when Mara was in the Broken Citadel, and we didn't know whether she would come out?" he asks. "Do you remember how that felt?"

"Of course," I say bitterly. "It felt awful. *Terrifying.*"

He nods. "It felt that way because you had no control over what was happening to her. You were helpless. Right?"

"Yes . . . ?"

"Well, I felt that way, too. When we waited for Uncle Edwarn. When *he* didn't come out."

I still, because Father never talks about that day.

"You waited?" I breathe. "How long?"

"A full day," he tells me. "And every minute was torture. Before then, it was my brother who I leaned on most for support, so as the wait got more anxious I kept reaching for him, only to be stung anew by his absence. The decision to give up on him and go in myself was one of the hardest I'd ever made. I had to close a part of myself down, and I'm not sure it ever opened back up. That's one of the reasons I was so . . . ungracious when we waited for Mara. I didn't want to ever go through that kind of excruciatingly drawn-out suspense again. That gradual surrender of hope. I preferred to cut it off early, thinking perhaps it would be easier that way. But it was only a different kind of pain."

In spite of myself, my hands unclench. "I . . . I had no idea," I say. "It must have been hard. Dealing with that."

"Yes," he says. "Especially when, mere weeks into my mourning, his son tried to end my life."

Any compassion that his words brought out of me collapses and my eyes narrow angrily. "So you say," I spit.

"I say it because it's true," he says, his tone almost gentle. "You need to come to terms with that."

But I'm already shaking my head. "I *know* him," I insist. "Alect wouldn't do that! He was my friend." Yes, he had trained his whole life to be Prime. But he wouldn't have tried taking it like that. Not the boy who brought me starsprouts.

My father is unperturbed by my denials.

"Everyone has their darkness, Mancella," he says. "Even Alect. Even you." He looks out the window at the stark cliffs flying by. Perhaps at the former Mountain Realm beyond them, decimated by the magic so many generations ago that the people no longer exist even in memory. "This world is cruel, and it will eat you alive if you let it. You need to learn how to control it. Tame it. The magic gave me a way to do that, so, yes. I value it."

I scowl at him. "You said the world, but it's *people* you're trying to control. Real, actual people."

"Oh, don't be so self-righteous," he says tiredly. "Everyone tries to control people. Kindness is its own manipulation, and sweetness its own breed of armor. Even one's status as a victim can be a weapon if wielded properly. There isn't a person in this world who doesn't try to puppeteer everyone else; we just have different ways of going about it. Mine at least is direct."

I stare at him, stunned. "So your apology today . . . ," I prod. "Was that manipulation as well?"

"Of course," he acknowledges easily. "All apologies are. People only say they're sorry when they want someone's feelings toward them to change. What else would you call it?"

I want to feel disappointed by his answer, but I actually feel relieved. His honesty, however terrible, feels safer than lies. Perhaps we really are having the frank conversation he promised.

Finally.

I lean against the frame of the carriage, regarding him.

"You didn't mean it, then?" I ask.

He looks back at me, taking in my expression. "I meant it," he says. "I *am* sorry. I wish the world wasn't what it is and that I didn't have to push you to do such difficult things just so we can survive in it. And, in this particular instance, I made a miscalculation. I hurt you deeply and we gained nothing. So I genuinely regret that it happened. But just because it was sincere doesn't mean I wasn't trying to manipulate you by voicing it. Human interaction, at base, is coercion. It's best if you learn that soon."

"But it isn't *true*," I tell him. "At least, not for me. I don't go about my day trying to control other people."

"You don't?"

"Not at all!"

He smiles like he's glad I said that. "Then tell me. Where is that girl's body?"

A chill runs down my spine and the carriage lurches beneath us. "Wh-what?" I choke out.

"Her body," he enunciates. "I looked for it after the fact, and it was nowhere to be found. So mysterious, don't you think? But you wouldn't know anything about that, would you?"

My stomach plummets and my palms get clammy. I wipe them on my dress, queasy. "I . . . I told the soldiers to give her body back to her parents. So she could have a proper burial."

He raises one large eyebrow, amused. "Did you?" he asks. "How considerate." Then he leans forward, leveling his gaze on mine. "Now tell me again that you're not trying to manipulate me, Mancella. Tell me that you *didn't* put on a show for me that day. And that you're not lying to my face right now."

I bunch the fabric of my dress in my hands, my heart racing.

Is this it? What I've been waiting for? Did he bring me out here to tell me that the trick didn't work, that now I need to kill for real? Or, worse, will he tell me that he's started executing Academy kids, just as he promised?

I've never been caught defying him to this degree before, and the uncertainty of how he might respond, how brutal he might get, leaves me lightheaded.

"That—that's different!" I protest desperately. "You were forcing me. I had to protect myself. To protect others. I had to take control of the situation."

"You see?" he says, triumphant. "You do understand."

Frightened, and more than a little disturbed, I hug my arms to my chest and turn away from him. Just as I do, we pass under an overhang in the cliffside, and my window darkens, my reflection flashing across the glass. I suck in a breath because I hadn't actually seen it yet.

I look sinister. Animalistic. Between the sharp lines, the added shadows and the pelt-like patterning, I look half beast. It's not the first time I've been made to look like this, of course, but it strikes me differently now. It hadn't ever occurred to me that most of the realm only ever saw me as *this*.

And Silver was one of them.

No wonder it was so easy for him to believe I was a monster.

I'm about to say something, perhaps make some kind of plea to go home, when we take a turn I don't expect, and the carriage starts tilting, clacking down the steep slope. My window brightens as we pull away from the cliffside, and I lean forward to peer out of it, concerned.

"What's going on?" I ask. "Shouldn't we be turning back?" After all, we passed the border of our realm a while ago. We're not far from the Grassland Realm now.

As soon as I think it, the walled city rises in the distance, causing me to stiffen. Last time I saw the place, a few months ago, its walls were painted with streaks of red, like dripping blood. An homage to their first spark of magic, just like our glass forest is a nod to my grandfather's powers.

Now the walls are pitchy, sooty black, and towering bonfires burn at their corners. Flakes of ash flutter down from them in waves, some coating the ground in a blanket of gray, and more flurrying through the air, a few even riding the wind all the way to our carriage.

I guess the new Prime wanted a makeover.

Kneading my skirts anxiously with my fingers, I wonder what it might mean that Azele wiped out her own realm's history.

It doesn't strike me as a particularly positive omen.

"We'll turn back in a minute," my father tells me. "First there's something I want to try, and it will be easier on flat ground." As he says this, the carriage levels out and comes to a stop.

With the wheels no longer clacking beneath us, we are plunged into a sudden silence. The fluttering ash gives everything an eerie feeling, and I don't want to linger.

"What exactly do you want to try?" I ask.

"Summon your animals for me?"

A premonition of danger slides down my spine, and I turn from the window to face him. "Why?" I ask carefully.

He gives an exasperated huff. "You know, I wouldn't *need* to manipulate you if you didn't fight me so hard at every turn. Believe it or not, I would prefer our relationship to be less antagonistic. You'll be my Seconde soon. Can't we have a fresh start? Work together on more level ground? I'll tell you what; if you humor me with this one request, I'll forget about the girl completely. We'll never speak of her again. All right?"

"And you won't ask me to kill another human?" I press. "You'll drop that, too?"

He huffs in exasperation.

"Yes," he says. "I will drop that, too."

Relief and continued suspicion war in my chest, and the animals within me are unsettled. But I doubt I'll get this offer again.

"Fine," I say. "Which animals?"

"All of them."

I hesitate for one more moment, but then I comply, flinging my creatures toward the space outside the carriage.

In an instant, the fields around us are bursting with life. My jaguar bounds through the open fields. My monkey frolics through the ash like it's snow. And they keep coming. A dog, a wolf, a raccoon, a bear, a bobcat, a fox, a horse, an owl . . . I lose count. I've never sent them all out at once before. I've seen them stuffed and mounted on walls, of course, but not all breathing and moving and *alive* like this. It's odd to think that I carry so much life inside me every day.

Then something cold wraps around my wrist.

I look down. It's a metal bracelet made of two semicircles that fit together, with a giant keyhole on the end of one of them. My father swings the other side shut, and it clicks past several notches until it lays uncomfortably tight against my skin. When I tug at the metal, it doesn't pull back apart.

"What is this?" I ask.

"Like I said, just trying something," he says. "Can you call your animals back?"

I tug at the metal again, not liking the way it's digging into me, but I do what he asks, pulling my animals back into my body.

Only they don't come.

My magic feels odd, like it's curdling just beneath my skin, unable to push past it. And while my animals still feel connected to me, it's like someone is stepping on the thread I use to pull them back and they can't feel my tug.

An unintentional whimper escapes my lips, and I dig my fingers into the bracelet more earnestly, trying to pry it off. "What did you do? It feels . . . it feels *wrong*. Take it off!"

"I will," he says. "Don't worry. It doesn't cut off magic completely. It just creates a barrier that magic can't pass through. Like your body is a fortress that has been secured. If they were within you when I put the bracelet on, they would be locked inside. But they're out, so they're locked out."

"I don't like it," I repeat. "Take it *off*."

"In a minute," he says, craning to look at something behind me.

I follow his gaze, and what I see stifles my response in my throat.

A group of soldiers approaches the border from the other side. Unlike our guards, who all wear insignia made from twisted glass trees, these soldiers have painted their faces in ash. Their armor is all in tones of gray as well. In the middle stands a woman significantly more decorated than the others. The pale gray soot traces her cheekbones, standing out against her dark skin. She regards my animals with steel-colored eyes.

"Is that . . . Prime Azele? What is she doing here?" But when I look at my father and his expression isn't surprised, my question changes. "What are *we* doing here?"

"Remember," he says. "Everything I do is to protect you. Our realm must be strong."

Dread slams into my chest.

Behind us, several more carriages stream down the cliffside, and soldiers disembark from them like ants forming lines. Foreboding stirs in my gut, and my animals shift restlessly all around me as my father sticks his head out of the carriage window.

Beside Azele, a crack opens up in the earth; then a shadow leaps upward from it and forms into a person. Her bodyguard, Rift. My breath catches as he surveys the soldiers before him, face stony.

"I called this parley as a courtesy," Azele speaks. "Explain your actions, or you risk war between our realms."

Her eyes land on my face, and as they narrow I suddenly remember what I look like and how she must interpret that. I cast around for a towel or a rag, anything to wipe the ferocity off me.

"Fire," my father says.

"*What?!*" No sooner is the word out of my mouth than an arrow flies from a soldier somewhere to my left. He's a good shot, but the second before his arrow hits the Prime square in the face, she holds up her hand. When the arrow meets her skin, it turns to cinders and blows away in the wind.

"So be it," she says.

She darts forward, pressing a hand to the helmet of a soldier right in front of us. It puffs to ash and she slams her knife into the space just under his jaw. Her bodyguard immediately follows suit, his body folding back into the earth, creating a chasm that rips through the grass and splits apart our soldiers' ranks, only for him to take full form again just past our front line. With a swish of his sword, three of them fall, spines sliced in half.

I scream as the bodies topple. Both sides rush to engage and soon the battle becomes a chaotic melee of fighting figures and flashing metal. Inside the safety of the carriage, my father grabs me.

"What have you done?" I gasp.

"Focus, Mancella. I need you to incite your animals to fight."

I look at him with a multilevel horror. "Are you insane? You know I would never do that, and you also know that I can't. They don't respond to my commands!"

"But they feed off your emotions. If you're angry, they'll react to that. Make them fight, now, or our men will die here."

"How . . . how could you? How *dare* you?"

He hasn't let the idea of an army go at all. Maybe he's dropped the idea of summoning a human, but he means to make me an instrument of war anyway.

Not one second of this ride was the open discourse he'd

pretended it was. For all his carefully crafted "honesty," we were always headed right here. To a battlefield.

Fury fills me, burning so hot I'm surprised I don't physically burst into flames.

"Good, good," he says. "Keep going."

What?

Oh no.

I scramble back to the window, and my animals are rampaging. My grizzly is ripping a soldier apart. My jaguar has her fangs buried in a man's skull, flecks of ash from his face peppering the blood. My wolf is dragging a man by his leg.

Only that's our man.

"They're attacking everyone! They can't tell the difference between our soldiers and theirs!"

"That's a good note for next time."

"Next time?!" My rage flares, and I hear my animals roar with my bloodlust. My heart lurches in alarm.

I have to calm down.

I squeeze my eyes closed and take deep breaths, but the sounds of carnage surround me. I try to think of calm things. The way it was before magic, before my father was Prime. Late-night games and warm smiles. Snuggling in Mara's bed. Ripples on a lake in the woods.

Something, it sounds like a body, hits the side of our carriage, making it rock on its wheels.

"Ripples on a lake!" I yell. "*Ripples on a lake!*"

"No," says my father. "Your mother, beaten. Your sister, tortured. Your people, slaughtered. Take your pretty lake and imagine it filled with blood and corpses."

"Stop it!" I scream. "What is wrong with you?" But his words are working and my anger feels like an inferno within me. Only I'm not angry with the soldiers from the Grasslands, I'm angry with *him*.

But, no. I'm stronger than this. I'm stronger than my father. I may not be able to control him, but I can control my own mind. I slam my mental walls down, shutting everything out, focusing on that last image, of a lake in the woods. A specific lake, one I haven't been to in a long time, but that I can still remember in detail. I focus on those details now. Soft ripples on the water. Dappled sunlight on the leaves. The gentle lapping sound. The smell of moss and earth.

And it's working. I can feel myself relaxing, feel the calm—

Then my father lays his palm on my forehead.

"You force my hand," he says.

And I don't understand fast enough, don't flinch away as immediately as I should.

In the next moment, my skin hardens under his touch.

The screams from outside the carriage grow more desperate, and if my eyes could widen, they would. I remember my snake writhing and lashing out the last time my father did this, remember how single-mindedly he attacked as I fought for air, and then I imagine my multitude of animals feeling that same level of desperate hostility.

As that primal need to live stokes my panic, it dawns on me that my father might not care if the whole field of soldiers is slaughtered around us. He may consider that a worthwhile cost. And no matter what he pretended at the beginning of this carriage ride, he doesn't care how this affects *me* at all.

My eyelids are locked halfway open, just wide enough to see my own hands frozen in my lap, but the sounds of carnage continue to assault my ears. Roaring. Slashing. Stampeding. Screaming. Tearing. Squelching. Begging. Clawing. Gurgling. Howling. Crying. Dying. The scent of fresh blood oozes into my nostrils. Ash flutters in and coats my face.

I have never felt so helpless.

When the magic moves to my lungs, stealing my breath, I almost welcome it.

14

Silver

|3 DAYS UNTIL THE ASSURANCE|

If I'd known that following Mance would lead directly to a frantic hyena launching itself at my face, I might have reconsidered the decision.

Then again, maybe I wouldn't have. The second I saw Mance in that makeup, I got a horrible, horrible feeling in my gut. Guerre's words echoed in my mind. I followed them until they got into the carriage. Then I saw soldiers climbing into additional armored carriages right after they left, and the next thing I knew I was pulling on one of the uniforms Mance stole and hopping in myself.

This is what I get for caring.

I fling the hyena back, making controlled swings with the standard-issue sword that I'm irritated to know how to use. I guess the Academy was good for something after all.

The creature lands on all fours and immediately launches itself into the attack again, caught in some kind of reckless, crazed frenzy. I throw my hands up into a block, but fortunately this time it targets someone else, just past my shoulder. I hear his shriek. Without looking back, I charge away, determined to stay out of the creature's path.

Which would be easy enough on its own, except that I also have to stay out of every *other* animal's path. And they're everywhere, all in the same hysterical rage as the hyena.

As I sprint forward I see the bear charging past me, swiping soldiers to the ground. The wolf has its head buried in someone's throat, and even though that someone looks very dead, it's still ripping the flesh to shreds, its snout coated with slick, slimy blood. Several birds are beating their wings frantically, clawing at soldiers' soft eyes and screeching like their lives depend on it.

So what *exactly* is that scum doing to Mance in the carriage?

Adrenaline coursing through me, I push for the back of the melee, dodging felled horses, panicked soldiers, and a neverending onslaught of unhinged, beastly wrath.

At one point, a horse's thrashing hooves knock me into another body, and when I reach out to steady the stranger, I realize it's Prime Azele. The soot on her cheek is streaked and her lip is bleeding. She has one sword drawn and another at her hip. As she takes in the carnage, for a second she looks vulnerable, like this isn't what she wanted either. But then I see the shadowy crack in the earth that indicates her bodyguard is about to appear and I drop her and keep running before either one of them realizes we're fighting on opposite sides.

When I reach the carriage, I lean against it, my breath coming in sharp pants. Then I steel myself for what I might see and peer inside.

At first I can't make sense of it. The Prime is just sitting there, his hand on Mance's forehead. Everything looks fine and for a desperate moment I wonder if I've grossly misread the situation. But then I notice how Mance's hand is suspended in the air at an odd angle, like she was just beginning to raise it, and the way her eyelids show a sliver of white at the bottom like she was in the middle of flinging them open.

My blood runs cold.

I back up, then charge the carriage, slamming my shoulder into it with as much force as I can muster. It rocks, and the Prime looks up, but his grip holds. I'm not strong enough to knock this thing over. The Prime looks away again.

So I pry a stone out of the ground and chuck it at the side of his head.

The glass window shatters, and the rock hits him above the ear with a sickening thunk. He falls sideways, cursing and letting go of Mance in his scramble to catch himself.

She's out of the carriage like a shot, gasping and stumbling to her knees. I grab her and haul her up, and when her eyes meet mine, the animals all around us fall to the ground in relief. She throws her arms around my waist and I wrap mine around her, too, as the din of the fight is replaced by a sudden, heavy quiet.

As soldiers on both sides reel back in bewilderment, Azele takes advantage of the break in the onslaught to sound the retreat. Men and women alike turn tail to run, grabbing for any horses that can still take riders, no matter what side they started on. Soon the ground rumbles with the thunderous sound of their flight.

"You came," Mance rasps into my shoulder. Then she pulls her head back and gives me this look of pure awe that cuts right to my heart. But it's gone in the next second as her eyes snap to the carriage. "We have to get out of here."

"Nah, I thought I'd stick around for a while," I say. "Seems like a fun party."

She groans but whether that's because she's in pain or because of my attempt at humor, I can't be sure.

The door to the carriage slams open, and the Prime emerges, walking down the small set of steps like he's descending a grand staircase.

"You did well," he tells Mance. Then his gaze darts to my arms still around her waist and he narrows his eyes.

Her head whips around, and creatures everywhere perk their ears, slowly getting to their feet as her attention focuses on him. My skin prickles and even the Prime looks a little unnerved with so many hateful eyes latching onto him.

"You *monster*," she spits. "I should have my creatures rip you apart right now. I promise you I have the rage for it."

The Prime takes one step back up the carriage rungs, frowning. "Seize her!" he cries at the soldiers.

"Don't you *dare*!" she screams, with such force and authority that many of the soldiers stumble to a stop in confusion. Even I almost flinch. Before they regain their bearings and decide their loyalty, Mance's animals rise up as one and begin to run.

This time I really do flinch, because it's a stampede like I've never seen, completely uncoordinated, fueled by nothing more than the desire to be anywhere but here. Some creatures sprint through the grass, others plunge into the edge of the forest, and still more scramble back up the cliffside.

In the pandemonium, Mance manages to grab her stallion by the mane and launch herself onto its back. Then she turns him around and gallops back to me, hand outstretched, hair streaming behind her.

I am not at all sure what I did to make her think I have the skill set to jump onto the back of an enraged runaway horse.

But I don't have a ton of other options, so after a desperate look around, I brace myself, run straight toward her, and hope for the best.

When I'm about at the horse's neck, I grab its mane with one hand, her arm with the other, and jump. She grips the beast with her thighs to anchor herself and tries to swing me behind her, but our limbs get tangled up and I hit the horse wrong, causing it to stumble. The ground rushes by way too fast, mere inches below my dangling feet.

By this point, a few of the soldiers have regained their composure and are bearing down on us, the Prime screaming at them to stop us at any cost. They reach for us. Their expressions are set. Drawn weapons are held aloft.

But then I pitch my leg over the horse's haunches and Mance digs her heels into its sides and we're shooting away, wind whipping in our faces, the horse straining below us, and my hands latched onto Mance's hips.

The soldiers, the broken battlefield, and the Prime's outcry all fall away behind us, drowned out by the steady thump of hooves in the grass.

She steers us toward the forest, and when we hit the foliage I have to bury my face in her shoulder to keep from getting smacked in the head with a branch. Even so, twigs scrape my skin and snag on my hair and clothing. She's not sticking to any path.

I press closer to her and say nothing, letting her guide us wherever she wants to go, trying not to think about the fact that the Prime definitely saw my face, and, given the context, will almost certainly remember it. It seems likely that if he sees me again, he'll kill me. I'll be another smashed-up body at the bottom of the cliffs.

But I'll worry about that later.

Right now the main priority is not falling off this horse.

❦✻❦

After what feels like miles, the heavy clop of hooves on dirt turns to splashing, and Mance yanks the horse's mane to bring it to a stop.

I have enough time to notice that sweat flecks its hide and its mouth is foaming before Mance slumps sideways. Given how intertwined we are, I go down with her, and we both careen headfirst into murky, lukewarm water.

I come up spluttering and gagging. She comes up like a water nymph, flipping her dark hair to make an arc of droplets that catch the sunlight.

We stand there for a second, soaked, breathing. Around us, the forest is still.

Then she dives under again.

"Mance?"

This time when she resurfaces, she's rubbing her face furiously with both hands, and I realize she's trying to get the makeup off. It's weird, but I actually forgot she had it on. I used to be so intimidated by the way she looked with those bold lines and darkened eyes, but now I just see . . . her. A girl clawing at her own face until it's a streaky, soppy mess.

"Here," I say. "Let me."

I take off my coat, with its glass buttons and shard-covered shoulder pads, and hold the softer inside lining against her cheek, wiping gently until most of the paint is gone. Then I drop the cloak in the water and ease away the rest with my fingers as she blinks up at me, midnight eyes searching.

Compared to the chaotic battle and the desperate escape on horseback, this moment feels so small. But there's something that passes over her eyes as she looks at me that doesn't feel small at all, like a single candle lit in the darkest part of the night, and my heart clenches.

A part of me, a large part of me, wants to lean in to that light. But there's also a not insignificant part of me that wants to blow it out and run. I don't know that I can be trusted to handle a light like this. I might get burned. Better to blow it out now, gently, than to let it get that far.

But even as I think those things, I don't drop my hands from her face. I keep smoothing my thumbs over the curves of her cheekbones. And her candlelit eyes stay fixed on mine.

"Do you, uh . . . want to talk about it?" I ask when the last smudge has finally been smoothed away.

She swallows, causing a rivulet of water to skate down her throat. "On the boat," she says.

"The . . . ?"

For the first time, I pull my eyes away from her face long enough to look around.

The lake we're in, if you can call it that, is tiny. More like an oversized puddle. And in the middle of it is a massive, greenery-covered boat. From hull to mast, every inch is coated with ivy, moss, and tiny flowers. In the middle of the deck, intrepid trees are poking through former portholes and winding around the crow's nest.

While I'm taking it in, Mance slips out of my hands and starts climbing, pulling on vines and rusty metal to haul herself to the top.

I flex my hands self-consciously, watching her. Then I splash some water on my face, shake my head, and wade after her.

The climb is easy going, with plenty of notches and roots to hold on to. It's almost comforting, doing something that feels so familiar. I start to relax, tension falling off me like the water that pours off my clothing.

Until my finger hits a metal band on the hull of the ship, and I have the fleeting thought that it reminds me of the stripe of metal on the hilt of the Victory's Herald.

And suddenly my limbs lock into place.

Because now that things have calmed down, my mind reminds me of a detail that I didn't examine carefully in the heat of the battle.

When I crashed into Prime Azele, she had two swords. One in her hand, and one at her hip. The former was clearly a practical, well-used blade, but the one at her hip looked ceremonial.

And it had that same band of metal on its hilt that the Victory's Herald did.

Not a similar one, but the *exact same* band.

On the exact same sword.

My fingers dig into the splintering wood, and I hiss, because I don't know what that means.

Or maybe I do, and I just don't want to think about it.

I look up, and Mance is waiting for me, her expression soft and affectionate. That warm, inviting candlelight still burning in her midnight eyes.

I wish I could erase the last few seconds from my mind and go back to believing I deserve the way she's looking at me.

But I was wrong to think I did.

She's only looking at me like that because she thinks I saved her, when in reality I'm the one who instigated that battle in the first place. My actions put her there. I caused the very hurt that I just soothed.

And now, no matter how much that little candle in her eyes lights up my chest, I *need* to snuff it out.

If I don't end this now, it will only get worse.

With gritted teeth, I put my head down and keep climbing.

15

Prospective Seconde Mancella Amaryllis Cliff

|3 DAYS UNTIL THE ASSURANCE|

Silver came for me.

As I lean over the railing of the boat, watching him scale up its side, I ruminate on that fact.

He actually came. I didn't even ask him to, but he was *there*.

I perch my chin on my arms, smiling down at him. Warmth curls in my stomach like steam over a mug of cocoa, and I revel in the feeling. The evening air is cool and my clothes are sopping wet, but I'm not shivering. I feel lit up from within.

When he nears the top, I extend a hand. He takes it, and his palms are rough and calloused beneath my fingers as I haul him over the edge. His grip is strong.

Once he's solidly on the deck, I swipe dripping hair away from my face and scan him up and down.

The poor guy is soaked, and with his overcoat floating somewhere in the water below us, he's down to just a white undershirt, which clings to him like it wants to weld itself to his skin. Unlike me, his teeth are chattering, and he looks decidedly uncomfortable.

Without thinking, I fling my arms around his neck, wanting

nothing more than to share my own warmth with him. But when my chest hits his I jolt at the feeling, and he tenses as well. The dress I'm wearing is thin, and his shirt is barely there, so when I wrap myself around him, it feels like we're skin to skin. As I suck in a breath, I feel his muscles go rigid everywhere our bodies touch. Which is . . . a lot of places.

Way too many places.

I'm about to pull back in embarrassment when a tentative touch at my waist causes me to still. Slowly, almost like he's fighting himself on it, he winds his hands around me, pressing me closer.

I sag in relief against him, leaning my head on his shoulder as my hands sink down to his chest. I breathe in and he smells like pine and woodsmoke. It reminds me of a crackling, comforting bonfire, and the uneasy tension I've been carrying for hours begins to lighten.

"Are you okay?" he asks, and his chest rumbles with the question.

I nod against his neck, so close I can feel his heartbeat thrumming. The solid, steady beat of it convinces me that the danger is past, that we really made it out, and I clutch the front of his shirt in relief. "Thank you," I say. "For being there."

He flinches. Then all of a sudden, he's pulling back, disentangling our limbs and running a hand through his hair as he releases a shaky breath. "Right. So, uh. What is this place?" he asks.

Cool air rushes into the space he used to occupy and now I do feel like shivering. Did I do something wrong? The edges of my lips pull down.

"Um . . . a cousin and I found it when we were younger," I manage to say. "He read about it in some book."

I move my hands up and down my arms, still chilled. Silver

watches the motion with knitted brows. He doesn't say anything, so I keep talking.

"It was a treatise on the line of succession in the Jungle Realm, and there was a footnote about some noble who was eligible to inherit for about a day and a half. He went to the Broken Citadel and gained the power to form a ship out of nothing, one that could ride on land as if it were sea. But he only got about halfway back home before he discovered the dark side of it—sail the ship too long, and it will drown you on its deck. Every single passenger suffocated where they stood. After the bodies were hauled free, the boat was left here, and someone else became next in line instead. Just another fun inheritance battle for the books."

I grimace and Silver nods, rubbing the back of his neck. I'm sure he's heard several other stories of this kind, some true and some embellished. The early days of the treaty were so chaotic.

"Anyway," I say. "Alect wanted to know if it was still here, and I begged him to let me come when he looked for it. So we packed a picnic and set out, with all the seriousness of actual treasure hunters. And here it was. We ate on the deck and then we went swimming in our clothes. When the sun set, we dragged ourselves back to the castle, soaking wet but triumphant. It was . . . one of the best days of my life."

Silver nods, looking nostalgic, perhaps for happier memories of his own. "So why did you take us here today?" he asks quietly.

I bow my head, looking at the moss that carpets the wood beneath my feet. "We never told anyone about it," I say softly. "It was our secret, but we'd steal away and visit from time to time. It used to be my sanctuary. I was picturing it when . . ."

I trail off, but Silver doesn't make me finish. He peers out into the shadowy trees before dropping his hand with a sigh. "Your dad's a real scumbag, you know that?"

I snort humorlessly. "I'm not a huge fan of him either at the moment."

There are tiny white flowers sprouting in the moss between my toes, so small and so sweet they look like a dusting of sugar. They're not starsprouts, but they'll do. I crouch down and pick a few, molding the moss into little bundles that vaguely resemble bouquets. Then I lean over the edge and drop them one by one into the water below.

My chest aches when I realize I don't know how many I need to make. How many died because of *my* magic.

Silver comes over and props himself on the railing next to me, watching the little blooming bundles bob away.

"Why do you do that?" he asks. "You made one for Vie, too."

I stretch my lips into a self-deprecating smile, but it collapses as soon as I form it.

"Because I have to do *something*," I tell him. "To show respect. To say that I'm sorry. But also . . ." I lapse into silence.

He turns his attention from the water to me. "What?" he presses.

I pick at a splinter on the railing.

"It's . . . a form of protest, I guess. The ones I usually use, the starsprouts, are actually just weeds that grow in our lawn. My father hates them. He has a standing order for them to be plucked and burned daily. But . . . they're so resilient. They just keep coming back. So using them to make bouquets is my way of saying that I find meaning and beauty in things that my father doesn't. Even in the darkest moments. And that, just like he can never stomp the flowers out fully, I won't let that spark of goodness in me die completely either. No matter how many beasts we bury in my heart."

My words get soft, and I slump against the railing as the day's events finally hit me. I swear I can smell the blood again, can feel the ash and hear the screams. Here I am talking about silly flowers when my magic took multiple lives today. Have I finally gone too far? Should I just admit that that spark of goodness has at last been obliterated?

Silver reaches out but hesitates. His hand hovers just above my shoulder, and through the curtain of my hair, I watch it clench into a fist. Then he drops it back to his side, and it feels like a condemnation. My throat gets thick.

"I used to think this place was beautiful, you know?" I tell him, spitting out words just to keep myself from crying. "Even after Alect left and I stopped coming, I would still think about it from time to time. I just . . . I loved how the trees grew back after they were trampled. I thought maybe I could be like that. I could take the harsh reality I was given and find a way to peacefully grow in spite of it. But what if I'm not the trees? What if I'm the boat? What if I plunge out into the world and fail and *kill* people, and then the world conquers me and all I can do is lie there helpless as it does?"

"You're not the boat," he says. "You're one of the strongest people I know."

His words cut straight to my core, and I tuck my hair behind my ear so I can look at him. His expression is sincere and open, like the words were easy for him to say.

"Thank you," I whisper.

For some reason, he winces and looks away. "You need to stop thanking me."

"Why?"

He shakes his head. "I . . . don't deserve it."

My eyebrows draw together and I twist toward him. "Why not?"

He runs a hand down his face, then pushes off the railing and paces across the deck. When he reaches the mast he turns back, leaning against it with his arms crossed over his chest. Whatever conflict was on his face before is gone now, locked away behind the same kind of placid smile he wore when we first met.

"So what's the plan from here?" he asks.

"Silver . . ." I take a step toward him.

"Are you going back?"

"No."

"You'd leave your people, then? You're supposed to be named Seconde in three days. You're just not going to show?" His voice is accusatory and it brings me up short.

"I . . . don't know," I answer.

"Where are you going to go?" he pushes. "What are you going to do? What's the plan, Mancella?"

The fact that he used my full name for possibly the first time ever feels like a slap. I don't know what's going on or what came over him just now, but it scares me. I take another step, and his crossed arms flex.

"I don't have a plan yet," I admit. "My main goal was just to get away. But . . . where's this coming from all of a sudden? What are you trying to distract me from?"

He inhales sharply, and I know I've gotten it right. Within seconds, his smirk is locked in place, but his eyes are burning with an intensity that hits me square in the chest.

I step forward again. "Whatever it is that you think makes you undeserving of my thanks, you're wrong," I tell him stubbornly.

But he doesn't seem cheered. He tears his eyes away from me, his mouth narrowing to a thin line.

"How can you say that without knowing what it is?" he asks, voice rough.

I close the rest of the space between us and tilt my head until I'm right in his eyeline.

"Because," I answer, dead serious, "of everyone in my life, you're the only one who was there for me when I needed you, and that *means* something. My mother might plead in private conversations I can't hear, my sister might lend me support in the aftermath, my Captain might try to be a force of reason, and my servants and soldiers might whisper among themselves that it isn't right, but when it comes to the moments I need help the most, no one has ever been around." I put a hand on his chest. "You *were*. And I don't know what you judge worth by, but I for one judge a person by their actions. And nothing else."

He clicks his tongue and tries to look away again, but I grip his chin hard, forcing him back. This time when our eyes lock, his are angry.

"Well, what if it's my actions that I'm worried about?" he demands. "What if I did something really . . . unforgivable?"

"Like what?" I ask softly.

For the barest moment, his eyes flick to my lips.

I swallow, and in a frightening burst of insight, I think I understand what he means.

It feels like we're on the cusp of something, just a step away from careening off a ledge. My whole body feels alive and I have the insane thought that falling might not be so bad, as long as we do it together. Does he feel it, too? That something? Is that what he thinks he's unworthy of?

"Something I couldn't take back," he whispers. "Something that changed everything."

"Maybe," I say breathlessly. "I wouldn't mind."

"Wait. What?" His brows draw together again and his eyes bore into mine. "What are you saying?"

I'm not sure myself. Admittedly, I haven't thought any of this through. But after the day I've had, the fact that anything at all can feel good is incredible. Beneath my hand, his heart is hammering, and my own is as well.

Without questioning my desire to, I lean in, tilting my face toward him in invitation.

When he realizes what I'm doing, Silver's face goes slack in surprise. His eyes flare, and the anger evaporates from them like water in a frying pan.

He puts a hand up to stop me, pushing gently against my collarbone.

"Wait," he says. But it comes out hoarse and low, and it doesn't sound like he wants me to wait at all.

I stop in place, my lips just a breath from his. His hand is an anchor, and there's no way he can't feel my heartbeat, too. The frenzied rhythm it pounds through my veins feels like an admission, one I can't take back. I wait for him to pull me forward or push me back, but he doesn't do either.

Instead, he closes his eyes as if praying for strength.

"Mance," he says, the word almost a growl.

"Yes?" I reply, my own voice barely more than a whisper.

But he doesn't respond right away. He just leans his forehead against mine and blows out a slow, tortured breath.

"I—"

Whatever he's about to say is interrupted by a peal of thunder so clamorous that for a second it feels like the boat is shaking. Then the heavens open up and a torrential, freezing downpour slices the moment in half.

I gasp and Silver staggers sideways, pulling his hands back like my body burned him. I let my own hand drop from his chest as well.

For a few tense seconds, the beating rain is the only sound. It drowns out my heavy breaths, as well as whatever Silver is muttering to himself that he clearly doesn't want me to hear. Finally, he raises his voice over the storm.

"Where do we go?" he asks.

I look around. "Captain's quarters. Come on!"

I reach for his hand, but he flinches, and I draw back, stung.

It doesn't matter. I turn and sprint across the deck, Silver choosing to follow behind me instead of running at my side. We have to tear undergrowth away from the door, but eventually we're able to fling it open, dive inside, and shoulder it shut behind us, blocking out the deluge.

The sound of the rain dulls to a steady, soothing rhythm, and I slide down the door to sit on the floor. The wood is smooth and sturdy, even though it should be rotted away by now. There must still be some magic holding it together.

Silver moves past me into the room, uselessly wringing out his shirt as he takes everything in.

It's a small room, but thanks to the fact that it was closed off from the elements, it remains mostly untouched. Just the way I remember it. Well, almost. The far wall is covered in windows, but they're coated in ivy now, making an odd, leafy curtain. Everything else is the same, though, from the cupboard and writing desk built into the wall to the bed tucked up under the windowpanes. It even still boasts a blanket and some pillows, which will come in handy if the rain keeps up like this.

"You asked about the plan?" I say. "I guess it's to stay here tonight."

"Here?" Silver asks, voice tight. "Aren't there crew quarters somewhere else on the ship?"

"Yeah, right about where that giant tree in the middle is," I tell him. "If it's not flooded already, it surely will be soon. Why?"

He seems incredibly uneasy, and I'm not sure what could possibly be upsetting him about this perfectly good shelter.

It's only when he glowers at the opposite side of the room that I figure out what the issue is.

There's only one bed.

I manage to suppress a laugh, but I can't help the smile that coils the edges of my lips, and I quickly duck my head to hide it.

Perhaps the moment doesn't have to be lost after all.

16

Silver

|3 DAYS UNTIL THE ASSURANCE|

This has got to be a joke. I stare at the bed, willing it to split in half and spare me. I can't *do* this right now.

When the bed fails to accommodate my wishes and stubbornly remains a single object, I squeeze my eyes shut, trying to make sense of the last several minutes.

If I hadn't seen the sword, if I hadn't realized I recognized it just moments before climbing onto this cursed boat, then everything that happened after that might have gone differently.

Against my will, my mind replays the feeling of her fingers clutching the front of my shirt, the way her voice got soft when she told me she didn't care about my past. The fact that she leaned in, and if I hadn't stopped her she would have . . .

Why did I stop her again?

My gut clenches and I grit my teeth. I turn my back to her and lay my head against the ivy-covered window, trying to get a grip.

I *had* to stop her. I have to stop all of this. I've tricked her, lied to her, and stolen from her family with her help, but I won't cross that line with her unless she knows everything.

So . . . maybe I should just tell her everything?

I glance back at her. She's slumped on the floor, her head in her knees, her shoulders hunched. She looks exhausted.

I can't tell her now. I don't even know the full situation myself yet, and she's been through enough for today. And, fine, a part of me wants to delay it as long as possible.

Because no one's ever looked at me like that before. Vie and Rooftop and I, we have one another's backs and we always will, but the core of our relationship is stark survival. It's not sentimental, it's necessary. If something happened to me, they would both be upset, but they would harden themselves and move on. They would do what they had to do.

Neither one of them has ever looked at me with the kind of vulnerability that Mance exudes so easily. It's all the more compelling because I know how strong she is. And I find myself drawn to that combination of strength and tenderness, wanting to be the kind of guy who could earn it.

But I'm not.

At least . . . not yet.

I straighten my shoulders as I try to scrape together some kind of desperate plan. I don't want to be involved with Guerre anymore; that much is clear. Tomorrow I'll figure out how to contact him, and then I'll get some answers. Maybe it's not too late to get out. Maybe I can even stop what's coming, because I have a feeling this was only a step to something else. Something worse. I do have one last task left, after all.

So that's the plan for tomorrow.

Tonight, all I have to do is not get too drawn in by the Prospective Seconde and the flickering candlelight in her vulnerable midnight eyes.

And that's it! One job.

Shouldn't be too hard, right?

"We should take off our clothes," Mance says.

"What?!" I jerk my head back, smacking it into the window frame, and swear under my breath as pain laces through my skull.

She raises an eyebrow at me, amused. "And put on dry ones?" she finishes.

I scoff, rubbing my head. "Does the magical ship also generate magical clothing?" I ask. "How convenient." The *least* it could do is generate a second bed, then, really. I check to see if perhaps the bed divided itself while my eyes were closed. Disappointingly, it did not.

"No . . . ," she answers, dragging the word out, "but after that first time, my cousin and I kept a few outfits here for when we went swimming and needed to change into something dry before going home. The clothes we stashed for me will all be too small for us now, but he was a few years older, so his might fit okay."

She crosses the room and opens the cupboard, revealing two small stacks of tunics and pants inside. She raises one of the larger ones up to her chest, careful to hold it out enough that it doesn't get wet.

Because her dress is . . . very wet. And the way that it clings to her body is—

I snap my gaze back to the window, seriously considering just gouging my eyes out entirely.

"Uh, I'm good," I say. Changing involves nakedness, and nakedness seems like a very bad idea right now.

"You'll get sick," she says sternly.

There's that frustrating compassion again. Vie or Rooftop would tell me to suit myself and laugh at me in the morning when my forehead was hot with fever.

Well, okay. Rooftop would make me soup or something. But he would still laugh at me while he made it.

"There's no place to change," I remind her.

"So don't look," she says lightly.

I'm gonna punch a fist through this window. She can't *possibly* trust me that much. *I* don't even trust me that much.

But when I look over, she's struggling to keep a straight face and there's a slight tremor in her hand that lets me know she's as nervous as I am. She's only pretending to be this cool.

Unfortunately, I find that adorable.

"Toss me a shirt," I say miserably. We might as well just get this part over with.

She lobs me a tunic, and a pair of pants after that, and we turn our backs to each other. Almost immediately I am subjected to the torturous sounds of wet fabric sliding along skin and falling to a heap on the floor. I try very hard not to let my mind form any kind of conclusion on what that sound might indicate regarding her current state of dress. I just whip off my own clothes and jam my limbs into the new ones as fast as possible.

"I'm ready if you are," she says.

"Same," I say. We both turn around.

And she bursts into laughter.

Admittedly, the fit of my outfit is a little snug. The sleeves barely reach my mid-forearms, and the pants extend only a few inches past my knees. Mance's outfit is small as well, but less in terms of length and more in terms of hugging certain unboyish areas very closely.

Did I ever find something to gouge my eyes out with, by the way? A dagger would be ideal, but I could make do with a spoon.

I grin sheepishly at her, because as embarrassing as the outfit is, her laughter is addictive, and I let it wash over me, wondering whether I'll ever hear it again after tonight.

"I'm so sorry," she says, still giggling. She walks over and tugs at my sleeves uselessly, trying to make them longer than they are.

I bat her off.

"I'll be fine," I say. "At least yours isn't, uh, so bad."

"Yeah." She looks down, then twists the bracelet on her wrist with a grimace. "I wish I could get this off." As she tugs at the thing, she reveals harsh red lines on her wrist where it bites into her skin.

I frown. "Let me see."

She holds the bracelet up and I grip her arm lightly, turning the metal band back and forth until I can understand how it works. It doesn't look terribly difficult to spring.

"Give me a hairpin," I tell her.

Obligingly, she pulls one out of her hair, causing several strands to come free and curl around her face, clinging to the curve of her jaw.

I will not be focusing on that.

I take the pin and bend the tip of it until it makes a decent lock-pick. Then I get to work, poking at the inside of the mechanism to see if I can get anything to give.

"A skill you picked up on the streets?" she asks, bemused.

"Vie's better at it," I tell her. "But I'm not bad."

The mechanism clicks open, and I unwrap it from her wrist. She rubs the now-exposed skin with her other hand and closes her eyes. Relief eases her features as, I assume, she calls all her animals back to her. I can almost feel them filling her up, settling back where they belong, and when she opens her eyes again, she looks significantly more relaxed.

"Thank you," she whispers.

I swear, if she thanks me one more time . . .

Guilt surges up my throat as all the things she doesn't know rise like a wall between us.

"You should get some sleep," I say gruffly. "I'll take the floor."

I grab a pillow and toss it down, but she snatches it out of the air.

"You can't do that!" she protests. "The floor is soaking wet now."

"Mance—" I start.

"*Silver*," she cuts me off. "It's freezing and it's damp. And the bed is plenty big enough. Besides, I used to share with my sister all the time. It's the same thing."

Once again, her body language betrays her. The way she bites her lip and plays with those stray tendrils tells me she knows perfectly well that it's *not* the same thing. But as endearing as I find her duplicity, it won't work on me twice.

I open my mouth to deny her more definitively, but she cuts me off again.

"Besides," she says. "I . . . I'd rather not be alone. With everything that happened today, I could really use the comfort of someone next to me tonight. If you don't want to, of course, you don't have to. But if you're trying to be polite, don't. I don't need politeness right now. I need . . . solace." Her voice is small by the time she finishes speaking, but her eyes are huge and imploring.

I swallow and my chest feels tight.

How does she do that? How does she just *say* what she wants like it's that easy? When I want something, I either try to trick someone into giving it to me, or I just take it behind their backs. If you express it, then they can say no. They can shut you down. Which is exactly what I should do right now.

But I don't *want* to.

I blow out a breath that feels like it comes from the depths of my soul.

And I plop down on the mattress.

She joins me shyly, easing down onto the bed with a slow deliberateness that tells me she's still worried I'll change my mind.

Her arm brushes mine and every hair on my body stands on end.

Suddenly possessed with the need to keep my hands busy, I lean back, wrenching the window open and breaking a hole in the vines so we'll have at least some warning if anyone decides to follow us. Then I pat down the pillows and shake out the blankets in case any bugs worked their way inside. And then I do it again, just to make extra, extra sure.

When it becomes abundantly clear that I'm just doing things for the sake of doing them, Mance rolls her eyes and crawls past me. She picks up the edge of the blanket and burrows under it, taking the side closest to the window. Within seconds, she's snuggled up tight, like a caterpillar in a cocoon.

I lay stiffly next to her, like a plank of wood.

"You can get under the blankets, you know," she says.

"I'm good."

"Silver, you're being silly."

"I'll be more comfortable this way," I tell her. "I promise you."

Unfortunately for me, my traitor body decides to take that moment to visibly shiver. Between the frigid rain and the rapidly cooling evening air, the temperature has plummeted in the last few minutes, and my child-sized clothing isn't doing much to fight it.

She narrows her eyes at me and I brace for her reproof. But instead of lecturing me, she tears the blanket off herself and flings it over my head. By the time I've wrestled free, she's already scooched all the way against the window and curled into a ball facing me, completely uncovered.

"What are you doing?" I ask wearily.

"If you don't want to share a blanket, I certainly won't make you," she tells me in a clipped tone. "But if that's the case then you should have it. *I'm* the one who dragged you out here, after all. And I won't be able to sleep knowing you're shivering next to me."

As if I'd be able to sleep with *her* turning to ice just a foot away.

I debate several options, only to reach the same conclusion at the end of every one of them. There's no way to win with this girl. I'm caught.

If I were a better person, that wouldn't thrill me so much. But I'm only me, and I can't help the dizzying feeling that I've won even though I've objectively lost.

With an exaggeratedly tortured sigh, I lift the blanket and scoop her into it, my hand at the small of her back.

She squeaks but doesn't struggle as I press her against my chest and wrap the blanket tight around both of us until every inch of her body is bound to mine.

"Happy?" I ask, and I should be alarmed by the rasp I hear in my own voice, but she feels so good there, so warm and so soft and so right.

She looks up at me through inky black lashes and nods, another smile curving over her lips, coy and victorious.

And I suddenly remember that she used to smile a lot. When she was a kid, every time her grandfather hauled the whole family out to look regal while he made some proclamation, little Mance would just stand up there beaming. As a boy, I couldn't take my eyes off her.

Slowly, hesitantly, I trace the edge of her mouth with the pad of my thumb, marveling at the fact that the smile she has on now is for *me*.

But even as I try to hold it, the smile falters and turns into something more serious under my touch.

She shifts closer, her legs brushing against mine in the blankets, and reaches up a hand to my face, grazing my cheekbones and the line of my jaw with a deliberate, featherlight touch.

I inhale, but that's a mistake, because I breathe in her scent.

Somehow, in the middle of all the rain, she still manages to smell like sunshine.

As her fingers skim closer to my mouth, I impulsively tilt my head, pressing my lips into the center of her palm, our gazes still locked.

Her eyes get darker. Bluer. Even more luminescent.

Then she returns the favor, pressing a kiss to the tips of my fingers, and I feel it all the way down to the pit of my stomach.

Reflexively, my hand curls, cupping the side of her heart-shaped face. With a soft pressure, I draw her toward me, heart hammering in my chest.

And it takes all my strength to tuck her head under my chin instead of pulling it up to my mouth.

As soon as I'm released from the intensity of her gaze, my expression collapses with an agony I can't let her see. An agony that I have to remember, because I deserve it.

Beneath the sheets I clench my hand into a fist.

"Get some sleep, Mance," I say roughly.

Because there's no chance at all that I will.

❧✻☙

I spend the next hour or so overly aware of Mance's every shift and movement as the sky outside darkens. Eventually, her breaths even out and her muscles go slack against me. I blow out a puff of air and wonder how long this night is going to feel, unable to decide if I want it to speed by or to linger.

Somewhere between five minutes and six eternities later, when I'm just on the edge of miraculously surrendering to sleep myself, there's a sudden glint of light outside, peeking between the greenery.

I stare at the space where I saw it, wondering if it was just my imagination, or perhaps the precursor to a dream. Then the light flashes again.

Carefully, without waking Mance, I lean over her and stick my head out the window to see what it is. There's another flash, and I rear back when I see what it illuminates.

A face in the woods.

One with familiar blue eyes.

Mance makes a sleepy noise at my sudden movement but doesn't awaken. Carefully, quietly, I extricate myself from her and slide out of the bed. An icy puddle chills my bare feet, and the air outside our little blanket fort is biting. I take the time to tuck the blanket closer around Mance and she snuggles into it, settling back down. Her face is open and peaceful as she rests, and I stare at it a little too long before I pad out the door.

It isn't raining anymore, but the deck is slick. Wishing my boots weren't too waterlogged to be helpful, I make my way to the side of the ship where one of the trees hangs low enough and jump up into it.

The leaves rustle as I make contact, spattering raindrops everywhere, and I whip my head back toward the door to the captain's quarters, dangling precariously. But when Mance doesn't emerge, I finish pulling myself up and ease my way across the branches and down the trunk.

Guerre is waiting for me at the bottom when my feet hit the muddy banks. He takes in my outfit with a derisive snort, and I glower, feeling like he's somehow intruding on something personal. I'm about to make some kind of snarky comment when I notice what *he's* wearing.

A general's uniform. In charcoal gray.

I lift my eyes to his face, noting the ash smudges on each of his cheeks. "So you work for Prime Azele, then?"

"I work for myself," he responds dismissively. "She's not the only one who believes otherwise."

I shiver as a brisk wind makes the cold night feel even colder.

"Were you there today?" I ask, rubbing my arms roughly with both hands. "Did you see what happened?" What I actually want to ask is whether he meant it to happen. Whether this was the plan or if something went horribly wrong.

"I was there," he acknowledges. "Though I'm hoping you can help me fill in some of the gaps."

"I will if you will," I snap.

He raises an eyebrow and takes a step back, appraising me. "Well, well, well. Something has changed. Is it the girl?" He peers through the darkness toward the ship and I have the reckless urge to jump in front of him and block it from his view.

"What's the end goal?" I ask. "What are you trying to do with all this?"

"I've already answered a question," he tells me, tone sharp. "If we're trading information, then I'm afraid it's your turn."

A gust of wind whips by and I tense. "What exactly do you want to know?"

He moves in closer again, an interested gleam in his expression. "How did he get her to attack with her animals?" he asks. "From what I've heard, she has a distaste for violence."

Frowning, I roll the question over in my mind, trying to figure out if answering it could harm Mance in any way. I don't think so.

"He had a bracelet," I say. "That locked her animals out of her body. And then he used his power on her to make them panic."

The moonlight catches on Guerre's ice-blue eyes. "Fascinating. Whose magic is that?" He thinks on it, mentally sorting through some kind of catalog in his mind before he must land on a name. "Ah. I see. Very clever. Where is this bracelet now?"

"I'm afraid it's your turn," I sneer, mimicking his earlier tone.

He scoffs, impatient. "My end goal? The betterment of the realm. And I'll make my next question more efficient to save time. Can you get the bracelet?"

It's in my pocket right now, cold against my leg.

He must see enough in my expression to satisfy him, because he claps a hand on my shoulder. "Excellent. Then this is your third and final task. Get the bracelet and put it back on the Prospective Seconde's wrist, this time while her animals are still within. If I'm right, then the bracelet is a barrier. It should be able to trap them in as easily as it can keep them out. Once it's on and it's locked, bring her to me."

The chill of the air feels like it's seeped into my bones now, harsh and constricting. "Are you going to hurt her?" I ask.

He leans back, studying my expression. The shadow of the branches falls across his face.

"I have no desire to hurt her," he says. "In fact, I believe she and I want the same things, and after today's events she might finally be ready to hear it. I want you to bring her to me because I'm going to ask for her help."

My breath mists in cold puffs around my face.

Can I believe him?

And even if I can . . . what does he want her help with? If whatever Guerre's doing resulted in the violence of just a few hours ago, then I don't want Mance anywhere near it.

"No," I say. "I don't want to do these tasks for you anymore. I won't bring her."

If I thought his eyes were cold before, it's nothing compared to the way his stare frosts over now.

"You'd give up your mansion, your papers, your future? When you're only one task away? When all I'm asking you to do is set up a conversation?"

I click my tongue, not buying it. If he just wanted to talk, he could climb up the boat and have a chat with her now. But he wants her leashed first.

It hurts to give up everything I've worked for, but I'll figure it out. Rooftop and Vie and I, we'll figure it out together. We always have.

"I won't do it," I repeat. "Give the house back to the family you evicted. I'm out."

I turn to go, but he grabs my wrist, wrenching me back, and then suddenly his sword is pressed to my throat.

"Do not misunderstand," he says through gritted teeth. "I will reward you for your help, but that does not mean you are free to stop providing it. If you refuse me, or if you breathe a word of my plans to anyone, *especially* Mancella Cliff, then not only will you never be able to afford a house, but I'll burn down the one you have. With your friends in it. In fact"—he tilts his head, considering—"that's where I'd like you to meet me tomorrow. I'll be waiting, all day, with sweet Rooftop and pretty Vie. If you bring the girl, you'll get the deed and the papers and everything will proceed as we've already agreed. But if you don't . . ." His voice lowers to a snarl. "Then you may as well never go back at all, because there will be nothing waiting for you but ash and corpses. Are we clear?"

I swallow against the blade as panic blurs my vision. In that moment, I hate him. Perhaps as much as I hate the Prime. Or maybe I just hate myself for getting into this situation. For how few options I have.

Anger flaring, I slam my fist into the hilt of his sword, knocking it aside, then turn and make a break for it.

But I barely go two steps before he grabs me and smashes me sideways into the nearest tree. Then he brings his forearm to my throat, before slowly leveling the sword back to the soft spot just beneath my jaw. It would take him only one movement to either strangle me or slit my throat.

"Don't make me ask again," he growls.

My breathing is harsh, but my voice is as sharp as his weapon. "All right," I say. "We're clear."

He pulls the sword back, sheathes it, and gives me an insincere smile, letting the arm at my neck fall away. "See you tomorrow, then, Silver. Sweet dreams."

As he retreats into the darkened forest, I hold shaking fingers against my throat, watching him go. The shadows seem to swallow him up, and I stare into the gloomy night long after I can't see him anymore.

Quietly, but not gently, I throw everything I have into a punch that I slam against the trunk of the tree. The pain is raw and searing, and I think I might be bleeding, but I manage to grunt instead of cry out, and the tree doesn't even shake.

It's not enough.

I want to scream. I want to knock the tree down completely.

I want my pain to *matter*.

I start to pace, shaking my arms out against both the cold and the sting that shoots up my right arm.

If I leave now, I could maybe be in the Outskirts by morning. Assuming I could find my way on foot in the dark, in a part of the woods I don't know well. Is there any way I could beat him there? I didn't see a horse or anything, but that doesn't mean he doesn't have one.

How *did* he get here, anyway? How did he even know where we were? How did he know Mance doesn't like violence when the majority of the population believes otherwise? And how did he figure out who made the bracelet when not even Mance knows everyone's power?

Who *is* this guy?

I should have asked these questions earlier.

But at least I may have gotten myself a clue.

I stop pacing and hold still, listening to the sounds of the night, making sure that Guerre is really gone. The wind continues to attack the trees, buffeting their leaves, and somewhere far off I hear the hoot of a lonely owl. But otherwise the forest seems to be at rest.

Satisfied, I open my cloak and pull out the bundle I took from Guerre's pocket when he was busy throwing me around.

Starting a fight is one of the most classic redirection tactics there is, and the bruises blooming on my back aren't the first I've gotten from trying it. Vie may be best at opening locks, but no one can match my skill at picking a pocket.

I just hope that whatever I managed to grab was worth it.

Slipping into a patch of moonlight, I ease the bundle open and spread its contents onto a dry patch of forest floor.

It's a pack of letters, with an array of broken seals—some, the bright ocher I'm familiar with, and others an ashy gray.

I suck in a breath, realizing that I'm about to find out what Guerre has been doing with the seal I gave him. The one he ripped off Mance's plea for peace. I lean in close, squinting at the scrawled script in the dim light.

It becomes clear very quickly that, for the last several days, neither Prime Merod nor Prime Azele has read a single word that genuinely came from the other. Guerre has been intercepting and rewriting every sentiment.

Prime Azele thinks Merod killed her captain with the Victory's Herald, a clear declaration of war. And Prime Merod thinks Azele wants nothing to do with an alliance, when in fact she's been begging for one.

The letters aren't complete—it's pretty obvious they're only a small subsection of the correspondence that Guerre has interrupted—but they're enough to paint a picture.

I've been helping Guerre start a war that neither party truly wants.

A war that Mance has been trying to prevent. That I *told* her she was preventing.

And all the while, I've been taking her well-meaning actions and using them to destroy the peace she craves.

The guilt burns so fiercely in my gut that I want to vomit, but I push it down, because I don't have time to dwell on how despicable I am right now.

I need to figure out what to do with this, preferably *before*

Guerre murders my friends.

Because I'm certain that threat was real.

If I don't show up tomorrow, he will burn my friends and my home to the ground.

And I can't, I *can't* let that happen.

But . . . I can't betray Mance either.

Can I?

I look up toward the boat, picturing her sleeping there. Trusting enough to get in a bed with me. To tell me her secrets. And caring enough to want sides of me that no one else has ever wanted.

I *can't*.

I run a shaking hand through my hair, gritting my teeth so hard it's painful.

On the other hand, Guerre did say he only wanted to talk.

He *did* say he wasn't going to hurt her.

That all he wanted was her help, and that their goals were the same.

Could that really be true?

I bite my lip, wishing I could believe it. But no. After these letters, I can't even pretend to. I know Mance, and she would never work with someone willing to do such despicable things.

Which means she would never work with me, either. Not if I told her what I know. What I've done.

This fragile thing we've built would be over immediately, shattered like glass in the Outskirts.

The pain of that realization rips through me, and I hate myself for even feeling it. I never deserved her affection in the first place, and I knew that. So there's no use mourning it now.

My only goal—the only thing that I have the right to care about now—is getting everyone out of this alive.

And that means that I can't tell Mance anything, because if I did she wouldn't trust me. She wouldn't do what I need her to do. So I have to go back up there, pretend everything is fine, convince her to put the bracelet on, and deliver her to Guerre. If I do otherwise, then Vie and Rooftop will die.

But once we're there, once my friends are safe, I will make sure that Mance gets out, too. I'll take the bracelet off her wrist, tell her everything, and fight by her side if I have to. But I *will* get her out.

Even if it kills me.

Even if she hates me.

Even if it ruins everything else.

As long as everyone gets out alive . . . then that's enough.

I pace for probably an hour more, but it's the bitter cold that finally forces me to climb back up the tree and drop onto the mossy deck. Before returning to the captain's quarters, I take several minutes to rub off every speck of dirt the forest flung onto me, and every smear of blood that streaks down my hand.

The door opens without a sound, but when I reach Mance, she's shivering, and the sight makes my heart clench.

I lift the blanket and tuck myself in behind her, waiting until my skin warms a few degrees before I let it come into contact with hers. She melts into me, a smile painting her face, and I hold her close.

Even though I already know I'm going to betray her in the morning.

17

Prospective Seconde Mancella Amaryllis Cliff

|2 DAYS UNTIL THE ASSURANCE|

When dawn wakes me, a weird breeze tickles my face, everything smells like rain, and there's something warm and solid at my back.

When the warm, solid thing shifts, my eyes fly open.

That is a person.

In my bed.

Why is there a person in my bed?

Obligingly, my brain fills me in with helpful reminders of my own brazen comments from the night before. They float through my mind like toy boats on a lake, bobbing mockingly along the edge of my consciousness.

...And the bed is plenty big enough.

You can get under the blankets, you know.

I need... solace.

I stifle a melodramatic gasp as the thoughts drop anchor. *I* said those things! To *Silver*! What possessed me?!

I throw the blanket over my head, suddenly extremely conscious of the flaming blush that paints my cheeks, the tangled, still-damp mess that is my hair, and the sour taste in my mouth that indicates possible morning breath.

I am conscious in an entirely different way of Silver's body pressed against mine, his pine-smoke scent wrapped around me, and the enveloping warmth of our shared space. It's all . . . really nice, actually.

This is too much to process. No one should be expected to process this many perplexing realities before noon.

"You awake?" Silver asks.

"Uh. No?"

There's some blanket rustling, and I think he's just propped himself up on one elbow. "So you just dove for cover in your sleep, then?" he asks.

"Yes," I tell him. "I'm a chronic sleep-diver. It's a very serious ailment. Incurable."

I expect him to shoot back some sly remark, or perhaps whip the blankets off me to prove I'm lying, but he just gets out of the bed, inviting a rush of crisp morning air into our formerly cozy cocoon.

"Take your time," he says.

His footsteps head toward the door, and I hear it open and shut behind him.

I stick my head out of the cocoon, frowning after him.

What was that about?

Did he not enjoy waking up next to me as much as I enjoyed waking up next to him? My stomach sinks at the thought.

After staring at the door long enough to determine that he's not walking back through it, I comb my fingers through my hair, doing my best to tamp down the mess into something vaguely presentable.

Then I swallow my nerves and emerge onto the mossy deck.

Only to find it empty.

Did he . . . leave? He seemed off, but I didn't think he'd abandon me in the middle of the woods without so much as a goodbye.

"I'm up here," Silver says, and I crane my neck toward his voice.

He's in the crow's nest, silhouetted against the bright morning sunrise, looking down at me with an expression I can't read in such obscured light.

I put a hand over my eyes. "Am I supposed to follow you?" I ask.

He shrugs against the sunshine. "You're welcome to try."

Um, all right, then.

I eye the rope ladder, which is as covered with vines as the rest of the ship, but opt to make a jump for the overhanging branches instead. It takes a few tries to pull myself up, and I can hear Silver snicker at my efforts, but eventually I'm able to scramble into the tree and start climbing.

Twigs scrape at my skin, sap rubs off on my fingers, and I run across more than one bug that crawls into my clothing as I'm evaluating my path. Even so, I stubbornly keep pushing until I'm on the edge of a branch that hangs at eye level with the crow's nest, giving Silver a triumphant smile.

He smirks at me with his chin propped on folded arms.

"Not bad," he says. "But now what?"

There's still about a three-foot gap between us, and no other branches are even remotely close by. Hearing the playful tone back in his voice again encourages me, though.

So I don't look down. I look at him. And that's all I need to look at.

"I'm gonna jump," I tell him.

His smile drops. "No, you're not."

"I am," I say. "And you're going to catch me."

He glances nervously at the deck below, then makes a hasty retreat to the other side of the crow's nest, hands raised to show that he's not ready.

"Mance, seriously," he says. "Don't."

"Count of three," I tell him, pulling my legs up onto the branch. "One . . ."

My heart is pounding, but I've come this far, and I want to make it. It's probably foolish, and in mere seconds I might really regret it, but I'm sick of being told what I can and can't do.

I let go with my hands and balance on my feet, but the branch is narrow and my stance is wobbly.

"*Mance!*" Silver's voice is desperate now.

"Two . . . ," I continue stubbornly. My foot starts to slip.

"I said *don't*—" Silver starts again.

"Three!" I yell over him, because at this point it's either jump or fall.

I launch myself at the railing and for all his protests, Silver throws himself forward immediately. I've barely started clawing the edge before he's on me, hands gripping, arms straining, expression tense as he hauls me over.

We collapse, panting onto the floor of the crow's nest, leaning against its sides. My adrenaline seems to kick in after the fact and my animals are going nuts in my chest. But there's an undeniable thrill to it as well. I feel more alive than I have in years.

"Why would you do that?" Silver asks. He sounds a little mad, but mostly incredulous. "You could have died!"

"You weren't gonna let me fall," I say between breaths. "I trust you."

Silver closes his eyes and leans his head back like my words cause him physical pain. "Do me a favor," he says. "Trust me a little less."

I laugh, but he doesn't, and the sound soon dies on my lips.

"What's with you this morning?" I ask. I thought we were past the weirdness.

"Nothing," he says, voice barely a whisper.

"Something," I push.

His eyes open and slide to mine but after a beat they skate away. "I've just . . . been thinking," he tells me. "I climb when I think. Always have. I didn't actually expect you to—"

"What were you thinking about?" I ask, because I don't want to talk about my stunt anymore. I want to talk about whatever's weird and fix it.

He pulls on the sleeve of his ridiculous shirt. "Next steps, I guess. I had . . . an idea."

I fold my legs under me, getting settled. "What is it?"

"Well . . ." His words fall off, like he can't even say them. I narrow my eyes and he flashes an apologetic smile. Then he takes something out of his pocket and it catches the sun, momentarily blinding me.

The bracelet.

I hold up a hand against the glare and sit up straighter. "I didn't realize you still had that."

He twirls it around his fingers, like he's considering what to reply, but finally something passes over his face and he continues in a voice that's more confident.

"I've just been thinking. If it can keep your animals out, it can probably keep them in, right?" he asks.

"That's what he said," I confirm. "Why?"

"Well, right now it's got a keyhole, and I assume your dad has the key, but what if . . ." He starts talking faster. "What if you used his own weapon against him? Locked your animals in and then welded the bracelet shut so he couldn't open it? If you did that, then he'd never be able to force you to summon again. He could never make your animals fight. He couldn't use you as this standing threat to other realms. He probably wouldn't even make you kill anymore, because what would be the point? You wouldn't have to be his tool any longer. You could just be . . . you."

It takes a couple minutes for me to process that idea. I gape at him, turning it over and over in my mind.

Willingly cut off my access to my own magic?

Be a normal girl?

Could that . . . really be possible?

Ever since I entered the Broken Citadel, I've wanted nothing more than to escape its clutches. My father's clutches. I don't even know what it would be like to not have to fight him at every turn. But still . . .

"I . . . I don't know," I say.

As my animals stir within me, reacting to my nervousness, I feel a pang thinking about never seeing them again. Never walking with them or running my hands through their fur. Never getting to express my feelings through their growls, chirps, hisses, snarls, or yips.

"I think it could help with the conflict," Silver says. "With the Grasslands, I mean. Clearly, taking the sword won't delay things for much longer. But taking his biggest weapon away might."

I bristle at being called a weapon.

And yet I can't deny that's what I am.

"Maybe," I say. "But it's a big decision. I just want to think it through."

Silver spins the bracelet on the tip of his finger and then stops it in place. "Tell you what. We won't weld it right away. Just put it on and see how it feels for a day. And then we'll go from there. If you don't like it, we'll think of something else. Together."

His words are kind, and yet there's something in his pushiness that makes me still and look at him sideways. His choppy hair obscures most of his eyes, but his gaze doesn't meet mine. Is he hiding something?

I shake off the feeling. Silver isn't like that. I'm too used to dealing with my father's manipulations and it's making me see subterfuge where there isn't any.

What he's offering is a way to get my freedom and autonomy back, to stop the endless cycle of death, to prevent whatever is brewing with the Grasslands Realm. His goals are the same as mine.

And after everything he did for me yesterday, I want to show him that he's someone I trust, even if it's scary. I just leaped out of a tree knowing that he'd catch me. I can do this, too.

It's like he said. We're in this together.

Without thinking any more about it, I pluck the bracelet from Silver's fingers and wrap it around my wrist.

His hand darts forward to stop me, then freezes in midair, and he opens his mouth, perhaps to tell me to wait and think it through.

But I know my choice.

Determined and, yes, perhaps still a little reckless, I snap the bracelet shut.

18

Silver

|2 DAYS UNTIL THE ASSURANCE|

"So being a normal person involves a lot of walking, huh?" Mance says, picking her way over yet another log.

"Yes, Mance," I say. "Normal people don't summon magical horses to carry them places. They just walk around on their regular, mundane feet."

She makes a face. "Does it always take this long?"

"Yes."

Sticks crack beneath our feet as we tramp forward, and the forest feels restless around us. There are birds cawing, bugs buzzing, and larger animals prowling in the brush. Not to mention wind whipping, leaves rustling, and a creek gurgling somewhere in the distance.

I have yet to see a creek of any kind, by the way. But the gurgling has followed us all morning. It's driving me crazy.

After climbing down from the crow's nest this morning, I told Mance that members of my secret organization were waiting at my house, and that we could talk about next steps with them.

She agreed so easily that it makes me sick. Because, as she so straightforwardly informed me after nearly flinging herself to her death right in front of me, she *trusts* me.

Guilt washes over me again as the bracelet seems to catch every scrap of light that filters into the dappled forest, constantly drawing my attention back to it with each mocking glimmer.

Mance makes cheerful conversation as we walk, oblivious to my inner turmoil. I'm half listening, throwing in quips as necessary and shooting her smiles. But whenever she gets distracted by a birdcall or a pretty flower and turns away from me, my smile slides off my face.

He said he wouldn't hurt her, I remind myself again. *It will be fine.*

And even if it won't be . . . I'll find a way to get us out. Escaping from impossible situations is my specialty, after all.

I should focus on the positive. When all this is done, I'll finally have my papers. Plus a real home, the one thing I've been striving for since the day I was dumped on the Academy's doorstep. Comfort, privacy, security, a future. It's all within reach. And this guilt, these lies, whatever's about to happen when we get to my house . . .

"It'll all be over soon," I say.

"What's that?"

I didn't realize I'd said the last part out loud, and I clear my throat. "The walk. Your anguish. It'll all be over soon."

Fortunately, that's true. The trees start to thin, and the ground gets rockier. Spindly houses begin cropping up, and the crunching under my shoes tells me I'm close to home.

But Mance is a little less familiar with the sound. "What is this?" she asks, pulling up one foot and examining the glittering shards lodged in the heel of her boot. At least she wasn't wearing slippers today. They probably weren't intimidating enough to match her makeup.

“Uh, glass,” I tell her. “From the trees.” I wave distractedly at one of the jagged stumps a little ways down the road.

She puts her foot down and approaches it slowly, her expression clouded. Then she raises one hand to touch it.

“Careful,” I say, drawing her hand back. “I know you haven’t seen a lot of your grandfather’s trees broken, but they’re sharp when they’re shattered. Even sharper than regular glass.”

She startles at my touch, like I’ve interrupted some internal line of thought, but lets me pull her away, studying the stump at more of a distance. Its vicious points glint under her scrutiny. As I watch her survey the glass-packed earth, the dirty, ramshackle houses, and the rest of the twisted, broken stumps, I see the familiar sights through her eyes.

It’s wretched. All of it. I’ve known that for a long time, and I guess I got used to it, but seeing the look on Mance’s face . . .

It makes me feel like I’m wretched, too.

“I always thought the trees were so beautiful,” she says. “But . . . people live in this?”

My face burns, even though her tone isn’t judgmental. “Come on,” I say gruffly.

She’s quiet while we walk, still taking it all in. I keep my eyes on my boots, partly because it’s generally a good idea to watch where you step in this area, and partly because I can’t stand to see her expression anymore.

When I reach the hovel that’s ours, I genuinely consider walking right by it.

But I’ve come this far. It’s almost done. I just have to see it through.

“This one’s mine,” I say. “Shall we go up?” My smile’s back on, but it’s stiff.

She tilts her head back, peering up into the branches. Looking at the place where I lived before I met her. The life I had. And it feels like peeling off a scab.

"No stairs?" she asks.

"Too difficult for you?" There's no bite in my goading, but I don't know if she notices. She takes it as a challenge anyway and rolls up her sleeves.

I beat her to the top, easily, but she determinedly wrestles her way up after me, just like she did this morning. Soon I'm grabbing her forearm and helping her onto the porch, my heart in my throat. Even though I'm not looking at it, I can feel the doorway looming behind me, and I know nothing will be the same after we walk through it.

"You'll want to take your shoes off," I tell her. "And beat them against the wall. To, uh . . . knock out the glass."

She steps out of her boots and into my house, then hits them against the outer wall once and sets them down. Once is probably not enough to dislodge what she's stepped in, but I'm too humiliated at this point to tell her so.

I close the door behind us—quickly and loudly, like I'm trying to cut off my own doubt—and Vie and Rooftop emerge from the back room and approach us. I expel a breath at the sight of them safe.

But Guerre isn't with them. That either means he isn't here, which seems unlikely, or he's waiting for the right moment, which worries me. I try to catch Vie's eye to convey something like "run now, please," but she breezes right by me.

"Hey, killer," she greets Mance with a sneer.

Mance raises an eyebrow like she's not sure whether the nickname is meant to be insulting or endearing.

"Hey, dead meat," she shoots back. Vie laughs, and Mance visibly relaxes, but I'm not so sure the laugh is kind.

"Prospective Seconde Mancella," Rooftop greets with overly formal, but still genuine, politeness. I try to catch his eye, too, but he's watching Mance pick up one of my candles. I wince when she smooths an uneven part of the wax down with her thumb.

"You said your parents made candles," she recalls. "Is this one of theirs?"

I can't believe she bothered to remember that.

I rub the back of my neck with one hand. "Actually, uh . . . I made that one," I tell her, distracted.

All my parents' property was confiscated when they were enlisted, so I don't have any of their original work. What she's holding is my best attempt to re-create the scent I remember most. Some kind of citrus and some kind of spice. I've never been able to nail it down exactly.

She holds it to her nose and breathes in, her face softening. "I love it," she says, and my chest tightens in response.

We don't have time for this. I need to get everyone out of here before Guerre shows up, and then maybe we can prevent the whole thing.

"Listen—" I start, but Vie cuts me off.

"What do *your* candles usually smell like?" she asks. "Gold and peasant sweat?"

"Leave her alone, Vie," I snap, annoyed.

She scoffs. "Oh no, did I hurt the tyrant's feelings?"

"What's your problem?" I seethe, and it comes out even more harshly than I meant it to because of how tense I still am. "We need to—"

The corner of Vie's lip lifts in distaste as she cuts me off again.

"Just don't know why we're playing with our food before we eat it, that's all."

My stomach drops.

"What?" Mance asks, looking at me. "What does that mean?"

"I . . ." I could kill Vie. Why does she have to be so rough and unsubtle? This is why I usually get the talking jobs. Of course, right now I can't think of a single thing to say.

Mercifully, and also devastatingly, we are interrupted by the front door swinging open, and even though I know who it is, my throat still goes dry when I see him and feel our chances of a peaceful escape evaporating before my eyes.

Today Guerre is dressed in the full splendor of a nobleman, dripping with jewels and fine silks that make even Mance's usual attire look simple. His bearing and demeanor are regal, too, and his hair is darker than I've ever seen it before.

Mance turns. Then she takes a step backward, clattering into our kitchen table.

"What . . . what are you doing here?" she gasps, her face paling.

She knows him, I realize with a start.

"Hello, Mancella," Guerre says, voice soft.

She rocks on her heels, as if teetering just on the edge of disbelief, blinking repeatedly to test what her eyes are telling her. I hold my breath, although I don't know what for.

She puts the candle down on the table.

Then she runs forward and flings herself into his arms.

19

Prospective Seconde Mancella Amaryllis Cliff

|2 DAYS UNTIL THE ASSURANCE|

As I look into the blue eyes I thought I'd never see again, it feels like looking into the sky itself. Like I've been living in a cave and someone just cut an opening in the ceiling. Like I'm a child again, and I still believe that people will take care of me. That things will be all right. That everything isn't entirely on my shoulders.

I haven't felt like that in so long. Not in about . . .

"Eight years," I say wonderingly. "It's been *eight years*."

"Did you miss me?" he asks, with an all-too-familiar smirk.

I falter because that expression reminds me of so much. Summer days and silly pranks and spinning stories and sneaking out. Simpler times. Easier friendship.

But . . . how *dare* he whip that smirk out now.

I extract myself from his arms, as the last eight years crash back in between us.

"Quick question," I snip, crossing my arms. "You ever heard of a letter? A few lines to let me know that you're safe? A quick, 'Dear Mancella, I'm not dead. Hope you're well. Sincerely, Alect'?"

"Wait," Silver interrupts. "Alect? You mean he's your . . . ?"

"Cousin, yes," I say distractedly.

He's grown about a foot, gained the muscles and stature of adulthood, and he's got a harder jaw and sharper cheekbones, but he's Alect. He looks so much like my uncle in every way. It's like stepping back in time.

But then Silver's confusion registers and I turn toward him, blinking. "Wait, you didn't know? Who did you think he was?"

Silver ducks his head, looking nervous, and I'm suddenly struck by the whole absurdity of Alect being *here*, in Silver's house, and not at all surprised to see me. Silver and his friends don't seem surprised to see him, either. They know one another . . . and yet they didn't know who he was to me.

"What exactly is going on here?" I ask. And then a thought occurs to me. "Oh! Are you in the secret organization, too?" That would explain everything.

But instead of nodding, Silver flinches, and Alect steps past him smoothly, putting one arm around my shoulder.

"We have time for all your questions," he says. "Why don't you have a seat?"

Under the gentle prodding of his hands, I sink into one of the rickety, mismatched chairs that flank the round table in the center of the room. I push aside a half-sliced apple with a dagger sticking out of it and prop my elbows on the wood, looking at Alect grimly as he takes the seat across from me.

"All my questions, huh?" I ask. "I've got a few."

"You always did," he says fondly.

My lips turn down and I fiddle with the bracelet on my wrist, still unfamiliar with its weight. Alect is smiling at me, like no time has passed, but time *has* passed. So much has happened.

One thing in particular.

"Alect," I start, voice low. "My father has . . . told me some things since you left. I have to know if they're true. Did you . . ." I swallow. "Did you really try to kill him? All those years ago?" Even I can hear the pleading in my voice. I'm sure everyone in the room can feel how badly I want him to reassure me that it never happened, as I've spent so many years insisting that it didn't. But now that the moment is here, I feel more fear than confidence in his response.

Alect doesn't look away, but he does tilt his head, regarding me carefully.

"Yes," he says. "I did."

My arms drop to the table in shock, both at the admission and at how easily he said it. The bracelet makes a hard thunk against the wood and it bites into my skin on impact.

"*Why?*" I ask. "How could you do that?" The Alect I knew, at least the one I thought I knew, would talk about better worlds. Kindness. Justice. All these years, I haven't been able to reconcile that person with the act of murder. It just doesn't make *sense.*

"Have you imagined yet what your life would be like if I had succeeded?" he asks, tone delicate.

I rear back, stunned to silence. His lips twist self-deprecatingly and he continues. "Your father is cruel. You know it as well as I do. Better, I'm sure. I entered the Broken Citadel and came back to kill him because I didn't want to see what would happen to the realm under his rule." He makes a sweeping gesture at the slums around us, shattered glass trees looming in the windows. "Can you blame me?"

"Murder is wrong," I say stubbornly. "Bloodshed leads only to more bloodshed."

"If I had succeeded, there would be no slums. There would be no Academy. You wouldn't have had to enter the Broken Citadel at eight years old. Or Mara at ten. And we wouldn't be on the brink of war when we're only barely beginning to recover from the last one. Can you really say it's better how it is?"

"I . . ." I try to protest, but my words trail off. I'm shocked at what he's saying, but even more shocked that it makes a cold kind of sense.

"You're starting to see," he says. "Why don't you hear me out?"

"Hear you out?" I ask. "About what?"

Beside me, Silver tenses, gripping the back of my chair. I hadn't even realized he was next to me until the sudden movement drew my attention. The other two are flanking him, their whole focus fixed on me and Alect. Rooftop looks anxious. Vie looks impatient. And Silver looks like he's going to be sick, his face pallid and his expression drawn.

"What exactly is going on here?" I repeat.

Alect folds his hands on the table in front of him, and I brace myself. "Your father is not a good man," he reiterates.

I raise my eyes to his but don't deny it.

"He's not a good ruler, either," Alect continues. "He doesn't understand relationships. Take this problem with the Grassland Realm. Instead of trying to sort it out, he immediately goes on the attack. He's training you for war because that's the only thing he understands. But I . . . I understand a lot more."

"Oh, yes?" I ask, folding my hands primly in a mimicry of his. "And what exactly do you understand? The contents of a pile of dusty textbooks?"

My own words surprise me. I've never talked to Alect like this before. But he's never talked to me like this before either, and what he's saying is scaring me.

I realize suddenly that my body is rigid, and that Silver is just as tightly wound behind me, clutching my chair so hard that it creaks.

Alect stands, then begins to pace the room while he talks, his rich fabrics swishing and ornamentation clinking as he moves. "Textbooks? No. I've moved so far beyond them. I've spent most of the last decade traveling from realm to realm, learning about each one. Just like we used to talk about. Remember? Understanding cultures, studying language and religion, even uncovering secrets. What I understand is people, and how they work. I don't just mean the ruling class, I mean the common people as well. I've worn many faces. I know how to negotiate a treaty, but I also know what basic needs our citizens are going without. I could make the world better. Create the one we used to imagine."

I bite my lip and stop tracking his movements with my eyes, choosing instead to look at my lap. I can't deny that what he's describing sounds better than what we have. But there's an undercurrent to his words that I recognize. That I can't stand hearing.

Ambition.

"Oh, Alect," I say. "You still want the throne. Even now."

"I've never stopped pursuing it. On the contrary, everything I hear about your father's rule has only strengthened my resolve."

I swallow, digesting that. "That's all well and good, but what, exactly, is your plan?" I ask quietly, even as a sinking suspicion stirs in my gut.

He stops, turning to face me. "Ideally, I'd like for us to work together."

I shake my head. "Be specific," I demand. "Work together to do what? And *how*?"

He regards me with careful eyes. "It's time to correct the failure of so many years ago. It's time for Prime Merod's reign to end."

My stomach drops as I clench my fists. "Kill him, you mean," I sneer. He may have fancier words for his reasons, but in the end it's all the same.

"I've already disposed of a tyrant once, Mancella. In the Grasslands Realm. And it's working beautifully. Sangua was a scourge, and she's gone now. I've been working with her successor, Azele, and you should see the improvements we've made to the realm. You *will* see; I'll show you!"

"Hold on," I say. "I thought Sangua ended her own life. Didn't they find her with all her blood outside of her body?"

"A fast-acting poison. As soon as she detected it, she tried to expel all the blood that was tainted. But within seconds, it was all tainted. So . . ." He makes a vague hand gesture, as though the explosive removal of a body's worth of blood was merely idle chitchat.

I'm shaking. Violently. This is *not* the Alect I know. What's happened to him? How could he have become the man in front of me, talking about murder with such a clinical lack of remorse? "You . . . you *killed* her!" I accuse.

"And in so doing, I saved and improved many lives," he tells me.

I dig my nails into the table. "You sound just like him. The man—the tyrant—who you're trying to destroy? You sound *just like him*." Tears sting at my eyes. "More importantly, you're not saying the rest of it. If Father died before naming an heir, it wouldn't be you who took power. It would be the closest living relative to the last Prime who possesses magic. It would be me."

"It would be Mara, if we're getting legalistic," he tells me patiently. "Or did you not know?"

My anger breaks off momentarily, replaced by confusion. His expression is serious, but his words don't make sense. I shake my head. "No, Mara doesn't have magic. It never manifested."

"Of course it did. Who do you think made that bracelet on your wrist?"

I don't realize I'm still shaking my head until he finishes speaking, and then I jolt to a stop. My mind goes blank, rebelling against this information. My hands shake, making the bracelet rattle against the table, and I hold up my wrist, regarding the contraption anew.

Could it be true? Why didn't she tell me? How does Alect know when I don't? And if she really does have magic . . . why did she use it to make a tool for Father to use me?

I spin the bracelet around to the keyhole, and when I do, I suddenly remember the stacks of locks and bracelets in Mara's room. The hoop and fastener in front of me look very similar. Similar even to the latch on Father's study, the one that's been there for *years.*

I'm finding it hard to breathe.

Is everyone in my life lying to me?

"I—that doesn't matter right now," I say, shoving the bracelet into my lap so I don't have to look at it anymore. "Except that it means you're actually third in line. So . . . what's your plan? Are you going to kill Mara, too? Kill me? Kill everyone between you and power?"

"I have no desire to kill you," he says, voice quieting. "You are not the poison your father is. You could be something much better. If you agree to work with me, I will gladly give you the throne. All I ask is that you name me your Seconde at the Assurance in a couple days. That way I can support and advise you with the knowledge I've gained, the same way I've been supporting Azele. As I said, I'd like us to work *together*. Like we used to."

"Right," I say. "Just as soon as I murder my own father. And . . . sister, too?" I notice he didn't say he had no desire to kill Mara. I can't remember whether they got along as kids, but surely she never did anything to him to warrant death. Has he really grown so heartless?

The smile he gives me is detached. "I don't need you to do that. It's already taken care of."

My blood turns cold. Even Silver and his friends seem startled at the revelation. One of them, I'm not sure which, inhales sharply behind me.

"What does that mean?" I demand. "What are you saying?"

He shifts, his feet apart and his arms folded behind his back, a stance that's almost militaristic.

"You don't need to concern yourself with the particulars," he tells me. "Suffice it to say that you *will* be Prime soon. The question is whether you're willing to work with me when you are."

"What did you do, Alect?" I press, voice dead calm.

"I'll tell you everything," he promises. "Once I have your agreement that you'll work with me. That we'll make decisions about your new reign together."

But I'm already shaking my head again, sharply. "I'm not giving you my word," I say. "Not like this. Not without all the information, and definitely not with a threat to my family underscoring our accord. *Tell me what you did*." The last few words are almost a scream. I realize I'm trembling, and I don't know if it's still in anger or because I'm afraid. He sounds so sure.

"You're certain?" There's a discordant note of regret in his tone, and his arms drop to his sides. "That you don't want to work together?"

I sit up straight and make my voice as firm as possible. "I've missed you," I tell him. "So much. I can't tell you how many times I've wished that you would appear with a plan to fix everything. But I'm not a child anymore. I can think for myself. I can see clearly. And if this is the plan? If this is how you're conducting yourself? Then I'm absolutely positive, yes," I spit.

He blows out a long sigh, running one hand down his face. He looks tired, suddenly. Like he aged another year in the last five minutes.

"Pity," he says.

Then his body suddenly breaks into two.

For a split second there are identical copies of Alect, one peeling off the other like a coat.

But then, no, they're not completely identical. The sad, tired look on the original Alect's face intensifies, the bags under his eyes seeming to darken and his frown becoming more pronounced.

The new Alect is leering at me with sick delight.

Right up until he evaporates into mist.

Someone gasps.

My mind races.

Then the second version of him materializes in front of me, sword held aloft.

Acting on instinct, I dive to the side, and his sword comes down through the space I just occupied, cleaving the chair in two. The other occupants of the room exclaim or take a step back as the two halves of the chair clatter to the ground. My heart pounds in my ears.

"Hold on!" Silver bursts out. He makes to rush forward, but

Vie digs her nails into his arm, restraining him. "You said you wouldn't hurt her!" he snarls as he wrenches Vie off.

"I said I had no *desire* to," the original Alect sighs. "And I don't. But . . . I will, if I have to." He turns back to me. "If you won't cooperate, then unfortunately you're in the way, old friend. I can't exactly have you running back home with my plans. It would have been nice to rule together, but I'm perfectly capable of doing it . . . on my own." He sounds confident until his voice falters on the last few words.

The clone notices it, too. "If you're going to be a baby about this, then get out," he sneers over his shoulder. "I can take it from here. In fact, it's better if I do. After all, if it weren't for you, I would have handled her father *years* ago. Don't mess this up for us again."

I take a step back, suddenly dizzy, as the room seems to lurch beneath my feet. This is too much at once. I can't even follow it all. I just know that I need to get out of here. *Now.*

Out of the corner of my eye, I see Silver having a furious whispered conversation with the others. I make a move to dash past them, but Copy Alect's sword comes crashing down in front of me and I barely skip back in time.

"I didn't say *you* could leave," he growls.

"It's not too late to agree," the original Alect pleads behind him. "I really don't *want* you to die."

"Well, I don't hear you calling off your creepy doppelgänger," I say.

As if to prove my point, the monster swings again, and I duck the blade before scurrying backward into a corner. Then I straighten shakily, leaning against the wall for support as my stomach clenches with what I'm about to do.

"I don't want to kill you, either," I say. "Not at *all* . . . But I will defend myself if I have to."

With bitter resolution, I locate my bear and my jaguar within me, feel their readiness to attack, and thrust them outward.

But when I try to push them past the boundary of my skin, it feels like they slam into a wall, and I flinch away from the feeling. The familiar, unnatural feeling.

Oh no.

I forgot about the bracelet.

I yank on it, scraping it against my arm, even to the point of peeling my skin.

The Alect in front of me chuckles darkly. "So it does work. Thanks for your help, Silver."

My hand freezes. Then the full impact of Silver's involvement in this hits me and I sag against the wall as though it were a physical blow.

Silver helped? He helped . . . cripple me so that I might be more easily killed?

Now that I'm looking, I realize that the sword Alect is holding is familiar, too. It's the one *I* stole. That I handed over to Silver along with all my darkest childhood stories. Did he ever even care about them, or was he only seeking to disarm me, literally *and* figuratively? Did he know as he took the weapon from me that my cousin would soon try to end my life with it? Has it hurt anyone else between then and now?

I look at Silver, eyes burning. He changed back into his regular clothes before we left the boat, but they're slightly damp still, and he has a small leaf plastered to his cheek from the ivy that coated the room we shared last night. His hair is even more tousled than usual, probably from the way we tangled together in the blankets.

He's in every way the boy I thought I knew.

Except that his expression is blank, as it has been a few times before, and I finally recognize that look for what it is. Silver is shutting me out. He betrayed me, and I'm not even worth his explanations. Why should he explain anyway? He brought me here to *die*.

Pathetic, useless tears prick my eyes. I hate him. I hate all of them. I hate *everyone*.

I feel a hardness come over me, as if I'm putting on my armor, and I let it settle onto my skin. I refuse to show him how much he's hurt me.

Instead, I clench my fist and smile coldly, turning back to Alect. "If you think my animals are my only weapon, then you have vastly underestimated me. I killed each and every one with my bare hands. I'm certain I can handle you."

I lunge, but he bursts away again and I'm left swiping at empty air. Alect's eyes get colder for a second, but then the coldness leaves again, like a wind just passing through. I spin wildly and get away from the wall, not sure where his copy will materialize next.

I was right to move. He coalesces in the space I just occupied, sword raised. When he sees I'm not there, his eyes flick around and his blade changes direction mid-strike, arcing back toward me. I fling myself into the table, and once again the sword barely misses me, only half a breath from my skin.

"*Stop it!*" Silver cries.

But I shut him out. I can't look at him, can't *think* about him right now, or I'll crumble. I need to stay angry, stay vicious, keep fighting.

I come out clawing, just as ferocious as any of my animals. I know vital points, I know my body, I know a thousand ways to hurt. I can win this.

But Alect is slippery. I throw punches, but they never land on anything solid; he merely dissipates from the air right before my fist enters it. He gets a couple hits in just by forming next to me, swinging his sword and immediately fragmenting away. But the stinging cuts only spur me on harder, only bring my magic roaring to the surface. I move faster and he increases his speed in kind until I feel like a whirlwind casting blows in every direction as I am pummeled in return.

Every time I miss, my magic burns through my veins, demanding contact. Demanding *pain*. My fury whips through me in a heady oblivion, and for once I embrace it. It hurts so much less than being a tool. I'm sick of being the one in pain. I want someone *else* to suffer. For the first time in my life, I know what it is to want blood.

I think even Alect is surprised. He manages to fend off my attacks fairly well, but I start to anticipate, start to predict where he might show up next, and soon I'm landing more hits than I'm missing.

I manage to slam my palm into his throat, hard enough to knock him back a few steps. He crashes into the wall, toppling a bookshelf and all its contents across the wooden boards. His body bursts into mist again and I make another guess, but this time I'm wrong, striking at nothing. Alect takes form across the room, next to his original body. Both of them are looking at me with the same inscrutable expression.

And then suddenly there's a hand on my wrist. Silver.

I jerk back, but he holds firm.

"I'm trying to help," he growls, pulling at my bracelet.

"Why would you—"

"*Silver!*" both Alects cry, the harshness of one voice mingling with the pleading tone of the other.

"The deal is off if you remove that bracelet," the sneering Alect snarls.

But Silver's already picking away at it.

I shake my head, not understanding, when the second Alect disappears again.

The bracelet falls away, and I pull Silver to the left.

Alect guessed that I'd move right and he appears there, slashing.

Wolf, jaguar, cougar, and bear burst out of me, and he glowers, but I school my emotions and hold them back. My creatures crouch, growling, ready to spring, feeding off my sudden wariness.

As the Alect in front of me tightens his grip on the sword, I turn toward the Alect I know, the one crouched in the corner, lips drawn into a thin line.

"You're outmatched," I say shakily. "But I'll let you go if you just tell me what's happening to my father and my sister. Please! Are they still alive? How long do I have?"

He straightens, fiddling with the strap of his bag. His mouth twists up like he can't decide on something, but then his expression clears, as he seems to come to a decision.

He slips the bag off his shoulder and drops it on the ground.

"*Don't—*" the other Alect spits.

"If you read the letters, maybe you'll understand," he says, jutting his chin at the satchel, which has fallen open to reveal a stack of letters and some sealed bottles. "Maybe you'll still side with me and we won't have to do this. In the meantime, we'll call this battle a draw. I guarantee you safety tonight if you don't leave this house. Read through the letters, think about what I've said, and we'll talk in the morning. All right?"

He extends a hand, but I make no move to take it.

The other Alect scoffs but still lowers his sword.

"Goodbye, Mancella," the original Alect says. "It . . . was nice to see you again. Even knowing how it turned out."

And this time it's the kind Alect who disintegrates into mist.

I look at the other one, but his sneer doesn't seem any softer.

"I'll respect that offer," he says. "Even if I do think it's overly sentimental. But if you step one foot out of this room, I cannot guarantee your safety. Understand?" He looks at the satchel, then scoffs again and looks back to me. "Same deal if you open the bottles. Leave them alone if you know what's good for you."

Then he bursts into mist as well. But where did they go if not into each other?

I run to the window in time to see a man bundled up in rags stand and start to hobble off. When he reaches the point where the trees get thicker, he, too, disappears.

A cold sweat runs down my spine. How many pieces can Alect split himself into?

I push back from the window, shaking my head.

It doesn't matter. None of this matters.

He wants me to sit quietly by while he enacts his plan? Wants me to understand? Wants me to wait for the morning without intervening in whatever happens during the night?

Not a *chance*.

I am done being a tool in the plans of someone else.

So without any further thought, without even a glance in the satchel's direction, I fling myself out the door, throw myself down the tree, and start running.

It might be too late, I know that, but he kept using words like "soon" and "will be." Which means they weren't dead when he got here. They might not be dead now. So if he refuses to tell me how soon "soon" is, then I'm not wasting my time riffling through some gaudy bag for answers.

I need to get to the castle and find out for myself.

20

Silver

|2 DAYS UNTIL THE ASSURANCE|

"Get the bag," I tell the others. "Figure out what's in there." Mance might be willing to leave a stone unturned, but I'm not.

Without waiting to see how they respond, I stuff my feet into my boots and grab Mance's off the mat before throwing myself down the tree and chasing after her.

"Mance, wait!" I call.

She's running through the Outskirts barefoot, completely ignoring the bloody footprints she leaves behind as her feet get cut apart.

And she's ignoring me.

"Come on!" I yell. "At least let me give you your shoes!"

She whirls, and I actually stumble back at the expression on her face. The *ferocity*. I've never seen her like this.

Then with a sinking feeling I realize that I have, of course I have. It's just never been directed at me.

I was certain there was blue in her midnight eyes, but in this moment they are hard, black, and blazing, not a single flicker of candlelight to be found.

"My shoes?" she sneers. "You betray me, deceive me, shackle me"—she shakes the bracelet at me and I recoil—"deliver me to a man who wants to kill me and my entire family, and you're concerned about my *feet*?"

"I didn't . . . I didn't know." In the face of her rage, I can't figure out how to justify myself. Because I know I can't, at least not completely. If this were purely a misunderstanding, I could clear it up. But the truth is that, at least in the beginning, I didn't care how all this would affect her. I was willing to destroy her.

And then when I did care, I was too cowardly to come clean about it, thinking that I could fix things before she found out the truth. I realize now I was trying to force her forgiveness by managing the situation myself until she no longer had a reason to be upset. For all the trust she put in me, I didn't give her any back.

How do you explain that?

How do you account for not doing the right thing to someone who *would've*?

She doesn't wait for me to figure it out. She stalks toward me and talks right over my stuttered rationalizations, a completely different creature from the girl who listened patiently on the boat. Who told me I was deserving of her thanks.

"You used me," she says. "But I'm accustomed to that. Everybody uses me and everybody lies, apparently more people than I even realized. So that isn't the part that hurts. What hurts is that you *saw* me first. You took the time to listen to me. To know me. You made me feel like the things I wanted weren't silly or irrational, but that they were noble. Worse, that they were *possible*." Her voice cracks on that word, and I feel like my heart cracks with it. "But you never meant to help me at all. You took every piece of vulnerability I gave you and you folded it into your plans so that you could use me better. I thought you were different, but you're not. In fact, you're worse. More willing to hurt me than even my father is, because at least he's straight with me about it when he rips me apart. You once called me a monster, and I can't tell you the pain that it caused me. But it shouldn't have. Because if there's a monster here, Silver . . . it's you."

"No," I whisper. "It's not like that."

For a second she looks like she wants to keep arguing, keep listing every way I've wronged her. And I wish she would, even though I know the list is lengthy. But then her expression shutters and she snatches the boots out of my hands.

"I don't have time to hear what you think it's like," she says. "And I'm not interested anyway."

She turns away and I grab her elbow. "Mance—" I start.

But she wrenches her arm free and shoves me back. "Don't touch me!" she screams.

I hold both hands up to show that I won't, even as my heart sinks.

"Hate me if you want," I say desperately. "Never talk to me again, but just don't go to the castle right now. *Please.*"

She shakes her head, disgusted, like this is just one more way that I've let her down. "Do you hear yourself?" she asks. "How could I possibly not go? My family is going to be killed! You want me to just wait it out?"

"If you go, you'll be killed, too!" I remind her. "You'll walk right into whatever trap he set for them and you'll be just as caught. Is that what you want?"

She gives me a look so cold that for the first time I see the resemblance between her eyes and Guerre's. Hers may be several shades darker, but right now they hold the same ice. The black ice of deepest winter, in the darkest part of the night.

"There are more important things than looking out for myself," she says, voice steel. "Maybe one day you'll figure that out. I told you once that I judge a person by their actions. Well, yours have been crystal clear. Allow me to be equally clear with mine."

She bends to scoop up a sharp section of branch by her foot and then flies at me. I expect her to plunge the glass into my chest—and I don't even try to stop her—but instead she slides it into my shirt and slices outward, ripping off the realm insignia that gives me admittance to the castle. It flutters brokenly to the ground between us.

She might as well have cut out my heart.

"You are not welcome in my home anymore," she says flatly, letting the shard fall from her hand. "And you are not welcome in my life. Goodbye."

I didn't flinch when she lunged at me, but that word makes me stumble back, slicing deeper than the glass ever could've.

Before I have a chance to recover, she summons her stallion and is already clambering onto his back and wheeling away.

It's obvious she doesn't want me to follow, but if I don't . . . she'll die. They'll *kill* her.

"Mance!" I cry out, my voice strangled. As she takes off, I break into a run, determined to chase her, determined to save her however I have to, even as the distance between us rapidly grows.

But before I make it three steps, something behind me explodes.

Debris shoots everywhere. Glass pelts me, and I fall to the ground, crying out as the air and the earth both conspire to pepper me with cuts.

Careful where I place my hands and my body, I turn over,

trying to figure out what happened.

And there's my tree, the gnarly oak that supported our little guard post, the one I climbed daily.

Absolutely destroyed.

Almost half of it is gone completely, shredded to bits. The house, my house, looks like someone took a giant bite out of it. Strange, spectral black flames lick at the splintered edges of the branches, caressing the broken outline of what used to be our front porch. The way the fire moves is unnatural, like it's halfway between liquid and smoke.

Before the shock even has a chance to sink in, I'm back on my feet and running again, but this time in the opposite direction.

Because the last time I saw Vie and Rooftop . . . they were still in the house.

Right where that gaping hole is now.

21

Prospective Seconde Mancella Amaryllis Cliff

|2 DAYS UNTIL THE ASSURANCE|

I don't even have time to grieve.

As I thunder up the cliffside on horseback, I swipe at my own eyes so hard that I scratch my skin, unwilling to let a single tear stay on my face.

Then I attack my clothes, clawing at the dirt that coats them. I rip leaves out of my hair, tearing them out so harshly that my scalp stings.

I want it all *gone*. Every physical sign of what happened today.

If I could tear apart the memories as well, I would.

Plunging one hand into my neckline, I withdraw a small leather bag, one I've been carrying around for days. Close to my heart.

My lip curls.

I can hardly open it fast enough, can't wait to shred the scrap of paper inside.

Because it's the note Silver gave me on the day we met. A memento of when my life started to change. I had thought it would give me strength, would remind me that someone believed in me. Someone was there.

With a scream, I reduce it to tatters.

Then, panting, I bury my head in the horse's mane and try to swallow everything down as the gates rise in front of me.

I'm used to burying things anyway. Every time I go into the arena. Every time I make small talk with my father. Huge sections of my heart need to be locked away.

This won't be any different.

I release the scraps of paper into the wind.

When I reach the gates, there are fewer guards than usual. Only two, where there are usually half a dozen.

I pull my horse to a stop and then dismiss him, wincing as I land on my cut-up feet, and both guards rush to my side in alarm. One kneels in front of me, searching my face, and the other fingers his weapon, scanning the street behind me for pursuers.

"Where is everyone?" I demand. It sounds like an accusation, and the guard in front of me flinches.

"They're . . . doing drills," the other replies. "The whole company. The Prime had some new tactics he wanted to try out. Why? Is there danger?"

I smile sourly. Drills, huh? That can't be a coincidence. No doubt my cousin found some way to put the idea into my father's head.

"Has anyone come in or out since they all left?" I ask.

"Not a single soul," the other assures me. He notices my feet and frowns at them in concern. "Should we call for a healer?" he presses. "What happened?"

I wave off his worry as I process his answer to my question. If no one's come in or out, then maybe whoever Alect was expecting to arrive isn't here yet. Maybe I made it in time.

Or maybe they just found another way in.

"You!" I say, jabbing a finger at the one kneeling before me. "Get the troops back here immediately. I have just become aware of a threat to the Prime and his family. Tell the Captain it's an emergency, and a direct order from the Prospective Seconde. And you!" I swing my finger to the other, larger one. "Don't let *anyone* through this gate. Or out. Unless it's my parents, my sister, or me. You got that?"

They both nod, finally picking up on my desperation.

"Good," I say. "Now go!"

Without waiting to see if they listen, I sprint past them, my mind already on the next task. They shout after me, but I filter out their words, too intent on getting inside and finding out what's happening.

Finding out if my family still lives.

My feet are killing me, dirt and gravel aggravating the cuts from the Outskirts, but my pounding heart is worse.

Where should I go? Where would they usually be this time of day?

I swipe hair out of my eyes and crane my head back to look at the sun. It's directly overhead, shining weakly through the clouds, so it must be around noon. Lunchtime, perhaps?

Our dining room is on the second floor, with a wall of grand, sparkling windows overlooking the realm, and I search it out, panting.

Then I rub my palms over my eyes to make sure I'm really seeing what I'm seeing.

They're there. Right there. All three of them. My father is slicing meat and talking boisterously. My sister is picking at her rice and nodding along. My mother's sipping a drink with a pinkie extended and not one hair out of place.

The way the windowpanes frame them, they look like a painting. Like the very picture of unalarmed normalcy.

My first feeling is relief, as I drink in my sister's face. But when my father throws his head back in laughter at some joke that no one else at the table seems to find funny, I'm surprised by a flash of helpless dismay.

I shove it down, horrified. That's my *father*.

But he's also the one who has made my life torture.

And some part of me wishes that it could be that easy. That he could just be . . . gone.

I shake my head hard to dislodge the thoughts. There's no time to unpack my web of complex feelings toward my father; I need to focus. Because none of this makes sense.

Was Alect lying to me about the threat? What would be the purpose of a bluff like that?

As I falter, replaying all the things he said and all the things he implied, a strange crack on the wall catches my eye.

It's a fairly large fracture, and I don't remember it being there before, but there's something familiar about it, something that gives me pause. The way it seems to pull in all the shadows around it is so peculiar. Almost deliberate. It reminds me of . . .

Of Prime Azele's bodyguard. When he disappeared into a dark crevice in the earth and tore across the grass. Right before he reclaimed his form and severed the spines of three soldiers at once.

As soon as I think it, the cleft begins to move, slicing up the wall and creeping into the open window, feet away from where my family dines. Then it takes form, first outlining the shape of a person and then flooding that outline with color until Rift is there, painted into the picture. Changing it irrevocably.

I hear screams.

I take off running.

My feet don't hurt anymore. I can't even feel them. I *have* to get up there. I throw myself at the stairs, charging recklessly, clumsily. Shouts and pleas, crashes and bangs assault my ears as I sprint down the hall, and I feel attuned to every sound. Was that ripping fabric a dress or a tablecloth? Was that shout one of injury or victory, and who made it?

Then, a few feet before I reach the door, all noise stops.

I jolt to a stop as well, my hands flying to my mouth. Anxious animals squirm beneath my skin as I strain my ears even harder, hoping to hear any sound at all. Any footstep, any voice, any indication that it's not over yet. That there's still hope. There's still life.

But I hear nothing.

I press my hands hard against my lips, swallowing the whimper that rises in my throat. Then I creep forward, trying to quiet even my ragged breaths as I press up against the door.

I don't want to look.

I have to look. I have to know.

But how can I?

Biting down on my lips, I extend a shaking hand and nudge the door forward. When nothing happens, I peer into the crack.

And all I see is blood.

Everywhere. So much of it. The smell hits me like a wave and I resist the urge to retch. Shattered glassware and toppled chairs make my heart sink into my stomach. But I don't see my family. Could they have . . . escaped?

Clinging to the pathetic hope, I lean in farther, searching the floor for bodies even as I pray not to find them.

Then suddenly my gaze collides with Rift's.

His expression is blank, despite the blood spattered across his cheek. His eyes are that same lifeless stone I remember from the battlefield.

For a second he just stares at me.

Then he folds himself into a fissure again, skating toward me across the bloodstained carpet.

I fling myself backward, crashing into the wall behind me. Then I bolt back down the hallway.

He's fast in this form. That shadowy split in the floor hurtles toward me, gaining every second. There's nowhere to go. He'll collide into me soon and then he'll take form and destroy me.

He's only a few seconds away.

Two.

One.

Squeezing my eyes shut, I jump, which is silly, but it's the only thing I can think to do. Incredibly, it works and he shoots past me, careening down the hallway.

I land and then falter, unsure of what to do with my momentary advantage.

But he soon seems to realize that he missed me, and he skids to a stop as well. Then he reverses, swinging rapidly back and forth across the floor, searching for my feet, making shadowy scars in the carpet.

I throw open a window and clamber out, hoisting myself up onto the overhang of the roof and bending my legs at the knees so they disappear from sight as quickly as possible.

Once safely over the ledge, I lean back and slam the window shut again. Then I go still, listening for pursuit and keeping an eye out for any trace of shadow. When nothing comes, I risk crawling over to a skylight and peeking in.

He's taken human form again, and he's searching the hallway and the adjoining rooms, but he hasn't checked the windows.

I hold my breath as he opens every door, overturning furniture and tearing tapestries off walls in his pursuit of me.

Eventually, he folds into his abyss again and skims away, returning to the dining room.

My mind races, not ready to relax yet. Has he really given up? Is he leaving the way he came? Maybe he's not actually supposed to kill me. After all, I wasn't supposed to be here.

On the other hand, maybe he'll be right back. Maybe he's laying a trap. Or maybe he's just taking the time to check the bodies and make sure they're dead.

The bodies . . .

My own thoughts echo in my mind, ripping through me now that I have a minute to process.

Did he really . . . kill all of them? My mother, my father, my sister? Was I mere seconds too late?

I realize I'm crying and wonder how long I have been. They were just right there. Eating. Talking. Living. And now . . . I'm alone.

My heart aches for my mother and my sister, for all the things left unsaid between us, but it's my father's death that I struggle to comprehend the most.

Because it doesn't seem possible. He's the most powerful person I know. It just doesn't feel true that he could be cut down with a sword in an instant like any other mortal.

And, despite all my anger and disgust toward him, I don't know who I am without him.

In that moment of hesitation in the courtyard, the one that possibly cost my family their lives, I thought I would feel some measure of relief at his death. That a burden would be lifted.

But all I feel is confused, and the burden is still there. And in fact, there's another one.

Am I . . . the Prime now?

22

Silver

|2 DAYS UNTIL THE ASSURANCE|

As I run toward the shell of our house, the side of the porch buckles and crashes to the ground, bits of black flames flickering around it.

Magic flame, of course. I've never seen this specific magic before, but I know it immediately. How could I not? It's what made the slums what they are. Prime Gore's magical explosions, the only thing that could shatter Prime Elod's glass trees.

And my house, apparently.

That must be what was in the bottles Alect warned us away from. Was he actually trying to protect us? Or did he know that telling a room full of teens not to touch something was the surest way to get them to do exactly that?

Shards crunch under my boots as I sprint as hard as I can toward the wreckage.

"Rooftop!" I yell. "Vie!"

I don't hear a response.

I grunt and run harder, my boots clomping on the hard-packed earth.

This is all my fault. I told them to grab the bag. And Guerre or Alect or whatever-his-name-is told me he was going to set my house on fire if I didn't get there in time. Where did I think he would keep his fire-setting materials if not his bag? I should have *seen* this.

I reach the bottom of the tree and pull myself up, skirting around the ghostly flames, some of which are floating in the middle of the air.

"Vie!" I scream. "Rooftop!"

There's still no reply, and I don't see them anywhere.

The only sound is the odd, spectral crackling of the fire as it licks at empty space.

Since the porch is gone, I have to make a pretty big leap, but I throw myself forward, grabbing onto the edge of the doorway and crouching in its frame. Wood splinters and crumbles around me.

The door is still there, hanging on one hinge, but beyond it is basically nothing. My house has been reduced to two walls, a sliver of flooring, and half the back room. And I can see from here that my friends aren't in it. Which means . . .

I look down.

Below me is a pile of rubble, familiar and unrecognizable all at once.

But I don't care about any of it.

Because I haven't heard a peep from Rooftop or Vie yet and it's feeling less and less likely that I'm going to find them alive.

My eyes stinging, I drop, landing on the couch, causing stuffing to spill out of it like innards.

"Where are you?" I cry, startled to find that my voice is hoarse. "This isn't funny. Make a noise!" I choke on the last word and the sound of my own panic makes my terror spike.

With an angry shout, I start throwing furniture, chucking

beams, overturning broken piles of things I used to value, looking desperately for an arm or a leg or anything, but there's no sign.

Did the magic obliterate them completely?

I punch the table and it buckles, so I punch it again. And again and again and again until it's nothing but a pile of splintering pieces and my knuckles are bleeding and tears are streaming down my face. It doesn't make me feel remotely better.

I just wanted a future. That's all. A safe place for us. Now the home I have is gone, I helped start a war, I hurt someone who didn't deserve it, someone I've grown close to, and Vie and Rooftop are . . .

Are . . .

My legs give out and I collapse, feeling more broken than the wreckage that surrounds me.

Why did I ever get involved in any of this?

What have I *done*?

I call their names one more time, half sobbing, and when they still don't answer I bury my head in my hands and cry, like I haven't done since my parents died.

I've lost everything.

Everyone.

And the worst part is . . . I deserve it. I got selfish and I tried to get a big payoff without caring who I hurt. I can't be too surprised when one of the people who gets hurt ends up being me. But why couldn't I be the only one? Why did Mance and Rooftop and Vie have to get hurt, too?

I cry until my shirt is soaked, my throat is raw, and the creepy black flames that hover over everything start to flicker away, like fading whispers.

But just as I feel like I might pass out from the weight of the grief pressing down on me, I hear the most beautiful sound in the world.

A cough.

My eyes shoot open and I hold my breath, terrified that I hallucinated the sound.

But then I hear it again.

I lurch to my feet, wading through the rubble toward a bed half propped on a wardrobe.

And when I shove it off, there's Vie, covered in dirt but completely whole, not even a finger missing.

"You suck at rescuing," she rasps. "I've been lying here forever."

"You suck at being rescued," I shoot back, tears dripping down my chin. "Make a freaking noise; what's wrong with you?"

"I *tried*," she croaks. "You were too busy crying like a big baby to hear me."

We grin at each other, and then she pushes herself up on one elbow and I drop to my knees and throw my arms around her neck. She grunts, but she hugs me back.

"Where's Rooftop?" I ask.

She clears her throat, trying to force out more words. "When we opened the bottle . . . there was this weird black stuff. Like liquid, but floating. Rooftop recognized it first and pushed me out the window. It blew up while he was jumping after me. Last I saw, he was thrown somewhere over there." She points to a collapsed wall, and my heart sinks. "I . . . think I passed out for a little. How long has it been?"

"Twenty minutes or so?" I guess.

She curses and tries to get up, but I don't wait for her. I rush over to the wall, tripping in my haste, and duck under it, crawling forward on my stomach.

Rooftop's there, lying limply on the ground, facing me.

His left leg is crushed under the weight of the wall.

His right leg is covered in black spots, like the magic is gnawing away at it, seeping further into his veins.

His eyes are closed.

And his head is covered in blood.

Vie appears beside me, and when she sees Rooftop her normally tough expression cracks and she looks like she's about to cry.

"Can you help?" I ask, putting one hand on the wall.

She winces, but says, "Of course."

We lie on our backs, brace our palms side by side and heave, pushing ourselves to our knees and then our feet until we manage to flip the wall in one big push. It lands with a crash, and then so does Vie, as she collapses next to me. I reach out to help her up, but she's already crawling back toward Rooftop, her hands outstretched to search for a pulse. I hang back, swallowing the lump in my throat, not sure I can handle it if she doesn't find what she's looking for.

When she gasps and then nods, a joyful smile on her face, I'm dizzy with relief, and I lean against the top three shelves of our cupboard for support.

Vie checks his injuries—clumsily, because it's usually Rooftop's job—and declares that the head wound isn't actually that bad; it just bled a lot. He might have a concussion, but he should be okay. The left leg is broken, but the bone isn't sticking out. I throw her my tattered vest and she wraps it above the injury to help stop the blood flow, and then I join her to go over the rest.

We don't know how to treat the magical wound, but at least it doesn't seem to be spreading, and it isn't bleeding either. It's cauterized, like it was made by fire, and yet every black spot is cold to the touch.

He'll live, though.

He'll definitely live.

And now that I know that . . .

I have to make sure Mance will, too.

I stand up.

"Get a healer to clean and dress the injuries properly," I tell Vie. "Plus some kind of painkiller to take the edge off. Whatever he needs; we'll figure out how to pay for it later."

"What exactly are you gonna be doing?" Vie asks, eyes accusing.

I heave a sigh. "Don't be like that, Vie. I *have* to go after her."

"Do you?"

"She could die!"

"So?" Her voice is as sharp as one of her many knives.

"So she doesn't deserve that," I tell her.

"We don't deserve a lot of things that have happened to us," Vie shoots back, standing up to confront me. "That's life."

"I think that's a convenient excuse to be a crappy person," I tell her. "I think a lot of bad things that happen have a little help from selfish people hiding behind excuses just like that. And I'm not going to be one of them. Not anymore."

"But if you—"

"Let him go, Vie," Rooftop says.

Immediately we're both by his side, pushing him back down as he tries to sit up, asking him how he's doing and whether he remembers what happened and what day it is and who we both are.

He shoos us off. "I'm fine, I'm fine. I remember everything. Enough to know that you need to see what I found in that bag before it blew up on us. Get it for me?"

Somehow, in the middle of running from the blast, Rooftop managed to shove the satchel down his shirt. I pull it out, and there's a stack of letters inside, just like the ones I lifted from Guerre's pocket. The other half of the conversation.

"What do they say?" I ask.

Rooftop has a coughing fit before he can answer, and I glare at the dust in the air that still hasn't settled. I glare at the weird magical flames, too, just in case they have anything to do with it.

"He's starting a war," Rooftop wheezes finally.

"I know that part," I interrupt impatiently. "What's the plan for tonight?"

He peels one particular letter away from the rest, this one without the seal of either realm. I skim it rapidly and my stomach sinks. Then I shove the letters back in the satchel and sling it onto my shoulder.

"I have to go," I say. "I'll be back as soon as I can. But I can't just let this play out like this. I can't let—"

"Just one more thing," Rooftop coughs. "One more letter." He pulls this one out of the inside pocket of his coat. "I found it shoved in the corner after that night you stayed over. And . . . I read it."

"Snoop," I say, snatching the paper out of his hand.

But I know what it is before I even look at it.

It's the letter Mance wrote. The one she gave to me what feels like ages ago. The one I didn't believe because it didn't fit with the brutal image I had of her.

The image that was false all along.

Skimming its contents again now, every word rings true, and my throat gets tight.

What might we have averted if I had just believed in her then?

"Go," Rooftop says.

And I do.

23

Mancella Amaryllis Cliff, Title Uncertain

|2 DAYS UNTIL THE ASSURANCE|

My first act as possible Prime of the Cliff Realm is to sob into my knees.

For a long, long time.

Some weak, traitorous piece of my heart wishes that Silver would appear, wrap his arms around me, and tell me again that I'm strong. But my more rational parts tamp that fantasy down, because there's no way to know if he even meant that or if it was just another part of the manipulation.

I won't ever be able to trust him again.

The next thing I wish is that my Captain would show up with her army, but as I search the horizon, I see no sign of them. Whatever "drills" are occupying them, they must have been a long way off.

Which means I'm on my own.

My forehead thunks against my folded arms and I take a shuddering breath. If I'm wishing for useless things as it is, then I wish Mara were here. I wish she'd just appear next to me with some snarky comment, like—

"See, now, this time I actually believe that you're desolate.

You've come a long way with the crying thing. Great work."

It takes me a minute to realize that the voice wasn't in my mind. I jerk my head up to see Mara stuck halfway out of a skylight.

At first I can only blink at her, thinking she must be a figment of my imagination.

But then a wave of jagged joy washes over me, and my eyes prickle with a renewed swell of tears.

With an incredulous half laugh, half sob, I hurry to help her, hauling her over the edge and onto the tile. Then I throw myself at her in a crushing hug, almost knocking both of us back into the skylight. She rubs my head tolerantly, pretending to be annoyed as I sniffle into her shoulder. But she doesn't push me away.

"Mother and Father?" I warble.

"Both alive," she says.

My head rushes with dizzying emotion. I'm glad, but it's also . . . complicated. A minute ago I didn't know who I was without my father, but having him thrust back into being doesn't feel good either. I can't go back to the way it was before. I won't.

It's uncomfortable. Not knowing how to feel. My animals churn in confusion, and it's so overwhelming that I feel like I might black out.

But then I force myself to sober, and my animals settle.

Because if everyone is still alive it means that today's events are far from over.

With one last shaky exhale, I loosen my grip on Mara and sit back. "There's a lot we need to talk about."

"You're right," she responds grimly, and her tone makes me snap to attention.

It's only then I realize that the arm I was just clutching has an enormous gash in it, and half-dried rivulets of blood coat her skin.

"You're hurt!" I cry, dropping her arm immediately, only to reach for it again to examine the wound. "Why didn't you say anything?" Then I shake my head, scolding myself. "No, I should have noticed. After all, I saw the blood in the room. I knew Rift had managed to hurt *someone*."

"Actually," she says. "Our dear old dad did this."

My fingers slow their anxious probing and I look up at her, brow furrowed. "What?" I ask. "Why?"

"Because—" She cuts off mid-sentence, suddenly looking nervous. It's an odd look on her, one I haven't seen in a while.

"What?" I ask again.

She frowns, though only half her mouth is visible beneath the ever-present scarf. "Mancella," she says. "There's a secret I've been keeping for a long time."

Oh, good. More secrets. "Is this about your magic?" I ask dryly.

She rears back in surprise. "You know?"

I go back to tending her wound, ripping a strip off the bottom of my dress to bind it. "Not much. Only that you have it and that you . . . made that bracelet? Is that true?"

Her face falls. "About that . . . I'm so sorry. I didn't know what he planned to use it for. If I did, I . . . well, I don't know. I'm not the best at standing up to him. Not like you. But I swear I didn't make it for that."

I pull the bindings tight, avoiding eye contact. "What did you make it for, then?" I ask.

She winces, although whether it's because of my question or because I'm binding her wound a little too snugly, I can't be sure. "I don't know," she says morosely. "I never know what any of it's for. He asks me to try to do something and I just do it. It keeps him off my back, keeps him from coming up with creative ways to force me. Besides, he usually spends most of his energy on—"

"Me," I interrupt. "You were hiding behind me."

She hangs her head, her mouth dour. "Yes," she admits bleakly.

I shake my head as I finish up the binding. "Thanks a lot, sis," I say, letting her arm fall into her lap.

"Do you hate me?" she asks, tone guarded.

"It's hard to say," I answer honestly. "I've been betrayed by too many people today. I'll have to decide later which blows I'm willing to forgive." She starts to respond, a question in her eyes, but I hurry on, not wanting to talk about all of that right now. "So how long have you been keeping this a secret?" I ask. "When did it finally manifest?"

She blows out a breath. "You remember . . . the tests . . ."

I nod, feeling sick. I thought Father had stopped conducting his experiments on her because he'd given up, or perhaps because he'd developed some compassion. I should have known he'd only stop when he got what he wanted.

"Tell me about it," I say quietly, bracing myself.

She looks at her lap. "It was when you refused the wolf," she says. "He got angry. He . . . often tested me harder when he was frustrated with other things."

I swallow a surge of bile in the back of my mouth. "I never thought—"

She holds up a hand. "I know you didn't. I've never blamed you."

I nod miserably, even though guilt still clutches at my throat.

Mara puts her hand back in her lap and twists her fingers together as she continues. "Anyway . . . you were bedridden, and Mother never left your side while you recovered, which means you were both out of the way."

"Wait . . . she didn't?" I ask, surprised.

"You know Mother," Mara says. "She always . . . tries. She *wants* to stop him. She's just never quite strong enough."

I *didn't* know that, actually.

To be honest, I don't know if it's better or worse than her not trying at all. But that isn't the point of this discussion, so I put it aside for another time.

"So . . . what happened?" I ask in a low voice.

She swallows. "He . . ." She falters on the word and it takes her a minute to be able to continue. I hold her hand, a pit growing in my stomach. "All the other experiments felt planned," she explains. "They took forethought. They were horrible, but they didn't feel entirely real. I knew he wouldn't actually let me die. But when you decided not to fight that wolf . . ." A tear leaks out of her eye and she swipes at it, annoyed. "He was so angry. And I was . . . there. He grabbed me by the hair and threw me against the wall, and before I could get over the shock of it, he had a knife. And then he just came *at* me. He wasn't holding back at all. He slashed at me over and over and over."

She clutches at her stomach, and I realize I haven't seen it in a long time. She always wears such high-necked, long-sleeved dresses that cover most of her body. I feel sick as I look at the one she's wearing now, wondering how much it's hiding.

"I really thought he was going to kill me," she says, voice trembling. "And then the magic in me snapped, just like he wanted. It craved my blood, too. It *liked* to feel me bleed out. It wanted more of me, wanted . . . my pain. But at least it also gave me a way out. When he reared back for another swing, I swiped my blood into a line in front of me, and when his hand came down it hit a wall. And he couldn't touch me anymore."

As she talks her breathing gets harsher and she struggles to slow it. "I finished the circle around me and just sat inside it shaking. I almost died anyway, because I didn't want to break the barrier long enough to let him heal me. I wasn't sure he really would, even though his words had turned sweet and congratulatory. Eventually he had to just leave the supplies in the room and go. I patched *myself* up. Then I limped my way to my room and locked myself inside. For weeks. He left food and bandages and medicine outside my room every day. But he never apologized. He never even implied that he regretted it."

I remember those weeks. I was bedridden myself as he put me back in the arena with wolf after wolf and I continued to refuse to fight. I had no idea what Mara was suffering at the same time.

"Why did you keep it a secret?" I ask.

She gives a dry, bitter laugh. "Why do you think? He liked your power a little better than mine. He wanted our realm to be strong, and he didn't think my magic was good enough. Of course, he tried to push it as far as it could go at first. In the last couple years, we've learned which parts of my body the magic accepts and which it doesn't. We've learned how to make it block magic and not just physical objects. We've learned how to infuse the magic into doorways and walls and"—she hangs her head—"bracelets. But when he felt he'd finally reached the magic's limit and found it insufficient, that's when he announced the Assurance, when he decided to make you his heir. Even though I knew what it would mean for you . . . all I could feel was relief."

As I take this in, I look at the already bloodstained cloth wrapped around her arm.

"So that's why he cut you today," I realize.

"Yes," she says, nodding. "To make us a shield around the

parlor. Mother and Father are still there. I slipped away while Rift was distracted looking for another entrance. Anyway. I could have used spit or hair or tears, but blood is fastest and strongest, and . . . Well, Father made the choice for me."

Of course he did. Disgust churns in my gut.

"You know, Mara," I say, voice low. "If you had told me . . . I would have acted as your buffer willingly. You didn't have to lie or trick me to ensure my protection; I would have given it to you."

Her face crumples, and again the expression is startling on her. My sister is always so composed. I hadn't realized how much she was dealing with all on her own.

"You're my little sister," she tells me. "I'm supposed to be the one protecting you. I'm . . ." She chokes on the words. "I'm so sorry. You don't know—"

I sigh, my own feelings complicated. "I wasn't trying to make you feel bad."

"You have every right to make me feel bad. I *should* feel bad. Listen." She reaches a hand into her pocket, fiddling with something there. "Before I lose my nerve and go back to being a coward, there's something else I have to tell you. Something Father doesn't know about yet. An experiment of my own. I've been saving it for the right time, and I thought that might be the Assurance, but maybe it's now."

Despite the certainty of her words, she hesitates before drawing her hand out of the pocket. When she does, she shows me a necklace, one with strange, oddly colored glass beads. Leaning closer, I realize that each is filled with something horrific. Hair, blood . . . I think I even see a tooth.

"What does it do?" I ask warily.

Her eyes trace each bead, lingering on memories I'm not sure I want to hear. Then she looks back at me.

"I've made a lot of barrier necklaces," she says, thumbing the two at her throat, which I now realize are the exact color of congealed blood. "Mostly they're just physical barriers that can trap a person in place. The bracelets I make trap magic. Some of my jewelry can block both. But this . . ." She leans forward, like she's afraid to even speak it. "It doesn't just block magic," she whispers. "It *takes* it."

My skin prickles. "Really?" I find myself whispering, too, even though there's no one else out here. But the idea is so unthinkable, so forbidden, that it almost feels sacred.

"Yes," she assures me. "At least . . . I think so. I haven't had a real test subject to work with for obvious reasons, but . . . I made it for you. Every time he did something truly awful to you, I made another bead. And when I heard about the fight with the Grasslands, well . . . let's just say it's finished now. It's your choice, of course, but . . . I *think* it can undo what the Broken Citadel did to you. Untwist what was twisted. Make you truly normal. *Free.*" Her hair falls in front of her face. "I owe you that. Especially if someone's running around killing those of us in line for the throne. If you get rid of your magic, well . . . you'd be ineligible. You'd be safe."

My mind sticks on the words "untwist what was twisted." I didn't know that's what it felt like to her, too.

And she's offering the chance to undo it. To go back to the moment in time when my life went down the wrong track, and straighten my path, my very soul.

"Yes," I say, without realizing I've spoken. The word isn't actual assent, just me marveling at the very idea of it. The concept is just so thrilling, so *enticing*. Far more than a mere shield in a bracelet, she's offering to make me whole.

But she must have interpreted the word as an agreement, because she holds the necklace up and it begins to glow, an unsettling bruise-like purple.

"All right," she says, "brace yourself."

Before I can react, she puts the necklace over my head and the glow surges into my skin, creating a sucking, hungry emptiness inside of me that gnaws at parts of me nothing else has ever touched.

It doesn't feel like fixing.

It feels like ripping.

In the space of a gasp, every insect I have is wrenched from my inner well and obliterated. They leak out of my skin in swarms, ignite in that same beaten purple, and then disappear. I can't feel them anywhere. While I scramble to process that, toads, frogs, lizards, and mice are thrown out next, convulsing on the ground as Mara's power eats them away.

Then the magic comes for my kitten. He tumbles out of my body, yowling as the glow ignites his fur, writhing like he's in pain, and within me, that emptiness begins to gobble up the space in my soul that is his.

"No," I scream. "No, no, no!"

I unclasp the necklace, flinging it off. That seems to stop it, but to be sure, I dismiss my kitten and then summon him again into my arms.

He looks as frantic as I do, but as I run searching fingers through his fur, I find no hair out of place, no residual magic clinging to his form. I bury my face in his warm, fuzzy side, breathing deeply.

"I'm sorry, I'm sorry," Mara says, wringing her hands. "What did I do?"

I try to summon the butterflies, the bees and gnats and mosquitoes that I've slapped throughout my life, but they aren't there. I call on my reptiles and rodents, but absolutely nothing comes forth. There are only spots of gaping absence where they used to be. And I feel . . . less.

"It's okay," I say, both to myself and to Mara, even though those pricks of emptiness feel like yawning caverns. "I just . . . I don't want them to go away. I may hate how I got them, but they are still mine. They are still me. I am who I am because of what I've been through, and while I wouldn't exactly do it over . . ." I lay my hand on my kitten's head, thumbing his ears. "I'm not giving up what I've gained, either. We'll . . . we'll come up with another plan."

Mara's face is stricken, and I soften, laying a hand on her knee. "Thank you for making it, though. I can't imagine what it cost you, and I appreciate that sacrifice. More than you know."

This seems to cheer her a little, and she gives me a small smile. Then she scoops the necklace up and presses it into my palm.

"In case you change your mind," she says.

I doubt I will, but I still accept it, sliding the beads into my pocket where they clink against the bracelet already there. If nothing else, it seems to give Mara a small measure of relief to be rid of it.

"All right," I say. "Now what are we going to do about Rift?"

❧✻☙

I secure my dress in place, concealing the armor now clinging to my skin beneath.

Mara stands in my doorway, having draped herself in jewelry

and scarves I've seen her wear a hundred times, never questioning why the black threads woven into the fabric are the exact shade of her hair, or why so many of the beads are filled with a clear liquid that looks like tears. These, she tells me, are her best barriers, capable of containing both physical and magical matter. They're not as powerful as the weaponized necklace that still sits in my pocket, but they'll make a nice trap.

"You ready?" she asks.

My eyes drift to the dirty saucepan sitting on my bookshelf. The starsprout I planted there has grown bigger now, multiplying so much that it barely fits into the handful of soil within. The poor thing will need more space to grow soon. With a wistful smile, I pluck one tiny bloom and tuck it behind my ear.

"I'm ready."

We steal back across the rooftop, trying to keep our steps light and soft, until we finally huddle around the skylight overlooking the dining room.

Rift paces below, prowling in front of a dark stripe of blood that paints the doorway to the parlor. My parents stand on the other side of it, unmoving. Watching.

The creak the glass makes when I wrench the skylight open shatters the tense silence, and Rift whips around.

"Good luck," Mara whispers, sinking into the shadows just out of view.

Feeling Rift's eyes on me, I don't respond. I merely drop down into the room below, and then stand tall, meeting Rift's gaze with my own.

As we predicted, he doesn't try to talk. He simply folds into shadow and skims across the marble floors toward me, leaving a dusky wake.

But this time I don't run. I hold firm, counting down the seconds until he reaches me.

Three.

I glance up at Mara, who has reappeared at the edge of the window, clutching a weighted chain.

Two.

Rift hurtles forward, closing the distance rapidly, and I tense, readying myself to sidestep at just the right time.

But before I can get to *one,* something slams into me from the side.

Unprepared for it, I crash to the floor, a considerable weight slamming down on top of me.

Rift veers to follow me, having somehow felt the vibrations of my movement, and Mara's chain clatters uselessly to the floor in the spot he would otherwise have been.

My mind races, and I need to recalibrate quickly, because Rift is still hurtling toward me and I'm now out of Mara's range.

Angry and panicked, I shove at the weight on my chest and look up at it.

Only to see Silver lying on top of me, wearing a sheepish grin.

24

Silver

|2 DAYS UNTIL THE ASSURANCE|

Okay, so Operation Fix Stuff is off to a rocky start. Between Mara scowling from the roof, the definitely-supposed-to-do-something chain that fell next to my head, and Mance glaring at me with a jaguar-level ferocity, it's clear I've managed to mess something (else) up.

Not to mention the assassin is still hurtling toward us.

Thinking fast, I roll to the side—an action that elicits infuriated shrieks from the girl in my arms—but that only causes the creepy shadow crack to veer again, so instead I leap up and haul Mance onto the table.

"What are you *doing* here?" she hisses. "Of all the—"

"Yell at me later," I tell her. "What's the necklace do?"

She kicks at a plate, sending it clattering to the ground, presumably in an effort to misdirect Rift. "It forms a barrier," she huffs. "We were *trying* to—"

"Got it."

As Rift springs into being, trying to figure out why we're not touching the ground anymore, I fling myself off the table, scoop up the oversized chain, and toss it over his head. He turns, and

Mance throws herself at the necklace on the floor, engaging some clasp. A breath later, when Rift's sword arcs toward her, it halts in midair, mere inches from her face. And it makes an odd . . . crunching sound.

He frowns, then tries to take a step forward, only to meet the same resistance. He folds back into shadow, but that doesn't work either.

Curious, I reach out a hand, and there's something solid in the air above the necklace. It feels weird and scratchy, like knots of matted hair. I look down and see Mara's black tresses threaded throughout the chain's metal links.

Gross.

Gross but cool.

Behind us, the Prime draws his own sword and slashes a cut in the ground, severing the line of blood that shields the doorframe. It goes from bright crimson to an aged brown in a second, and he storms past it.

For whatever reason, he heads to me first.

"*You!*" he bursts out. "What are *you* doing here?"

I knew he'd remember me.

As he stalks forward, I straighten, my gaze leveling on his. Through the power of my scowl alone, I try to convey something like, "Look, I still think you're a monster and if it were up to me you'd probably be dead, but I doubt your daughter would forgive me if I killed you and at some point her happiness became more important to me than my hatred of you, which is kind of a big deal for me so I'm trying not to mess it up."

I doubt all that got through, though.

I glance at Mance for help, but she only crosses her arms. "He's no one important," she says cuttingly. "And he's leaving now."

"Hold on," I say, shoving down the well of hurt that rises at her words. "I understand why you don't trust me, but I promise I'm here to help."

"You're doing a great job," she scoffs, and I'm once again struck by the difference in the way she's treating me now. Struck by the fact that I deserve it.

"Just give me a chance, okay? I'm not even here to talk to you. I'm here to talk to him."

I jab a thumb at Rift, who has taken human form again, and Mance narrows her eyes. "About what?" she asks, each word edged.

In answer, I turn to face Rift, opening the satchel and withdrawing a fistful of letters. "Do you recognize these?" I hold up the slate-gray seals and he narrows his eyes at them.

"Of course I do," he says stonily. "Why do you have them? For that matter, who are you?"

I once again wave away the question and kneel down on the ground in front of him, laying out the letters so he can see them. At first he just scowls down at me, but eventually he lowers himself enough to look. Mance glowers over my shoulder, but even she leans forward.

I take a deep breath, relieved that they're at least hearing me out.

Now I just have to make sure I convince them.

"These are the letters your Prime wrote," I explain, fanning one of the stacks. "But *these* are the ones our realm actually received." I leave the second stack unfolded and facing toward him, so he can skim for phrases like "unwilling to negotiate" and "building battlements" and "inevitable war."

Rift squints at them, careful not to touch the wall, his frown growing more and more pronounced. "Why?" he growls.

"Her advisor, Guerre," I tell him. "The one who has guided her so dutifully since she took the throne. He's been swapping them out for as long as she's been writing them, trying to convince her—convince *you*—that our Prime was a warmonger and her only chance at peace was for you to kill him and his savage daughters. He promised that the next successor would give her the alliance she craved, never letting on that *he* was that successor."

Rift sucks in a breath at this, and behind me I hear an outraged bellow from the Prime, then Mance's urgent shushing.

I'm briefly encouraged that she's at least letting me talk.

"He killed Sangua." I brandish a letter with the recipe for a fast-spreading poison followed by a receipt for the purchase of its ingredients. "And then he made himself indispensable to Azele by helping her broker an agreement that both sides already wanted. Finally, when those falsified negotiations got to a breaking point, he tried to use *you* to get him the throne here, so he'd essentially be ruling two realms at once. It's all there . . ."

Rift scans the pages, brow furrowed, occasionally asking me to turn one over, or hold it up. Finally, he meets my gaze.

"I knew there was something suspicious about Sangua's death," he says. "And yet I never cast those suspicions on Guerre. He always redirected them, toward more convenient targets. Clearly, I was a fool to let him. But even so . . ." His eyes flick over my shoulder, where Mance and her father still hover. "Let's say I believe you, and that all the letters we've received have been lies. What then? What's the truth? You say your realm wants peace, but I've seen no evidence of that. Perhaps our conflict on the plains was the result of our disrupted communications, but when we first met with you, your Prospective Seconde summoned a beast in the middle of dinner, and there were no falsehoods between us then. You've explained away some words, but how can you explain away those actions?"

Frankly, I'm glad he asked.

I unfurl the last letter and press it up against the invisible wall, which gives slightly beneath my fingers.

"This is the letter Mance, uh, *Mancella* wrote later that night, one that she tried to send to you." I swallow, remembering that I'm the reason her words never made it, and the small gasp Mance makes behind me tells me that she's putting that together, too. I wince but press on. "If you want truth, this is it. There's no more accurate record of her intentions."

Rift crosses his arms and leans against the other side of the circle, a move that does not look possible and—I now know—probably feels incredibly weird. But Rift's expression is cool as he takes in Mance's curling script.

Finally, he turns his head sharply to the side. "I've read enough. Release me and I will return to my Prime with this new information. We will talk about what she wants to do."

"How do we know you're not just going to try to kill us again when we let you go?" the Prime asks.

It's a legitimate question, but the snide tone in which he asks it makes me ponder very seriously whether I'm feeling treasonous enough to slap the Prime upside the head right now.

"You'll have to trust me, I suppose," Rift replies, somewhat testily. "The way I am being asked to trust you."

The Prime frowns, but Mance hurries forward. Even though I read most of the letters and I know that peace is Prime Azele's primary interest, I still hold my breath when she unclasps the necklace and tosses it to Mara, who has now dropped into the room as well.

Rift snorts like he thought she wouldn't really do it. Then he sticks his foot out slowly, putting it down when he meets no resistance.

He angles a look sideways at Mance, one hand on his sword, and my heart leaps into my throat. But she meets his gaze with one of her sunshine smiles and my anxiety eases a little. Only a heartless person wouldn't trust that face.

Thankfully, the bodyguard must not be one, because he folds back into shadow, splitting across the room until he plunges out of the window he came through. The shadowy cracks he left in the carpet flicker and slowly start to fade.

Everyone in the room releases a breath, me included. Then Mance turns that sunshine smile on me, and my breath catches all over again. It's not her usual full-force beaming—really just the edge of dawn breaking around the corners of her lips—but it's still the first time she's smiled at me since my betrayal was revealed. It's the first time I might deserve it. And it's the first time she's given me a glimmer of hope that forgiveness might be possible.

My chest swells with warmth and I grin back, taking an unconscious step toward her as her smile draws me in.

"Well. That was heartwarming," says a voice by the door. "Truly, what a touching moment. You all must be very proud."

I freeze in place.

By the time I rip my eyes away from Mance's rapidly crumbling expression and look, Alect is already strolling inside, a disapproving frown on his face.

"I told you to stay out of it, Mancella," he says, drawing his sword. "It didn't have to come to this."

"Alect?" Prime Merod gasps, his large eyebrows drawing together in surprise.

Mance steps forward, narrowing her eyes at her cousin. "Which Alect are you?" she asks. "The real one or the twisted one?"

For a moment, conflict flashes across his face.

But then it sets.

"They're all real, Mancella. They're all me. Splitting just lets certain parts of me take fuller control. Sometimes . . . I need that."

Her eyes widen and her head shakes in denial.

He only gives her a self-conscious wince. "I didn't tell you before because I wanted to preserve the faith you've always had in me. But now . . . it's too late. You've tied my hands. I have no choice but to proceed from here alone." His grip on the sword tightens. "Goodbye, Mancella. For what it's worth . . . I'm sorry."

His form begins to split and Mancella cries out as the body that's peeling itself away shoots her a sadistic grin.

Thinking fast, I draw two daggers from my boots and shoot forward. Maybe he's vulnerable as he's splitting.

I aim for both chests, but one body twists away as the other dissipates into mist.

Cursing, I dive in front of Mance before the second one materializes, and when it does I point a dagger at each.

"If you want to get to her, you'll have to go through me," I say.

The first Alect looks upset, but the second one turns, looking at me curiously, his face deceptively pleasant.

"I'm not sure why you think I'd be opposed to that," he says.

Then he lunges.

25

Mancella Amaryllis Cliff, Title in Jeopardy

|2 DAYS UNTIL THE ASSURANCE|

I grab Silver and yank him out of the way as Alect strikes the air and then disintegrates in front of us.

Only to reappear behind us.

And beside us.

And . . .

Wait.

As Silver and I press our backs into each other, multiple Alects peel off the first two and pop up throughout the room. One is laughing, one is clenching his fists, one has tears streaming down his face. One backs away in fear, one reaches for me, and one starts barking orders at the others. One sneers, one cringes, one cracks his knuckles. One stretches, one crouches low to the ground, and one seems to pray. The final Alect is the one with the smirk and the sword.

Altogether there are thirteen. Thirteen copies of my cousin, spread throughout the room.

I have a breath to take them all in, and then everyone starts moving at once, and the room becomes a battlefield.

Only one of them has the sword, but that doesn't mean the

others are useless. Two pairs of hands grab at me as the sword-bearer advances, and it's only because Silver plunges a knife into each of their backs that I'm able to squirm out in time.

As the sword-bearing Alect mists away, I throw myself at another, kneeing his stomach and headbutting the bottom of his jaw. There's a crack as his head snaps back and I feel his jawbone give. Then he sags to the ground at my feet.

The way his limp body hits the floor makes my stomach roil, but another Alect attacks before I get a chance to dwell on it. Or to check if he's still breathing. A lump in my throat, I turn away from him and focus on the new opponent.

Silver stays by my side, lashing out with his daggers any time an enemy gets too close, his anxious amber eyes constantly checking on me.

My father weaves through the melee, freezing Alects in place and then slitting their throats with his own blade. He targets the versions that look the least likely to fight back.

Mara flings the rest of her necklaces and manages to entrap three of them before she runs out. Then she looks at the still-oozing gash in her arm before wincing and clawing it open again, making blood flow in rivulets down her arm.

My mother backs into a corner, cowering. One of the Alects tries to assure her that he has no intention of harming her, since her lack of magic makes her ineligible to rule, but Father cuts him down before he can finish the sentiment.

Mara pushes both parents farther into the corner before painting a line on the ground around the three of them.

"Mancella, come on!" she says, stopping her line while there's still enough space for Silver and me to slip through before she closes it. I grab Silver's hand and we sprint toward them, dodging fists and snatching fingers.

"Wait," Father calls. "If we all just take shelter again, nothing will be solved. We need to end it. Use this!"

He tosses me something and I leap for it, snatching it from the air as Silver plows into an Alect who tried to get there first.

In my hand is a familiar crescent-shaped bottle. Sleeping gas, the kind the healers use to make me go unconscious after a fight in the arena.

I clutch it gratefully. Hopefully it's enough to knock out the rest of the crowd. Briefly, I wonder if they'll each have different nightmares.

"Remember to cover your face!" my father shouts as Mara finishes the line and hems the three of them in.

"Sleeve over your mouth," I tell Silver. "Don't inhale." He complies.

A couple of the Alects hear me and cover their own mouths as well, so I uncork the bottle and throw it in a panic before they have a chance to spread the message to the others.

Then several things happen at once.

Instead of the pearl-colored mist I'm expecting, a sooty substance somewhere between liquid and smoke leaks from the bottle as it arcs toward the middle of the crowd, leaving a trail that stays unnaturally suspended. It's like the air is water and someone's dribbled ink all through it. I haven't seen this substance before, and my mind doesn't work fast enough to process what it is.

Silver's does.

"No!" he cries. "*Mance!*"

The next thing I know, he's slamming into me, pushing me out of the way with urgent hands and desperate, wide-flung eyes.

Then the air itself explodes.

I am hurled backward and hit the wall. Around me, I hear several smacks, slams, and thuds as various other objects and bodies make impact, but I can't see anything. Sinister black flames hover in the air, obscuring my view, and my ears are ringing. My mind seems stuck, unable to process what just happened.

I was only supposed to be throwing knockout gas.

The entire room wasn't supposed to *explode*.

Silver is slumped over my chest, and where the inky matter coats his back, it eats holes into his clothes and then keeps going, burning into his skin. I whimper. My hands hover over the wounds, not sure if I should touch them. Then I realize that he isn't moving and lose all hesitation.

I frantically feel for a heartbeat, my trembling fingers probing his neck and his wrists. Everywhere the blackness touches feels deathly cool.

Finally, just as I find a reassuring pulse in his throat, he groans and his eyes flutter open to meet mine.

"You okay?" he asks. His voice is hoarse.

I want to shake him, but it seems unwise. He still looks one step away from total collapse. "Why?" I gasp. "I have armor, Silver!" I roll up one sleeve to reveal the black suit. "Why didn't you dive *behind* me?"

He makes a noise that's half laugh and half cough. "Hasn't anyone told you?" he croaks. "Some things are more important than looking out for myself. Some things . . . like you."

He barely gets the words out before he sags onto me, his body heavy and slack. I close my eyes and swallow back the emotions rising in my throat.

I was holding on to my hurt and anger even through Silver's

reveal of the letters. I couldn't be sure that it wasn't another act or another part of his plan. And besides, I just wasn't ready to let it go yet.

But if there's any action to judge a person by, risking your life to save another has to be one of the most telling. I believe him. Whatever else the circumstances might have been, in this moment, I believe that he cares about me. That he doesn't want to hurt me anymore.

I just need him to wake up so I can finish yelling at him.

Blowing out a long breath, I adjust his weight to a more comfortable angle and settle in for however long it might take for help to come, determined not to leave Silver's side until I know he's being cared for.

But then, out of nowhere, a feeling slices through me that I didn't expect.

And as soon as I recognize it, the breath evaporates from my lungs.

My magic.

It's surging.

It's . . . thrilled.

It only feels this way when . . .

Sick dread washes over me and I scramble to feel Silver's neck again, my fingers shaking so violently I have to grip one hand with the other before I can get a good read.

It's there. That steady, reassuring rhythm.

Which means it isn't him. He isn't the one dying.

But it's someone.

Mara finished that line, right?

"Mara?" I call.

"We're fine," she calls back. "We're all fine."

Still my magic surges up my throat, choking me.

Which means there's only one person left who it could be.

I guess it shouldn't be too surprising. Alect's bodies are strewn all over the room, hovering black flames flickering around them. When I threw the bottle, I did my best to hit as many of them as I could.

One by one they blink away. Whether they go back into Alect or whether they're gone for good, I can't be sure.

Nausea washes over me, but there's something more important.

If the magic hasn't stopped surging yet, it means that at least one of him is still alive.

I move Silver off me as gently as possible. Then I grit my teeth and crawl straight into the flames.

The floating blazes dance around me, and I avoid as many as I can. But I'm still rushing, desperate and hopeful, so I can't avoid them all. When they touch my armor, I don't feel a thing. But when they touch my hands, or brush up against the side of my face, my skin stings with a strange, deep chill that eats at me, burrowing into my flesh until my very bones feel coated in ice.

I ignore it, filtering through the bizarre magic haze as I search for any sign of life, examining body after body with my cousin's blue eyes, even as some of them disappear in front of me.

Some Alects are missing limbs. Some are missing parts of their faces. The blast—which I now realize was one of Prime Gore's magical explosions that someone, for some reason, put into the wrong bottle—obliterated everything it touched. The bodies look like they were made of no more than clay and someone sliced chunks of them away, leaving only cauterized, black-tinted flesh.

Finally, I find an Alect with his eyes open.

And a gaping, coal-black hole in his chest.

His gaze crashes into mine, and he looks vulnerable. Unsure, like when we were kids.

"Which Alect are you?" I whisper.

He opens his mouth to respond, but the words won't form. All he can manage is a low rasping noise, like a dry whimper. Still, I can tell from his eyes. Whatever other parts of Alect this body might have held, his love for me was one of them.

Tears track down my cheeks and I curl up next to him, laying my head on his shoulder like I used to when I was younger. It's nostalgic and horrifying at the same time, and I squeeze my eyes shut.

He still smells the same. Like ginger tea and old books.

I heave a breath and open my eyes again, leaning back. With one shaking hand, I take the starsprout that I tucked behind my ear earlier and hold it out to him, unsure if he'd even want something so silly.

But his gaze softens and his hand lifts an inch off the floor.

He manages a weak smile, and I grip him tight, pressing the flower between our clasped hands. And then I watch, shattered, as his light fades away. Soon those sky blue eyes of his, the ones I only just got back in my life, the ones I still haven't figured out yet, are staring at nothing at all. And this body doesn't fade away. Which means he's . . . really gone.

I have exactly one second to mourn.

Then his spirit rushes into me, all at once, and I scream.

I scream like I'm being tortured. Like *I'm* the one who's dying, because that's how it feels.

It's never been this powerful before. No animal had a soul complex enough to fill me up this much. Alect's emotions, his personality, his essence form within me, attaching themselves to my very soul as more useless tears stream down my face and I claw at my stomach, fighting the feeling.

He was right about all the experiences he'd had. I crave foods I've never tried and miss places I've never been. I used to long for adventures like these, and I find it bitterly ironic that I am getting a taste of them now, but it's only an aftertaste. Just the remnants of someone else's journey.

At the core of all of it, I feel Alect's pain. The loss of his father, the powerlessness he felt, and the relentless drive he had to get that power back. I understand all the different Alects at once, the way he split himself, and even the way that some parts of him were shocked and revolted by what other parts had done. The way he feared himself. And the way he kept trying anyway, kept fighting for what he wanted, for the world he thought he could build.

I weep for me, and I weep for him, and for all his unfulfilled ambitions, all his unhealed wounds. As I weep, his sightless corpse stares back at me, with a yawning, grotesque hole still growing in his chest.

Behind me, my father laughs.

Not a bitter laugh, but a jubilant one. A triumphant one. One that reminds me of the sick victorious feeling my magic forces into my body with every kill, the same one it pumped into my veins just moments ago.

The sound is so odd, so out of place, that it stifles my sobs in my throat.

I sit there, breathing, clutching my stomach, the tears I've already shed still dripping down my cheeks.

I hope with all I am that I heard wrong.

But then my father laughs again.

"I knew it!" he crows. "I *knew* that would work. You can feel him, right? I can tell that you can. Summon, summon! Let's see what happens!"

I hear him scuff the floor with his boot, presumably breaking my sister's barrier, and approach.

Slowly, I rise, my back still turned to him, my breaths getting shallow. Fury buzzes through my veins.

"After your stunt with that girl, I knew I'd never get you to end a life willingly," Father gloats. "So I made the bottle, hoping for an opportunity. *Finally*, those plans have paid off."

My hands clench, and my animals riot within me, so violently that I almost can't see straight. The idea of him carrying a bottle of death in his pocket, just waiting for the chance to paint my hands with blood, makes me want to scream.

And he's *still* talking. "But that's not all; we've made two discoveries today!" he continues, delighted. "Now we know that your magic works on humans, *and* that you can use magic to kill so long as your foe also possesses magic. A fair fight, right? If you're fighting an animal, then *of course* a fair fight means no weapons. But an armed human you could perhaps use more force against. That's what I was hoping would happen when we battled the Grasslands Realm. But magic against the magicless still proved to be too unbalanced. Fortunate for us, then, that a victim with magic volunteered himself, right?"

I tilt my head to the side, still not looking at him. "Silver was here, too," I hiss. "Does it matter to you at all that he was caught in the blast? That he could have—"

I cut myself off mid-sentence because the answer is clear.

It doesn't matter to him.

It never has.

Every collateral consequence has been completely worth it in his twisted mind, so long as the dark power within me could keep growing stronger. The power that I never wanted, that he forced on me to begin with.

There's no point in listening to his justifications anymore.

His actions have spoken for themselves.

And it's time to let my own actions speak for me.

I whip around, my expression fierce, black flames flickering on either side of me as my predators surge into being around me, snarling and snapping their jaws.

My father falters in the middle of whatever explanation he was offering. His eyes dart from one to the next.

"Now, Mancella," he starts. "You wouldn't do anything to hurt me, would you? Not you. Not the girl who mourns ladybugs and kittens."

My creatures growl and my own voice joins them as a hiss. "Why not?" I ask. "Isn't this what you taught me? Violence? Power? Did it really never occur to you that I'd unleash your lessons back on you?"

He recoils and begins to look worried. "Let's take a minute to calm down," he implores me. "You don't want to do anything rash."

"Rash?" I breathe, advancing on him. My animals move with me, our motions scarily in sync. "This isn't rash. This has been building for years. *You* have been building it, with every death you forced on me, every creature you condemned, every experiment you thought up in your mind, and every human being you threw away in pursuit of your sick quest for power."

I step forward and flames lick at my side, but I welcome the chill. It matches the cold certainty that has gripped my heart. "I understand now," I continue. "You will never stop. Whatever love you have for me, or for Mara, it's clear that it's not enough to keep you from breaking us, or even from killing us should you deem that necessary." I gesture behind me at Mara's still-bleeding arm. "So if you won't stop yourself, then I will stop you."

My animals charge forward, snarling, and he draws his sword to fight them.

But they are only a distraction.

Alect is knit to my soul in a way the animals aren't, and when I tug at his spirit I don't expect him to appear outside of my body as they do. Just like the first time I slapped a fly on the way back from the Broken Citadel, there is a sudden, basic understanding that settles around me as far as how this new magic will work.

I could put on his body like a cloak, stand here as Alect instead of as myself. But his physical form isn't what I reach for because it's not what I need right now.

I have a new ability, too.

His ability.

And his perfect clarity on how to use it.

I feel his magic inside of me and it's dark, like mine, but sharper and more precise. For a second, my stomach lurches when I think about using it, but my father will only be unguarded for a moment. With a deep, shaky breath, I gather his magic up . . . and I release it.

Pain rips through my every pore, and I would scream if I could. The feeling is indescribable, as though each and every bit of me is ripped in half. It's so fast and so fierce that my mind rebels against it, and even when the pain stops, I stagger back, biting my lip until it bleeds.

But even though I'm reeling and nauseous and, quite frankly, a little scared, I'm also right where I want to be.

Behind my father's back.

And also right in front of him.

I blink at myself. The other me shakes her head and puts her hands up to her mouth, but I didn't make her do that. I'm not in her head at all.

The dissonance doesn't worry me, but it must worry her, because half of my animals skid backward in fear. The other half, the ones who must be reacting to my emotions, continue to advance on my father, growls in their throats.

I put my passion and conviction in this body and left my hesitations and deliberations in her, so nothing holds me back now. I feel focused and free. Even eager.

Ready to make him *pay*.

Magic blazes through my every vein until it feels like I'm lit up from within. It's more vicious, more bloodthirsty than ever before. I don't know if it's because I've added Alect's power to my own, or because this is the first time I'm initiating an attack myself, but whatever it is, the magic is revoltingly pleased, overpoweringly eager.

I reach into my pocket. The bracelet Mara made for Father and the necklace she made for me are still there. I clutch them both in a fist and draw them out.

Then I jump onto my father's back and wrap the necklace tight around his throat.

With a gurgling noise, he drops his sword and reaches up to claw at it.

The beads beneath my fingers grow hot, glow purple, and my father's screams become even more desperate as the beads steal not only his breath, but his magic, too.

I remember the feeling, that scorching, ripping sensation of power being torn away, and I can only imagine adding burning lungs and slow suffocation to the experience. He must be in agony.

The thrill of my magic burns my throat, glazes over my eyes, eggs me on as my father's choking grows more garbled and wretched. It wraps itself around my mind, urging me to keep going, to end it, to feel his death beneath my hands.

Then suddenly my two bodies slam back together, both of us now clinging as one to my father's back.

The rejoining doesn't hurt, but it's psychically jarring. All at once, I have two sets of memories that cover the last few seconds. I know both my own rage and my own fear of that rage, the sensation of my father struggling beneath my hands and the way it felt to watch myself do that, to see the look on my face and on his. I know that one part of me forced our bodies back together to stop the other one.

The necklace around my father's throat loosens.

He gulps in air, but then grabs at the beads, trying to get free. For a moment he manages to buck me and I fly backward, but the necklace catches on his chin and I'm able to clamber my way back and pull it tight again.

He wheezes, clawing at it, and this time I don't feel any of the excitement that part of me felt a moment ago. Instead, my stomach roils in revulsion.

But still I hold the beads tight.

He reaches for me, trying to freeze me in place with his magic, but I slam the bracelet on his wrist. By the time he touches me, his fingers are nothing but fingers, and my body is my own.

After a couple more minutes, his face tinges blue and his swiping gets weak. The magic surges in glee and bile rises in my throat. I only have to hold on for a few more minutes to end this man for good.

But that's never been what I wanted.

Not really.

I let the beads loosen again. Just for a moment. Just enough to let him get in a breath. Long enough for him to start clawing at me in confusion before I draw the necklace taut once more to continue draining his magic.

This goes back and forth a few times, with him pressing every bit of leeway I give him, and me keeping a tight rein while still allowing enough air to keep him alive. Despite his best efforts, I maintain control. I cling to his back, my knees digging into his sides, and I loosen and tighten, loosen and tighten as needed. Until the whole work is done.

It takes . . . a long time. Endless moments of nothing but his ragged breathing, the restless pacing of my animals, and the clack of beads against beads.

At one point he reaches for my mother, croaking out a cry for her help.

She looks at him, at me, at Mara, where she tends to her bleeding gashes.

And then she turns away.

He reaches for Mara next, but she never even looks up.

When the beads grow cold and the purple glow disappears, I finally let the necklace go. He flings it across the room, and I slide off his back as he collapses to the ground. I dismiss my animals and back up a couple steps. Then I prepare myself for whatever his response might be.

At first, he just clutches his throat, rubbing the red marks I left there.

"I thought you were going to kill me," he rasps.

I give him a humorless smirk. "I thought about it. It was my first thought, actually. And part of me wanted to very much."

He narrows his eyes, glaring back over his shoulder at me. "Why didn't you, then?"

I look at him there on the ground, stripped of his magic, and he's never looked so human. In this moment, it's strange to me how afraid of him I used to be.

He's just a man after all.

"Two reasons," I tell him. "The first is that I'm not like you. I don't consider death to be worthwhile collateral, and I don't want to build my power on bloodshed. It's not that I don't think you deserve it. If anyone does, it's you." I give him a bitter smile. "But if I'm going to run things differently, then I can't start them the same way. The second reason, is, admittedly, a little more selfish."

He pulls himself to his feet, still eyeing me warily. "What's that?" he asks gruffly.

I straighten to my full height and face him directly, summoning all the strength and surety I've gained in the last few moments, making sure that my voice is clear and strong.

"Because if what you said about my magic is true, then no matter how I killed you I would never be rid of you. You'd be part of me as inextricably as Alect is now. But I want you to know that I'm done. I'm free of you. And I'm freeing the whole realm along with me. You'll never have power over us again. I'll *show* you how to build a better world. You'll get to see it all." I tilt my head. "From your prison cell."

He shakes his head, his anger finally sparking. "You can't throw me into prison. I'm the Prime!"

"Primes have to have magic," I remind him. "Unfortunately, you're ineligible."

His face goes pale, and then red. He thunders toward me,

getting right in my face. "You can't change the leader of a realm based on a technicality like that! Even if you could, I haven't named you heir yet. Which makes *Mara* the Prime, not you."

"Pass." Across the room, Mara is pulling herself to her feet. The black flames have mostly dissipated by now, leaving only wisps where they once were. They dance around her, framing her resolute expression as she approaches. "I've kept my magic a secret for years. I see no reason to stop doing it now."

"It doesn't matter, anyway," Father splutters. "I'm the Prime. Even if you explain your convoluted reasoning, the people are used to following my rule. As long as I live, they will obey *my* orders."

Almost as though in response to this statement, the door bursts open, and the Captain charges in, followed by a small battalion that quickly swarms to fill the space.

"Good timing," I say.

"Actually, about an hour ago would have been *better* timing," Mara mumbles.

"What happened here?" the Captain demands, surveying the dark smoke in the air and the bodies strewn about the room.

I square my shoulders, nervous. Is my father right? Will no one follow me? Will they see a mere girl and not trust me? Will they remember my kills and fear me? Is my reasoning too weak? Is my inexperience too unsurmountable?

"There has been . . . a change of leadership," I inform her, with all the gravitas I can muster. "I am the Prime now, and my father is stepping down. You see—"

The Captain holds up a hand, cutting me off. A smile, one more relaxed and girlish than I've ever seen on her, paints her wizened features, making her look decades younger. "Don't much care about the why or the how, actually," she says. "All due respect, of course. But I've been waiting a long time for this, and I'd rather not put it off. You can fill me in on the particulars later."

Without further ado, the Captain drops to one knee and swears her fealty to me as my father gapes. Behind her, every soldier in the battalion kneels as well, some hesitantly at first, but then more and more confidently, and when the Captain finishes her oath with the words, "I and all my soldiers with me," the synchronized assent of the gathered troops resonates through the room, bringing tears to my eyes. I smile and hold my chin high, accepting their allegiance, their faith, and their hopes for my reign gratefully.

And then it really is time to end this.

"Thank you," I say. "Now seize him."

26

Silver

|1 DAY UNTIL THE ASSURANCE|

In my dreams, my mind rakes me through the worst parts of the day, over and over. The way Mance's expression crumpled when she realized I'd betrayed her, how she turned to me and I had nothing at all to say. The explosion, and how it felt to tear through the wreckage of my home looking for my friends, not knowing whether they were dead or alive. Inky blackness hovering through the air in front of Mance's curious face, and the fear that I wouldn't get to her in time.

I am thrown through these scenes so often that I can't remember how they turned out, can't remember whether I managed to explain, whether I ever found my friends, whether I protected Mance from the blast.

When I bolt awake, it's in a bed with scratchy sheets, in a room that smells like medicine and lavender, and even though everything is calm and still around me, my heart is pounding as the claws of the nightmares refuse to unclench from my mind.

Where am I?

What happened?

I'm about to fling myself from the bed and burst out of the room demanding answers.

But then I see Mance.

She's asleep in a chair next to me, slumped onto the side of the bed. Her face is slack and peaceful, no sign of injury or even pain. Her dark hair is splayed on the white sheets and one hand is clutching the edge of the blanket.

The other hand is clutching mine.

My heart clenches painfully at the sight, because I don't think I've ever seen anything so beautiful, so immediately soothing. I gasp out a chuckle at my own panic and force my mind to slow down enough to remember the rest of what happened. I did explain. I did find my friends. I did save Mance.

I don't know yet whether she forgives me, though.

I examine our entwined fingers like they might hold the answer, wondering if she took my hand on purpose or merely reached for it in her sleep. Heck, maybe I reached for her.

As the tension eases from my shoulders, I stroke my thumb over her knuckles, drinking in the sight of her unharmed. The sound of her even breaths. The soft scent of honeysuckle soap in her hair. It's all perfect.

If I could, I would linger in this moment forever.

Instead, I force myself to disentangle and pull back.

Because if this isn't what she wants, if she yanks her hand away in disgust when she realizes what it's doing, that would break me.

I blow out a breath.

Then I tuck a strand of hair behind the shell of her ear and whisper her name.

She blinks awake, looking at me blearily, and I dig my nails into my leg as I wait for her to smile or frown.

She does neither. She just sits up, slowly. Her gaze drags across my face and I tense at the feel of it, like she's brushing fingertips across my skin.

Yet her eyes never quite meet mine.

"What did you dream?" she asks.

The question throws me. I put my elbows on my knees, stalling, and the sheets slide down my bare chest.

Weirdly, there aren't any black marks. I know the magic hit me, am sure I remember its cold burn, and yet it isn't there.

"We gave you healing magic," Mance explains, reading the confusion on my face. "But it's known to give nightmares. True ones. What did you see?"

I'd rather talk about why she's here, why she waited at my bedside long enough to fall asleep, and the still-pressing matter of who specifically reached for whom and when. But I sigh, supposing that I owe her an answer.

"Just . . . today," I tell her. "Over and over again. Betrayal on your face, my house exploding, digging through debris and not being able to find . . ." My mind catches up to my words, and all of a sudden it occurs to me where I am and how much time has passed. There are windows on the far wall, and they show nothing but darkness outside. It must be the middle of the night. "Vie and Rooftop!" I cry. "We have to go get them! They—"

"Are in the next room," Mance assures me. "About an hour after you got knocked out, Vie showed up at the front gate hauling Rooftop and screaming something about how if I'm still alive and I'm really as great as Silver thinks I am, I'll treat them both immediately."

Fond pride hits me like a hot brick to the chest. "And you did," I say confidently.

She makes an affirmative noise and then looks down, playing with the hem of the sheets as something vulnerable leaks into her expression. It's the same broken face she made earlier, like an echo of my nightmare playing out in front of me.

It *kills* me to see it.

"Mance, I—"

"*Don't* tell me you're sorry."

I reel back, her words like a slap.

So that's it, then.

She doesn't forgive me.

My throat constricts and my body suddenly feels ten times heavier. I close my eyes and try to breathe, try to convince myself that I'm okay with her decision. I never deserved her forgiveness in the first place, so I can't blame her for withholding it. But I still feel the cut somewhere deep within me.

I must have been the one who reached out after all.

"Fine," I hiss. "Although I am. What do you want me to tell you instead?"

She's silent so long that I open my eyes again, unable to stop looking at her, even when the looking hurts.

Her face is pale, her shoulders hunched. I have to bite the inside of my cheek to keep from taking her into my arms and smoothing away the creases on her brow.

Because that's not my place anymore.

"Just tell me," she says finally, "how much . . . um. What I want to know is . . . when we . . ." She trails off, her hands wringing the edge of the linen again, making shadows in its creases. "Did you lie about . . . everything?" she asks.

"Not even most things," I tell her, voice low but forceful.

She purses her lips. "What about last night?" she asks.

The question tears through me. It's cruel to make me linger in those memories if they're the last ones I'll have with her, but I suppose I deserve that, too. I'll drag myself through it if that's what she needs me to do.

I give an unsteady laugh. Without meaning to, my gaze latches on to the curve of her lips. "Are you asking if I wanted to kiss you?" My voice sounds strained even to me.

Her cheeks flood with heat, but she nods.

And the fact that she doesn't know already is so comical that it almost makes me angry.

"When?" I grit out. "Do you mean when we were on the boat and you leaned in . . . this close . . . ?" My body moves on its own, bending toward her until we're only inches apart, as though if I could only reenact the moment well enough, we would fall back into it.

I brace for her to pull away.

But she doesn't.

Instead, her eyes widen and finally meet mine.

And something between us shifts.

My chest tightens in disbelief, and I study her obsessively, hungrily.

She studies me back, her eyes just as searching.

Slower now, testing her response as well as my own restraint, I reach up a hand to frame her face, my voice softer. "Or do you mean when you were wrapped around me in the blankets?" I ask, my touch trailing down her jawline to trace her lips, just like I did then. Her breath hitches and I feel it flutter across my fingertips.

I clench my teeth, scared to push her too far. "Actually, it doesn't matter. The answer is yes. You could pick any moment out of last night, and my answer would be yes. I definitely wanted to kiss you. And I haven't stopped thinking about it since."

I thought I knew what wanting was. After all, I've spent most of my life yearning and desperate, fighting in the dirt.

But I've never wanted anything as viscerally as this before. I've never felt it as a physical sensation in my body, cutting through my stomach and curling my toes.

With a colossal effort, I wrench myself away from her, intending to fall back onto the pillows with a groan.

Until she grabs my chin, holding me in place.

"Me too," she says breathlessly.

I still beneath her touch, deathly afraid that I'm misunderstanding her, even as a thrill of anguished hope burns through me.

I tamp it down, determined. Because she *can't* really mean—

She reaches back to twine her fingers around the hand cupping her face, and I'm certain she's going to remove it.

But then she guides it lower, running our tangled fingers down her skin until we reach the hollow of her throat.

Where her heart is beating as fast as mine is.

My eyes flicker up, shocked.

And hers are blazing. Far beyond a flicker of candlelight, it's like there's an inferno in her midnight eyes, making them bluer and brighter than ever before.

Bright enough to incinerate the last of my resistance.

My lips crash into hers and it's like dawn breaking over me. The sunshine of her smile—which I can now feel the curves and edges of up close—lights up my every nerve ending until my whole body feels alive. I think I groan, but I don't have time to be embarrassed because she's burying her hands in my hair, tilting the corners of my jaw upward and kissing me back like she really has wanted this just as badly as I have.

I drag her into the sheets and we become a tangle of blankets and limbs, searching hands and searing mouths. She takes hold of my shoulders, pulling me into her, and I take hold of her hips, marveling at how good she feels against me.

There are no secrets left between us anymore. There isn't anything left between us, not even space. Her chest is flush against mine, so close that I can feel our pulses pounding together, a frenzied rhythm that reassures me with every beat that we're finally, *finally* on the same page.

When we pull back, our breaths are ragged.

"All right," she says. "I forgive you."

The kiss had been a bit of a giveaway, but relief still makes me lightheaded. Idly, I smooth down the wild tangle of her hair. "Are you sure? I feel like we could run over some of the finer points of my apology again."

She chuckles, her eyes lingering on my mouth in a way that makes me feel like I might still be on fire.

"Later," she says. "I promise. But right this minute, I need to go. I wanted to be here when you woke up, but since you have, well . . . Now that I'm the Prime, there are a few things I need to take care of."

She sashays out of the room, softly humming under her breath, and I'm so dizzy with elation that it's not until she's halfway down the hall that I fully process what she's said.

"Wait, hold on!" I call after her. "Now that you're the *what*?"

27

Prime Apparent Mancella Amaryllis Cliff

|THE NIGHT BEFORE ASSURANCE|

That evening, Prime Azele and her bodyguard both arrive for dinner, on my invitation. Our usual dining room is currently out of commission, what with the explosion and all, so I had to relocate the meeting to another venue.

I lead them into the arena.

Or, well, that's what we used to call it.

It has been transformed. Everyone on the serving staff deserves a raise, and they'll get one. Where this morning there were bare floors marred by claw marks and dark splatters, there are now ornate rugs in tones of gold and blue. The windows are unboarded and opened wide, to a breathtaking view of the surrounding mountains that I never knew was there. The giant cage is draped with curtains, making the whole space feel softer and more intimate. They even found and rehung the chandelier, a grand and glorious piece, dripping with crystals, that gives the whole room a soft glow.

Of course, I know the cage is still there, just beneath the rich fabric. In the same way that the bloodstains remain just beneath the soft, colorful rugs.

I can't undo what my father did, but I can choose what I build upon it. I can seek redemption. Standing here in a place restored to its proper purpose, I feel my own sense of purpose settle upon me, just as the corsetless dress I've chosen settles around my body in a way that armor never could.

Dinner goes well. At least, it's significantly less confrontational than the last meal Prime Azele joined me for.

Of course, I have help. Silver has reprised his role as servant for one last evening, and he keeps slipping me notes of encouragement. Sometimes he adds a thought or two about Azele's body language and how he thinks she might be taking my statements. If Rift notices that Silver is the same person who showed him the letters, he doesn't call his Prime's attention to it.

But the conversation doesn't need too much push. There's a reason Prime Azele tried a parley first. It's the same reason she sent one bodyguard instead of a battalion. She wants to avoid war as much as I do.

Negotiations wind down by dessert, which is pistachio cream puffs. They were made by Rooftop, who has just taken a job on my kitchen staff, and they look delicious. I notice one missing on the plate Silver carries out to me and shoot him a dry look. He grins at me with full cheeks.

"Are we in agreement, then?" Prime Azele asks as she swallows the last of her pastries. Her expression and tone are appropriately regal but tinged with a decided edge of hope.

"Almost," I say. "There's one more thing I would ask. But to be honest it's more of a personal favor than anything else."

❦✻❦

An hour later, in more practical attire, Prime Azele joins me on a walk through the Outskirts, glass crunching beneath our boots.

"I thought this was an odd request," she says. "But I see now why you asked. And I take it as proof that you are sincere in your wish for peace."

We stop by a jagged stump, and she lays her hand on it. Beneath her touch, the sharp edges disintegrate into harmless ash.

"You'll have to do something about the shards in the dirt, though," she muses. "I can't find and touch every single one."

"I know," I say. "It will take time. But uprooting the main cause is the first step. We'll figure out how to deal with the shards left behind after that."

She nods. "One thing I have learned is that ash makes excellent fertilizer."

"Is that so?"

"Yes. Once you've burned everything down, it's the perfect time to help new things grow. I hope that turns out to be true for both our realms."

"I do as well," I say.

We clasp hands, and then Prime Azele moves to disintegrate another hulking stump, this one with half the branches still intact. The resulting ash flutters down in a shower, and Prime Azele catches some in her palm, smiling.

Behind her, her shadow warps slightly, betraying the presence of Rift, guarding her. My own shadow, Silver, is trailing much less subtly, watching the most painful parts of his neighborhood unravel with an inscrutable expression.

Finally, when the last tree is puffed away and Prime Azele and I reiterate our promises and then say our goodbyes, I linger and let him approach.

"What do you think?" I ask.

He threads his fingers through mine. "I think you're going to be a better Prime than your father."

"I feel like we could set the bar a *little* higher than that," I protest.

"I think you're going to be the best Prime in the history of this realm or any other," he says. "And if there are any other planets or universes out there and *they* have Primes, you're going to be better than all of them, too."

I roll my eyes but smile anyway. We fall into step heading back to the castle, still hand in hand. I will never get tired of the way his palm feels against mine.

"So," I say. "I've been thinking of your housing situation."

"Oh yeah?" He looks amused.

"I can't help but notice that your previous home is in a somewhat . . . less than desirable condition."

"What do you mean? Two walls is plenty."

"You're welcome to stay in the castle with me," I offer. "Or I could get you a house in town. One in a safer area."

He kisses my hand, but shakes his head. "I appreciate the offer. But I think I want to earn it honestly this time. Build something myself, you know? Like you're doing. Besides." He leans down and scoops up a handful of ash from one of the piles Prime Azele left, letting it run through his fingers and catch on the breeze. "The neighborhood's getting a lot better." As the last of the ash falls to the ground, he looks back at me with a hooded expression. "If you could get me papers, though? So I could get a job?"

"Actually," I say, "that's one thing I can't do. Seeing as papers are no longer required for employment, we won't be issuing any more of them. You're free to apply wherever you'd like."

His features relax into a relieved smile, and as we pass a candlemaker's shop, his eyes linger on the awning. I squeeze his hand encouragingly and he shoots me a wink.

As we walk back to the palace, we chat about the events of the last few days. How Vie has none of Silver's aversion to my generosity and has been gleefully requesting every dish she can think of from the kitchens, most of which end up being prepared by Rooftop. How the Captain approached me about taking a break from combat, since the main reason she's stayed on so long was to push back against my father, and how I asked her whether she'd be in charge of reforming the Academy, raising up the kids there the way she always mentored me. How she loved the idea.

By the time we're strolling through the courtyard, we're laughing, wondering whether there are any cream puffs left over in the kitchen that we could swipe for a late evening snack.

Silver kisses me, and the action is so sweet and so open that I linger in it for a minute, reveling in the way it feels to know that this is real. That there's someone who will be there for me, even if it's dangerous and hard. To feel his hand cupping my cheek and my fingers in his choppy hair, warming each other even as the evening cools.

But then we say good night, because there's one last thing I need to do. I grab the dirt-filled saucepan from my room. Then I hike up my skirts and pick up a trowel.

28

Prime Apparent Mancella Amaryllis Cliff

~~|DAY OF ASSURANCE|~~

|DAY OF ASCENSION|

The next morning, in the minutes before dawn, when the night is just starting to turn gray, I walk through the front gates to meet my people, and a confused hush goes over the gathered crowd. Torchlight casts distorted shadows. The streets are stuffed with people waiting to see me become the Seconde, some even spilling up and down the cliffside, or perched on outcroppings of rock to witness this historic moment. I can feel them squinting at me in the dim light, trying to make sense of the picture before them.

They expected to see me marched out on the arm of my father. But I walk alone. Instead of the black, twisted glass corset my father picked for me, consistent with my reputation as a brutal killer, I wear a simple lace dress. Instead of the dark, animalistic makeup I was supposed to have painted across my features, my face is bare. And instead of the surly scowl they are accustomed to seeing me don at official events, today I wear a small, confident smile.

The Captain begins reciting her vows, with her soldiers

echoing them from atop the walls behind me. Only the vows she recites are those acknowledging a Prime instead of a Seconde. When the crowd realizes this, there are whispers. I feel people shift. Rumors, theories, and suppositions skate up and down the cliffside. But when the Captain kneels before me, everyone and everything goes silent.

It's time for my own vows.

I can hear my father's voice, drilling me on the vows he composed.

Like the glass trees of Prime Elod, I vow to be mighty and unbreakable, both a stalwart defense and a deadly weapon.

"Like the glass trees of Prime Elod," I start, stretching my arms to indicate the glittering forest around me, "I vow to be rooted and reflective. Both a stalwart defense and a testament to beauty."

As long as I am Prime, I pledge to reign in glory, and to make the renown of the Cliff Realm my foremost concern.

"As long as I am Prime, I pledge to serve in humility, and to make the well-being of the Cliff Realm, and every person within it, my foremost concern."

After giving me a soft smile of approval, the Captain opens a steel-plated box and offers me a crown nestled in a bed of velvet. But instead of the weighty glass crown my father commissioned, adorned with sharp, wicked points that mirror the glass pines towering on either side of me, the crown she offers is a circlet I braided out of starsprouts.

Behind me, dozens more of the tiny blooms sparkle delicately from the lawn, breaking up its harsh uniformity with tufts of light. Their pointed petals stretch joyfully toward the sky, and as the sun rises behind me, the blooms catch the colors of the sunrise and display them back, creating a breathtaking kaleidoscope of orange and pink pinpricks dancing throughout the grass.

After striving for so long, the flowers finally get to see the sun.

And so do I.

I lift my chin high.

Then I place the crown on my head.

Prime
Mancella Amaryllis Cliff

EPILOGUE

It's midmorning by the time I finally slink into my rooms. The second I cross the threshold, the exhaustion I've been ignoring pummels me like a fist. I've barely closed the door behind me before I'm sagging against it, almost breathless with the weight of what I've just taken onto my shoulders.

But I'm breathless for another reason, too. With gentle, reverent fingers, I disentangle the delicate woven stems from my hair, easing my crown off my head. Cupping it in two hands, I hold it up to my face, breathing in the sweet, floral scent that I could never detect from a single bloom. Yet with a handful—with an entire lawn of them—the scent is heady and comforting all at once. Like tart apples and dulcet honey.

A smile flits over my lips. Because exhausting or not, I did well out there. I'm proud of the way I started my reign.

A harsh thump from my closet wipes the smile off my face.

My eyes lift to the source of the noise and then lower immediately, the sweat on the back of my neck turning cold.

Then there's another thump, louder.

And a third, hard enough to make my closet handle rattle.

"Stop that," I say sharply. But I can hear the note of fear in my voice, and it makes me wince.

The banging ceases, and I swallow in the sudden silence. My fingers flex, and the scars that cover them seem somehow starker now that the petals' soft glow has faded.

"Was it fun?" a voice asks into the silence.

I flinch, unsure if I should respond. But I do anyway. "Was what fun?"

The person in my closet shifts, and I hear the clack of hangers rearranging. "Putting flowers in your hair," the voice says. "Prancing around before your adoring subjects. Spouting your pretty words. Did you have a nice time while I was locked away in here?"

I gnaw on the edge of my lip, guilt acidic in the pit of my stomach.

"I'll . . . I'll get you more comfortable accommodations soon," I promise. "Once I can get the appropriate barriers from Mara."

There's an unkind laugh, and it cuts me. "Oh, you're making me a *cushioned* cage. How thoughtful."

It's only then I realize my hands are shaking so hard that the crown is shedding petals. I hastily hang it on the corner of my vanity and cross my arms behind me, nails digging into my elbows.

"You have to understand," I plead.

"Do I?" the voice retorts dryly.

"Yes," I say. "I'm going to be different. I *have* to be different. My father and my cousin had parts of them that were . . . dark. And they allowed those parts too much freedom. I won't make the same mistake." Bile rises in my throat as I remember the way I (she?) felt when I-she-we closed the beads around my father's throat. That thrill. That desire to make him pay for what he put me through. It *scares* me. "I'm not going to hurt you. I just need to make sure that you won't hurt anyone else."

There's another bang, and this one breaks the top hinge. My throat closes with dread, but before I can do anything there are two more hits in quick succession. The first causes the door to splinter and crack, and the second sends the upper half toppling to the floor.

There, in the shadows behind the newly formed hole, framed by ragged, broken wood, is a girl who looks like me, my magical armor wrapped around her clenched fist.

Only I've never seen my features twist like that. I've never known the way that anger curls my lips and sparks in my gaze. I've never witnessed a predator in my own face.

My heart racing, I retreat a couple steps, until my back hits the wall and my arms are pinned behind me. But I still want to try reason. After all, this person is *me,* isn't she? Or at least a part of me?

"Until I know I can control you, it's safest to keep you locked up," I say, trying to summon the Prime-like authority I displayed at the front gate just moments ago.

For a second, something like hurt flickers across her features and the acid in my stomach burns even more deeply.

But then her expression hardens and she sinks back into the darkness.

"Lock me up?" she echoes faintly from the shadows. The words are low and yet I hear them as clearly as if they were whispered directly into my ear.

Then the bottom half of the door goes flying. With one kick, she smashes the other hinge, and I hold my arms over my face to block the splinters spraying in all directions, just barely wrestling a scream into submission before it escapes my throat.

She emerges from the tattered opening with languid grace, like she's strolling into a throne room instead of slipping through a pulverized mess.

Her lips curve into a mocking smirk.

And then she speaks.

Just two words.

"Try it."

ACKNOWLEDGMENTS

I have wanted to publish a novel since before I even knew how to write. As a young kid, I would draw pictures and then tell my mother what to transcribe below them so that I could bind the pages together into vaguely book-like things. I would then proudly add a little title page with my very own, carefully selected pseudonym. (No, I will not tell you what it was. It's embarrassing.)

All of this to say, it's been a long journey, which means I have a lot of people to thank.

Let's start with the obvious. To my agent, Catherine Cho—when I got the email that you'd read my whole novel in less than a day and wanted to make me an offer, it really felt like my life was changing because someone (you!) believed in me. And looking back, I can't say that feeling was wrong. Signing with you was one of the best decisions I've ever made. From the beginning, you have been so dedicated to pushing my writing to be the best it could be, and you have been such a champion for it as we put it out into the world. I am so grateful to you, and to everyone else at Paper Literary, especially Melissa Pimentel, for her sharp editing skills and astute problem-solving.

To my editors, Brian Geffen, Emma Jones, and Carina Licon—it has been such an incredible pleasure working with you. I think about the early stages of my writing when I was desperate for feedback and I just feel so honored to have had not one but *three* incredible minds willing to spend months in a world that I built. Your kind words, thoughtful insights, probing questions, and constant, constant encouragement are things that I will genuinely treasure forever.

To my copy editor, Linda Minton—I've never met anyone

more pedantic than I am and I love you for it.

To everyone else who worked on this book—I'm sure I don't know half of what you did, but please understand how incredibly grateful I am for your efforts. Especially Ann Marie Wong, the editorial director; Kristen Stedman, the production editor; Jie Yang, the production manager; and Alex Blaszczuk, my authenticity reader. You are all rock stars.

To the people responsible for the incredible UK cover, Kieryn Tyler, the designer; Rachel Vale, the art director; and Kate Forrester, the jacket artist—you all made my little book look like a beautiful fairy tale, which is so perfect because that's exactly what this whole process has felt like. Thank you.

But of course I also want to thank a lot of people who were there for me before there was ever an agent or a book deal. When writing was just this thing that I loved and couldn't stop doing.

To Joe Williams—you were the very first person who believed in this story, and you're STILL probably the person who has read the most drafts of it. I can't thank you enough for how much time you put into giving me feedback during a stage in my life when I craved it so badly. This book wouldn't be what it is without you.

To VS—my love for you all cannot be expressed in words. We met because we all cared enough about our writing to apply for a mentorship program, and we bonded as we waited for the results, feeling like our futures depended on them. Most of us didn't get in (myself included), but we still won because we found each other. You are not only the writing community I've always wanted but you are also some of the best people I know. Where would I be without your brainstorming magic, your spiral support, your chaotic humor, your aggressive encouragement, your craft recommendations, and your selfless feedback? Not where I am, that's for sure.

To my mom—bless you for thinking even the early drafts were good, and for being my unwavering cheerleader through all of this. I'm sure you had concerns when I told you I wanted to quit being a lawyer for a while so I could work on a book, but you never expressed those concerns to me. You let me dream and you supported me, just like you did with those handmade picture books when I was four. For that and for many other things, I will always love you.

To my kids—the thought of you reading this book someday and having opinions about it truly intimidates me, but in many ways I did write it for you. At this age, you probably have no idea how much your smiles and snuggles encourage me, but hopefully one day when you read this, you will know. You are, and always will be, the light of my life.

To my husband—I am constantly floored by the level of support you give me as I try to pursue this thing. I love you for reading my story about teen magic, even though you'd probably rather read something nonfiction. I love you for getting stressed out when you tell me you like a chapter and I tell you I've already cut the whole thing. I love you for telling me to take more time to write even when it means that you'll be watching all three kids by yourself at the end of a long workday. I love you for who you are and for who you allow me to be when I'm with you. Basically, I love you.

To all the other friends and family members who have always given me support and love—there are far too many of you to list individually, but hopefully you know who you are and how much I love you back.

Finally, to God—Psalm 34:4 puts it best. From the deepest part of my heart: Thank you.